MW01555096

The Rising

The End Time Saga
Book Three

★★★

Daniel Greene

Cover Design by Christian Bentulan
Formatting by Polgarus Studio

ISBN: 978-0-9976096-4-6

I dedicate this novel to my Grandfather Victor. Thank you for introducing me to Prince Valiant as a young man and piquing my imagination for lifetimes to come.

THE PASTOR

Northern Michigan

Thick leather cowboy boots clopped over the finely polished wood floor. His weary body felt every step he had taken in his soul's sixty-four years of mortal existence. His weathered hand fell on the head of the hammer that hung from his hip. Its metal head was tarnished with rust. The face was dinged and the claw on the back stripped from a long life of use. The shaft was worn and dirt had been ground into the old fading wood; it swung as he walked. The hammer of a simple carpenter.

He whispered a prayer under his breath. The words hid inside his mouth, sticking to his tongue. *I am your servant. Your word gives me strength in the darkness.*

The muted sounds of a sobbing woman were muffled through a closed door. The crying lured him forward through the clean wooden hallway adorned with framed family pictures. Light shone beneath the door, and as he drew near, the crying grew in volume.

The echoing of his footsteps stopped. A small metal crucifix hung slightly off-kilter. He took a wrinkled, knuckled finger and gently straightened the bottom of the cross upright. His finger wavered below, waiting in case it swung back. He surveyed his handiwork another moment before moving on.

Continuing down the hall, he eyed family photos that had been taken all over the world: Stonehenge, the Eiffel Tower, the Great Wall of China. All were photos of the same family. Mother, father, son, posing, smiling and living. A young blonde-haired woman appeared in some next to the son and eventually the father disappeared.

Reaching the door, he grasped the gold door handle and tenderly opened the door inward as if he respected their privacy. The room was dark but for a series of flashlight beams shining on a distraught couple. The large bedroom was extravagant and filled with the possessions of the affluent. Large expensive furniture. An equally large king-sized bed in a thick wooden bedframe.

He acknowledged a large man resting on the wall, arms folded against his wide chest. The man's sandy blond curls bounced when he looked his way. The two men were almost of equal height but the pastor still looked down on the broad man.

"Peter, how are they doing?" His voice hardly rose above a whisper. He knew he would be heard when he spoke.

The gold-haired man straightened upright, and he flashed a beam of light tentatively on the crying woman. Her face frowned at them and she squinted her eyes, turning her head away. Her face twisted and her lip curled through her gag. Peter removed the light from her face.

"They seem pretty shaken up by everything, but I have faith that God will show himself here tonight."

"God always shows himself. It's only the matter of us seeing him."

Peter bowed his head in deference. His curls shifting. "This is true."

Three more of his followers stood expectantly in the room. They held flashlights on the two people. One trained a shotgun on them and the other two held long knives.

The captives sat on the edge of the bed, hands bound behind their backs. Blankets and sheets lay tangled behind them. They huddled close together and the woman's shoulders shook as she cried. The man nursed a swelling eye with blinks, his other eye darting frantically at the men surrounding him. Humans were pitifully weak and sorry creatures.

They may not be ready. They may yet be castaways, vestiges of the old world unwilling to embrace the new. We do not choose when he calls, but we must answer. "Gabriel, release their gags," he said, waving one of the men with a knife forward with a curt gesture.

The pastor turned toward his broad-chested lieutenant. "Peter, a chair if you will. My back." A chair was set behind him, and the wood of his hammer gave a dead thump on its side as he sat eye level with the man and woman.

The man before him exercised his gray stubble-clad jaw. He wasn't as old as the pastor and he wasn't young. He was probably in his late fifties and unaccustomed to wearing a beard. The woman, her face wet with salt-laden tears, had gray streaks running through her once blonde hair. She stared at him, defiantly afraid.

The pastor leaned backward, stretching his back and allowing the chair to support him with its frame.

"You need not be afraid. We are not here to hurt you." His voice was soft and gentle.

His two captives did not appear soothed by his forthcomingness.

"Why are you doing this?" the woman stammered. She sniffled back tears. "We haven't done anything to you." The man next to her only stared.

The pastor cocked his head. "The chains that bind you are only of earth, but what chains bind your soul?"

The older woman wiped the side of her face on her shoulder. She blinked confusion. "I have no chains on my soul."

The pastor grimaced. "You do. You sit here in all your opulence, refusing God's call to service, for service is where we find him. You are a doctor, are you not?"

"Yes. How did you know that?" She looked over at her partner, confusion on her face.

The pastor smiled, brushing his thick white hair back from the front of his head. He rubbed his hand over his hair in a second effort to keep it out of his eyes.

"A man does not lead a parish for thirty-five years without getting to know a person with just a glance."

She looked down before she answered. "I'm a doctor at St. Anastasia's North Shores Hospital. I am the chief of surgery there."

"It appears that you are a woman God has blessed with many gifts." He nodded as the left side of his mouth curved upward.

"And you, good sir?" His eyes took in the other man. *Another doctor, no doubt.*

"I am an oncologist at St. Anastasia's," the man said flatly.

The pastor grinned inwardly. These were very special people. People that would be such a great asset to his parish.

"Two very gifted people indeed," he said, folding his hands between his knees and leaning forward.

"Gabriel, get them some water."

Gabriel bobbed his flat brown-haired head in confirmation and pulled a bottled water from a green backpack on his back and cracked the top. He was a young man from his parish, not more than eighteen. He did as the pastor bid and stepped forward, pouring water in their open mouths.

"That's a good lad," the pastor said. *At one time he feared death. Now he embraces his place here on earth with the willingness of an old man.* The young man finished and tightened the cap back on the bottle. He stepped back and the pastor gave him a nod of appreciation before addressing the doctors.

"I want you to join my church community. I won't ask you for much, and you will be safe from those who would do you harm, but I think we would both benefit from getting to know each other better."

The man looked indignant. "You come here and hold us hostage at gunpoint. That's some way to welcome someone."

"Some introductions must be harsher than others," the pastor said, spreading his hands and folding them back together.

The woman looked away as if she didn't want to say it, but she turned back to him, resolution settling on her face. Her eyes filled with angry tears. "We've seen what you've done to the Millers." She looked out the window. "The bodies. The fire," she spit out softer, her lips trembling. "You and your people are monsters," she hissed.

"The only choice we have is to see God's will be done. I will release you when you repent and join. No harm will befall you. You will join the hundreds of good people of my parish. People that you called neighbors once. You will be safe and a valued member of our community. You will be a part of something so much greater than yourself. You need not work only for your own gratification. You can truly be God's servant, helping him to build his new paradise on earth."

The captive male doctor snorted. "Paradise? Have you looked outside? The world has gone to hell." The pastor leaned back stretching and stood up. Even with support, standing always seemed better. He put his hands on his lower back and pressed in the center of his spine.

"One may call this world hell, yes. This world has only ever been hell, each and every misery put here by God to cull his flock. To drive his flock forward. Throughout mankind's history, he has wrought us with the Four Horsemen of the Apocalypse: Pestilence, Death, Famine, and War, if only to test us. Pestilence was only the beginning. Before this is over War, Famine, and Death will fall upon us with their wicked arrows and swords. Most will perish. This is known. It is also known that God's people will rise up stronger," the pastor said, letting his voice rise as if he stood at the pulpit.

"Amen," his men said in unison. The pastor nodded to them in praise.

"His victory will be ultimate for we who are destined to bring an end to hell here on earth. We are his champions, his instruments, and Revelations reads that his victory will be complete over Lucifer and his minions, and God will bring paradise here on earth."

The woman shook her head. "This has nothing to do with God. This is a disease," she shouted. The pastor held up a hand as one of his men, with an unkempt thin beard and long hair, stepped forward to strike her.

"No, Luke. She is confused."

"I'm not confused." She sneered at him. "It's a virus. People are sick." She shook her head. "This is madness."

The pastor lifted his chin a bit as if he were lecturing a child. "This is a crusade. We will wipe the spawn of the devil from the earth, bringing peace to our world. Will you not join in something greater than yourselves?"

The woman frowned and the man grimaced. They glanced at one another, condemned lovers on their way to the gallows hand in hand.

"I can't be a part of this madness," she said, shaking her head. She nudged her partner with an elbow.

"No," he whispered. They looked at one another, gaining strength in their defiance.

The pastor paced a moment. *These are excellent minds that could greatly further our cause. But God's will is his word. Yes, he challenges us all. They are tempting to appease for their expertise, but I will not fall into that viper's pit.*

"Repent and join. You can see God's will before you, why do you not grasp it?"

"False prophets will show themselves. They dress like sheep, but inwardly they are ravenous wolves. You've corrupted yourself, Pastor," the woman spat. The pastor grimaced, his skin drawing tight over his skull.

"A misinterpretation of Matthew's gospel. I had faith that you would see the light, but God knew you would not join him when he made you. The Lord despises those with hearts of pride and they will not go unpunished." The pastor nodded to Peter.

Peter bent down, pulling the plug from a red can of gasoline. The aroma of fuel engulfed the room. Peter swung the can, splashing the liquid onto the man's face and body.

"What are you doing?" the man screamed. He scooted back on the bed, falling onto his shoulders.

The pastor took a deep breath, sighing out loud. "Your choice has been made."

"No, you mustn't!" the woman yelled at him. Peter continued to slosh the liquid around the room.

"Purification by fire," the pastor said, almost disinterested by them.

Peter finished the can off by dousing their clothes and bodies.

"Please, Pastor. You can't do this," the woman cried.

The man spit gasoline onto the floor. "We will join you. We promise," he sobbed.

The pastor looked down upon the groveling doctors, people that held high societal status in the old world. A world created by man, rotted through by mankind's greed, lack of piousness, and self-gratification. Now that world had crumbled away, leaving only the righteous and those marked by the beast.

"Our Crusade is one of the righteous. Mankind will survive on the backs of God's chosen people. You are the children of sin and will be washed away in the flames of time."

The pastor and his followers marched outside, the clopping of their boots echoing off the wood floor and hallway walls. Pickup truck headlights illuminated over a hundred armed men that waited outside. They stood talking and waiting, holding their weapons ready. Shotguns, hunting rifles, clubs, bats, and hammers were held loosely in their hands. They were a mere fraction of his crusaders. His army of believers. They bowed their heads to him as he drew near. A few men knelt on the ground.

The pastor's hands rose to the sky.

"Praise be to God."

"Amen," his followers said in return.

"Look at this house. This mansion. The people who live here have lived in affluence for years, hoarding their wealth, sitting on their pedestal, peering down their noses at the poor and uneducated in disgust. Feeling bad when they heard about their struggles on the radio. Horror when they watched the poor marching in the streets on television. The only action they took was turning the channel when they'd had enough." His men watched him intently, nodding their heads in acknowledgment here and there as his words rang true with what they knew as worldly fact. "They milked a rigged system that exploits the lower and middle classes to line the pockets of the rich."

His followers howled in the night, enraged by the injustice. The pastor raised his hands, and his followers quieted down in reverence. He pointed at the house.

"These people were doctors. Healers. Talented and intelligent individuals. God bestowed great gifts upon them in the hopes they would use them to serve." He dropped his hands to his sides in disappointment. "Yet here they hide while good people such as yourselves that need their help suffer." He turned and pointed at his young follower. "Gabriel's new wife languishes, ravaged by illness. Yet, they would not help." Gabriel, more of a boy than a man, gritted his lips, pained by the mention of his wife.

"They refuse to see the light. They refuse to do God's will. They refuse the opportunity, no, God's command, to remake the world in his image. Their mansion gives them no shelter when Heaven rains from above. Their science gives them no answer when God ordains those below."

His men jeered the house and the rich inside. Brother Mathias walked forward and spit at the structure. The pastor took it in, feeding on the holy fervor of his followers. His soldiers of the apocalypse.

"They have turned their backs on God and now will pay the eternal price." He nodded to Peter. The man hustled to the front of the house and flicked a lighter. Little orange and yellow flames leapt. The fire burst along a path leading inside the house. Soon the flames grew into a roaring inferno, the blaze of light conquering the darkness of night.

"God's light triumphs over the darkness," Peter said as he returned.

"You have done well, Brother Peter. Every day we grow the Kingdom of God," the pastor said.

His men cheered the fiery collapse of the old order.

The pastor raised his eyes upward, looking at the smoke-filled night sky and a smile settled on his lips.

I was placed on earth for this.

STEELE

Shores of Lake Michigan

A gold cliff rose up over a hundred feet on Steele's right-hand side. It was covered with small shrubs and stunted trees. Thin green palms of dune grass bent backwards in the wind, holding on to the hill with long shallow roots. The wind whipped off the far-stretching lake, forcing itself up the beach and into the hill. It buffeted the dune grass as it went, blowing sand, attempting to erode the hill away one cool breeze at a time.

On Steele's left, waves crashed onto the shoreline, beating the sand with no remorse. The water was almost black, and the sky reciprocated the dreariness, reflecting a gray sunless sheet from above. The weather had been dismal since Colonel Kinnick and Joseph had left them on the beaches of Grand Haven.

"How much further?" came Gwen's voice from behind him. The heavy packs weighed down on them, and the loose sand fell away from their feet. Each step felt like a battle against the elements, like they were walking on ground that could turn to quicksand at any moment. It wasn't a nice little day hike but a soul-draining trudge enough for him to want it to be over soon. He looked over his shoulder back at Gwen. Her hair was pulled tight in a ponytail, her face set in a determined line of worry. Behind her trudged lanky Kevin and stout Ahmed, both looking equally as miserable. He stopped, facing them.

"We got about ten miles to go," Steele said, pausing. "As long as we keep the cliffs on our right and the lake on our left, we will eventually get there."

"Is there like a sign or something?" asked Kevin. The beanpole high-school teacher looked like a college student in an ROTC course with his too large Army Combat Uniform on.

"There's an old dead tree that sits just below the hill on our beach. It's big and gangly and ours. I'll know it."

Kevin strained against his pack and bent his neck to the side trying to relieve the stress. "I'll keep my eyes peeled because I ain't walking any further than I have to."

Steele smiled, ignoring the complaining of his comrade. Instead, he focused on the land trying to recognize something from his past. A house sat on the cliff above them. It leaned dangerously on the bluff as if prospecting its own private beach. All whispers of a different time. Echoes of summer in the midst of a dying fall.

Wood stairs with landings every fifty steps raced up the sandy cliff leading to it. Clean naval-gray painted wood lined the house. A wooden deck lining the back of the house sat empty. Long rectangular panoramic-style windows were broken in. Behind the windows was only darkness.

"I figure we will trek another three miles up the coast and find a house to overnight in. That will give us about seven miles tomorrow." He readjusted his thick pack that adorned his back, trying to free up some slack for his M4 carbine sling so it would stop chaffing the skin on his upper back. He shifted his tactical carrier vest, trying to regain some level of comfort from the weight of the black magazines of 5.56x45 mm NATO rounds. His chipped tomahawk hung from his right hip. In front of the hand axe rested his holstered M9A1 9mm Beretta. It wasn't his preferred sidearm, but it had a similar double-single action design as did his former duty SIG he had grown accustomed to over countless hours of training in the Counterterrorism Division. He hadn't had a choice. It was take whatever Colonel Kinnick had to offer him or have nothing for the long march home.

"Do you think she'll be there?" Gwen said softly as if worried her words might reach him. Regardless, the wind carried her words away. Loose strands of her hair danced atop her head as she watched for his response.

Steele drew his mouth tight.

Steele pointed to the top of a short dune on their right. "Kevin, can you post up on that sand embankment and scout that way?"

"You got it, Captain," Kevin said. He leapt up the sand dune with long strides and a groan of discomfort. Steele gave his back a dirty look. He hated when Kevin would call him "Captain," a title he didn't want or deserve.

He breathed through his nose and looked at her. "She was there six weeks ago. That's the last I heard since phone service died." *The last you heard of your mother. What kind of son am I? She was here alone with no one, and I don't even know if she's alive.*

"A lot has happened in the last six weeks," Gwen said. Her words were pained and filled with worry. He gave her a flustered look. The puckering wound atop his skull reminded him that a lot had happened since the beginning and he still hadn't fully healed from his last scrape with death. "I'm trying to forget."

"Me too." Her pretty lips frowned. "I'm only trying to manage expectations. A lot of horrible things have happened since the outbreak..." she trailed off.

The wound complained. The wind touching the exposed healing skin still sent weird pain and other shooting sensations through the nerve endings and into his neck. He gingerly ran a hand along the top of his head where the bullet had decided to spare his life. Instead, it left him with a wicked going away consolation prize.

"It doesn't matter. I have to find out. If it were your family, you know we would do the same."

"Would we?" she said. Her words took him aback. Unrepentant gray-green eyes stared at him.

Of course we would, but I can't save us all. That's one thing I know for certain. Then why do I keep trying? It was only another layer of stress piled atop him. It was hard enough to bear the losses he already had.

"But we're here. So we're checking on my family." Waves continued their assault on the beach, roaring onto the shore.

"How will I ever know about my family?" Gwen said, her voice rising with emotion. He was taking them as far from people and cities as he could think of and basically the opposite direction of her family in Iowa. He considered them lucky to only have killed twenty or so infected in their entire four-day journey up the coast of Lake Michigan.

"I promise we will make sure they're okay," he said. Her face remained perturbed, her eyes almost matching the dark gray skies like a green thundercloud. Her eyes always seemed to change with her mood and the lighting. They spoke volumes of her soul and had only shown severe darkness since Pittsburgh.

He gave her a smile from underneath a beard that hung down to his chest like a castaway. Unwashed and unkempt save for lake water, it grew wild and free without oil or wax to keep it healthy. Just testosterone, sand and dirt fed the mangy animal on his face.

Her gaunt face paled as blood drained from her cheeks and lips.

He reached for her. "Gwen?" Her eyes grew wide and she smacked his hand away.

"What's the matter?" he said as she spun around. She darted up a sandbank, clouds of tan sand springing up behind her. She bent in half at her hips, puking into the dune grass.

"Gwen? What's wrong?" he called out. She continued to get sick as the swaying grass lapped her ankles.

Still bent over, she wiped her mouth with her sleeve. "It's just something I ate," she groaned.

Steele's stocky Egyptian ally sidled up next to him. With his previously shaved head needing a trim, he looked a bit like a chia pet experiment gone wrong.

"What do you think it was? The fish?" Ahmed asked. He held his gun uncomfortably as if he wished it were a baseball bat instead. They both watched her heave, the two of them concerned. Ahmed had saved her life early in the outbreak, and his attraction to Gwen had caused tension in the small group. The two men bonded over their mutual care for Gwen while destroying the bridges of Pittsburgh at the behest of Colonel Jackson.

"We all had it," Steele said. He watched the woman he had been in a relationship with for years heave.

"I haven't been feeling that great," Ahmed confirmed.

"The only other option is the MREs with enough sodium and preservatives to back you up for about a month."

Steele's eyes ran from Gwen back to Kevin. Kevin crouched in the grass, only his head sticking out. The lanky man gave no signals of approaching dead. Steele's eyes never rested. He was always scanning for something out of the ordinary. *Go with your gut feeling.* Last time he had ignored his gut screaming, "It's a trap!" he had almost lost his head. *Not again.*

"I'm just thankful we have food," Ahmed said.

"A little variety couldn't hurt. Let's go check on her."

The two men hiked up the embankment. Gwen held her abdomen, hunched in a miserable position.

Steele placed a hand on her back, rubbing her gently.

"Babe, you okay?" he said.

"I'm fine," she snapped. She spit hard in the sand. She stood upright, wiping her mouth with the back of her hand. Color returned to her cheeks in uneven blotches as if they still weren't sure she was better.

"I can carry your pack," Steele said, reaching for her. It would be horribly inefficient and exhausting, but he would do it. She dodged him, throwing a shoulder out of his reach.

"I got it. You have enough."

"I could carry it. I got less," Ahmed offered. Steele was already maxed out, having been forced to ruck most of the ammunition for the group generously offered by Colonel Kinnick.

Gwen straightened her back.

"No. I can do it myself. I don't need either of you carrying my pack for me."

Ahmed gave her a sorry smile. "Just trying to help."

"I'm fine. Let's keep moving," she said with an apologetic smile for Ahmed but nothing for Steele.

I cannot wait for this conversation later, he thought.

"Steele, come look at this," Kevin half-shouted. Steele scanned the beach quickly, looking for movement. That was one of the only good things about their enemy. They were noisy and moved like blacked-out drunks. He ran along the dune ledge, bounding alongside Kevin. Steele quickly took a knee, decreasing his profile next to Kevin. The gangly man pointed down the beach.

"Well, I'll be damned. More than we've seen yet," Steele said as more of an afterthought. A ragged pack of infected hobbled down the beach a couple hundred yards away. Wind whipped their torn clothes. Fractured bones protruded from gray dead skin, and intestines peered out from open gut wounds.

"What about up the stairs?" Kevin asked, straight brown hair flipping around his head. The beach had provided them with ample protection from the infected. Something had now driven them this way. Steele was wary to find out. Every time they engaged the infected, they chanced infection themselves or expended too much ammunition putting them down. Ammunition was a finite commodity at best. *Only a headshot will do. Save the bullets for when you need them.*

Steele nodded to Kevin. "Up the steps. We'll follow the coastline up top along the cliff."

They jogged along the sand embankment. When Steele reached Ahmed and Gwen, he slid down the dune, letting the collapsing sand take his weight down a few feet.

"We got infected incoming. We're going to take the cliff," Steele said.

Gwen eyed the houses as if they were wolves, peering down upon them from atop the lake cliff. "What if there are more up top?" Gwen insisted. His girlfriend was a voice of concern and reason in a sea of doubt, but doubt bred doubt. Indecision got men killed in warfare all the time. Indecision when facing the infected was a final mistake.

"Then we will have to come back down to the beach."

"We could get pinned between two groups," Ahmed said. Steele stared at him. Sometimes he wondered if he was even in charge, or if this was some cruel prank where if the infected didn't kill him, their nagging would. The Arab man looked expectantly at Steele.

"That does look like a lot of steps," Kevin said. His eyes fluttered up the cliff as he counted.

Steele took a deep breath. "So you're telling me, you would all rather risk fighting a whole pack of infected with the possibility of dying than walk up some damn steps?"

Kevin shrugged his shoulders. "Just saying. That's a lot of steps."

Steele gave him a snort of a laugh and a shake of his head.

"If you weren't carrying so many bottles of booze in your bag, this wouldn't be a problem."

Kevin smiled. Mirth filled his half-open eyes. "You don't seem to be complaining."

Steele grinned. "I'm not one to complain about a drink at the end of a long day."

"Hey, you guys. We don't know it's safe," Gwen said. Her carbine was angled downward in a safe position, but her eyes continued to watch the cliff, untrusting of what might lie in wait above them.

"We don't know what we don't know. Eventually we are going to bunk in one of the houses. No better time than now," Steele said.

"Fine," she said, glaring at him as if she had let him win this time but wouldn't the next.

Steele made for the red wooden steps at a jog, not looking behind him, knowing that one way or another they followed him.

KINNICK

Airborne somewhere over Illinois

Whop whop whop. Two helicopters' rotors thudded as they raced one another across an angry sky. Clusters of gray clouds crowded above them, pushing on one another for space. Below them, patchwork fields of brown and yellow created the land quilt of rural Illinois. A wide chocolate brown snake curved over the land, crawling as far as Kinnick could see north and south. The Mighty Mississippi River. *More like the Muddy Mississippi,* he thought to himself. Wind cut through the open doors of the UH-60 Black Hawk that ferried his men to the United States Government's last rally point in Colorado. Those were the last orders he had received from General Travis before the Pentagon was bulldozed under the dead.

Brown-bearded Special Forces Master Sergeant Hunter, his senior non-commissioned officer or 18Z, slept in the seat across from him. His beard crept down the front of his tactical gear like a neck protector, and he wore sunglasses that covered his sleeping eyes. His head leaned back against the helicopter wall with his mouth slightly open. If they weren't in a helicopter, Kinnick was sure he would hear the man snoring. The M4 carbine, the shorter, lighter variant of the M16 assault rifle, leaned muzzle down, resting against his thigh between his legs. A gloved hand rested on the pistol grip, his index finger straightened out just above the trigger. He was still safely handling his weapon even when sleeping.

Next to him sat the elusive Center for Disease Control doctor, Joseph

Jackowski. His shaggy brown hair swept low, almost into his eyes that were concealed by glasses with cracked lenses. The doctor had evaded them for over a week in the remains of Pittsburgh, Ohio, and Michigan. Kinnick's squad had finally caught up with the squirrelly doctor on the lakeshore of Michigan. Now, Kinnick's unit was a lot lighter than when they had first started. Almost half of his pieced together search and rescue unit were gone.

The doctor had brooded since they left Michigan, even as he studied Patient Zero from across the Black Hawk cabin. His eyes blinked rapidly, taking in every breath, twitch, and movement of Patient Zero.

Patient Zero mumbled something unintelligible through his gag.

Special Forces Weapons Sergeant Turmelle hit Patient Zero with his shoulder. "Shut up, Jody." He gestured to the defeated man with his head. "Jesus, this guy is such a fucking pussy."

Patient Zero hung his head in defeat, revealing his sparsely haired bald head.

Kinnick's men called Patient Zero a Jody, in reference to the military man's civilian nemesis featured in military cadence calls. Jody was medically unfit, not squared away, or brave. In military lore, a Jody actively worked against the men by stealing their girls and living a luxurious life while the servicemen fought. For Kinnick's men, Patient Zero fit the bill on everything they despised. While they had been serving their country, Patient Zero, a pathetic, infected, out-of-shape man, had destroyed their world.

When Patient Zero was coherent, he went by Richard Thompson. The man had only had one relapse since they were airborne. His body writhed and he launched himself violently at Kinnick's men. A relapse was an ugly thing, dangerous all the time and potentially deadly while in the air.

Green socks stuck out from underneath the duct tape covering Patient Zero's mouth. His men had been generous with their application of the tape. Whatever little hair Patient Zero did have would be gone when they ripped it off. His hands were gray-taped nubs, the tape wound so many times around that no part of his hands was exposed. He was seat-belted in tight as possible. He wore an extra harness clipped to the side of the helicopter in case he decided he was tired of this world and wanted to throw himself out, plummeting to the ground. Kinnick was pretty sure by the sorry look of him, he didn't have it in him to do the job right.

Turmelle nudged Hawkins, sitting next to him. The half-Asian intelligence sergeant's face was stoic as stone.

"What's the matter, Hawk? Jody's got your tongue." Turmelle snickered at his own joke.

Hawkins didn't take the bait but blinked acknowledgment. "No," he said.

Turmelle shook his black curly-haired head in irritation, staring at Patient Zero. "What?" Turmelle yelled at Patient Zero, pumping his head at him. Patient Zero flinched and looked downward. Satisfied with his level of intimidation, Turmelle leaned back with a smirk. His hand stroked his kukri. The wicked knife at his hip was enough to make Kinnick nervous that Turmelle might use it on the infected man.

Kinnick's radio clicked on in his headset. "Colonel Kinnick, we're getting low on fuel. I believe it would be prudent to set down in Hacklebarney. There's a small airfield there," the pilot said.

"Hackle-what?"

"Hacklebarney, sir. A small airfield in Iowa."

"There's an airfield around here?" Kinnick said. He leaned to the side, looking at the rectangles of brown farmland below.

"Yes, and they're responding to our radio chatter."

"There are people down there?" Kinnick leaned forward toward the cockpit. "Here I was thinking we were in flyover country. Put me through." The radio crackled and went silent.

"Hiya, this is HAK. Grady here," came a rural accent, not a drawl like the south and no elongated vowels of the northern Midwest. They stretched their sentences enough to let you know they weren't from the city and sounded off on their O's a bit so you knew they were from the Midwest.

Kinnick smiled. *Now this is a down-home country boy.*

"This is Colonel Kinnick, United States Air Force."

Hunter perked up in front of him, visibly snorting himself awake. He swatted at Turmelle's knee with his hand.

Hunter yelled over the rotors. "You sure you're still in the Air Force, boss?" A deadly smile carved out his lips.

Turmelle yelled his way. "We were thinking about adopting you, sir. You know, make you an official Snake Eater. Get you a Skins patch made." His eyes closed to almost slits as he smiled fiercely.

"You know. If you'll take us," Hunter said like a wolf trying to be sweet.

"Later," Kinnick said, covering his microphone.

Grady spoke over the line. "Flyboy, huh. I was a Marine Corps Crew Chief '78 to '86. I see your birds on radar here. Been awhile since we heard from any of you fellas."

Kinnick shook his head in disbelief. *Cannot believe these guys are still operating.*

"You think you can help out a couple of squads of knuckle-draggers with a refuel?"

Grady's laugh on the other end eventually turned into a cough. "Things must be really messed up if they are putting an Air Force full bird colonel in charge of a bunch of baboon bootlickin' grunts. Come on down. All I got left is Jet A-1 fuel." Jet A-1 was a civil aviation fuel, but it would work in the many military aircraft that preferred the Jet Propellent or JP-8 because of its anti-corrosion and anti-icing additives.

"That'll have to do. See you in five mikes." Clicking a button on the side of his headset, he switched channels. "Put down in Hacklebarney." He turned to his men. "Everyone get ready to put down. We don't know what's going on down there, so prepare for infected or otherwise."

Hunter addressed his unit. "You heard the colonel. Get ready to be in and out like a swabbie on shore leave."

Turmelle grinned, nudging Hawkins. "Faster than Hawkins at prom."

Hawkins's face was flat. Turmelle shoved him with his shoulder again. Hawkins brown eyes stayed even. One eyelid twitched. Turmelle held his hands up. "Alright, Hawk. I'll lay off. Geez, no need to get so defensive."

His men checked the status of their weapons. They patted down their vests, making sure their magazines were fully loaded and easily accessible.

Turmelle turned to Kinnick. "Sir, you think a bunch of farmers are going to try and jump us?" He finished with a laugh. "Good luck."

"A bunch of farmers took it to the invincible British in 1776."

Hunter and Turmelle smirked and shook their heads.

"But this is home field," Turmelle said.

"For who?" Kinnick said.

Both of his men shut their mouths.

"Whatever you say, Colonel," Turmelle finished. He looked back out the helicopter at the fast-approaching airfield.

***

Kinnick's soldiers spread out from the helicopters led by the Special Forces soldiers. The men knew the drill. The infected were everywhere. No place was safe. The living were sparse but dangerous. It was hard to tell what was the greater threat: man or the infected.

Each soldier covered a different sector, guns pointed outward. Three hundred and sixty degrees around each helicopter was covered by the remnants of Kinnick's unit.

The single-gated airport had only a lone runway, just long enough for a single propeller plane. A man hobbled out from a low one-story brick building.

A dusty mellow orange Allis Chalmers hat perched atop the man's head as if it were only resting there. He used a free hand to hold the hat on top of his head. His overalls were covered in grease stains and a mishmash of dried grime. The older man's eyes crinkled around the edges as he stepped up to Kinnick.

"Welcome to the Hacklebarney Municipal Airport. Name's Grady." Grady gave Kinnick a lazy salute. Tired of wrestling with his hat that didn't want to stay put, he removed it from his head. He held it in front of himself, thumbs creasing its worn bill.

Kinnick scanned the perimeter. No infected lined the chain-link fence surrounding the airfield. *Good sign.* The farther inland they went, fewer signs that the infected had conquered were there. *It's only a matter of time before they come here as well.*

Kinnick returned the older veteran's salute with a crisp hand to his forehead. Saluting still felt awkward, even after his volunteer non-official reenlistment from retirement.

"Good to see this facility up and operational," Kinnick said.

Grady scratched some white stubble on his chin, thinking about his words.

"The single-engine Cessna planes ain't flying no more. Been almost two months since we seen 'em, on account of the plague. None came back from Chicago or St. Louis. But I'm sure you boys seen enough of that." He gestured with his stubbly chin at Kinnick's men. "You can tell 'em to relax. None a' the sick ones are 'round here. Sheriff Donnellson seen ta dat."

"Hunter, take Turmelle and check the building." The operator whistled through his brown beard at the other magazine-clad soldier, and they jogged off inside the brick building.

"Hawkins, you're on zero duty." The half-Asian intelligence sergeant's eyebrow twitched, the only indication that he was unhappy with his new tasking. He pointed his M4 carbine downward, taking an outward position next to the helicopter near Dr. Jackowski and the arguably more important Patient Zero.

"Can we get some fuel? We still have a long way to go."

"Ah, of course. Where abouts you boys headed?"

"West." Kinnick gave eastward a glance over his shoulder as if he knew evil lurked on the horizon.

Grady's brow furrowed. Worry deepened his creases.

Kinnick turned back and Grady glanced at him as if he expected Kinnick to give him an explanation.

"We're in a hurry. Our mission is vital to national security," Kinnick said. He didn't want to be terse with the man assisting them, but lingering was not an option.

Grady nodded and turned away. He limped over and grabbed a yellow hose dragging it near to one of the helos.

Kinnick pointed. "It goes over there."

Grady wheezed a laugh. "Ain't my first rodeo, Colonel. I'll get you boys back on your way. Always happy to help our fighting men and women." He snapped the hose into the UH-60 Black Hawk. Grady looked over the helicopter. His hand found a string of quarter-sized bullet holes lining the fuselage.

"Looks like your bird took some pretty heavy rounds out there. Reminds me of Grenada." Grady looked back at Kinnick. The man knew they were facing a heavily armed foe. Grady's eyes danced to the other soldiers and then stopped back on Kinnick, apparently satisfied that Kinnick and his men were real soldiers and not imposters. "What's going on out there? Don't get much info since they stopped the news broadcasts." His eyes were uneasy about the things that were taking place all around him.

Kinnick gulped down dryness in his throat. *Do I give this man hope?* He rubbed his brow. *Do I tell him the East Coast has collapsed? Do I tell him the fuel he is giving us may give us hope that the doctor sitting in that helicopter can make it back to Cheyenne Mountain with Patient Zero?*

"It's complicated."

"Figured as much. You boys at least dishing it out to the bastards?" The infected army grew, and the only boundaries were those left breathing in the United States.

Our army dwindles to a handful of battered souls as we speak. "The infection spreads very fast, but we're still in the fight," was all Kinnick could muster.

Grady eyed him, gray eyes weighing the truthfulness of his words. The old crew chief gave him a knowing nod. "Sometimes all we can do is pray." He patted the side of the helicopter. "Got plenty of jet fuel here. I can keep your boys flying for awhile. Provided things don't get too ugly down here."

"We thank you for your help, but we must continue west."

Grady pulled himself upright using the helicopter. He picked his hat up and scratched his head. "Seems like the fight would be the other way."

"The fight is everywhere," Kinnick said.

Grady nodded, eyes scanning the skyline. Kinnick didn't know if the man realized that he was on the frontier of a breaking world.

"Looks like a storm is a brewin' to the east." Grady covered his eyes as if to block the impeded sun. "Better get the other bird topped off," he said with a nod. He hustled over, unhooking the hose and dragging it over to the other helicopter.

The sky blackened. Black birds flapped their wings in the distance as if they fled the storm. *Or they go to where the fresh bodies are.* Wind picked up on the tarmac, ruffling Kinnick's uniform. *A storm is coming, and we aren't ready.*

GWEN

Coast of Lake Michigan

Alternating white and blue bathroom tiles reflected her sorry face. Pulling her pants up, she fumbled with the buttons of her military ACUs in the dark. Her mind raced. She moved toward the sink, hands finally fastening her pants. She swatted blindly for the toilet in an attempt to flush it. Nothing happened when she found the handle. She jiggled it until she remembered the toilet had been devoid of all water. It was just instinct at this point to continue to try and use modern luxuries such as indoor plumbing.

She looked up in the mirror. A ghost stared back at her, illuminated only by the moon that shone through the second-floor window. She locked her hands on the counter, leaning toward her rough image. Beneath her puffy eyes, a large red spot jutted out from her chin. *Acne now? Really? Am I in junior high?*

Exhaling loudly, she stared at a mellow pink stick about five inches long. Her hands never wanted to leave their safe place on the counter edge to pick up the dreaded object. She shook her head at herself. *You have to know. You have to.*

She snatched the stick up and waved it in front of her body as if fanning herself with it. Her heart beat furiously in her chest. *This can't be happening.* She looked at the stick impatiently. The clear plastic encapsulated diagnosis screen lay void of its impending verdict.

Her mind scattered in a dozen directions as she waved the stick. *What will*

I do? Where will I go? It won't be. I can't be. She laughed nervously out loud. "Don't be silly."

Guilty eyes stared back at her, blaming her, in the mirror lined with big round bulbs along its edges. Glancing at the stick again, she saw that it still revealed nothing of her impending fate.

"Come on," she said. Her impatience grew with every second of not knowing.

Pacing, she wiped sweat from her brow. *Jesus Christ.* Her stomach had been queasy for weeks. She couldn't touch her breasts without wincing in pain, and they were noticeably larger despite her restricted diet. She had been hiding it from the others, but after the incident at the beach, they must be suspicious. Her head pounded and her skin became slick in a cold sweat.

"Goddamn it," she swore. Bile rose in her throat for the second time since they'd been in the lake house for the night. Puke spilled into the empty toilet, splashing up onto the sides. Ripping a soft yellow towel embroidered with blue sailboats from the rack, she dotted her mouth with it.

The stick lay on the counter, a poison viper waiting to strike her if only she looked at it.

"Really. You are just going to stare at it?" she said to herself. Clenching her jaw, she snatched up the evil little stick.

A large plus sign filled the little diagnosis box. Shock filled her and she blinked rapidly, trying to digest the prognosis she had known for weeks. Tears rolled down her face. She wiped one away from her eye, letting her hand cover her mouth. It was something she had wanted so badly before and had looked forward to for so long in life, and now, it was happening to her at the worst possible moment.

"Everyone is dead. Everyone else is trying to kill us. And I'm going to have a baby. This can't be happening to me."

She tossed the stick into the waste bin, disgusted by its prediction. Tearing open another package, she squatted down on the toilet again. The sound of tinkling water filled the room. She repeated the process again after that. And each time a large purple plus sign mocked her. It was as if the gods were showing contempt for her deep desire as a woman, waiting until the most inopportune time to drop a bomb of sweet infant joy on her.

An unexpected rapping on the door made her jump.

"Jesus, you scared me," she said at the door. She smoothed her clothes, exhaling loudly.

The knob turned and stopped. It twisted again.

"No need to lock the door. It's just me," Mark's voice said from the other side.

"You know I get nervous. Give me a minute. I'm getting cleaned up," she said, looking for a place to hide her personal shame.

"Do they have running water in there and you aren't sharing?" he asked.

"Ha. No running water. Give me a few minutes, okay, Mark?" Silence met her from the other side.

"You sure you're all right?" he said through the crack. "Why don't you let me in?"

"I'm fine. Now go away." *I can't tell him. If we can get to a pharmacy, maybe I can find some drugs to take care of this. A sense of dread struck her. I don't want that, but what choice do I have? Risk being pregnant and on the run during the end of the world? What kind of monster would I be bringing a child into such misery?*

Opening the window, she picked up the trash can and tossed its contents outside. The sticks were swallowed up by the night and tall grass. Straightening her camouflage, she took a deep breath to calm herself. *Everything is going to be fine.* "It's fine," she repeated to herself. "It's fine," she said into the mirror.

She tiptoed down carpeted steps to the living room. Ahmed lounged on the couch, hands behind his head. Steele sat nearby, his gear laid out. He took a cloth and oil to the receiver of his gun.

He looked up, his blond, snarled beard covering a bothered face. "Are you okay? We left you some chow in case you were still hungry." A small tan ripped MRE package sat on the ground next to him.

"Thanks, but I'm all right."

She sat down cross-legged on the carpet. The house had been untouched since the apocalypse. Closed up for the coming winter. This lake home probably belonged to someone that never made it out of the Grand Rapids metropolitan area alive.

She watched Mark work the gun, cleaning it with a rag and reapplying oil to different pieces.

"Lots of sand on that beach. Shouldn't hurt the guns too much, but long-term it might degrade their functionality. Here, let me see yours." She checked to see if the weapon was safe and handed it over to Mark. He shifted the two pins out and removed the upper receiver from the lower receiver of the black military carbine. He began disassembling the pieces from the bolt carrier group.

"These are your hotspots. Here and here. Gotta keep these as clean as possible." He wiped the pieces hard and then blew on them.

He always has been a caretaker and protector. He always had the makings of a great father. Can I ask him to do that now?

"Wish I had an air compressor." He looked up at her and smiled, mere curves of his features visible in the darkness of the house. His hair separated in the dark, revealing a nasty scar covering his skull from the front to the back.

He's still handsome with his wounds. Scarred but handsome.

"Then you slide this back in here and reconnect here, and you're back in business. Not a professional cleaning, but it'll get us by in the field. Keep us in the fight." He checked the safety of the weapon, and without pointing the barrel in anyone else's direction, he handed it back to her. He gave her a grim smile. "Don't want to flag you."

She took the weapon back, cradling its weight in her arms like a newborn. "Thank you," she said softly.

Hope lined his eyes. "Tomorrow we should be there. Check on Mom, make sure she's all right. Her house isn't ideal for defense, but I bet I can make it work in the short-term. Barricade the living room and get a sniper nest on the top floor."

He still has hope that she's alive. I still hope she is, but how can we believe that? "Where's Kevin?" she asked, trying to change the subject.

"Top floor looking out for problems," Mark said.

Could he have heard me getting sick?

She could lie to him if he asked, deny the whole thing, or she could blame it on the food again. They were men. They wouldn't take notice of minor mishaps like this. Better to root and stamp out such inquisitive thoughts early.

"I'm going to go help him."

Steele rested his head back on the white plush couch like a pillow.

"Okay. I'm going to crash for a few. Wake me up if something's going on."

"You look like you need it," she said, watching to see if he caught onto her bluff.

"I know. I know," he said, leaning back to get comfortable.

He did need the sleep. How the man operated with so little rest bewildered her, but better for her to talk to Kevin alone.

She left the two men snoozing and drifted up the stairs. Kevin stood at a window, his M4 carbine resting in the corner. He paced nervously back and forth. The moon glinted off a bottle traveling to and from his lips as he walked.

"Hi, Kevin," she said lightly. Kevin splashed alcohol onto the carpet in surprise. He looked down and back at her, disappointed.

"Gwen. God. Jesus and the saints. You scared the crap out of me. Make an announcement or something. I spilled the good stuff." He gave her a half-smile.

She stepped inside the bedroom, looking out into the window.

"Sorry," she said.

"No worries," he breathed and turned back to the window.

They were quiet, watching the night. Waves thundered below in the dead of night. The moon glowed on the water, revealing the whites of the caps as they crashed on the shore. Moans drifted from below. *The wind or them?*

"Wild and beautiful," Kevin said, startling her from her mesmerized thoughts.

"Wha-?" she said. She shook her head, folding her arms beneath her tender chest. *Try and act normal,* she reminded herself. "Yeah, it is. Almost two months ago, it would have been warm enough to go in. Perfect weather. Fall comes fast and hard up here. When we come for Thanksgiving, there's always snow," Gwen said.

Kevin took another swig from his bottle and stopped, muttering under his breath and reprimanding himself. He wiped his lips with his sleeve.

"Sorry. Where are my manners? Want some?" he asked. He shifted the glass bottle in her direction, offering her some.

"Ahh, not tonight Kevin." She held her breath, waiting to be discovered.

He took the bottle back. "Not feeling so hot, huh?"

"No, not really," she mumbled, avoiding eye contact.

He shrugged his shoulders and looked back out onto the giant fresh-water lake. "I heard you getting sick. I always say we have to be more careful about the food we eat. Tons of bacteria and parasites in the water and with no refrigerator, we are just asking to catch something."

She exhaled a bit. He was a typical man. Oblivious to the obvious. Unobservant at best. Couldn't find the ketchup if it was on his burger.

"Sure you don't want a swig?" he said with a smile. His features were long in the moonlight, his eyes only drunkenly half-open.

"No thanks," she said, avoiding his gaze. She adjusted her arms beneath her chest trying to get comfortable. *I need a new bra to hold these gals.*

Kevin broke the silence. "I have this feeling you didn't come up here just to hang out. Is there something else you want to talk about?" He gave her a side-glance.

"No." She looked away. Anger welled up in her followed by the fear of being alone. Bearing her burden alone made it so much heavier. She feared being unable to hold it all together.

"I'm pregnant, Kevin," she blurted out. Kevin stood in silence for a moment, slowly nodding his head. He took a quick swig of his whiskey as if he forgot he was holding it. He turned her way and spread his arms wide.

"Come on in for the real thing," he said. She let herself be pulled in for a hug. He smelled like whiskey and body odor. His lanky arms brought her some comfort.

After a moment, Kevin pushed her away from him. "Are you sure it's mine?" he asked. She felt a pang of guilt in her gut.

"Of course it's not yours." She laughed a bit, wiping a tear from the corner of her eyes. He released her.

"Just checking. I like to throw a few back. Thought maybe you snuck one by me," he said, chuckling. "But between you and me, it was pretty obvious. How long have you known?"

She folded her arms back beneath her breasts. "About thirty minutes. But I've suspected for a couple of weeks. How could you tell?" Her eyes watched him for recognition.

"I was a high-school teacher in a poor rural district. You aren't the first woman I've seen puking her guts out for no reason. Combined with not drinking, it doesn't take a rocket scientist or a history major."

"History major?" she laughed.

He smirked. "Yeah, we're the smartest. We know why everything is the way it is."

She stifled a laugh.

They stood in silence, the reality of her pregnancy during the apocalypse hovering over them.

"Please don't tell Mark. I'm not sure what's going to happen yet."

He made a mock symbol of locking his lips together. "Lips are sealed my dear, but on the down low, you should tell him. I would want to know, and I think he has a right to know." He pretended to throw away the key.

She pursed her lips together.

"When you're ready, of course. That's only my two cents."

She looked off to the side, avoiding the idea of an even more serious conversation with Mark. "I will, but I have to get my feet under me. Thank you, Kevin."

"For what?"

"Listening."

"That's why I'm here," he said with a smile. He gave another glance out the window. "Wait a second." Closing in on the window, he cupped his hands attempting to block out the glow of the moon.

"What is it?" she peered out, seeing only dark water.

"I thought I saw it before, but now I'm sure. Look there through those trees and down the coast." His finger thudded off the window glass.

Small slivers of orange light danced between far away trees.

"Fire," she said.

"Fire means people," he said.

She nodded, turning for the door. "I'll get Mark."

JOSEPH

Cheyenne Mountain Complex, Colorado

Water trickled down the rock walls in tiny streams. It followed the outlines of the coarse and jagged rock. The walls were uneven as if the creators of the facility were more interested in completing the complex than making it uniform. Every ten feet, metal-encased lights with exposed wiring poked outward attempting to illuminate their way with minimal effect.

A dozen soldiers' boots echoed down the corridor as they marched. The soldiers were dressed in all black tactical gear, giving them the appearance of a SWAT team. For all Joseph knew, they were. They surrounded him and Patient Zero, making Joseph feel a bit like he was a mastermind serial killer on death row. Patient Zero's head had dropped all the way to his chest. His head bobbed from side to side in defeat as he trudged.

They walked through open three-foot-thick nuclear blast doors. Circular six-inch metal locking mechanisms stuck out from the side of the door. Beyond the giant door they entered a better lit corridor, and after another thirty feet, a duplicate nuclear blast door. *Would the mountain not be enough?*

The mountain complex was a multilayered hive. Each floor gave way to another layer of the complex. Military officers passed them. Civilians with ID badges on their belts walked past. The farther Joseph walked into the safety of the bowels of the earth, the more Joseph felt the anxiety of his task. Each step took him farther from the dangers of the outside and infected but brought him closer to his molecular battlefield and the insurmountable task at hand. It was a game of chess at the microscopic level; he was the novice and the virus was the mastermind. He wrestled the doubt into his gut and settled for a permanent state of distraught uneasiness.

A black-helmeted soldier stopped and pointed to a metal door on the right. His goggle-covered eyes ignored Joseph.

"Put the subject in there," came his voice from underneath his black ski mask.

Two soldiers disappeared with Patient Zero through a doorway on the right.

Patient Zero emitted a muffled "Ow." The middle-aged beer-bellied man gave the soldiers a dirty glare as they shoved him inside the room.

Joseph pointed with his non-injured arm. "Where are you taking him?" He had been stitched up when he had arrived on site, hastily given a bottle of pain pills, and whisked away with a heavily armed escort.

"Observation room." The soldier waved a gloved hand. "Follow me, Doctor." The soldier gestured forward and a placed a firm hand on Joseph's back. A white door was opened nearby, and Joseph stepped inside with some assistance from the soldier into a dimly lit room.

A cluster of white-coated individuals gathered around a one-way glass mirror that they could see through, but the person on the other side could not see them. They ignored Joseph, enamored by the subject on the other side. They murmured and whispered to one another in careful consideration.

Joseph walked to the window and stood near a taller than average shoulder-length auburn-haired woman with pointed black glasses. Her nose stuck out farther than average and came to a sharp point. One arm was folded across her chest, propping up the other held thoughtfully under her chin. A long finger ran up her cheek.

Joseph shoved his free hand into his pocket, joining them in their observation. Richard Thompson sat attached to a metal chair. Bright lights beat down on him, glinting off his almost bald head and causing him to squint. He sobbed softly to himself, his whole body jiggling. Every few moments he would look up at the lights and mumble something. His head would then fall again and he would cry. The soldiers had removed his duct-tape-and-sock gag and replaced it with a folded surgical mask. His eyes regarded the reflective window with fear, knowing that unknown people on the other side were watching him.

"Amazing, Dr. Weinroth. Look at his facial distress. He is showing what appears to be both behavioral and physical manifestation of emotions," an older heavier-set white man said, leaning over near the auburn-haired woman.

"All of our subjects so far haven't expressed any sort of remorse or fear, only uncontrollable violence," she said, letting a finger tap the side of her mouth as she watched. She pressed her lips together as she thought. "This is interesting. Are we sure he's infected?" She looked down the line of white coats.

The fat doctor leaned away, considering her question. "We haven't run any tests. He arrived not long ago." He picked up a piece of paper, peering down at it. "It is a field subject." The doctor looked over his glasses. "Discovered by a Dr. Jackowski? Hmm, states here he is a CDC virologist. I'm not familiar with any of his work."

Joseph watched them from the corner of his eyes as he stared at Patient Zero. He cleared his throat. "He's infected. I can assure you of that."

Dr. Weinroth turned her head in his direction and gave him a curious glance from the corner of her glasses. The fat doctor leaned around her, staring at him.

"You know, if you take the gag from his mouth, he can talk too."

"He can talk? That's different than all of our research. Every other subject has lost all ability to orally communicate."

"Fascinating," the fat doctor said, his belly almost touching the window, as he got closer to it.

"Of course he can talk. He's alive," Joseph said, raising an eyebrow.

The doctor at Dr. Weinroth's side leaned past her, his fat jowls seeming to stick out farther than his belly. "Wait, who are you? How do you know this?"

"Forgive me," Dr. Weinroth said. She gave Joseph a pleasant smile with clean white teeth. "Dr. Hollis, this must be our CDC virologist, Dr. Joseph Jackowski. Our newest associate."

Dr. Hollis gave him a nod of approval, his double chin tripling. "Incredible fortitude, doctor. We had written off this scenario much earlier in the pandemic."

"Thank you," Joseph said. He removed his glasses and gently rubbed them on his clothes with one hand. The crack in one lens reminded him of the Battle of Steel City where his gun had recoiled into his face. *Could have been worse. You could have died. Many times.*

"We're ecstatic about this discovery. I'm Dr. Weinroth, infectious disease specialist with the United States Army Medical Research Institute of Infectious Diseases, USAMRIID." Keeping an arm folded beneath her, she offered the other and shook his hand. "I'm a civilian. No need to salute," she added with a little laugh. "How long have you been studying the subject?"

"We found him in Michigan four days ago. My observations have only been outward conversations."

"Conversations? He can put together complete thoughts? This is unlike anything we've seen," an Indian woman said. She stood on the other side of Dr. Hollis, blocked by his girth save for her head.

Dr. Weinroth touched his arm. A gentle and somehow comforting gesture as if he were her longtime friend. "Forgive me Dr. Jackowski, let me introduce my team." She gestured to the gray-bearded heavyset gentleman next to her.

"This is Dr. Hollis. He is with the Biomedical Advanced Research and Development Authority. They assist in stockpiling biomedical resources nationwide." *No vaccine for this,* Joseph thought. He nodded to the obese doctor.

"Next to him is Dr. Desai. She is a leader in research for live attenuated vaccines from Johns Hopkins Hospital. Her research into the CCR5 receptor of white blood cells may help us find a cure for AIDs one day." The young Indian woman smiled at him.

"Next to him is Dr. Nguyen. You may know him from the CDC." The short Asian doctor tilted his chin downward. Joseph knew him. In the hierarchy of their organization, Dr. Nguyen was second only to Dr. Williams; both were experts on bioweapons. With Dr. Williams most likely dead in the bunker of Mount Eden, Joseph supposed that made Dr. Nguyen number one in the world.

"Loved your work on weaponized anthrax," Joseph said. The Asian doctor bowed his head lower in thanks.

"If only this were that easy," Dr. Nguyen said.

The man on the far end didn't acknowledge Joseph as he stood scrutinizing Patient Zero. His hands massaged his smooth chin while deep in thought. His close-cropped white hair gave him the look of a military man.

Dr. Weinroth smiled and spoke a bit louder. "The gentleman on the end is Colonel Byrnes, M.D. We are colleagues from USAMRIID. His research in biosynthetic viruses and vaccination is top-notch." The United States Army Medical Research Institute of Infectious Diseases was based out of Fort Detrick in Maryland. Joseph knew them well. A secretive group, but they were some of the best minds against any biological threat to the United States.

The gaunt colonel regarded Joseph with intelligent gray eyes. His camouflage combat uniform revealed itself from beneath his white coat as if it were hiding.

Joseph was confused. "I thought Fort Detrick was gone? I was under the impression that everyone had met up at Mount Eden in Virginia."

Byrnes spoke as if he were annoyed with Joseph's existence. "Fort Detrick is gone. We were annihilated in under an hour. Our HAZMAT suits did nothing to stop them from ripping through the protective plastic. If I had half of my staff from there, we would be making some serious headway instead of standing here watching Patient Zero cry."

Dr. Weinroth's smile faded into a pretty close-lipped grin. "This has been a difficult experience for many of us."

"Tell that to my staff I watched get butchered alive," Byrnes said.

Dr. Weinroth's eyes pleaded with Joseph for understanding. Her eyelashes beat each other furiously. "Fort Detrick was horrible, but all of us have lost friends during this difficult time." She directed a glance toward the colonel. He was already ignoring them, back to analyzing the subject.

"We're all glad to have you here. Someone with your experience will be essential in our research and development against this global outbreak. We've adopted the facility staff and name as our own. I think it has more meaning now that we have come from all over the country to work together. Welcome to the Mountain Integrated Medical team."

Joseph nodded. It was an impressive team for research, and perhaps, the only team.

"We call it MIM for short." She pointed to a patch on the sleeve of her white coat. A doctor's caduceus, a staff with wings and dual serpents running up its shaft, sat in the middle of two M's that looked like mountain peaks. The words Mountain Integrated Medical curved beneath the design.

He took a deep breath and gulped. "Thank you, Dr. Weinroth."

"Call me, Rebecca."

"Thanks, Rebecca," he said with a faint smile.

Her smile in return made his arm hurt just a little less. He supposed that was all the comfort he could ask for in a time like this.

"I can take a look at your arm later if you'd like. How'd that happen?"

"I was stabbed," he said. The cold steel inside his arm still haunted him.

Concern flooded her eyes. She visibly gulped.

"It was an accident," he hurried out. She gave him a quick smile.

"Of course," she managed, seeming uncomfortable.

"I would appreciate you taking a look." She nodded and turned her attention back to Patient Zero.

The team stood watching the tears stream down Patient Zero's stubbly cheeks. These were his band of fellow warriors in the battle for mankind. They had come from all different backgrounds. They had all lost friends and family to the infection. They had all watched, helpless as the world crumbled around them. Now it was time for them to strike back.

KINNICK

Golden Triangle, Colorado

Kinnick rode in a Humvee down a wide residential street. They passed newly built single-family homes, some still with turned earth in unfinished front yards. Humvees sat in a few of the driveways. No other cars drove on the road aside from military vehicles, giving him an eerie feeling in the depth of his gut that he was in the Green Zone of Iraq.

Three eight-wheeled Strykers grumbled past traveling the other way. The big green personnel carriers had been effective at protecting soldiers in Iraq and Afghanistan from IEDs and small arms fire, and he imagined they were being put to excellent use against the infected.

Hunter sat behind him, sunglasses on, beard fluttering in the wind, staring out the window. An airman from Peterson Air Force base sat in the driver's seat and another soldier stood in the center turret, manning the Mk 19 grenade launcher on top of the vehicle.

"He ever hit any of them with that?" Kinnick asked, throwing a thumb at the turret.

The driver smiled. "Yup. Shreds the bastards. Sometimes they crawl, but it does good work against large groups and makes it easier when the bastards aren't quite as fast."

Kinnick nodded, wiping a hand through his hair. He had never lost the short, military-style hair even after he retired. Some things just stick with you, but now, his hair was as long as it had been when he was in college at Purdue.

Probably a lot more gray than before the outbreak.

They zipped by long stretches of fences lining the roadways. The fences engulfed entire neighborhoods in sturdy chain-link steel with razor wire spiraling around the top.

"How far does the Safe Zone span?"

"We call this the Golden Triangle, sir. We've been able to control the area between Peterson Air Force Base, Fort Carson, and Cheyenne Mountain. It cuts off the southern part of Colorado Springs which we now use to house extra troops and civilians."

As far as Kinnick could see, there were green and brown mountains, trees turning shades of yellow and brown, and housing. "I understand the triangle, but why Golden?" he asked the airman.

"Cause if you are inside, you're golden, Colonel," the airman said with a grim smile.

"I see," Kinnick responded, clamping his mouth shut. The Pentagon died without military support, and portions of the United States Armed Forces sat in Colorado, not even lifting a finger to help their fellow brothers and sisters in arms. Soldiers and civilians all over the country were being overrun and murdered. *Can I blame them for creating a base of operations to continue the fight? That's what I would do. Consolidate my forces and strike back out.*

The Humvee stopped at a fenced-in checkpoint that clearly kept civilians from the military base housed within the safe zone. A soldier waved them through layers upon layers of fencing, concrete barriers, fortified buildings, and machine gun nests. A sign that looked like six mountain peaks read *U.S. Air Force, Peterson Air Force Base.*

They rolled to a stop near a modern building with white sides and dark bluish-gray glass reflecting outward, preventing anyone from seeing in. The building had a cold government look to its architecture made with long lines.

"Here's your stop, Colonel," the airman said, sounding a little nervous.

"Thank you, Airman." Kinnick and Hunter dismounted the vehicle and walked down the white concrete sidewalk leading to the building. Kinnick could sense the master sergeant's uneasiness next to him even with the swagger in his step, but it was as if he were repelled by the thought of being inside an office building.

"I'm Colonel Kinnick," he said to two lightly armed, black-beret clad airmen standing outside heavy glass doors. The area was quiet, untouched by the chaos engulfing the nation. The airman on the right whispered in his radio.

"You have clearance to enter, sir."

The door audibly clicked and the security specialist pushed it open, revealing a large lobby with a shiny polished granite floor. Airmen in Airman Battle Uniforms sat at a large reception desk. Officers swept through the room, holding red folders with papers sticking out of either end.

Weary from his journey, Kinnick took a seat on a long bench on the wall. Hunter let his carbine rest in front of his body and joined him. Not more than a moment after sitting down, his foot began to tap repeatedly. It was the most uneasy Kinnick had seen him since they'd met.

"I fucking hate offices. Just something not right about 'em," Hunter said.

Kinnick looked around. "Safe and clean. Living men and women. What's not to like?"

"All of it. The people. The conformity. The life-sucking vibe that goes along with it. Some guys love the smell of fresh carpet and computers, but not this one."

"Just be thankful we aren't still stuck in the field. We'll get a nice break now."

"I'd take the field any day of the week over this nine-to-five hell."

An officer walked by, eying Hunter with his carbine.

Hunter leaned forward. "See?" He gestured at the man with an elbow. "Look at them. Did you see the way that guy looked at me? Like he'd never seen a gun before. Fuckin' Powerpoint Rangers rule this unholy prison."

Kinnick grinned at the Green Beret. "Just wait until we get inside. They got some nice toys in here. Maybe you'll learn something."

Hunter shook his head. "The Chair Force and their gadgets. No offense. At this point, you are basically a grunt by association, and I'm not saying they don't have their place, but you can't win a war from the sky. You need boots on the ground if you want a…" He paused thinking for a moment. "Resolution."

"I suppose we should be thankful they're still in the fight. I'd rather have them than not."

They waited five minutes and a short officer with oak leaves on his shoulders and black hair on his head and glasses greeted them. "Good afternoon, sir. You must be Colonel Kinnick. I'm Major Thomas, 10th Special Forces Group, based out of Fort Carson."

Kinnick stood up. "Major Thomas, good to meet you." They shook hands.

Hunter piped up behind Kinnick. "Figured you would have bought the farm already?" He stood up behind Kinnick. "And somebody promoted you to major?"

The major narrowed his eyes, focusing past Kinnick. Kinnick thought the major might shove him to the side.

"Holy hell, Master Sergeant Hunter. I thought you got taken out by a goat herder south of Kandahar," Thomas said, grinning.

The two men shook hands. "Would have rather been taken out by a goat herder than be in your shoes. Look at you with your shiny oak leaves." Hunter pretended to brush his friend's shoulder off. "A bit dusty too from sitting inside all day."

"Promotions are a bit expedited these days," Thomas said.

Hunter shook his head. "You used to be a hard charger, and now, here you are pushing pencils with the best of the computer junkies."

"I would go back into the field in a heartbeat," Thomas said. He addressed Kinnick. "You were in good hands, Colonel, coming in with this alley cat. Tough as nails and mean as a bear with a toothache."

"Yes, I was. I owe my life to him on more than one occasion." Hunter had fought like the devil himself against hordes of infected and rogue military units. The rogue units still left a sour taste in Kinnick's mouth even now. Kinnick had no doubt he would have been killed without him. He would be in a ditch feeding the worms or the infected. It didn't matter much, because either way, he would have been dead.

Most of Kinnick's search and rescue squad had perished during the mission. The tomb of Mount Eden's underground bunker had claimed most. The bunker that had sat about an hour outside of Washington, D.C., and doubled as an emergency evacuation facility for Congress during a disaster had turned into a pit of hell.

"Let me get you inside to NORAD. We'll get you up to speed on the ongoing operations."

"Ongoing operations?"

Thomas gave him a questioning look. He blinked in rapid succession behind his glasses. "Yes, sir. We are at war here. Operations are currently underway to take back the United States."

Kinnick couldn't hide his look of puzzlement. "Carry on, Major." *We are at war, but I was under the impression there weren't that many of us left.*

Three card-access doors and two ID checks by soldiers and secret service agents and they ended up inside a large operations center.

The wall was covered in giant projection flat-screen televisions. The huge televisions tracked flights. Others displayed jostling cameras of troops on the ground. Another was a map of the United States, displaying green swaths over large parts of the country. The green seemed to pinch the middle inch-by-inch, starting from the coasts.

"You still have ongoing flight missions?" Kinnick asked, looking at the flight radar screen.

"Yes, sir. We are funneling supplies mostly to and from Elmendorf Airfield. It has been largely unaffected by infection. Most of my boys from Fort Carson ended up there. Put some hurt on some bastards and locked that place down." Faster moving blips on the map caught Kinnick's eye.

"You're still flying combat sorties?"

Thomas looked at him, confused. "Why yes, sir. Most of our combat runs are in the Colorado area. I don't understand. Did someone tell you otherwise?"

Kinnick ground his teeth. "I was at the Pentagon before it fell. We only had local air support. Eventually that stopped. We could have used some help." He stared at the man for a moment. "Any help."

Thomas looked down at his feet before he spoke. "I'm sorry, Colonel Kinnick. Those decisions are above my pay grade."

Kinnick's mouth twisted. "Whose decision was it?" *So many lives lost. So many great minds.*

"That came down from the vice president." He stopped himself. "Well, the President now."

"The president's dead?" Kinnick said louder than he wanted. People wearing headsets turned from their computer monitors to stare at him. Hunter whistled a high-pitched note in surprise behind him.

Kinnick gave him a nasty look. "Not helping, Master Sergeant. The president is dead?" he said softer.

"It's unknown, sir. He went missing during the initial evacuation of Washington, D.C."

"Are you kidding me?" *The bastard's been missing this whole time.*

"No, sir."

"We had no idea." Kinnick clenched his jaw. *The American public has no idea. Most of the American public has been left for dead. Entire military units have been left for dead, and we don't even know who the hell is leading us.* "Is that bastard vice president here?"

"I am," came a voice from behind him.

STEELE

Northern Michigan

Steele peered out into the night as the waves of the giant lake collided with the shore. Fire gleamed in the dark miles down the cliff.

"You see right there?" Gwen said, pointing out the window. Miniature flames spoiled the encroaching night. Steele crossed his arms over his chest, thinking. *This isn't good.*

"What do you think is going on?" Kevin whispered as if the flames miles away could somehow hear him.

"Someone set a fire, and it isn't the infected," Steele said. He pulled on a snarl in his beard. *People always mean bad things.*

"What are we going to do?" Gwen asked on his other side.

"A fire that size in the night. Must be a building." His eyes couldn't leave the flame. He was a moth to its blaze. It lured him. It beckoned him. It was dangerous and primal, but he couldn't pull his eyes away. "We will wait until morning and take a look."

"We shouldn't go now?" Gwen asked. Worry plastered her face. He gave her a second glance. Her face was pale like a ghostly shade.

Must be the food poisoning. "No, tomorrow."

"Why?" she asked.

She will be the death of me. I would have bet on the infected, but the longer I live, the greater her odds.

"Because it's dangerous and I don't want to walk into another trap like we did in West Virginia. Even if it means people who need help have to wait." He reminded himself of his training. It seemed like a past life, as if generations had come and gone and yet he still lived. *Make sure the scene is safe before helping others.*

Is she disgusted or uncomfortable? He couldn't tell.

***

The next morning they set out early. Dawn cracked the horizon like an egg sitting sunny-side up. The beach was peppered with the tortured faces of the infected, so Steele opted to lead them along the edge of the coastline cliff. They ran through overgrown leaf-covered yards from lake house to lake house.

Most of the houses were already boarded up for the harsh Michigan winter that lay ahead. Only a few die-hard Michiganders would brave the lake-effect snow the Great Lakes State had to offer. One thing a Michigander always knew was that, no matter what, winter was only a few months away.

Steele's mother was one of the brave. She never seemed to mind the cold that winter brought, opting for wood fires instead of sunny Florida or dry Arizona. Most of her friends and colleagues were snowbirds, usually retirees that migrated from the northern states to the south in the winter to avoid the harsh weather. Perhaps the isolation of a Michigan winter was worth it now.

Steele left his friends near the side of a brown boxy house. Crouching, he ran to the cliff line. Spying down his optics, he zeroed in on the pack littering the beach. *They know we're here. Something keeps them lingering.*

He watched as one tried to climb the hill. After shuffling up four feet, the infected man stumbled, crashing onto his hands and knees. Clawing his way up the sandy cliff, he tumbled backwards, rolling down like a log.

How are we losing?

Sand flew into the air as the infected tumbled, arms flailing. He got up again and repeated the clumsy process.

They will never surrender. They will never give up until we are all dead. How do we continue this fight knowing our enemy will never give up? The only option is for us to never admit defeat. Go toe-to-toe with the bastards. Until we win or we all disappear. Maybe we're the crazy ones to want to continue on in this world.

He lowered his M4 carbine and gave a quick wave to his comrades with a quick bend of his fingers in their direction. Kevin groaned when he saw all the steps to the bottom of the beach.

"We can't go along the cliff?" Kevin whispered.

"The beach is clear ahead of them," he said. He waved down the beach. Most of the infected clustered near the steps they had gone up the night before. "Now, let's move, soldier."

"I'm not a soldier," Kevin retorted.

"You want to read history or make it?" Steele said.

"I prefer a more leisurely pace with fewer steps."

Steele gave him a grin and gentle shove. They rucked down to the beach in single file.

Reaching the bottom, their feet sank into the loose sand of the pristine beach. Their footprints would be swept away by fresh water in the night. The weight of their packs pushed them deeper into the sand, making each step more difficult than the last, as if each tiny grain of sand wished to slow them down by crumbling and giving way beneath them.

"Wish we would have stayed at the top," Kevin complained.

Steele ignored him. Within no time, sweat trickled down Steele's back settling into his military loaned already sweat-stained ACUs.

A plume of smoke rose in the distance, a dissipating black snake in the sky. A smoky stink hung in the air, refusing to fade away. It worried him. He knew it was from the fire they had seen the night before. Not knowing who had set it or why started to pummel his nerves. *Burning bodies?* He sniffed the air hard. The sickening scent of burnt human flesh was not present. *Were they smoking someone out of hiding?*

Plowing forward underneath the weight of their packs and the impending dread of what they might find, the small group trekked across the sand. The clouds of billowing black smoke grew larger, warning them to stay away, but they kept moving. Idleness was death. Step by step, they marched closer to his mother's lake house. Each step made his heart hammer faster, and an excited fear rose up inside him.

Miles later, Steele halted them with a tight fist in the air. The smell of burnt timber was thick. The smoke was a visible fog enveloping the surrounding sandy cliff.

A single dead oak tree sat upright in the sand. It had been there as long as Steele could remember. As a kid, he would throw his towel over its low-hanging branches that had been eroded by wind and rain over its decades of life. These low sun bleached-white branches had still been sturdy enough to support the weight of their beach bags and belongings, keeping them from getting sandy in the summer.

This is my beach. That is my old oak. We're here. He watched the beach, trying to digest the thousands of thoughts shooting through his mind.

"What's the matter?" Gwen asked. She hadn't been there enough to know the difference between the miles of beach they had traversed.

"This is my beach," he said, voice flat. Almost as if he didn't believe it.

She coughed, covering her mouth from the smoke. "We're here? I thought we were still a few miles out."

"So did I."

A lone moan floated along, gliding to their ears. Steele ignored the unhallowed voice. He was fixated on the bleached tree and the palm-like dune grass that led up his hill. One hundred and twelve wooden steps that he painted summer after summer led up the cliff to his family's home.

"Up those stairs is my mother's place." The deep lonesome moan was echoed by a second and a third.

All of Steele's party scanned the dunes looking for the culprits. Their carbines were held in the low ready. The undead offered nothing but more death.

"Nothing too drastic. Stay together in a tight group. Don't let any get behind us," he said, tasting the smoke in the back of his throat.

A head wobbled near his dead oak tree. *That's my tree.* He made for the lakeside steps only to see the bobbing heads of more infected crossing the dunes for him. His hand found the tomahawk on his hip. It screamed for the blood of the dead, electrifying beneath his hand. He let it free and it almost hummed in anticipation.

"Let's keep it quiet as long as we can," he said over his shoulder. He crested the top of the dune. The number of dead surprised him. They clustered over the dunes farther down the beach. *Must be the fire drawing them in.*

Steele cut into the group of infected. He chopped down hard, his tomahawk sticking for a moment before he ripped it free again. He sliced diagonally through the air left and right, catching another infected in the face. The blade stuck in the creature's cheekbone, and Steele felt the rotting bone shatter. A hand blurred by Steele's face as Ahmed jabbed another under the chin, his blade running into its brain. Gwen grunted as she jammed the point of her dagger into an infected rounding the tree. She pushed the body back down. The infected knocked into the tree and collapsed.

"Steele!" Kevin shouted, his voice low. He pointed down the beach. Infected bounded up and over grassy dunes, many more than Steele cared to get up close with.

Steele glanced over at Gwen and then at the others. "Go hot," he shouted, slipping the tomahawk back into his belt.

Steele moved at the high ready, keeping his carbine pressed to his shoulder, his left hand grasping the fore grip, right hand resting on the pistol grip stock of his M4 carbine. The first infected down the dune crumpled into a pile of gutless meat, its eye disintegrated by his hot 5.56 round. Crack. Crack. His shoulder easily accepted the recoil of the piston-run long gun. His body was built for fighting. Bounding up the dune, he reached its crest with a snarl.

"This is my beach!" he screamed at them. Dead soapy white eyes stared at him, unknowing of anything except death. Fleshless decrepit fingers spread wide for him.

Again and again his carbine barked, followed by the pops of the rest of his group behind him. Still more came over the sandy dunes.

"Forget it. Make for the stairs," he shouted and they ran. "Move, move, move," he yelled at them. He pushed them up the steps and they huffed by him. He took the rear. Press. Pause. Press. A moaning infected, its skin hanging from its chewed open jowls fell forward, feet kicking up behind it as it dropped headless to the ground.

Feet clicked off the brown-stained wooden steps as they ran for the top.

Steele checked his six a few times making sure they were not followed. His thighs quivered as he churned out step after step. Soon he caught up with the rest, everyone's bodies exhausted by their heavy packs, dogging it up the steps.

The last flight of stairs was shrouded in smoke like a gray funeral shroud, an acidic chemical burning their eyes and stinging their nostrils. Gwen coughed, covering her mouth with her sleeve as she walked.

"A few more steps," Ahmed said, breathing hard and pushing up Gwen's pack as they crested the cliff. Steele's heart thumped in his chest trying to get enough blood and oxygen to his muscles. His three comrades stood on the top landing waiting, all eyes preoccupied.

Steele bent down, sighting up the infected that struggled even slower up the stairs. He exhaled and squeezed the trigger. The lead infected fell backwards, mangling the other infected in a mass of limbs as they rolled down the steps. He turned around when he heard Gwen gasp.

"What?" Steele shouted, pounding out rest of the steps.

Ahmed looked at Steele fast approaching with fear in his eyes.

"What?" he said. He took the final few steps in groups of two.

He crested the cliff edge.

Gwen's hand instinctively covered her mouth. Kevin peered at the ground. Ahmed put a hand on Steele's chest. "Steele, man. Let's take this slow." Steele removed his hand with more force than he would have liked, unable to take his eyes off the destruction before him.

"Don't," was all Steele could squeeze out.

The house was a charred, blackened foundation of what used to be an exquisite log cabin. Around the edge, tan, round full logs lay scorched, cracked, and broken. His childhood sanctuary lay in ruins before him. His only place of refuge. The place where he found peace. He ran forward.

"Mom?" he said at the rubble.

"Mark, no," Gwen said softly. He breezed past her.

"Mom?" he shouted louder.

Heat emanated from the structure like he was next to a blazing fireplace. He raced around the sides of the building looking for any signs of her. The woman that had raised him. The woman that had loved him unconditionally as only a mother could. The mother that supported him when he decided to join the Division instead of playing it safe as a teacher or lawyer.

He looked over at her neighbor Jim's house. The large white-and-green lake house stood, still intact. Hope bubbled inside him. *Maybe she's there. Or somewhere else.*

"Mom?" he called out.

Gwen walked near the ruins. "Mary?" Gwen called out behind him. "Kevin and Ahmed, check that house," she said. The two men jogged off.

No one returned his calls. The only sounds filling the air were the soft crackle of wood, the waves of the lake, and the moans of the infected at the bottom of the steps.

He paced near the burnt down home until the two men returned, unable to comprehend the scene ahead of him. A somber Kevin shook his head no, and the bubble of hope in Steele's chest popped. He stopped pacing and his eyes felt distant and unfocused. His M4 dropped from his hands. The sling did its job and the gun swung down at his side. His hands dug into the smoldering charred wood as he searched for anything to solve this mystery. He threw pieces to his sides, looking for something to prove him wrong, something to prove that this wasn't his house.

"Mom. I'm here!" he shouted. His voice was absorbed by the black hole of the ruined structure. He could hear the others shouting his mother's name, but he ignored them. Piece after piece he tossed behind him until his hands were black and scalded, and his clothes filthy with soot.

Exhausted, he dropped to his knees in tall grass badly in need of a cut. *What happened? Where is she? Who did this?*

"Steele, check this out," Ahmed yelled from the garage.

Steele pushed himself up off the ground and stumbled for Ahmed. His mind was a foggy mess of confusion and questions.

Ahmed stood near the garage next to the front lawn looking down at the ground. "Look." Ahmed pointed at the ground. Deep tire treads lined the grass and earth, not bothering the driveway. Long ago, his father would have murdered whoever had destroyed his well-groomed lawn.

"Over here too," shouted Kevin. The lanky man kicked at the ground.

Steele was a bloodhound on the trail, his mind a blind haze going from track to track.

"Must be at least a dozen vehicles," Ahmed said. Steele bent down, feeling the earth that was now a clue to finding his mother.

"There's some single tracks over here," Kevin shouted.

Steele stared at him. "Someone knows what happened here, and I will find them," Steele muttered with bloodshot eyes. "Come on."

TESS

Northern Michigan

Squeezing her knuckles, Tess pushed them in until they popped one by one down the breadth of her hand. Faces formed a continuous crowd around her. Just outside their rowdy ring was a tall maroon-bricked lighthouse that spired for the sky. People at the top leaned over the black railing, ringing the observation deck.

The faces around her laughed, yelled, and pushed, trying to get a view of the entertainment. Tess wiped a hand through her thin short hair, letting the grease from not bathing hold it slicked back.

A big fat woman stood across from her. Big Bessie was a truck driver and new to the camp, bringing in a large supply of non-perishable food from the local grocery store Edmund's in Muskegon. Her chins doubled up upon other chins. "Bring it on, you fuckin' twat," Big Bessie shouted at her. She raised her big bloated arms up and down beneath a crudely cut off long sleeve shirt to fire the crowd up.

They cheered.

"I got a can of tuna on Bessie!" shouted a man.

"Double or nothing Bessie breaks her tiny little arm," said another.

Ye of little faith.

Two gamblers shook hands on the wager.

Tess gave Bessie an ever-so-sly smile.

An attractive lightly-bearded man stood behind her. She turned toward him. He gave her a wide grin, his strong hands taking her slender shoulders in his hands. He massaged her like he was prepping a prize fighter for a fight.

He leaned close to her face. "You think you can take her?" he said under his breath.

"She's all fat. No technique. She's already lost," Tess said. She wobbled her neck from side to side while he rubbed her back. *Keep it loose.*

"I put a week's worth of food on it with Randy, so I hope you are right," he said. She looked over the crowd, locating Randy. He laughed with the rest, already celebrating his victory.

"What a dick," she muttered.

Glancing down at his hands touching her shoulders, she laughed short melodic notes. "I don't lose, Pagan."

"Oh look at the little baby. Needs a little back rub from her pool boy before she gets her *arms* ripped off," Bessie roared at her. Bessie's voice was deep and cracked, having been scarred by years of smoking.

Tess raised her tattooed arms over her head, stretching. Speed, leverage, and timing were her only weapons. A hundred-and-ten-pound woman wasn't going to stand a chance against all of Big Bessie's weight for long. Size mattered, but it could be mitigated with proper technique.

Tess stalked up to a table that had been set in the middle of the encampment for this single activity. Big Bessie positioned herself at one end and Tess took the other. Wedging her elbow into the table, she locked eyes with Bessie. Bessie's eyes were the color of a fresh turd. Ugly yellow hair hung down in dirty curls around her shoulders.

"Look at this girl here," Bessie wheezed with a sneer. "Little mosquito bites for tits." The crowd laughed at her insult. "I remember my first beer."

"Pagan," Tess called over her shoulder. "Vodka," she said coolly.

Bessie thought this was hilarious and laughed uproariously with the crowd around them. Bikers and woodsmen were the loudest, but most of the people were refugees with nothing to do.

Pagan slammed down a bottle of 150 proof Whitetail Vodka and set down two shot glasses. The harshest vodka found in the Mitten State. *Better off drinking pure gasoline.* He poured the vile, clear liquid in both glasses. It smelled like a blend of fuel and rubbing alcohol; it probably could be used as both in a pinch.

Tess grasped a glass with slender fingers. *Don't think about it.* She threw it back and the booze burnt the length of her throat like she had swallowed fire. Bessie reached for the other shot glass, but before she could wrap her pudgy fingers around it, Tess had scooped it up. She smiled at Bessie and tossed that one back as well. Bessie smirked.

"So the little thing can drink a bit," Bessie grunted.

Tess smirked back. "Fill it up again," Tess commanded. Her eyes never left Bessie's round, plump face.

"Hahaha," Bessie chuckled. "Fill it up, pretty boy." She made kissing noises at Pagan.

Tess inwardly laughed at his discomfort.

Pagan leaned close, filling them up. "I hope you know what you're doing. I'm not sure getting drunk is going to help." He tipped the bottle once and then twice. Bessie swatted at Pagan's behind. He tolerated her with a mild grin.

Tess belched rancid fire. "Eyes over here, Big Bessie," she said, pointing her index and middle fingers at Bessie then back at her own eyes. "He's mine." The crowd laughed.

"Come on, Tess," Gregor shouted. He was a broad-framed welder from a construction company in Cadillac. Long black hair hung down to his shoulders.

"Drink it up," added Garrett. The tall biker smiled in glee through his salt-and-pepper beard. He wore the same black leather vest as the other bikers from the Red Stripes Motorcycle Club.

Tess threw the next shot back and tossed the glass onto the ground. Before it hit the earth, she was sucking down the next. Shaking her head like a dog, she was ready.

"Whew," she shook out.

Bessie laughed. "Look at her. She can hardly sit in the chair."

Tess placed her elbow on the table, exhaling loudly. She glanced from her hand to Bessie and back again.

Bessie's elbow thumped down, shaking the table. It trembled under her weight. Her sweaty hand engulfed Tess's, letting Tess carry the brunt of her fatty arm.

Thunder, a grizzled gray-bearded biker, pushed his way through the crowd. His leather vest was covered in patches. The largest one was a black skull with its mouth slightly open encased in a diamond of blood-red. Stripes of the same blood-red color lined overtop of the skull. Four small blue naval stars decorated the background.

He cleared his throat. "Ladies, and I use that term loosely." Bessie laughed uproariously at the comment, coughed to the side, and hacked a glob of phlegm on the ground.

"I see plenty of 'em round here," Tess said, staring up at him. Her eyes dared him to say otherwise. Thunder's patch-covered motorcycle club vest hung open, revealing a basketball-sized hairy belly. A red bandana held his long graying hair back behind his head.

"We still can't confirm if you're a girl, Miss Tess," he said with a grin beneath his bushy beard. "Only rules are, feet can't leave the ground and hands must stay locked together for the entire match. Do you understand?"

"I do," Tess responded.

"Let her stand up, won't matter," Bessie said.

Tess rotated her body so her hips were in line with her shoulders and arm. *I must pull fast and hard toward myself to negate her great strength and size.*

"Then let's begin." His weathered, cracked hand rested briefly on the two women's.

"Ready. Set. Go." He raised his hand with a flourish, standing back to watch the mayhem with a smile.

Bessie grunted as Tess hooked her hand, pulling Bessie toward the edge of Tess's side of the table. The booze was starting to kick in and she felt invincible. Bessie saw it too, glaring intently at their hands as Tess moved her inch by inch, her thin muscles straining as hard as they could in her arm.

Bessie turned red with effort. "Rarrr," she screeched, focusing her energy on bringing their hands back toward her. Tess's arm quivered as Bessie gained the advantage, pushing Tess's hand further and further from victory.

Tess's arms were skinny at best. She wasn't going to win a pushing match.

The pressure on her forearm made her think her arm was going to fracture and explode.

Bessie exhaled and sucked in more air, her face looking like a red balloon. One more inch and Bessie's weight would finish Tess over the top.

Tess twisted her hips in her seat, using her shoulder to gain leverage. With a slight maneuver of her hand, which Bessie would never notice, she forced her competitor to grip the bottom of her palm. Then she pulled Bessie's hand directly in toward her body, displacing her challenger's center of gravity. Using her momentum, she slammed Bessie's hand home, letting the table be a backstop. Releasing the woman, Tess stood to the cheering of the crowd and the jeering of her defeated opponent.

Tess held her hands open wide in the air and spun around in a circle.

"Are you not entertained?" she yelled at them.

Pagan wrapped an arm around her. "That was great, babe." From the side, Thunder nodded his head approvingly like a proud father.

"You never cease to amaze me, Miss Tess," he said.

Bessie rubbed her hand. She stared at it, confused as to why it had betrayed her. "Bessie, you can leave those supplies by the camper."

"How did you do that?" Bessie said. She cradled her hand in the other.

"If I told you, I'd have to kill you," Tess said, raising an eyebrow.

Bessie stood up from the table. "I'll drop off the food. You are a strong little bitch; I'll give you that," Bessie said.

The crowd dispersed to their separate campsites. Tess and Pagan crossed back to their camper, his arm hooked around her waist. Tess stopped, turning back to Bessie.

"Bessie, you are free to stay here as long or as short as you would like. You need not be alone."

Bessie smiled faintly. "Thank you, Tess. I'll stick around for awhile, but I want a rematch."

"You're welcome to try," Tess said with a smile.

Back in the camper, Tess had sex with Pagan. The combination of her victory and the pleasure made her feel alive again if only for a fleeting moment.

They lay next to one another in their musty camper from the '70s. Fake wood made from plastic covered its interior panels. Long thin vertical lines of brown, tan, and white decorated the couches. It was the worst color scheme she'd ever seen, but the camper was home. She looked up at the yellow-stained ceiling, hands behind her head, naked aside from an old patchwork quilt covering her lower half.

The man next to her was lean and hard. His body had more muscle when they first had met during the beginning of the madness, and now he was only thin muscle. She had been with Darren Pagan ever since. Tess would never call it a relationship—she didn't have relationships—but it was a mutual agreement they had fallen into. More of a person to pass the time with. She felt the former Marine although there were no former Marines, only Marines, stir next to her as he woke up.

"Can't sleep?" he whispered. He shifted his weight in the futon-style bed and the whole camper creaked.

"You know I don't sleep."

"You want to talk about it?"

"Nope."

He paused. "Thunder and his gang said they saw torched homes along the lakeshore again while they were out collecting."

"Who do you think is setting them?" she asked. She rolled over to pull a joint from a baggie beneath her pillow. Lighting it up, she took a hit and passed it to Pagan. He burned the weed, its deep red embers glowing brightly. It always surprised her that the Marine would smoke weed with her, but then again she never expected to be a de facto leader of a group of survivors in the apocalypse either.

"From what I can gather," he said, his voice rose as he tried to hold it in before exhaling the light blue smoke through his mouth, "it doesn't seem to be diversionary or random. The fires seem to be set on purpose."

"But to what end? You don't think it's those nutjob Christians."

"I'm not sure. This is pretty far north for them, but I won't know unless I get up close and investigate." He passed the joint back to her. She placed it in her mouth and inhaled.

"I don't want any surprises from anyone. Tomorrow you should go check it out." She put out the weed in an ashtray. Her body felt light and relaxed. The only way she could feel relaxed now was by smoking. Survival was a constant anxiety that never went away. That's what happened when everywhere you went people tried to kill and eat you.

The Little Sable Point community had started with her and Pagan holed up inside the lighthouse. Narrow steps led upward three floors to the lighting chamber. They had slept on the top-level observation deck, wind howling around them with views of the lake and dunes for miles and miles. It was breathtaking in more ways than one. The land had been summer green, the dunes sandy gold, and the water ocean blue. The old age of the lighthouse had made her wonder if it would even stay up in the gushing wind.

Within a week, others had found their way to Little Sable Point. Refugees that fled the infected were drawn to its rotating lights while there was still power.

The surrounding woods and few houses isolated it from most people. Soon after the people came, the infected found them. She and Pagan had killed the most, gaining them the loyalty of the others.

Now it was a refuge for roamers and the unaffiliated, the lost and the broken. They all came here and found a bit of solace from the storm. While the power still worked, the light shone, calling to the fleeing people. No one made them stay. A loose rule of law was set forth, mostly from the Red Stripes who enforced it. It was enough to keep everyone safe.

They came in campers, semis, buses, pickups, and cars that all encircled the lighthouse, providing a protective barrier to the outside world of the infected. When one left, the others closed ranks. Any large packs of infected were sighted from atop the lighthouse, and the small groups or individual infected that came upon them were forced up against the sturdy ring of vehicles.

Gunfire echoed from the edge of her camp.

Pagan pulled the blinds back, eying the outside suspiciously.

"Infected?" she asked, slipping on her loose tank top.

Bullets sounded off in quick succession.

"No." Pagan hopped out of the bed, slipping pants on over his muscled legs.

"We're under attack."

JOSEPH

Cheyenne Mountain Complex, CO

Joseph stood at the end of a reddish wood conference table. The MIM team of doctors looked exhausted after hours spent debating the future of Richard Thompson, patient zero of the worst pandemic in the history of mankind. Soda cans and coffee cups lay scattered around the table. Stale, dried out sandwiches sat on a platter in the corner. No one's appetite was very big today aside from Dr. Hollis. With his unslung hand, Joseph pointed at the projector screen. He cleared his throat. "Let's get back to the basics."

Clicking a controller, the slides switched on the screen with a lazy-blinds transition. The people before him looked tired to say the least. Colonel Byrnes sat on the side of the table farthest from Joseph. Dr. Weinroth sat closest to Joseph. Dr. Nguyen next to her. Dr. Hollis nodded off next to Colonel Byrnes, and Dr. Desai sat on the other side.

"Since we are all in agreement that a cure cannot be found, we must attempt to move forward with the development of a vaccination. There are four different types of vaccines that are possible: the first is a live virus attenuated vaccine. Measles, mumps, and chickenpox operate like this."

"Is this even feasible for the subject virus?" Dr. Desai said. She looked down at her papers. "The virus is highly contagious with bodily fluid contact."

"If Patient Zero is any indicator of behavior associated with live virus inoculation, then it's not a plausible method of vaccination," said Dr. Nguyen.

"I agree," said Dr. Weinroth.

"As do I," Joseph said quickly after her. He smiled something only meant for her. He pushed the button again, and the device made an audible clicking noise.

"How do we feel about a killed or inactivated vaccine option?" Joseph asked the group.

"We don't know the affects pieces of the virus may have in a live host," Colonel Byrnes said. His mood never changed from a natural glower.

Dr. Nguyen tapped his pen on the paper in front of him. "The mutations are too fast. You've seen infected blood work. We are lucky the computers can keep up with such fast mutations. How can we possibly defend the host cells while the virus mutates?"

The doctors looked down at their notes. Papers shuffled. They took swigs of coffee, tea, and soda, hoping that a jolt of caffeine might somehow push their drained brains beyond the fog to find an answer.

Byrnes frowned up at Joseph, rubbing his forehead. "Joseph, we don't need an explanation on how vaccines work. Why don't you take a seat?" He gestured with a free hand. "We already know your next few slides: nanoparticles, toxoids, and biosynthetic vaccines."

Joseph sighed and took a seat, letting his arm settle on the armrest. He tossed the controller on the table. His knife wound was healing with Dr. Weinroth's help. Joseph made sure to give her a friendly smile.

"When stuck, it can't hurt to go back to the basics," Joseph said.

Byrnes exercised his fingers in front of him, his scowl deepening. "I'm not sure we have the technology here to create a virus-like nanoparticle. Toxoid vaccines are primarily used for bacteria-related illness. That leaves a biosynthetic vaccine as the best option. We will change the antigen that the virus injects into the cells. The immune system will recognize the virus upon infection and respond positively, providing defense against the virus."

Dr. Weinroth coughed into her hand. "With all due respect, and I mean all due respect. Do you know how long it takes and how much live testing we have to do in order to create a biosynthetic protein that not only does what it's supposed to do but is safe for the patient?"

"About fifteen years," Byrnes said. His face was flat as if he had already lived every day of those fifteen years, watching all those around him die in the process.

"And we have at most a month," Dr. Weinroth said. She peered down at a piece of paper. "Two. If the military holds."

"That's a big if," Byrnes said.

Dr. Desai looked perturbed by their assumptions. "I'm not sure we can even discuss it. It isn't realistic."

"None of this is realistic, doctor, but we have to try. I am advocating for open surgical tissue harvesting to increase tissue mass available for analysis.

Joseph's brow creased. *Patient Zero is not an autopsy.* "Hold on, Colonel. Patient Zero is still alive. He's a person, not a walking corpse like the others. An open mass tissue harvest will greatly increase his chances of mortality."

"That's true," Byrnes peered down at his notes. "But we don't have time. We must extract lymph nodes, liver tissue, and lung tissue from the host immediately. We will need a quick analysis of the material and original virus if we want to stand a chance at getting something. Really anything." He eyed Rebecca as though speaking to his daughter. "Put him under. He's dangerous anyway. Take the needed specimens and keep him in an induced coma. He won't feel a thing."

Dr. Weinroth shuffled her papers, uncomfortable under his gaze.

"I don't think that's necessary. I believe we can get all the information we need from non-invasive testing." Joseph nodded his head in agreement. "If that doesn't work, I will agree to more *dangerous* harvesting methods."

"Time is our enemy. Dr. Nguyen needs time if he is to—work his magic. Don't have a bleeding heart over this man. If we can still call him that."

Joseph frowned. "You can't just cut him up into pieces. He's a human being." He adjusted his glasses up the edge of his nose. The crack in his lens split Byrnes into two unhappy pieces.

"He's infected. It's between us and the virus. The faster we can figure out how this thing ticks the faster we can defeat it. Plain and simple," Byrnes said, letting Joseph know his displeasure at being debated with a frown.

"If you want to kill infected, go outside this mountain, Colonel. There are plenty of infected to hack up out there. We need to exercise some caution. Potentially killing Patient Zero does us no good either."

"And what would you know about what's happening out there?" Byrnes said. His voice was sharp and poignant.

"Plenty," Joseph said. His eyes met the colonel's. His gut went from a simmer to a boil.

Byrnes gave him a sneer. "Like you've killed a thing. Please back me up on this one. You understand the importance of gathering good expedient data. The more data we can get the better."

Joseph cut in. "Infected aren't the only things I've killed." Joseph fixed his eyes on the two Byrnes. Both of them infuriated him.

Byrnes ground his teeth at the other end of the table, his eyes reaching out to slap Joseph's face. *I don't care if he tries to whoop my ass.*

Dr. Nguyen's eyes grew large underneath his small round glasses. He coughed into his hand, breaking the stalemate. "Colonel Byrnes is correct, Dr. Jackowski. During the Ebola outbreak in West Africa, we made the most progress when conducting high volume tissue harvesting through more intrusive procedures." Dr. Nguyen flattened his lips. He didn't need to spell it out.

More intrusive operations on patients to contain the outbreak were easier to authorize when the disease was abroad, in a jungle, infecting people that weren't Americans. Doctors would eagerly use the data, ignoring the higher risk operations conducted as a necessary risk.

Dr. Weinroth flipped her auburn hair over her ear before she spoke. "Although, I too would like an expedited solution to this pandemic," she said. She gave Joseph a glance out of the corner of her eye. "I believe we should try non-invasive testing as a medical priority. The patient may benefit, and more importantly, may provide us with even more clues with less trauma to his body. Clues that if he has expired, we may not find."

Dr. Desai's long black curls shook around her shoulders. "Yes. Perhaps he will provide us with a way to manage the disease."

"Manage? That's ridiculous. We need results now." Byrnes slammed his fist on the table. Exhaling sharply, he calmed himself. "People are being slaughtered," he said softly.

"He's not some sort of lab rat for us to grow an ear on. Those that can feel, judge best," Joseph said.

"His humanity is debatable." Byrnes crossed his arms.

"Regardless, we have a responsibility to find a vaccine for this disease. The last data report we ran, inoculation of the surviving populations and military forces, will bring our success rate up to seven percent."

"Up from what?" The words tumbled out of Joseph's mouth.

Dr. Weinroth picked her papers up and straightened them out. Her throat moved as she swallowed tentatively. She thumbed through her stack and slid a single sheet over to Joseph. He hesitated a moment before he touched the paper as if he reached for the virus in eight-and-a-half-by-eleven standard letter form.

He lifted the paper up to his eyes and bent his head downward so he could look over his glasses. The paper was filled with charts of data and corresponding graphs. Everyone was silent as he read.

Dr. Weinroth broke the silence, her voice rushed as if she were trying to outspeak his internal reading. "Within the Cheyenne Mountain Complex, we have stockpiled a host of vaccines for every known infectious disease. Enough for tens of thousands of people. If we can find one that we can modify, we may have success." Joseph ignored her, digesting the numbers on the sheet.

"That's a big if," Joseph said, studying the information. He felt his gut drop inside of him.

A list of calculations ran down the sheet. A pie graph was one hundred percent red. The next graph had a sliver of blue in it, time tables and numbers in separate columns.

"Our success rate is between zero and seven percent," Joseph said under his breath.

"That is correct, Dr. Jackowski," Byrnes said from across the table. His hard-as-bullet eyes softened a tiny bit. "If we move fast, we only have a small chance of success." He capitalized on Joseph's digestion of the morbid information. "One man's life means little in the face of this threat. We should bring this to a vote."

Everyone around the table nodded in agreement.

"Should we move forward with invasive testing for mass volume harvesting or continue with less credible non-invasive procedures?" Byrnes said.

Joseph locked eyes with Dr. Weinroth.

"All in favor of invasive, say aye." The colonel nudged Dr. Hollis with an elbow. Dr. Hollis stared around the table, blinking rapidly, entering the conversation for the first time. "Doctor, we are taking a vote."

"Yes. Of course we are," Dr. Hollis said.

"Aye," Byrnes said. His mouth clamped shut as if it were an order to the rest of the doctors. He raised his hand slowly in the air.

Dr. Nguyen glanced at Joseph. "Aye." His hand went up.

"Dr. Hollis?" Byrnes said.

"Aye," Dr. Hollis said with a nod.

Byrnes glared at the rest of the table. Dr. Desai sat quietly examining her hands. Joseph knew Dr. Weinroth was on his side. Byrnes frowned, unable to get his majority vote. The doctors put their hands down.

"All those in favor of less invasive tissue harvesting on the human subject, say aye," Joseph said.

"There's no need. Neither group will get a majority," Byrnes said, disgusted with the outcome of events.

"Let's see," Joseph said.

Byrnes snorted and looked away.

"Aye," Joseph said. His voice was clear and loud.

Rebecca gave him an affirming smile. "Aye."

"Aye," Dr. Desai said.

"Aye," Dr. Hollis mumbled.

"What was that, Dr. Hollis?" Joseph said.

Dr. Hollis's second chin trembled. "I said, 'aye.' I believe we should move forward with as much testing as possible."

Byrnes's face soured as though he were sucking a lemon. "Dr. Hollis, you cannot vote twice," he growled.

Dr. Hollis shook his head. "Who do you people think you are? Of course I can vote twice."

"Dr. Hollis, please. Vote for one or the other," Joseph said. Dr. Hollis folded his hands over his belly and stuck his receding chin outward. "I will not. Forward or not at all."

"You can't change your vote, Hollis," Byrnes said.

The heavy doctor stared at the colonel and raised his eyebrows. "Then I won't vote."

Joseph smiled. "Then that settles it. Three to two. Non-invasive testing of Patient Zero."

Byrnes sighed impatiently as if he were dealing with children. "Goddamn it." He stood up, and for a second, Joseph thought that the slender colonel would race around the table and pummel him. The colonel strode for the door. When he reached it, he pushed down on the doorknob and stopped.

He spoke down to Joseph. "What are you waiting for? We have tests to begin."

Joseph smiled at the soldier doctor. "Yes, we do."

TESS

Little Sable Point, MI

Tess slipped on the tan leather shoulder harness that held her semi-automatic Colt .45 1911 handgun and two spare magazines over her tank top.

Her feet dug into the sand as she ran. Pagan sprinted next to her, holding his M27 Infantry Automatic Rifle fitted with a bipod and a 3.5x Squad Day optic. The gunshots grew louder as she got closer to the entrance of Little Sable's protective ring of vehicles. Men shouted at one another.

Thunder's voice rose above the rest. "Keep your heads down!"

She squatted behind a trailer tire, still far enough away to stop and think. She drew her black 1911, holding it in both hands and pointing it to the sky.

Looking back at Pagan, he gave her a nod and they burst into the opening. Thunder and five of his Red Stripes took cover behind trucks and cars. They pointed guns across car hoods at four soldiers in tan, brown, and gray camouflage. *The military? Where did they come from? The lighthouse should have seen any trucks on the road.*

Tess lined up her sights on a blonde woman standing twenty-five yards away pointing a carbine in their direction.

"Put your guns down," a blond-bearded man yelled, rapidly transitioning his aim from biker to biker. His head had a horrific scar that ran down the top of his skull like a divot on a golf course fairway.

Thunder pointed his twelve gauge short-barreled Benelli at him.

"Fuck you. You throw your guns down," Thunder growled.

"I got a shot, Thunder," Rat-Face shouted. The skinny biker with a shaved head squinted down the barrel of a scoped 30-06 Springfield bolt-action hunting rifle.

The tension rose every second the standoff continued. Pagan set his M27 rifle on the back of a pickup truck, letting the bipod fling out from near the end of the barrel.

"Everything is going to go bad unless we do something," he said softly. He closed one eye, using the other to line up his shot.

"I can see that," she said sharply. Tess exhaled heavily. *Sometimes I wonder if I'm the dumb one.* She stood up and shouted. "Hey, you."

The disgruntled soldier aimed in her direction, looking for the voice.

"Beard guy," she said, lifting her chin at him as if she were picking a fight. The scarred, bearded man pointed his weapon at her. Tess pointed her gun back at him with a nice little cock in her wrist.

"Where is she?" he blurted in her direction.

This guy is off his rocker. "Where is *who*?" she retorted.

"What did you do to her?" he yelled. *What is wrong with this guy?*

"We didn't do anything to anyone. Everyone is welcome here."

"Where's your leader?" Beard Face said, eyes darting back at Thunder with his shotgun. His eyes said he would carve the big biker to bits in a second. Tess doubted he could, but the crazy guy looked insane enough to try.

Thunder faced her way, his gray beard resting on his chest like a bib.

"That's all you, Tess," he grunted.

"You sure you don't want to talk to crazy pants?" she said to him.

Thunder laughed. "He may be a bit more receptive to the words of a woman. But if he gets antsy, maybe we will see what a couple of slugs does to him."

"This isn't 'Nam, Thunder," she said, lowering her handgun and holstering it up underneath her armpit. She clipped the retention flap over the handle of the gun so it wouldn't fall out.

The unsettled man breathed hard while he stared their way. *He's like some sort of bull. Time for him to meet his matador.* She hoisted herself up and hopped over the cars then stopped, collecting herself. *Am I insane for stepping between these guys?*

"If you meet me in the middle, we can talk," she yelled out at him. She gave Thunder a glance over her shoulder. "Then if you want to play guns with Thunder and the Red Stripes, you can be my guest...after I get out of the way, of course." The bearded crazy lowered his M4 a bit, watching her from over his sights. The weight of his presence hung in the air. Seconds clicked painfully by, and she feared she had made a mistake by stepping into the open.

"Lower your weapons," Beard Face commanded. His military crew moved to a low ready, guns pointed downward. Beard Face marched across the weak grass that had started to turn brown, purpose filling his strides. He kept his chin slightly downward as if he expected to be sucker punched at any minute. She could see his eyes scanning the defenses for threats.

She walked his way, trying to keep her posture erect but relaxed as if she didn't have a care in the world.

They met in the middle of the two hostile groups for a moment, standing and watching one another, making a quick assessment of what the other was dealing with. She put a hand on her hip.

His steel blue eyes pierced her almost jet black ones. His cheeks were sunken and a thick snarled beard hung almost as low as Thunder's, but he was forty years his junior. His camouflage was stained with sweat and dirt, making him appear if he had returned from the horrors of a World War I trench. *The whole world is one battlefield.*

"A handsome man lies beneath all that hair, scars, and muscle," she said. He blinked rapidly. *I've caught him off guard.* He was a different version of Pagan. Tenser. He instinctively ran a hand along the length of his healing head wound. She shifted her weight to her back leg like a cat waiting to pounce.

"Well, what do you have to say for yourself?" she demanded.

His jaw clenched. Fury lay beneath his almost flat features waiting to emerge. It was as if it took all of his energy to control his own emotions. "Where is she?" he breathed. "Tell me."

"You know, you aren't very polite. The least you could do is say thank you for the compliment." She gave him a heavy sigh.

He was silent.

Her eyes judged him. "I'm a forward woman, but you don't have to be such a sourpuss," she said.

The mustache of his beard twitched. "I'm Mark." He expected to be heard when he spoke.

"That it? Usually you army guys love to talk about your rank, unit, and cock size. So what are you? Like a general or something?" she said.

She glanced back at Pagan over her shoulder. The lightly bearded Marine looked up and over his gun watching, ready to fire his weapon at any moment. She could barely make out his finger tapping the trigger guard of his gun. He only did that when he was nervous. *If I hit the deck, he'll light them up. He's a good shot.* Then it would be whether or not Mark could get rounds into her before he was destroyed by hot lead.

"I have no rank."

She raised an eyebrow at him. "What's with the uniforms? Former military?"

"We're not former military either; they were a gift. I used to work for the federal government."

She laughed and grinned at him. "I knew it. You douches are all the same. Always have to be something sexier than the last guy, thinking you are going to pick up chicks. It's like you all read the same friggin' book."

"I'm not here to get *laid.*" He looked over her shoulder at the bikers lining the entrance. More Red Stripes were gathering.

Still sizing us up for a fight. Back to me, tough guy. "Sure you aren't, Mark. Every man wants to get laid." She narrowed her eyes a bit. "I'm down here."

His eyes regarded her with indifference. "Are you in charge of this place?" he said, gesturing with his head.

She looked down at her small chest. "What you afraid of? A woman ruling the roost?"

His lips tightened.

"No. I'm here to find," he paused for a second, but the look in his eyes said it all. "I'm searching for a woman. The tracks led us in this direction."

"Can you be more specific? A lot of people come and go from here," she said.

"Mid-fifties, blonde hair, petite. Her name is Dr. Mary Steele."

"Lost your mom, huh?" she said. She immediately wished she hadn't. Pain crossed his features and then anger.

"Are you mocking me?" His face filled with disgust.

"A man of your stature? Nah. Wouldn't even think it."

His jaw tightened beneath his beard, the tendons on the sides of his face hardening. "Have you seen a lady that matches that description?"

"Thunder, you seen a Dr. Mary Steele?" Tess called back.

Thunder shook his head. Skinny Joker laughed next to him. "Sure did. Kept me warm last night."

Mark squinted his eyes. "What did he say?" he growled.

Tess put a hand out toward Mark. He dodged her, bringing his gun up slightly. "No. Don't worry about him. He's just an asshole," she said.

"Real nice," Joker taunted, thrusting his hips out and rolling them in a circle.

Thunder shoved him. "Shut up, you idiot."

In a split second, the barrel of Mark's firearm was an inch from her face.

Tess licked her lips and looked into the black hole of his gun barrel. The bullet wouldn't have to go far to evaporate the back of her skull.

Mark stared at Thunder over her. "Give her back and nobody has to get hurt," he called to them.

Tess blinked, trying not to piss herself. *Cool as a cucumber.* "Joker's a big prick. Got a little one, but he's fucking with you. Cruel, yes. But that's the boy of a man he is. You can come inside and look around. If she's not here, I'll help you find her."

Mark's eyes jumped from vehicle to vehicle of their protective ring.

Slowly, Tess let her hand rise up and rest on the barrel of his gun. "I would prefer if you stuck that thing somewhere else." Her lips curled into a smirk. She met his angry blue eyes.

He let his gun be lowered inch by inch, and the two parties visibly exhaled. He pointed his carbine downward and shook his head. He ran a hand through the hair on his head that hadn't been carved off. He sighed, letting his hand fall to his thigh.

"Long day?"

He nodded. "When's it not?" He gestured down the coastline. "About eight miles south of here. Her house was burnt down. There were a lot of tire tracks. Some led this way."

Tess gulped, trying to hide her discomfort.

Steele's eyes pierced her face looking for deceit.

"What is it? What do you know?" he said.

"Not much. This isn't the first time this has happened. We can talk about it inside."

His look was serious but relieved. "Can we keep our weapons?"

"Of course. You're free here."

She stepped closer to him and leaned in close to his face. She didn't know if she made him nervous or if he didn't like people being that close. "But don't shoot anybody. Okay?" she whispered. She patted him on his shoulder and it felt like she patted a pet rock.

Mark exhaled. "Thank you." He relaxed, but his eyes mistrusted the circle of vehicles. He looked as if he expected an ambush at any moment.

He waved his group forward. "Come on."

His crew walked up. Tess gave the blonde an eye. The woman returned her glare, and Tess turned away and walked back to Little Sable Point. The Red Stripes let them pass unhindered, their patched vests and guns making them an intimidating sight.

"I don't like him," Pagan said, falling in at her side.

"Of course you don't, babe. He's like you, rough and ready for a roll in the hay," she said. She bumped her shoulder into his playfully.

"Military?" Pagan said. He gave the newcomers a look out of the corner of his eye.

"No, some sort of Fed." She wrapped an arm around Pagan's waist, sticking a hand through his belt loop. She gave a look behind her at the others. Mark and his crew followed behind her like a pack of feral dogs being tempted by the whiff of a free meal. She could feel Mark's eyes on her.

"There's food over there. If you want extra, you can trade something for it." She waved her free hand at a semi-trailer stuffed with boxes, its doors open. "Bessie, give them a day's worth of my winnings."

"You got it, Tess," Bessie shouted. She hacked a cough into her hand.

"Everyone is on their own for lodging. I'm sure if you ask around, someone will take you in for the night."

"We have tents," Steele said.

Her eyebrows lifted. "Suit yourself. Soon it will be too cold for that. In the meantime, come over to my camper and talk with us."

They followed her to her camper. Pagan opened the screen door. "After you," he said, his head leaned back and his chest out.

Everyone piled inside. With more than two people, the camper seemed like a crawl space. Thunder and his sergeant at arms or enforcer, Garrett, stood sideways their girth filling in the narrow space. Mark's crew stood crammed together on one side; the Arab man stood halfway in the doorway.

Tess hopped onto her fold-out bed and scooted back into the corner. "You wouldn't mind sending some of your crew outside, would you?" she said to Mark.

Mark nodded, his beard smashing on his chest. "Can you guys leave while we talk? Kevin and Ahmed can grab some water and food." Quieter he said, "Gwen, can you check out about trading for more food?"

A tall lanky man stepped outside following the stocky Arab man. Gwen stood her ground.

"I'm not going," she said, voice level. Mark gave her an evil stare and met her eyes.

She's his woman, and she's as stubborn as a mule. Don't make it too easy on yourself, do you, bearded man? A glutton for punishment.

"I think we're good. She can stay," Tess said, feeling behind her. Patting under a pillow, she pulled out her weed stash and rolled a joint, licking the paper so it would stick. Thunder plopped down on a built-in table bench, shaking the camper then placing a hand on his knee like a gorilla.

"Want a hit?" Tess asked the two newcomers.

"No," they said in unison.

Tess laughed. "Straight-laced even now? You two must be a real joy to be around," she said, with a smirk at Pagan. "Probably strict missionary too."

She laughed. The emerald-green-eyed blonde stared at her coldly.

Steele brushed it off, his emotions hidden beneath his stonelike unamused surface. *He's a man that's to the point. No frills. Just action.*

Tess sparked up her joint and took a long drag, letting the smoke fill her lungs. She closed her eyes and let the joys of the apocalypse dim a bit. His voice brought her back.

"What can you tell us about the fires?"

Tess opened her eyes and passed the joint to Thunder, who took it in his fingers, sucking in the smoke. Pagan stood in the kitchen, his arms folded over his chest, M27 resting near his leg.

"Before we get all cozy, who are you?" Pagan demanded. Dislike shone on his face.

Tess rolled her eyes. *Jesus.*

"I'm Mark Steele. I was a counterterrorism agent with the Division before the outbreak."

Recognition passed over Pagan's face. "I've heard of you guys. Pretty tight outfit."

"We get the job done. You?" Steele said.

"Force Recon," Pagan said.

"Tough bastards. High-speed shit," Steele said.

"They're all right." Pagan looked up at Steele's head. "How'd you get that scar on your dome?"

"Some asshole shot me in West Virginia."

Pagan smiled and lifted up his shirt. A golf ball-sized discolored scar stuck out on his abdomen. "Snuck through the vest in Fallujah."

Tess let the smoke come out her nose to mask her slight irritation. *These two and their posturing are boring me.*

"Okay, guys, you done jerking each other off? If I wanted to watch bro-bachelor in apoco-paradise, I would have stayed in the real world."

Steele ran his hand over his head scar again, and Pagan let his shirt fall down

"All right. Tell me what's going on here," Steele said. He rested a hand on the tomahawk in his belt.

Tess tapped the end of the joint in an ashtray. "Since we've been here, we've only run into one other large group. They're a bit religious. Call themselves the Chosen." She stopped and looked at Steele for acknowledgment that he understood. He kept his face flat.

"We're talking medieval Christians." She raised her eyebrows at him. "Very uncompromising to say the least."

"What's the matter with the Christians?"

Maybe he would be better off finding them on his own.

"Nothing is wrong with being Christian. If that's where they find salvation, then so be it. I'm surprised they still believe in anything at this point. But these guys," she said. She shook her head and took a drag off her joint. "These guys have taken worship to a whole new level. We're talking about waging a holy crusade against the living and the dead. Like they think they're some sort of army of God or something. I dunno."

"I'm not objecting to waging a holy war against the dead," Steele said, his brow furrowed as if he dared her to say otherwise. "The infected have caused enough grief, and giving some of that back would be nice."

Thunder coughed, his beard almost seamless with his gray chest hair. "Nobody minds bashing in a few skulls more than me, Steele. The fewer of the bastards the better, but these folk are none too friendly to outsiders."

Pagan rubbed his short beard. "A couple that came in the other day said the crazies burnt down their house. They hid in the forest for hours before they could escape," he said.

Mark's eyes widened.

"Young couple," Tess said, shooting him down.

"When me and the Red Stripes first rode up this way weeks ago, we drove past several burned-out buildings along the coast. And it ain't just a few of 'em. We seen dozens," Thunder said.

Mark took a deep breath. "My mother's home was torched."

"Then it don't look good," Thunder said. His hands rested on his knees and his gut hung down the middle as if he could breathe better that way.

When there was only a tiny prick left, Tess mashed the joint out in her ashtray.

"Mark, you should spend the night," Tess said. Gwen's eyes flamed. *A jealous one, huh?* "You and your group can rest here, take a load off. Maybe Thunder here would be willing to loan you one of his bikes then you, Pagan, and maybe a few of the Red Stripes can scout around a bit, see what you can discover regarding your mother."

"I wouldn't just loan you a bike," Thunder boomed. He twisted his head to the side. "But Lenny's gone now. Bugger got butchered taking a shit in the woods. I told him not to go that far." Thunder shook his head in disgust. "You can borrow his old chopper, but don't get any ideas about keeping it."

Steele sat, contemplating the overture.

It's a good offer, knucklehead, Tess thought, smiling at Steele and then Gwen. *I'm giving him what you can't,* her eyes said to Gwen. Tess met Steele's eyes with ease, feeling coy and mellowed out.

"I appreciate your help." He gave a curt nod of thanks.

Of course you do. Her lips curved. "You're smarter than you look."

STEELE

Little Sable Point, MI

Late morning came on slow and dragging like an infected's leg. The sun hid behind a sheet of cloud cover, and waves splashed onto the shore as if they were reluctant to touch the land.

Steele had been up with the roosters and had been waiting for the arrival of his reconnaissance escorts. Across the vehicle enclosure, he watched the arrival of Pagan and Thunder. They both looked over in his direction. Steele stood.

"What do you think they're talking about?" Gwen said. She sat cross-legged on a blanket in the sand, her M4 resting upright against an RV, almost as if she were at the beach in the summer. Ahmed leaned on the RV nearby, muscular arms crossing his chest. A bat leaned up next to him like a tired lover.

"Probably the best way to kill me," Steele responded, watching the men.

He lifted his carbine sling up and over his shoulders, letting the gun hang low on his back. With a twist of his hips and a reach rearward, he could have the gun back up and ready to fire. He wouldn't carry a pack today; it was too heavy for a recon mission on a motorcycle. Some extra mags shoved in his pockets made his pants hang low on his waist. His sidearm on one side and his tomahawk on the other were all he needed.

"You sure you don't want me to go with? We could ride together. I'll watch your back," Ahmed said, hefting his bat and holding it nonchalantly.

Steele glanced at the man. "Not today, buddy. If we were looking for a fight, I'd bring you with. And I don't want to give the Red Stripes the wrong idea."

Ahmed nodded with a grin. "Since when do you care what other people think?"

"Since I decided to roll out with a motorcycle club I know nothing about."

Steele eyed the bat. Ahmed's last one had been lost in the hills of West Virginia. "Where'd you get that?"

"This?" Ahmed held it up. "Traded one of the kids for it."

"Traded them what?"

Ahmed lifted his eyebrows. "What every kid wants. Candy." Ahmed gestured ahead and Steele turned.

Pagan made his way toward them walking across the shared grounds. He held an M27 IAR casually draped downward in front of his jeans and a dirty checkered long sleeve. He stopped and stood tall in front of Steele. "You ready?"

"Yes, sir." Leaning down, Steele kissed Gwen's cheek. Her cheek was a cool bottle of milk beneath his lips.

Her demeanor bothered him. *Is this all we have to look forward to? Short goodbyes? Is this all we have until I fall on some soon forgotten battlefield?* Her indifference made it a little easier to focus on his mission. *Do I fight only to fight? Or am I actually serving a greater purpose?*

"Come back," she commanded, green eyes pained. Her arms enclosed her stomach as if she protected it. *She must feel the same way. She has to feel it. Despair. Fear. But not of death. Of the unknown.* He nodded to her and Ahmed. Ahmed understood. He would watch out for her. *Just like Mauser had done?* Steele swallowed his worry.

Steele joined Pagan and they walked through beach sand past the rusty-brick colored lighthouse. A thin black gun barrel stuck out of the top like a metal toothpick high in the air.

"Everyone volunteers to take a shift up in the lighthouse," Pagan said.

"Everyone?"

"Yeah, why?"

"Because I know everyone here isn't a marksman. Probably more likely to fall off the lighthouse than hit anything or anyone."

"We have some hunters who are pretty good shots. They don't have the same formal training as a sniper, but you should see some of the shots these guys take. A lot of them grew up with bolt-action hunting rifles in their hands."

"Yeah, my dad used to hunt up here," Steele said.

Pagan nodded and patted Steele's shoulder. "We'll find them."

Not him. Maybe my mother.

They approached a gang of motorcycles near the entrance to the community. Two pickup trucks parked grille to grille sealed them off from the rest of the world. Despite the lack of adequate cleaning supplies, the gang's choppers reflected what little pieces of the sun had managed to penetrate the earth's atmosphere. Silver exhaust pipes shined, gas tanks and fenders were polished bright, and the engines were immaculate.

"'Bout damn time. I was beginning to wonder if our prodigal son wasn't going to show for his scouting trip," Thunder said. He wore his leather motorcycle club vest over his riding leathers. The Red Stripes tag sat above another that read President on his left breast. Below that, a tag read Thunder. Just below a diamond 13 sat a skull and crossbones on his other breast with an FTW patch below that.

Steele ground his teeth. "We can take the bikes if you don't want to risk your neck for us."

The club members laughed loud and mean led by Thunder. These men weren't the least intimidated by Steele's presence. He had no doubt the club would gang beat him if not kill him if they had the urge. Motorcycle clubs had a strict code of honor that only a member of one could understand, and it was clear Steele was not a part of them.

"Fucking A, you think I'd let you take one of the bikes?" Thunder's belly jiggled with mirth. He turned toward his men. "This guy doesn't know shit." He grinned at Steele and shook his head with the amusement of a father watching his toddler. "I'm going to make sure my choppers come back in one piece. Take a look at Lenny's old bike," Thunder thundered into a rancorous laugh.

A motorcycle sat unmanned.

"This is a sweet ride," Steele said. He ran a hand along the gas tank. "May I?" he asked. His eyes darted at Thunder, seeing if the man would allow it.

"Since you asked nicely," Thunder said, talking down to him. "'Cause I don't want you doubling up with any of my guys."

Steele threw a leg over the seat, letting his hands rest on the handlebars.

"Lenny spent every penny he had on Marissa. If I didn't have my own hog, I'd snatch up this one." It had a navy blue gas tank accented by two reflective silver exhaust pipes that were shadowed by all black wheels and tires.

"What kind is it?"

Thunder laughed. "I'm embarrassed for you. This bike deserves better than you. It's a Harley Davidson Blackline." Thunder circled the bike. "Twin Cam 103 V-Twin engine. This thing will ride. Go ahead." He nodded at Steele.

Steele turned the key in the ignition. He flipped the kill switch to run, kept it in neutral, and hit the starter. The engine growled to life underneath him. He let it settle on a nice hum.

"Listen to her purr," Thunder said with a grin. "Give her some love."

Steele twisted the throttle. The engine roared, showing the power of the bike.

"She's a beauty," Steele said.

"Let's keep her in one piece," Thunder said. "Alright lads, mount up," Thunder called out.

Three more Red Stripes—grizzled veterans of wars, bar fights, and gang life—saddled up.

"I want to search north of here," Steele said.

Thunder nodded. "All right. Pagan, you roll with Rat-Face and Joker take the south shore. Half-Barrel, you and me are with the FNG. We're going to have to find you a nickname if you can manage to ride with us."

Fucking new guy. Not the first time he'd been called one. Best to let it slide.

Half-Barrel smiled at Steele. Everything about Half-Barrel suggested he was procreated by bowling balls. His head was the size of a basketball and his body resembled a beer keg. "This wannabe," he snorted. "Fuckin' pigs can't ride. Ha," he laughed.

"FNG is fine with me, but let's go," Steele said. He added, "We've waited long enough." He could care less about their MC outlaw biker code and nicknames. He wanted to be on the road. He needed to be on the road. If his mother was in danger, then minutes could be the difference between life and death.

"We're going to ride up the coast, cut inland, and cross back and forth. About a forty-mile circuit. We should be back by nightfall," Thunder said.

"We'll find her," Pagan said with a nod. Steele nodded his appreciation.

"Let's roll!" Thunder shouted, revving the throttle, and they were off.

"Keep the rubber side down," Half-Barrel said. He placed a skullcap atop his melon-sized head.

"You steal your helmet from a kid?" Steele mocked.

A disgusted look crossed Half-Barrel's face. "You'll be laughing a different tune when you horizontally park that hog. Then Thunder will finish off whatever's left of you."

"Okay, big guy, show me how it's done."

Half-Barrel rolled forward and Steele followed with a rev of his engine.

They cut down a sidewalk to a parking lot with a single entrance leading into a forest of white pine and maple. The motorcycles glided over the roadway, winding through the trees for over a mile. They reached a green and white sign that read Lakeshore Drive. They took a left and headed north.

Steele rode behind Thunder and Half-Barrel, feeling the freedom of the road as the wind blew through his hair. The coolness on his bare scalp combined with his wound sent a myriad of nerve sensations through his skull.

From behind the bikers, their gang colors were clear. A black skull with its mouth slightly open was encased in a diamond of blood red. Stripes lined overtop of the skull were the same blood red color. Four small blue naval stars decorated the background. Above the center patch in red-outlined black letters was their gang name: Red Stripes.

They sped past fields of tall grass. Forms shambled toward the motorcycle riders, but they were easily passed. The motorcycles rumbled down the road, and the two club members navigated obstacles with ease. They would use hand signals to let Steele know of upcoming obstructions in the road.

They traveled north for miles. The road disappeared beneath their two-wheeled stallions. As they got closer to a town, they started to pass rows of old Victorian-style houses. Thunder slowed down when a cluster of buildings emerged in the distance. Short structures, which only a small town would have, were topped off with a slightly newer and taller residential structure.

"Pentwater is up ahead. Been through there a few times. Nothing but the dead. We'll drive around Pentwater Lake and cut back down the main highway. There are more cars over that way. You good to navigate through them and the junk that was left behind?"

"I should be alright. My dad had one of these growing up and he taught me to ride." *A total of about two times.*

"Waxer," Half-Barrel smirked.

Steele had no idea what he meant.

"That's enough Half-Barrel. Let's keep moving."

They circled around Pentwater Lake. Three-story modern condos sat along the water by a marina. An aqua-colored water tower rose up on end of the town. Only a few white boats still sat in their slips, seemingly abandoned by their comrades.

Crossing the southernmost tip of the town, they slowed their bikes down to look for any signs of anyone living. A white utility van with a ladder on top had been driven into the storefront of a pharmacy. The blue and orange sign above read Gerkin's Pharmacy and Shop.

Thunder slowed his bike to a stop.

"We should check out the pharmacy and see if they have anything useful for Little Sable." Steele figured this would happen. *How can I expect these guys to put their necks out on a limb for me and not try to find some positive in the matter?*

"I wouldn't mind stretching the legs a bit," Steele responded.

"Good man. I'd rather not come back empty-handed." Thunder gave Steele a glance to see if he had offended him.

"I ain't mad. I only want some answers," Steele said, dismounting his bike and swinging his M4 to his front.

"Half-Barrel, stay with the bikes," Thunder commanded. Half-Barrel nodded, releasing a sawed-off shotgun from his riding holster and setting it on his lap.

Steele and Thunder approached the van with caution. Thunder held the short 12-gauge Benelli shotgun in his hands. Guns in the low ready, they scanned the outside of the two-story brick building for anything that moved. They pointed guns at either side of the brand-new apocalypse doorway created by the van.

Steele and Thunder locked eyes, steel blue with dark brown for a moment, and Steele gave him a slight tilt of his chin. The Vietnam vet scooted around one side of the van as quick as his tactical girth would allow and Steele followed a step behind him. A hand reached out of the driver's side window. Fingers curled, grasping Thunder's leather vest.

Thunder beat down with the stock of his entry shotgun, unable to get a shot off at the infected. Steele twisted to his side behind Thunder, aiming his carbine over Thunder's shoulder. With a squeeze of the trigger, he put a bullet into the infected's brain. Thunder ripped his vest free from its dead hand.

"No one touches these colors." He hacked a loogie on the decaying body of the infected still pinned in the driver's seat. He adjusted his vest and gave Steele a nod.

"We're good," Thunder called out to Half-Barrel.

They continued cautiously inside, step by step.

The electricity was out in the small hometown pharmacy. Shadowed ramshackle shelves sat barren, raided by looters at some point since the outbreak. Black blood stained the thin hard carpet. More blood had been smeared over the carpet leading behind the counter as if someone had dragged a body that way.

Steele's boots crunched shards of glass and chunks of rubble alike from the destroyed wall. Flicking his tactical light on, he shined it along the walls, its beam lighting up empty packages, trash, and wrappers. He heard them before his eyes caught them. Inch by inch they stood, specters materializing from the ground up. They stood behind the counter, undead pharmacists motionless for a moment, blood causing their clothes to cling to dead gray skin.

"Ugly cocksuckers, aren't ya'," Thunder said behind him. Steele sensed him taking aim and before the man could fire, he thrust his gun up, tapping the trigger on one and driving his hips, firing again into the other. Both infected collapsed onto the counter.

Steele gave Thunder a sidelong glance. *FNG. I been through enough.* He held his tongue. Rounding the counter, they went to work, collecting whatever they could get their hands on.

Steele dumped them all in his bag not caring what they were. Round disks, packs, and bottles of pills that read simvastatin, omeprazole, metformin.

"Ain't much here. Most the good stuff has been picked over. No oxycodone. No azithromycin. What the hell are these things?"

Thunder held a round yellow package in his hand. Steele had recognized it as something that Gwen had in her purse all the time.

"Birth control. Put it in. I know somebody who might want it." *She will be happy to have a fresh supply. Keep us from putting a loaf in the oven.*

"He, he, he. You kids and your pills. Back in my day, we didn't have all that shit. There was only one method of birth control. Pulling out."

Steele laughed. "Thanks for the advice. I'll keep it in mind."

"Worked for me." The older man shrugged his shoulders. "I think." He scratched at his beard and went back to cleaning out the shelves.

Steele dug through boxes, shaking them to see if there was anything left inside.

"Tell me about the club."

Thunder smiled. "We got some history." He shoved more pills in his bag. "The Red Stripes were founded in 1952 by United States Marine Corps Lance Corporal Michael Abbott, 2nd Raider Battalion, 1st Marine Division. He was the only survivor of the captured raiders on Makin Island in the Pacific."

"Sounds like a tough SOB."

Thunder smiled. "He was one of a kind. A legend. Him and eight men were left behind at Makin. In 1945, after years of captivity, the Japs knew they were going to lose and were trying to get rid of any extra liability. The story goes they beheaded his raider team one by one until Abbott was the last one left. They shoved him in front of the garrison commander. The evil bastard looked down at him with a nasty grin. That particular bastard loved that shit. The commander swung his samurai sword high above his head, waiting for Abbott to cry out, but he didn't. He just looked that mother fucker right in his slanty eyes. Then you know what he did?"

"No."

"That bastard, Abbott, leapt up and killed the commander. Ripped out his fucking throat with his teeth. Took that fucker's own sword and put a bunch of the other Japs down like dogs. Problem was, the island's radio equipment had been destroyed in a rainstorm weeks before, and he was stuck there for years after the war."

"The Navy never conducted a rescue operation?" Steele said, massaging packages of medicine for scraps.

"They claimed they did, but he had been declared KIA in 1942. Seven years later, a fishing boat ran aground in a nearby reef. When a ship came out to tow it away, they saw a man on the beach. Wasn't waving or nothing. Just standing."

"Abbott?"

"Yup. But he wasn't alone."

"Who else was there?"

"He had three of those slant-eyed fucks as captives, all linked together with some sort of vine rope that he had made by hand. Government denied the whole thing." Thunder shook his head. "After he got back to the states, he retreated from society, embittered with his own government, mistrustful of people he had sworn to defend. Tossed all his medals here into Lake Michigan. In '52, he met up with some other Marine Corps members, and they formed the motorcycle club."

"Geez. That's a hell of a story."

"Proud to call him our founder," Thunder said.

Boom. Boom. Gunshots roared outside on the street.

"Half-Barrel," Thunder said under his breath. Gripping their guns, they ran for the street.

KINNICK

Peterson Air Force Base, CO

Kinnick turned around. They had never met, but he had seen the man on television enough to recognize his face: Vice President Patrick Brady.

The vice president was taller than Kinnick, hovering about six feet in height. His hair appeared to be fleeing the front of his head for the back and sides. Long wisps of brownish-gray hair were brushed across the top. His tie was loosened, and his collar stained yellow with sweat. A patchy beard had grown on his face, focusing around his jawline and chin. He was flanked by a four-star general in blue and a three-star in a slightly darker blue uniform. Their uniforms were crisp and clean.

Brady's eyes were intelligent with a glint of unsettledness, almost as if he enjoyed chaos. Kinnick hadn't remembered that look in his eyes before when he saw him on television. *Has he always been like this?*

Brady leaned closer to Kinnick. "Which part of my fearless armed forces are you from, good sir?"

"Air Force, sir," Kinnick said.

"You have the look. What's your name?" His eyes narrowed in judgment.

"Colonel Kinnick, retired, sir."

"Retired?" Brady's eyes narrowed.

"Yes, sir. In light of recent events, I found myself back in service," he said. The whole interaction made Kinnick uneasy.

"As long as you remember that you are here to serve."

The words slipped off Kinnick's tongue before he could reel himself in. "Like General Travis at the Pentagon?"

Brady's eyes widened. "You came from the Pentagon?"

"Yes, sir. General Travis sent myself and two patched-together squads on a search and rescue mission for a CDC doctor. We found him and Patient Zero and brought them here."

The vice president's eyes gleamed with gratitude as he nodded. The four-star general leaned in and whispered into the vice president's ear. The vice president nodded. "Yes, I recall the report. Your country owes you a debt. You have my thanks."

"It doesn't owe me, but the men who sacrificed their lives to make it so."

"Many men have made sacrifices since this started," Brady said. He gave Kinnick a wave. "Come into the War Room. We must speak in private. Generals, please see to the ongoing operations." He dismissed them nonchalantly with a shooing motion.

The two generals glanced at one another and only a fraction of dissatisfaction crossed over their faces. The Air Force four-star general looked Kinnick up and down, a sour look on his face, but left with a slight bow of his head.

Kinnick followed behind the vice president into a conference room attached to the operations floor. A long, oval wood table sat in the middle. Twelve large black leather chairs surrounded it, unoccupied.

"You may close the door behind you," the vice president said. Kinnick complied and stood at attention near the edge of the table.

The vice president strolled to the end of the room to a long waist-high cabinet. He pulled a crystal stopper out of a decanter and poured two glasses. He walked over to where Kinnick stood and set one down in front of Kinnick.

"Pick it up and drink," he commanded. Brady took a big swig from his.

Kinnick hesitated. One didn't have a drink with the acting president every day. "Mr. President, I would rather not drink at this time."

"Colonel, if you want to keep your rank and stay inside the fences, you will sit down, pick that glass up, and take a drink."

Kinnick momentarily debated the option of quitting on the spot. The de facto president eyed him.

"I know it's bad out there. Have a glass of nice scotch. We don't know how much longer we will be here to enjoy it."

Kinnick sat hesitantly in a leather chair. He picked up the crystal glass and took a sip. The scotch was smooth and rich with a smoky peat flavor and a hint of sherry and fruit. It didn't burn his tongue at all but only warmed his insides.

"Mr. President, you know your scotch," Kinnick said setting the crystal glass down.

The de facto president raised his eyebrows as he swallowed the alcohol. Sitting for a moment in silence, he stared at the glass.

"Bowmore's." Brady held up the glass, looking at the deep mahogany liquid. "Between you and me, I could care less about how good it is."

"Mr. President, surely a man of your standing would care?"

Brady shrugged his shoulders and held up a finger. He leaned in toward Kinnick. "You know, I never signed the paperwork transferring the power of the presidency over to me." His eyes met Kinnick's. They were a vibrant brown like the scotch he drank. "The man is missing, not known to be dead." He leaned back again, taking a sip of his alcohol.

"I see, sir."

"Drop the sir. We are behind closed doors, and I heard what you said back there. You don't have to like me, just do as you're told."

Kinnick nodded. "Understood." He took a sip of the brown liquid.

"I prefer the vice presidency to the presidency anyway. It's like being the backup quarterback on a winning football team. You get to get all dressed up and win, but you don't have to put in all the blood, sweat, and tears. No one blames you for losing the game."

Kinnick breathed a laugh into his drink.

"Unless the starter goes down in the fourth quarter and the home team needs a score," Kinnick said.

Brady laughed.

"You're only one play away from starting." Brady sighed. "But between you and me, I never liked the guy that much anyway. Too much of a tight ass, by-the-book kind of fellow. Not really my thing."

"Me neither," Kinnick said. He laughed outright, almost feeling ashamed for laughing at the most certainly dead president. He stifled his laughter by taking another sip of his scotch.

The vice president scrunched his forehead together. "Would you want to be the president when the country went under? If some smart asshole ever writes a history book about the end of the world, they are going to have all sorts of horrible shit to say about me."

Kinnick quietly shook his head no.

Brady leaned back in his chair one hand on a leather arm, the other holding his glass. "I was hoping for a second term out of the guy, pad my stats. No one likes to say it, but you make a lot more money if you're a two-termer. Speaking engagements. Book deals. Businesses want you for your political connections. That's when you make the big bucks. Then it's the easy life," Brady said. He stared vacantly at the wall.

"The easy life," Kinnick said to himself, muttering into his booze.

"To the easy life." Brady held his glass up. Kinnick did the same and Brady slung back the rest of his scotch. He leaned forward to the table. "Slide it over. I'll get us another."

"I'm not finished," Kinnick pleaded. Half the brown liquid remained.

"Slide it over. That's an order, Colonel, from your commander-in-chief," Brady said, snapping his fingers together. Kinnick tossed the rest of the mocha-colored liquor back. The sheer amount of the booze stung but still didn't burn his throat. He was never a lightweight, but he hadn't drank in awhile or eaten for that matter. He slid the glass over the table to the vice president.

The vice president snatched up the glass and headed over to the decanter. He poured a tall glass of scotch in one and stopped mid-pour of the other as he thought of something.

"You know, General Travis chose to stay behind. We tried to get him to evacuate early on." Brady peered back over his shoulder at Kinnick.

Kinnick's head buzzed a bit, and he felt more relaxed than he could remember. "I know that, sir."

The vice president brought the topped-off glass back to Kinnick and set it down in front of him. Brady plopped back down into his chair.

"Within two weeks we had lost global communications. Power grids are a touchy thing. Our fail-safe measures weren't prepared for this kind of strain on both resources, especially the people." He shook his head. "We assumed the worst about the Pentagon and fell back to our contingency facilities. When those went down, we moved to the next facility."

"The Pentagon is gone. I spoke to General Travis as it was happening." The fear in the old general's voice would stay with Kinnick to the end of his days.

"I'm sorry to hear that, but maintaining operations on the East Coast was not a viable strategic option."

Kinnick broke in. "The vice president must know what was happening to his men. Not only that, but units were rallying in the Midwest with no orders. Hundreds and thousands of soldiers were stranded when the C-130 Hercs stopped coming."

Brady gave him a grim smile, staring down at this drink. He jutted his chin out a bit.

"Not a fun decision to make. I heeded the advice of my generals here, but I gave that command. Their lives are on my shoulders."

"You left them hanging. No orders. No hope."

Brady pounded his fist on the table. "I fucking know that. Communications were limited. Most of our military has been annihilated. Most of the nation has been eradicated. We needed to focus on something that we could hold."

"So you threw men in their way. Mere speed bumps as the enemy rolled over them?"

Brady leaned his elbows on the table. "And we are grateful for their sacrifice. It gave us breathing room to figure out what the hell was going on. Now we are fighting back and securing our future, however shitty it may be." He threw one hand out and took a swig with the other, daring Kinnick to contradict his words.

Kinnick set his glass down. "Our soldiers deserve better than that. The American public trusts us to help them."

The vice president shrugged. "We can't help them if we can't help ourselves. This is it. We're surrounded. Let me show you." He snatched up a remote control and flicked on a large TV that hung on the wall. A map of the United States appeared.

"Come over here. See this for what it is. Look," Brady pointed with his liquor glass.

Kinnick stood up and walked over to the vice president. Brady stayed seated as he gestured at the map. Every major city was red. The eastern half of the United States was all red.

"We consider all of the eastern half of the United States of America unsalvageable. We will not conduct operations east of the Mississippi River until our situation has drastically changed. My generals are projecting five to ten years."

"Five to ten years?" Kinnick said in disbelief. "That's a long time for the people out there to survive on their own."

"We don't have the manpower to control the area, so we're leaving it alone until we do. Could be sooner, I don't know." The vice president turned an eye on Kinnick which he ignored.

Kinnick pointed at spaced-out red lines that ran through the bulk of the prairie Midwest. Iowa, Nebraska, the Dakotas, Kansas. "What are the lined areas?"

"We've been calling it the MidDeath. Because of the low population and lack of large cities, those areas are considered within a salvageable area of operations. After we spread our reach here, we will work on pushing through and clearing out those areas. Hopefully, we can use it to resettle misplaced persons and continue agricultural operations to keep the living fed. Unfortunately, for now, they are on their own. With limited resources, we must focus on the survivability of the mountain region first."

"What about the West Coast?" The West Coast was also painted crimson. The bloody edges splashed up on the Rockies.

Brady took another drink of his scotch and ran a hand over his thinning hair. "There's been a lot of debate over the West Coast."

"What's the debate?" Kinnick asked, fearing the answer. He couldn't tell if it was the booze that was making him woozy or the predicament of the nation.

Brady got out of his chair and went back to the scotch decanter. His back turned to Kinnick as he spoke. "Whether or not to nuke it." He tipped back the crystal decanter and topped off his scotch. "Another drink, Colonel?" he said, holding up the decanter. Only about a quarter of the liquid remained. He clinked ice in the glasses.

Kinnick nodded, dumbfounded, staring at California and the Western Seaboard. Brady placed a glass back in his hand. He stood near Kinnick, eyes judging the map.

"Almost sixty million people live between here and there." Brady shook his head. "Whew. Good stuff." He looked at his glass. "Sorry, lived there. Past tense. General Daugherty tells me that if we can eliminate the smaller threat that flanks us, we can more safely address the threat from the East."

"There has to be a better way," Kinnick said softly. He shook off the idea. The alcohol and the thought of nuclear holocaust gave him heartburn rising up rapidly in his chest.

"I'm open to suggestions, of course, but when you are surrounded by enemies on all sides, my plays are limited.

"There must be people still alive out there."

The vice president patted Kinnick's shoulder and walked back to his seat. "Trust me. It's not something I'm happy about. I'm no expert on fallout, but my generals tell me the Rockies give us a natural barrier from radiation, fallout poison clouds, and the like. Not to mention it keeps the breadbasket of the nation safe from contamination for rebuilding efforts, and most of our military bases are in the east. You aren't the first person to find this option *drastic*."

Kinnick knew the man spoke the desperate truth; his rationale was that of a man on the brink.

"You want to drop nukes on American soil. You want to drop nukes on Americans," Kinnick said aloud. He wasn't sure if he said that for himself or the acting commander-in-chief.

Brady cocked his head. "Former Americans. You've read the executive order. Both of us know that those aren't Americans anymore, and even if there were living, breathing people trapped inside those zones, they're as good as dead within the month anyway. No clean water, no food, hundreds of thousands of the infected trying to kill you. It's a death sentence if you live there."

Kinnick turned away from the map and took his seat, using the arms to help himself down. "You can't do this." The scotch had loosened his tongue quite a bit.

Brady's eyes grew large. "What else would you have me do? The remainders of the Joint Chiefs are recommending this. It will shift the tide of the war more in our favor. It clears our strategic flank, giving us a single front to focus on. This isn't normal war, Colonel. This is make the right play or checkmate you're dead. No one will be left if both coasts overwhelm us here."

"Please." Kinnick shook his head and rubbed his hands across his brow. "Let me think on this. I will find a better way. I brought Patient Zero here. Give the doctors some time to find a cure."

The vice president's eyes narrowed. "Those doctors in Cheyenne? Find a cure? Ha, that could take months, even years. Or from the latest briefing, never."

"We can hold until then." *Is that the booze talking?*

Brady's eyes lit up as if Kinnick had proposed a dare. "Can we? The decisions I make are for an entire nation. It's not just the West Coast. I have to consider the survivability of this government and the people that depend on it." Brady took a long sip of his scotch.

"No one envies your position. Dear God, it's a terrible one, but please give me time. I will come up with something," Kinnick begged.

Brady gave him an unnerving smile, and for a moment, Kinnick thought the man had cracked.

"Well, you want the responsibility so bad. Come up with something," Brady said.

Kinnick's mouth stuck open.

"Don't stare dumbstruck. That's an order. Make me a plan to save millions. The generals say it's impossible." The vice president shrugged his shoulders. "You say it's not. Prove it. Be daring. Be great." He raised his eyebrows. "Do something worthwhile for Christ's sake." He slurped up some scotch and crunched the melting ice from the bottom of the glass.

"I. Sir, I'm not sure what to say." Kinnick could feel the sweat beading on his forehead in little droplets. The smell of the scotch was making his stomach turn over, or was it the scotch in his stomach?

Brady guzzled the rest of his golden-brown alcohol. "Don't say anything." The vice president stood up abruptly. His glass banged loudly on the table as he set it down. Kinnick tentatively followed, standing upright.

"You have twenty-four hours, Colonel, to come up with a plan to save the Western Seaboard."

STEELE

Little Sable Point, MI

Two pickups parted ways so the motorcycle scouting party could drive back through the entrance to Little Sable Point. The pickups rolled back into place, sealing the ring of vehicles as if they were settlers in covered wagons on the wild frontier. Tess was there waiting for them.

Tess stopped pacing as they flicked off the engines. Wrapping a thick arm around Half-Barrel, Steele strained to lift the heavy biker off the back of the motorcycle.

"What happened?" she demanded. Her eyes were a sparkling obsidian.

"A pack of infected got in too close while we were stopped. Half-Barrel had a heck of a time."

Steele helped the 300-pound plus man limp to a nearby chair.

"Must of been at least a hundred of them," Half-Barrel breathed as he got settled.

"Prolly get that knee propped up and ice if someone has any. Take a couple of these," Steele said tossing the man a bottle from the satchel.

"Where'd you get those?" Tess asked him.

"Came across a pharmacy in Pentwater and took everything that hadn't been picked over. Not much. Generic anti-inflammatories, a few painkillers people couldn't identify, none of the good stuff, heartburn medicine, diabetes meds, anti-fungal cream. Figured it's better to have it and not need it than need it and not have it."

Tess watched him, her eyes unwavering in her judgment. "I'm glad you came back." Her lips curled upward as if she held in the funniest joke ever told but didn't want to share it.

Steele leaned out of Half-Barrel's earshot. "Between you and me, the pack was like six infected, and Quarter-Barrel fell off his motorcycle when they closed in, pinning himself underneath it."

She gave Half-Barrel a sly glance, rubbing her tattooed arms. Scaled green and red dragons crawled up her forearms all the way to her shoulders.

She looked amused. "I'm glad you brought him back in one piece. He may be a simpleton, but he's our simpleton."

Steele nodded. "Everyone here has been generous. It's the least I could do."

She peered up at him. "You should think about staying for awhile. We could always use the help."

"I'll consider it, but I must find her." He looked over her shoulder at the camp.

"Is Pagan's crew back?" Steele asked, looking down at her.

"No. We haven't heard anything. I was hoping you would have an idea."

Steele checked his six. "I don't." He looked out at the ring of vehicles surrounding the lighthouse. His eyes ran over the mishmash of whatever vehicles and supplies people had when the outbreak started or what they had acquired since then. *Could we defend against a horde? What about a determined enemy force? These people were mere nomads. No, they are only refugees.*

"He'll be back if he knows any better." She reached up, tugging at his beard playfully.

Steele could only stare back in surprise at this woman he hardly knew holding his beard hostage with her fingers.

She released him. "We'll talk later," she said, walking away. Steele watched her go, confused as men are with women. *Is she hitting on me? No, can't be. She knows I'm with Gwen. Girl Code, right?*

A light finger on his shoulder drew his eyes away from Tess's backside.

His beautiful blonde stood there. "Gwen," he said with a smile, feeling shame but not knowing why.

"What'd she want?" she asked. Her eyes watched Tess and turned back toward him with suspicion.

"Checking on our supplies we found."

"Did you find any signs of Mary?"

"Nothing." Frustration cloaked his insides.

She straightened his coat, staring down at it then back up at him. "You'll find her. I know you, and I know your will." Dark circles had formed around her eyes. Combined with her pale skin, those dark circles made it look like a terminal illness was lurking inside her.

He reached out and touched her face gently. "Are you okay? You don't look well."

Tears rushed to her eyes, and she looked like she wanted to break down and cry. It scared him a bit. She hadn't shed any tears since Pittsburgh. She was a strong woman, and it was easy to overlook that she had been through so much between the outbreak, her captivity, and the loss of friends and family. When she became vulnerable, it was difficult for him to watch her struggle.

She had hardened over the last few weeks, and now, he was on the verge of getting the exact opposite. The mystery of this female continued to elude him. *Will they ever make sense?* In fact, the more he aged, the more he realized he would never understand them, only learn to skim the watery surface of the female mystique.

She wiped a teardrop from the corner of her eye. "I'm fine. What was she saying to you?" she said, eyes still watering and her face set in a pout.

"I was only telling her what we found out there."

Her eyes narrowed as if he were in a conspiracy against her.

He reached for her and gently gripped her shoulders. "I'm not sure what I can do to help."

She removed herself from his hands by shifting her shoulders. "You can't." She covered her chest with her folded arms closing him off. She looked away from him toward the ground. "What's our plan?"

"I'm not sure." He gazed around the camp. "Not sure I want to drag myself back out in the wilderness without more information on where my mother went. This isn't a bad base to search from."

Her eyes shifted. "You remember what happened on Mount Eden. No place is truly safe." Mount Eden, a giant military base and government continuity of operations center atop of a mountain in Virginia had been overrun in thirty minutes.

"You're right." The idea of a false sense of security was always in the back of his mind. Little Sable Point would get swarmed under in thirty seconds by a horde half that size. The thought soured his whole mood.

She looked like she was about to tell him something, but she choked it down.

"Pagan still hasn't returned yet with the other Red Stripes. If he doesn't return tomorrow, that's a bad sign. Something bad is happening south of here."

"What does that mean for us?" she said.

"More running. Either way, we're in danger. As nice as these people have been, they could turn on us quick."

Her eyes flitted up to his. "I mean *us*."

"We keep fighting until we find a place for us."

"We should stay," she offered. She glanced at the vehicles around them. "We could live here. There's food, water, safety," she said.

He eyed the crude ring of vehicles with disgust.

"We are further from the cities. Maybe it's far enough away to be safe. A place like this, free and safe, but organized and cohesive in purpose." Her words sounded like a pipe dream, when in reality, they lived in a nightmare.

"That sounds amazing, but this place is lucky to exist and wouldn't stand a chance against a horde."

She looked at the ground. "I'm not sure, but we have to reach for something better than survival or we will die tired, beaten and our spirits crushed. I need something. I need to believe in it. Back there in West Virginia, I saw people at their worst. Not like the infected. People like you and me, and it crushed me. It took away my hope. When you rescued us, a glimmer of hope was there, but when you left me again and Lucia died, I knew I was wrong to hope. People are evil. They lack morality and conviction. They don't even have a sliver of compassion for others. It makes me sick to be like that. I've seen the good in people in the past, and I want it back. Even if it's just a lie I tell myself so I can sleep at night."

Steele's jaw dropped a little, his mouth hanging open a crack. It had been days since she had said more than a few sentences at once to him. "I…I understand. I want all those things too, but I'm not sure where they even exist at this point."

Her eyes grew impassioned. "We can run trying to find them, or we can make them. I may not be the same person I was, things might never be the same in our relationship, but we can only reap what we sow. We either build a society we want to live in, or we perish in the flames of someone else's."

Her words burned inside him. "The world will never be the same. I've accepted that. But everything I've done was to keep you and others safe. I'm no saint, but I'm trying to do the right thing."

Her eyes narrowed. "You never would have left me in Pittsburgh if that was true," she said.

He shook his head no. *I am going to be paying for that decision for awhile.* "I thought we were over this."

"No. You have to understand why you were wrong."

"I had to leave. It was the only way Colonel Jackson would let us go."

"We should have left then, escaped."

He threw his hands in the air. "With Mauser on crutches. No vehicle. Mountains to climb. Hundreds of thousands of infected between us and here. There was no way. We needed them."

"You left me alone." She looked away, trying to compose herself.

"You weren't alone. Mauser was there along with Kevin and Joseph." Mauser's name was a bitter mint on his tongue.

"They aren't you."

"They aren't, but if I thought there was a better way, I would have done it. Colonel Jackson threatened your life if I didn't do it, and you and I both know he meant it. We're lucky to be free of the man."

She was silent. "I understand you have your duty, but remember you have a duty to come back to me. You have a duty to include me in your life. You have a duty…," she stopped, her sentence trailing off.

"I'll always come back to you. I've always promised I would."

She sniffed hard, rubbing her nose. Awkward tension filled the air.

He reached into the cargo pocket of his pants, removing the yellow, packaged birth control pills.

"I found these for you. Probably won't need these, but," he said, giving her a careful look. He placed the plastic wrapped package in her hand.

She stared down at the package and back at him. It was as if she held Pandora's box in her hands, infinitely tempting but only woes were locked deep inside.

"That's the right kind, right?" he asked, confused by her response, thinking she would be appreciative or at least want them.

The disc-shaped object sat atop her open palm. She eyed them poisonously.

"Are they not right ones?"

She quickly put them in her pocket and wiped her hands on her camouflage pants.

She gave him a short smile. He was confused. He expected some sort of thanks.

"Of course they are. Thank you," she said quickly.

"Okay, good. Can't be too careful. Jesus, can you imagine if you got pregnant now?"

Her throat jiggled up and down as she swallowed.

"I can't."

JOSEPH

Cheyenne Mountain Complex, CO

An air-pressure resistant door closed behind him with a whoosh. It sealed closed and the air was sucked out of the chamber, leveling the air pressure with Patient Zero's containment room. The low pressure made it difficult for pathogens to escape. A rubber bladder inflated, making the seal tight along the door edges.

Joseph's blue HAZMAT suit wrinkled and scrunched as he turned toward Dr. Weinroth. Behind her plastic faceplate, she flashed him a nervous smile.

Their section of Cheyenne Mountain was a Biosafety Level Four Laboratory (BSL-4), meaning they could handle any and all known diseases that were fatal and had no known vaccine or cure. In this case, their current viral enemy was both, unknown with no known treatment.

"Are you ready?" he asked Dr. Weinroth. Her eyes were anxious beneath her fogging glasses.

"Of course," she said. Her voice shook a bit in his headset earpiece. "My glasses are kind of a pain," she added softly, pushing on her plastic faceplate.

"Mine too," Joseph said into his microphone. They both wore headsets to communicate effectively inside their suits. She stared at the metal door as if it were the gate to Hell. A red biohazard sign covered the middle of the door, reading Authorized Personnel Only over the glass.

Whether or not she was ready, it was time. He timidly pressed the flat of his palm onto a large, circular red button on the wall. This was his first day without a sling, and his arm was shaky at best. When he let his mind drift at night, he could still feel the blade sticking into his flesh and through the muscle, the cold foreign metal inside his body.

The button depressed and an orange siren on the ceiling spun. It honked away like a submarine under attack from above. If they were exiting the lab, vertical banks of nozzles would be spraying them with a decontamination shower for over seven minutes.

The doors rolled open. With a look at one another for courage, the two doctors hesitantly stepped inside the white room. The overhead fluorescent lights shone down with extreme brightness. They were encased in airtight boxes to prevent viruses from collecting along the edges. Epoxy was lathered over any fixture where a pathogen could hide.

Richard Thompson lay on a single shiny metal table in the middle of the room. His arms were bound at his sides. A white sheet covered his lower body. His head was strapped down with a band across his forehead. Machines lined the head of the bed. They beeped out Richard's heartbeat and other bodily functions with robotic consistency. A miracle in itself, he was the only infected person still alive.

The doctors' blue biohazard suits crunched step-by-step like they were walking across a bubble wrap covered floor for Patient Zero. The room's ceilings were high, well over twenty-five-feet tall. The room was all white except for the two-way mirror on the wall. The other doctors observed from the opposing side.

Richard's eyes, the color of chalky chocolate milk, moved from one doctor to the other. "Who are you? What are you doing to me?" Richard stammered. His chin shook with fright and his breath quivered from his lips.

"Richard. It's me, Dr. Jackowski. I found you at your home in Grand Haven." *There were others. Your wife and daughter. Dead.* Joseph digested the thought hoping the man couldn't read his thoughts.

Richard closed his eyes. "My wife? And Helen?"

"I am so sorry, but they have passed," Joseph said.

Richard stayed with his eyes forced closed for a moment. "No. No," he whispered. When he opened them, they blamed Joseph with angry tears.

"I wish there was something I could have done for them."

"You could have started by having your friends not shoot them," Richard spat. Richard tried to turn his head away but had to settle with averting his almost white eyes.

Joseph swallowed hard. *No choice, but how could we ever make this man understand?* "If you cooperate with us you will be able to save the lives of millions of people." *If that many are left.*

Richard twisted his face. Joseph touched Richard's shoulder. "Everything is going to be okay."

"Who's the girl?" Richard said. His eyes turned to Dr. Weinroth like a predator.

"This is Dr. Weinroth. She is an infectious disease specialist with the U.S. Army Medical Research Institute of Infectious Diseases. We are going to run some very basic tests in an attempt to learn more about the virus."

"Hello, Richard. We are here to help," Dr. Weinroth said with a sad smile.

"What's wrong with me?" Richard cried. His arms pulled against his restraints. His normally nonexistent veins became vascular, crisscrossing his forearms. "Why am I strapped down? Let me out of here." His hands rolled in a circle as he searched for a way to free himself. Dr. Weinroth took a step back. Joseph locked eyes with her, trying to give her strength. Her pretty face was stricken with worry.

Joseph nodded to her. "It's okay. He's harmless in his current state."

She shook herself. "I've…" She looked at him again. "I haven't been this close to an infected patient yet."

"You haven't? How?"

"I've been here since the outbreak. I wasn't with Colonel Byrnes at Detrick. They only sent us samples, but no live specimens."

Joseph gave her a comforting smile from behind his suit mask. He glanced over her shoulder at the mirror. He was certain Byrnes scrutinized him on the other side.

"Let us begin. Richard, I am going to give you a topical anesthetic, and we are going to biopsy some of your poxes."

"Okay," Richard said quietly.

Joseph picked a syringe up and pressed it into Richard's shoulder.

"Ow," Richard uttered. Joseph ignored him and injected his shoulder. He removed the needle and set it down.

"Now that's not so bad is it?" he said to Richard.

"It stung." Richard's eyes kept going from doctor to doctor.

"Dr. Weinroth. Can you hand me the scalpel?" His eyes briefly grazed her plastic-covered face. She handed Joseph the surgical knife. He tapped Richard's skin.

"Do you feel that?" Joseph looked at Richard's whitish-hued eyes. It was unsettling to see a live person with such a dead stare. Joseph tried to smile.

"No. Only pressure," Richard said.

"Good."

Joseph went to work like a sculptor. He carved a centimeter-wide pox off Richard's shoulder and placed it in a glass tube.

"I am going to draw his blood," Dr. Weinroth said. She tied a rubber tube around Richard's arm and pushed a needle into his skin. Joseph massaged around Richard's neck with his fingers, locating a golf ball-sized node.

"I would like to have one of his nodes as well," Joseph said. He looked up at Rebecca. She filled vials with Richard's almost black-red blood. Richard tensed underneath their probing hands and needles.

"I...I...I can feel it," Richard shouted. Joseph stopped what he was doing.

Richard let out a groan and his neck stretched. The veins bulged along his throat. Dr. Weinroth looked at Joseph, eyebrows creased upward.

"I can feel it inside me, bubbling beneath the surface of my skin. It's crawling in *my* veins." He twisted his head toward Joseph. His restraints dug into the skin of his forehead. For a moment, he let out a low moan. "Ooooo." His lips then curled into a snarl. "It only wants to get out!" he screamed. His shoulders rocketed against the table. His torso thrust upward as if he were trying to bend in half the wrong way.

Joseph instinctively took a step back, holding the scalpel in the air. Richard writhed on the table in deep affliction.

"You're going to be okay. I'm going to give you a sedative. It will make you feel less anxious."

Richard's body banged back down on the metal table. His hands and feet still moved in their restraints. "That. Would. Be nice," Richard said, his body relaxing a bit.

"Dr. Weinroth, can you hand me the benzodiazepine dipthopham? Thirty milligrams."

She stared at him for a moment, eyes wide. "Joseph. That's three times the recommended dosage for the average adult."

"I understand that, Rebecca, but this is no normal man."

She nodded. She picked up a syringe and stuck the tip inside a small vial. She extracted the clear fluid from the bottle and handed the syringe to Joseph. Their hands touched as she handed it off, and her hand lingered for a brief moment. *Was that on purpose?* She looked back down at her work. *My cruel imagination.*

He put the syringe into the drip chamber and pressed the fluid inside. Richard blinked rapidly. Joseph held his breath for a moment, and Richard's eyes closed.

"How are you feeling, Richard?" he said down to him.

"I'm…fine…," he mumbled.

"That's better. I would have liked to have spoken with you more, but we will have more time. Perhaps when you're less agitated." Joseph gave Rebecca a smile which she returned, her plain pink lips flipping up on the sides.

"I agree. I'm thinking that we should take that lymph node biopsy while he's sedated," she said.

"I concur. I'll prep the large gauge needle for you?"

Patient Zero's foot twitched. At first, it was a small jerk. Joseph and Rebecca stopped. It swung wide in a rotation like a windshield wiper.

Rebecca stopped her preparation. "Did you see that?" she whispered.

"Uh, yeah. Must be an involuntary muscle spasm."

Unsureness crossed her features. "I've never seen that before with dipthopham." She continued at a high whisper. "And never with such a high dose."

"Neither have I," Joseph uttered. He leaned his face close to Patient Zero. The man's chest rose and fell at a slow rate. One, two, three, up. One, two, three, down. The heart monitor beeped an even, controlled double beep. Joseph stood upright.

"His breathing is normal—." Joseph was cut off as Patient Zero started to shake uncontrollably. The metal table rattled beneath him. His body appeared to be in some sort of hypothermic involuntary state. Every single portion of the man vibrated. The heart monitor fired up with a hurricane of mini-heartbeat waves.

"What's he doing?" Rebecca shouted. Patient Zero's body convulsed, and stopped. The heart rate monitor toned down as the man's heartbeat came under control again. The room became quiet save for the monitors beeping. Joseph found himself holding his breath.

"I think that did the trick," he said. He tried to give her a smile with some swagger behind it. "Shall we continue?"

Rebecca gave him a nervous smile. "Of course."

Joseph glanced over at the two-way mirror, knowing the other doctors were critiquing his every move.

Joseph's breath steamed up his mask. He pushed on his clear faceplate with his blue plastic-suited hands. It did nothing but knock beads of condensation down his mask. The only sound in his head was the beating of his heart in his chest. He took a step closer.

"Richard is restrained. We have nothing to fear from him," he said.

Rebecca nodded fast, but her suit didn't move.

"Let's continue," he managed with more bravery than he felt.

"Okay. Where were we? Ah yes, the lymph node biopsy." Joseph gave the monitor an uneasy look. The blips were coming too slow. The beeping slowed as Patient Zero's heart rate dropped.

"Jesus, his heart rate's crashing," Joseph said. He reached for Patient Zero's chest restraints. He undid the straps, throwing them to the sides. "Loosen those restraints. We can't have anything impeding his blood flow."

Joseph's hands fumbled along the wrist straps. Rebecca did as he asked, loosening Richard's other arm restraints.

"Let's get some oxygen in him." Rebecca turned and twisted a knob atop an oxygen tank. She quickly handed the mask to Joseph. He placed it timidly around

Patient Zero's face. He folded his hands and placed them on Patient Zero's chest and began giving him compressions. Within thirty seconds, the heart rate monitor was back to normal. Joseph leaned back, watching the monitor.

"See. There we go," he said, breathing hard.

Joseph picked up the biopsy syringe off the ground. *No need for a new one. Sterile facility.*

He inched the twenty-gauge needle point against the lymph nodes in Richard's neck that sagged to the side through his skin, too heavy to remain in place. Rebecca bent in and, with her finger and thumb, and forced his eyelid open.

Patient Zero's eyes glared at her. They darted to Joseph and back to Rebecca in a few blinks.

"Raahhh," Patient Zero snarled. His mouth worked open and closed. His hand shot from its confines and grabbed Rebecca by her wrist. He twisted and turned beneath the other restraints. Joseph watched in horror.

"Joseph!" she screamed. She bent in his grasp, pulling like a dog fighting in a tug-of-war with hard jerks for her arm back. Patient Zero kicked one leg free and then the other.

"My hand," she said, frantic.

Patient Zero stood upright.

"Joseph," she cried. She cowered, his hands wrapped tightly around hers. Alarms blared overhead. The other doctors had seen. Help would be coming soon.

"Let me go," she cried. Yellow sirens swirled above them. "Joseph," she mumbled.

"Richard," Joseph commanded. Richard turned his head to the side, and his whitish eyes judged him for a moment. "Get back on the table." Richard ignored him and turned back to Rebecca, driving her forward.

"No," Joseph yelled. He ran around the table and lunged for Richard. He wrapped his skinny arms around Richard's shoulders. He barely felt his stitches tear as he clasped his hands together.

Richard shoved Rebecca down. He bucked Joseph, but Joseph refused to let go.

"Stop," Joseph managed to sputter.

Patient Zero backtracked and rammed Joseph into the sterile white padded wall. Joseph's breath was forced from his chest and he wheezed. Patient Zero spun in a circle like a madman.

Byrnes was donning his HAZMAT suit inside the pressurized chamber. He pointed at a soldier dressing himself. He screamed at the man to hurry. Rebecca pushed herself up the wall near the two-way mirror.

Joseph found himself flying through the air and crashing into the ground. He could even feel the blood trickling down his arm. Richard lumbered away from him.

"No," Joseph said. His eyesight was disoriented as though he'd had too many vodka sodas at the bar.

Rebecca made a run for the pressurized door, but her blue HAZMAT suit made her clumsy and she tripped.

Richard leapt onto her body. She rolled on her back, fighting and pushing him in desperation. His hands ripped at the seams of her faceplate. Blood erupted from his fingertips as he clawed her. She screamed.

"Please," she screamed. Joseph's arms felt like lead, but he pushed himself off the floor. He wobbled as he found himself upright.

Plastic flew in the air as Patient Zero ripped her faceplate to the side in a cracked mess. Joseph stumbled toward Rebecca, his hand reaching out for her, but he moved slowly as though he were under water.

Patient Zero leaned in close to her face, and she let out a bloodcurdling cry. Patient Zero's head jerked back, Rebecca's flesh in his mouth. Blood dribbled down his lips. His jaw worked as he chewed.

The pressurized doors whisked open and a scowling Byrnes stepped through with two soldiers armed with tasers and long batons. The colonel ran forward and struck Patient Zero in the face with his baton. Patient Zero flipped onto his side, sprawling across the floor. He convulsed, his limbs stretching in painful strained positions. One of the soldiers used his baton to pin Patient Zero and he writhed against the constraint. Joseph raced for Rebecca and wrapped an arm around her with the help of Byrnes. They dragged her over the floor into the pressurized chamber.

They set her down and the doors rolled closed behind them. Rebecca's hand covered her cheek. Blood seeped between her fingers. Pressurized air hissed as it was driven inside the chamber. Ghostly white air fogged inside enveloping them.

Joseph got close to her face, holding her. "Are you okay?" Joseph shouted.

She nodded, tears streaming down her face.

Byrnes pounded on the door. "Open this thing up. We don't have time for decontamination." Batons flailed inside the other room, the faint zap of tasers reaching their ears. Patient Zero's screams sounded like the old Richard Thompson, but Joseph's only focus was on Rebecca.

Rebecca's eyes read Joseph's, blinking her pain back. Her eyes were wide like those of a scared doe behind her bent glasses. Watery tears engulfed them and fear surrounded them.

No, not her.

Byrnes reached past Joseph and gripped her face with hard fingers. "Let me see your face," he commanded. Her hand shook as she removed it from her cheek. A blood-filled crater defiled her.

Byrnes mouth downturned into a fierce snarl. He held his baton with two hands and shoved her into the corner.

She held up a hand in defense, covering her head. "Please," she cried.

Joseph's heart dropped because he already knew.

"She's infected," Byrnes hissed.

STEELE

Little Sable Point, MI

Gwen's eyes were distrusting; and their color had changed to a drab mossy green. Single blades of blonde hair hung down around her face, outlining her high cheekbones.

"Why are only you two going to look for him?"

Steele removed boxes of ammo from his pack and set them on the ground. "I don't know. She asked and I said yes."

"Why'd you say yes?" Gwen asked.

He continued to replace the ammo with MREs from Gwen's pack. "Must I ask your permission to search for my mother and Pagan?"

"When you go somewhere without me, yes. Were you even listening when we talked yesterday?" Her eyes set in a steadfast position, unmoving and unwavering.

"Of course I was." *Listening to the parts I wanted to hear.* He met her eyes and clenched his jaw tight, causing the top of his skull to ache. *Is it the gunshot wound that makes my skull ache or the continuous clenching of my jaw brought on by her everlasting woman's tongue?*

He shook a box of ammo at her. "Make sure to hide these, and make sure your pack stays with you at all times. These people have been kind, but they are a very loose confederation. They come and go, and I wouldn't put it past any of them to snatch up one of the packs if left unattended."

"We'll keep them nearby, but why did you say 'yes' to her?"

Steele stopped packing. "My mother is still out there. At least I think she is." He gestured behind him. "Pagan went on a limb for us, and I have a responsibility to bring them both back." He stood up and pointed the weapon angled safely upward. He twisted the carbine and grabbed the changing handle with his left hand, pulling it back to view in the ejection port. A brass round rested inside.

"What about all those biker guys? Can't they help?"

"I don't know. I'm not in charge." He released his magazine from the carbine and looked inside. With a rectangle to rectangle alignment, he seated the magazine back inside the gun. "I will be back, one way or another."

Gwen didn't laugh. Her face gave away that she wasn't amused by his morbid humor. He bent down face level with her and kissed her cheek. He pulled himself upright and shouldered his pack. It was better to have cold goodbyes. If he lingered long enough, he might never leave. He walked the short distance to the entrance of Little Sable Point.

"You can't keep doing this," she yelled after him.

"I'm building our world," he growled back at her over his shoulder.

The ring of vehicles sat parked around the lighthouse. Inside the ring, tents were set up in a haphazard manner. Trash littered the ground. People that were there yesterday were gone today. Others idled in front of campers and cars in lounge chairs watching the others come and go. Some grilled. It didn't look like much. *Fish?* Steele couldn't tell what they were grilling, but it stunk like campfire smoke.

Tess awaited him at the entrance, her shorter black hair combed straight back so it ran down the back of her skull. She wore a shoulder harness that held a 1911 and extra mags over a tight-fitting black thermal and black hiking pants. A small pack hung off her back.

"You have a big pack there," she said with a smile as he drew near. He chose to ignore her quip.

"Can't be unprepared. Don't know how long we'll be out there."

"You're right, but I don't suspect long. That idiot Pagan will wish he was dead when we find him."

Steele nodded. "What are we driving?"

"I would take a motorcycle, but if there are wounded, those are useless. So we'll have to settle on one of the gas guzzlers." She slapped the metal side of a boxy red 1980s era Ford Ranger pickup.

"That's a gas guzzler?"

"Anything that ain't a motorcycle." She tossed her small pack in the pickup bed. "We won't be hauling a ton of rocks in this thing, but it does well enough on gas, and we could lay multiple injured in the back if need be."

Steele nodded. "Or shooters. Good choice." He tossed his pack in the truck bed then reached for the driver's side door handle, popping it open. "Keys?" He raised a stiff eyebrow at Tess, hindered by the scar tissue on his scalp.

"Sorry, soldier. You get shotgun. I know the area, and no one drives this puppy except for me. It got Pagan and me out of a few tough spots in the beginning, and I don't let anyone else drive Red Rhonda." Steele was a bit taken aback but nodded his acknowledgment.

"Your car, your rules," he said, trying to hide a grin. He circled around and hopped in the passenger side. The seats were a worn faded gray fabric that originally may have been black. It was hard to tell. Steele cranked the window down, resting his M4 carbine across the truck's windowsill. He felt a bit like he was riding shotgun on a stagecoach in the Wild West.

Tess turned the key and the pickup sputtered to life. She waved at a couple of Red Stripes and the entrance pickups rolled away, giving them access to the outside.

She gassed the old pickup away from Little Sable Point Lighthouse and onto a large sidewalk. They rolled down the sidewalk and a sandy field of dune grass and small trees that lay between the lighthouse and a thicker forest. The sidewalk took them into a state park parking lot, and finally, they turned onto a sand-blown road leading away from Little Sable Point Lighthouse. For over a mile, they wound back and forth down the forested road until they hit a green and white Lakeshore Drive sign.

"This is where we split the other day," Steele said. He leaned near the dash, peering left and then right.

"Right. South we go." She twisted the steering wheel, taking them to the right.

The pickup rattled down the deserted road at about thirty-five miles per hour. Yellowish brown leaves leapt up behind them as they cruised down the two-lane road. Fall was in full effect in Michigan. Turning leaves became falling leaves, and a deep, bone-chilling cold would soon coat the coast of Michigan.

Tess turned a knob and the radio clicked on. Static blared as she switched from station to station. Nothing came through. No DJs spoke. No music played. Bored, she clicked the radio back off and slapped her hand on the steering wheel.

"Guess we'll have to talk."

"I'm not a big talker." He made sure to look out the window after he spoke, outwardly making sure she knew he wasn't interested in the fine art of small talk. He could feel her eyes on him.

"Sorry, bud. You get to be a good listener then."

He was silent. Cold air blew through the open window and rippled his beard.

"I never would have gone for Pagan before the outbreak." *Fucking relationship talk. Is she serious? Kill me now. Six thousand ways to die out here, and I get talked to death about feelings.* He continued to avert his eyes out the window.

She sat in silence as if she expected him to respond. He didn't say anything. Relationships were not his strong suit and to add input on a relationship he knew nothing about was bound to make someone upset. He watched the coastal trees instead.

"I don't know," he mumbled under his breath.

"Hmm. You got nothing?" she prodded him. He could feel her glancing over at him every few seconds before looking back at the road.

He gave her a short glance and brought a hand up in defense. "I'm not a leading expert on relationships. Best to leave me out of it."

Tess ignored his words. She looked at him and back at the road a few times before she continued. "Let me explain more."

Please God no. What have I done to deserve this?

"I'm always down for a good time, but you know, more of a long-haired rocker in a band type. Never thought I'd shack up with a goofy, smiling all the time Force Recon Marine. Never saw the man not smile, even when we were facing a horde of infected. It's like he's always laughing on the inside. Ya know. Like nothing could get him down. I guess he was just made for this."

"The Marines have a twisted sense of humor, but you definitely want them on your side."

"You aren't one of them, are you?" She glanced over at him. "But you've seen some shit. I see it on your face."

"I've seen enough to know better. I don't enjoy it. I'd rather be somewhere else, but most of the time, I don't have a choice."

She draped a single hand over the steering wheel. "You in the business of playing hero?"

Steele half-laughed and ran a hand down his beard. "No. I'm in the business of keeping my folks alive."

"So? Like going out of your way to help a Marine you've only met in passing."

"He did the same for me." Trees passed by, waving dying leaves like parade flags.

"He did. But I have a feeling you would be out here either way. Some people, that's all they know."

Steele sat silent for a moment contemplating his reasons for his actions.

"I would." *It's the right thing to do. Pagan could be an ally. It could gain your group's trust. It may lead to a clue to finding my mother. The reasons went far beyond being helpful.*

"Those are the markings of a leader."

He shook his head, still scanning the trees and the two-lane road.

"I wouldn't call leading a group of four a leader. You have a band of a couple hundred people. You're the leader."

She snorted. "Nobody there follows me. They're there because it's safer together. No one else volunteered to help me search for Pagan. I make decisions, but I don't lead. A man like you inspires."

"I only do what I have to do to keep my folks alive. Not leading some rebellion."

She gave him a half-smile. "A warrior with a heart of gold. I assume that's how you got that nasty scar?"

He tenderly ran a hand over his scar as if he still didn't believe it had happened. "The results of an ambush in West Virginia. Good people died because of decisions I made," he said. He finished with a look at her to see if she understood his survivor guilt. He gave a painful smile under his bushy beard as if thinking about the wound somehow reopened it. "I was hoping my hair would cover that up."

"You're going to have to grow a hell of a lot more than that to cover that puppy."

"I suppose I should be thankful to still have a head." Darkness from his peripherals made him look ahead quick. "Tess, look." He pointed out. A thick-trunked tree lay across the road, blocking their path forward. He pushed his carbine up to his shoulder and scanned the fallen tree. Clear chainsaw cuts and grooves cut through the bark revealing the white of the inner trunk. Shiny bits of metal lay in the brush on the side of the road.

"Looks like a motorcycle," Tess pointed.

"Someone has set this up. I don't like it. We should get the Red Stripes and come back," Steele said.

A determined look fell upon Tess, and Steele knew he was going to regret whatever happened next. "If he's here, I'm not leaving him." *Jesus, they're all trying to get me killed. Either by infected, bullets, or a heart attack.*

A shaved-head infected stood up near the tree and hobbled through the ditch then up onto the roadway. White creamy bone had been forced through its riding leathers. Red Stripes motorcycle club colors covered his torso. Pus oozed from large wounds covering his legs where the skin had been worn off by sliding on the pavement uncovered by leather. Lower layers of epidermis were exposed and reddish pink.

"Damn. Looks like Joker and he's all fucked up."

Steele peered hard at the trees looking for anything and anybody that could pose a threat. Their exposure in the middle of the road gnawed at the back of his mind. "I don't like this." He spun in his seat, looking out behind them and trying to get a three hundred and sixty-degree grasp on everything around them. "I'll go put him down. But then we go."

"No," she asserted. Her eyes were the darkest of brown. "We put him down, and we search for the others. I will not abandon Pagan when we finally have a clue to as to what's going on." She stared at him, mind made up but waiting on him to respond. *Are these people worth the danger?*

"We put him down. Take a quick look around and then come back later from a different way."

"Deal," she said with a smile, slipping out of the pickup's driver side. Steele hopped out and put his carbine to his shoulder in the high ready. He eyed the trees. Soft-needled white pines grew between jagged-leafed bigtooth aspens; a few thick-trunked oaks grew amongst their smaller brethren.

Ambushers could be waiting behind every tree and rock to put bullets in him again. He steadied his breathing with some tactical breaths, drawing up alongside the slender woman. He let himself ramp up into a heightened state of readiness.

"I'll do the honors. Payback's a bitch," he breathed.

"But," she got out. He ignored her and charged the former biker. Letting his carbine swing to his hip, he drew out his tomahawk, and with a heavy downward strike, he sunk the rounded axe blade through the front of Joker's ugly hairless skull. Joker stopped mid-step, his body almost suspended in the air. Steele let the man fall back. Joker's jaw clicked open then closed one last time and he went limp. Steele wrapped his other hand around the shaft and ripped it free with a spray of brain matter.

He put the tomahawk back and his carbine whipped back up to his shoulder.

"Look here." He pointed with his gun to a red streak running along the pavement toward the tree. Small chunks of flesh made it look like he had hit an animal, turning it into roadkill, but in reality, those were pieces of Joker.

"What do you think happened?" Tess asked.

"It looks like Joker laid his bike down back there going pretty quick. You see?" Pieces of metal, engine fluid, and Joker lay scattered along the cracked branches of the fallen tree.

Steele circled the downed tree, stepping around branches. He frequently checked his flanks expecting the shit to hit the fan at any moment.

"I got nothing over here," he called over at Tess. The trees rustled in the wind and the drying fall leaves crackled together like ten thousand pieces of crinkle paper. He bent down, putting a finger on a deep gouge in the flesh of the tree.

"Somebody definitely did this on purpose," he muttered.

"Come quick," Tess called. Gripping the giant tree trunk with one hand, he hopped over the log, landing near Tess.

"Jesus, Rambo." She gave him an intense stare. "Check this out. Tracks." The leaves were pushed out of the way. Sand and dirt had been scraped to the sides. Something had been dragged through the ditch into the woods.

"They went this way," she said, holding her 1911 pointed toward the ground.

Steele bent down trying to read the tracks like an ancient message written in the sand. He could make out a dozen distinct footprints. "At least a dozen people." He gave her a glance. He already knew what she would say.

She didn't hesitate. "I'll grab our packs."

KINNICK
Golden Triangle, CO

Kinnick watched Hunter as he slurped up chicken soup by upending his bowl. Yellow liquid dribbled down his wild brown beard, running along the whiskers as if they were canyons. He gave Kinnick a wolfish grin as he chewed up the meat and noodles in the broth.

Men and women moved in and out of the cafeteria while the din of plates and silverware clanked in the background. They were allowed full kit in the cafeteria. Kinnick supposed if they weren't allowed, no one would tell them otherwise.

Kinnick's men consumed as much of the non-MRE food as they could get their hands on. It was the only taste of civility he had experienced in what felt like forever. He picked at his food, sick to his stomach about what was going to happen to the West Coast.

"What's got your goat, Colonel? Can't be too mad about the food. It's hot. It's free, and there's plenty of it," Hunter said.

Kinnick pushed his bowl in front of the master sergeant.

"Be my guest," he said with a dismissive wave.

"You sure?" Hunter questioned him with raised eyebrows.

"Take it." Hunter grabbed the bowl and started to shovel its contents into his mouth

"A lot more food to go around since Lewis left us," Hunter said, between bites.

"I'd rather have his SAW pointed downrange than the extra food," Turmelle said.

"Me too," Hunter said. "But, I ain't gonna turn down the extra rations." Hawkins sat next to Turmelle, quietly eating his food. The man was meticulous even in his eating. His mechanical, robot-like chewing irritated Kinnick.

"What's the problem, Colonel? You got the egghead and that Jody into the secret mountain base. Humanity's got a chance. My mission don't change, but surely your life's a bit better now," Turmelle said.

Kinnick met the man's hard blue eyes. "My life didn't get better by coming here. My family's dead. My men have died, and I have to figure out a way to prevent the vice president from nuking the West Coast."

Hunter choked on his food and went into a coughing fit. He wiped his nose and stared at Kinnick.

"With all due respect sir, you don't mean nuke, nuke, do you?"

Kinnick gave him a flat look. "That's exactly what I mean, Master Sergeant. He's going to pound every city center along the coast with 400-kiloton warheads to eliminate the infection with a heavy dose of fire and brimstone."

Hunter's eyes narrowed. "He can't do that. This is America."

"He can't?" Kinnick ground his teeth. "He will. He has promised me that."

"That's like using a shotgun to shoot a fly off your foot," Turmelle said.

"You can begin to understand my reservations," Kinnick said.

"We can't let him do that," Turmelle said, growing excited. His short black curls trembled. "I have family out there."

The men looked at one another and back at Kinnick as if they expected an answer to their problems.

"I have twenty-four hours to come up with a plan to protect our western flank or the VP is going to do it."

Kinnick stared at the remnants of the "Skins" Operational Detachment Alpha 51. Each man wore a patch on their sleeves of a skull wearing a wolf headdress, two red arrows behind it. They were on loan to him from General

Travis, brought up from Eglin Air Force base. General Travis was dead. They had started this war with twelve men. Now, they were down to three. Kinnick considered them lucky for that. To die was a release from their nation's never-ending demand of duties.

"Strategic planning is not part of our responsibilities. My job is to teach indigenous folks how to tag 'em and bag 'em and maybe sneak a few kills in when the boss ain't looking," Hunter said. Soup continued to run down the long hairs of his beard, flowing down the indents and ridges made by his thick bristly brown hair.

"God has given you a fine set of skills, Master Sergeant, but I need you to think outside your box. We have to figure out a plan to stop roughly sixty million infected from crossing the mountains in our rear and presenting the other one hundred and fifty million from the east coast an anvil to smash us on."

"What about the other hundred million people in the United States?" Hawkins asked.

"Well, I'm assuming they're dead, but I'm sure they will find their way up here somehow," Kinnick said, irritated by the sight of Hunter's soup-filled beard. "Wipe your beard, Master Sergeant."

He stared at Hunter's beard. Little droplets sped down the long hairs, following the curves and outlines made by the coarse hair. Hunter took a napkin, running it along his beard as if he tried to straighten it.

"Did I get it all?" Hunter asked with an unrepentant smirk.

"No. You didn't, but you just gave me an idea." Kinnick pulled out a rolled-up map he had taken to study and stretched it across the table, pushing bowls and cups out of the way.

Hunter ran a sleeve across his face and shrugged his shoulders, leaning in.

"Hear me out. The infected are like a river, much like the soup flowing down your beard. It travels down the easiest path. If you block one way, it will flow through the path of least resistance. So find me pinch points. Passes. Anywhere we can hold an enormous force of infected without deploying too many resources."

"Can they even get through the mountains? They don't seem too agile," Turmelle said.

"I'm not sure. Some will make it through, no doubt, but we will assume most will struggle, trapping themselves in the mountains. The parts we have to worry about are established routes through those mountains that they can easily traverse. Highways, tunnels, and passes through the Rockies."

"So we're going to dam 'em up?" Hunter said.

"More like push them along until the snow takes care of them for us. Once those passes are covered in snow and no one plows them, the dead will be trapped on the other side," Kinnick said.

"What about next spring?" Turmelle said.

"If we make it that far, we will deal with it then. Specialist?" Kinnick waved to a broad soldier, a green and tan ivy patch on one sleeve, walking by with a food tray in his hands. His name tag read Rogers. He stopped at their table. "Specialist Rogers. You based out of Carson?"

"Yes, sir. I am."

"Good. You go skiing around here?"

Specialist Rogers looked a bit uncomfortable. "Yes, sir. Not recently."

"No need to worry, soldier. When does the season start? When does it usually begin to snow in the mountains?"

"Ah, well, it depends on the year, but I would say by mid-November we usually get enough snow to really hit the slopes."

"Perfect. Carry on, soldier."

Specialist Rogers nodded and left.

Kinnick pointed at the map. "We only need to hold the choke points until mid-November and then the snow will do all the work for us. Who knows maybe the snow will kill 'em."

Hawkins studied the map silently then spoke. "That's a lot of ground to cover. Exactly how many resources are we thinking?"

"There's me, you, the master sergeant and ah, Turmelle, maybe a couple of the boys from the squads," Kinnick said with a weak smile.

The master sergeant laughed. "I love those odds."

"Sign me up," Turmelle said, leaning over the map.

Kinnick jammed his index finger on the paper. "Look here. You see this tunnel? The Eisenhower Tunnel. We'll have to shut that down." He dragged his finger to Highway 70. "That's the fastest way through Colorado from the West."

Hawkins pointed, touching his finger south of the Eisenhower tunnel.

"Independence Pass. And here, Mosquito Pass. And there, South Fork." His finger touched each pass of a major roadway through the Rocky Mountains.

"And here." Kinnick jabbed his finger downward, feeling the pain in its tip. "When we block the Eisenhower Tunnel, they will funnel through this way," Kinnick said. His finger dragged along the map all the way to a single spot. He tapped it with his finger. "What does that say?"

Hunter got his face close to the map. "Dunluce Pass."

Kinnick's three men looked back at him. Expectant. Inspire us, they seemed to say. *No, they don't need inspiring.* They were used to this. They had gone into the field of battle countless times, always expecting to return.

Kinnick took a deep breath. "That's the spot."

Hunter grinned. "You really know how to sweet talk the girls, Colonel."

"Luckily, it's only you three stooges I have to worry about."

"If we can get some token forces in place at the smaller passes, hold them there, and plug Dunluce, we can stop the West Coast infected from breaking through."

Turmelle jumped out of his seat, twirling his kukri in his fingers like a hibachi-trained chef and then slammed it blade first through the map into the table. Soldiers from a nearby table looked up, considering the operator's outburst. Their eyes quickly went back to their meals.

Turmelle gave them a wicked grin. "When do we start?"

JOSEPH

Cheyenne Mountain Complex, CO

Dr. Weinroth's auburn hair lay sprawled across her white pillow like sugar-plum rivers on a field of freshly fallen snow. Joseph brushed a strand of hair behind her ear. White surgical mask straps wrapped around the back of her head pinning her hair down. Thick white bandages covered the bite wound on her cheek. The rest of her was curled in a ball as if she were a little girl nestling into her mother for warmth.

Joseph sat next to the bed, his hands clasped in front of his body. Filled with fear and regret, he had watched her sleep for hours, and his heart hung low in his stomach. *You should have saved her. She was afraid and you continued on with the experiments anyway.*

She rolled over, her sheets rustling around her. Her eyes opened and creased along the edges. A hand rose to her face and she pushed on the bandages. She let her hand drop onto the covers, and a small voice came out. "I thought maybe it was only a nightmare, but it's real."

Joseph didn't know what to say to console her. "I'm sorry."

Her eyes held tears but no answers. "Can you hand me my glasses?"

Joseph jumped up for them. His heart raced as he tried to help her.

"They are on the table behind you."

He quickly walked over, snatched them up, and handed them to her. She took the glasses and placed them on her thin face. Their frames were slightly bent, resting crooked on her face.

"Thank you," she whispered. Her brown eyes were still brown beneath the lenses, regarding him. They hadn't yet begun the process of changing colored pigments to white.

"How are you feeling?" he said, sitting down and adjusting his own damaged glasses.

Her mouth moved underneath her surgical mask. "As good as somebody who is infected with a fatal super virus can feel." Even now, after everything that had happened, she smiled underneath her mask, and it made him feel so much worse than he thought was still possible.

He sighed. "We'll figure something out."

Her eyes looked sad. "I'm sure you will."

Already writing herself off. "We will," he corrected.

Dr. Weinroth's eyes closed slowly. "Don't be foolish. We know what this means. The virus, however slow it changes a person in its original state, is infecting my cells one by one. You shouldn't be here. You should be working on a vaccine so this doesn't happen again."

"I know," he muttered. He chanced a glance at the door and whispered, "Colonel Byrnes has taken over the research. He's pushing to begin massive tissue harvesting. Without you and your vote, he will succeed." Joseph ran his hands up, over, and through his hair.

"Joseph." He looked up. "Without you there, he will succeed. You know what you're doing is right. Find a way."

"I'm going to need your help," he said. He looked to her for affirmation. She nodded. "Take a look at these first test results." He handed her a manila folder. She pushed herself upright with her elbows so she was seated. She adjusted her light blue medical gown over her shoulders.

Rebecca flipped open the folder as if she were the doctor and not the patient. Her eyes skimmed down the page.

"This can't be right," she said, looking over her mask at him.

"Every test result is the same."

Her finger poured down the page. "Did you see the genome of this virus? It's not monkeypox. At least not in its entirety."

"I know." He leaned in and pointed at the page. "Look here. These sixty pairs of DNA match the genome of monkeypox. But here." He pointed again. "And here."

"Those are entirely different genomes," she said excitedly.

Joseph couldn't help but be excited by uncovering its inner workings that were like a puzzle with a billion pieces. "It's true. We're looking at a satellite virus. A virus that uses the platform of another virus to pass on its genetic code." He scootched his chair closer.

She eyed him. "Don't get to close," she said.

"I don't care about that. You have time yet. I need you to hold on. We need your help to unravel this nightmare." Her eyes judged if he meant what he had said. She knew that he knew she was doomed and that she would rapidly degrade over the next few weeks, maybe even faster.

"Look at the DNA. I know it's a lot. Try to untangle its evil code. Monkeypox was only a vector to whatever this," he tapped a finger on the paper, "whatever this thing here was trying to do."

"I'll try," she said. As if her body realized she was making promises she couldn't keep, she coughed hard into her hand. He watched her squirm in pain with suffering.

"I have a meeting with Colonel Byrnes and the team in a few to discuss our options. I will check in a bit later." He stood and made for the door.

"Joseph."

"Yes."

"You can't let it win."

"I won't," he said, softly closing the door behind him.

Joseph stepped outside, noting her room number C-3EB before walking away, trying not to think about the monster she would become. His feet padded down the white sterile hallway, unique to this part of the facility, installed with the purpose of making it feel like a lab or hospital and not the deep windowless mountain cavern it actually was.

Joseph stopped at a room with a sign on the wall that read BSL-C1. He pushed the handle down and walked inside. From the first step he took into the room, his senses were pounded by the force of the man already there. Colonel Byrnes sat at one end of the conference table. His hands were neatly folded in front of his body. His ACUs were neat and crisp as if he feared a superior officer would inspect him at any moment.

Heads turned toward Joseph. Dr. Desai peered guiltily down at her hands.

"Sorry I'm late," Joseph mumbled.

"Dr. Jackowski, thank you for coming to this emergency meeting. How is Dr. Weinroth?" Joseph pulled his chair out and sat down. Dr. Nguyen eyed him through the tiny slits of his eyes and Dr. Hollis appeared adrift, lost in a sea of his own thoughts.

"She's doing well, all things considered." Her infection hung over the Mountain Integrated Medical team like a black cloud of locusts. It was only a matter of time before they landed for feeding on their lush plant-stalk minds and souls.

Byrnes lips pursed. "What happened was very unnecessary." He took a pile of papers in his hands and stacked them on end. He continued to do so until they were straight and orderly. Joseph envisioned that the colonel was shaking and straightening him out until he had fallen in line.

"Yes, it was. A most devastating accident," Joseph said.

"Accident. And preventable. Joseph. The team has been in deep discussion about the way forward from here." *I bet you have.*

The rest of the team looked at Joseph as if they expected him to give them an explanation of what happened to Dr. Weinroth or some sort of glorious speech about the merits of human life. He gave them nothing.

Byrnes's head lowered and his eyes narrowed.

"The team believes that we should change tactics to a more aggressive approach, one that keeps the patient in a more comatose state. It will help prevent any further *issues.*"

Joseph shook his head. "No. We voted before that we should try a less lethal approach. Patient Zero is not like the other infected. The information we discovered only yesterday points us to a satellite parasite-like virus attached to the host monkeypox virus." He collected himself and sucked in a deep breath. "If we can unlock the genome behind the satellite, we may be able to figure out the riddle behind the epidemic."

Byrnes nodded. "While this is true, there is much more that needs to be discovered before we can move forward. We need more information now."

Dr. Nguyen nodded his agreement, his eyes larger than normal behind his thick but small round glasses. "We should move forward with invasive tissue harvesting. Since Dr. Weinroth's infection, we not only lost an important asset, but it set us back on our research timeline. We don't have a choice now."

"We always have a choice," Joseph said. He quickly scanned the room. They all avoided his eyes like he was one of the deadly infected.

"Dr. Jackowski, the time for half measures is over. He's only one man. Certainly you can see the higher mortality rates associated with high tissue harvesting mean little compared to the lives of millions," Dr. Nguyen said.

Dr. Hollis rubbed the corners of his mouth and flicked away a crumb. "He is right. The risk is worth it."

"He's alive, Dr. Hollis. We've only scratched the tip of the iceberg with our first few tests, and the data is fantastic."

"But not enough," Dr. Hollis said.

"He also assaulted and infected Dr. Weinroth." Byrnes's index fingers sprung up in front of his folded hands, running up the center of his mouth to his nose. "We do what we must. You said yourself you would support more intrusion if non-invasive harvesting did not work. It hasn't worked, Doctor. It's time to move forward." His eyes brained Joseph. There was no debate in them. "All in favor, say aye."

A resounding echo of "ayes" met Joseph's ears. Not one person voted to continue less invasive procedures. Dr. Desai couldn't look Joseph in the eyes. Joseph took his glasses off and rubbed his tired dry eyes. He had been up with Dr. Weinroth all night and was losing his will, not to the virus but to his peers, to fight the battle. He was beginning to accept the fact that he was going to assist in dangerous procedures in the name of "science."

"I can't argue this any longer. I defer to the team. But let me speak to Mr. Thompson. Perhaps I can make him more compliant to our research needs."

Byrnes nodded. "I believe that's fair. Dr. Desai, will you start analyzing the lymph node biopsy? Dr. Nguyen and Dr. Hollis, please prepare for surgery." He said nothing to Joseph.

Joseph stood up and left, leaving them behind. He walked down the hall and alone to the changing antechamber. He stripped down his clothes and hung them up in his locker. The locker next to his had a brown nameplate on it that read *Weinroth*. It sickened him to think of her as one of the infected. He slammed his locker closed.

He grabbed a fresh pair of green scrubs from a white cabinet near the edge of the lockers. They would be incinerated later, never reaching this room again. He washed his hands and picked up a soap brush. He picked his nails with one end and then vigorously scrubbed his fingers, hands, and forearms. He reapplied soap that was a nasty bile color, and it left his skin orange until he scrubbed it off. He tossed the brush into a biohazard trash bin. He repeated the process again with soap. The other doctors began filing in and he left them behind. Soldiers followed them in scrubs.

He entered the next chamber. Blue HAZMAT suits hung on the walls. He pulled his down and put his legs inside, pulling it up and around his shoulders. He said nothing to the lab technician as she checked his suit for leaks. He ignored the other doctors as they prepped to go inside the room with Patient Zero.

Thirty minutes later, they all stood silent as the air was sucked up and out through ventilation ducts and pumped outside the facility. The doors rolled open and the team of doctors, along with two soldiers, walked inside.

Patient Zero was strapped to a table. They had doubled down on the bindings and kept the man under a different twenty-four-hour sedation. Joseph's blue suit crinkled like a flapping tarp in a windstorm.

He stopped next to Patient Zero. His eyes were closed. His skin pale. *He infected her. He killed her with his bite. He deserves what is coming. No.* His ethics battled his need for revenge. *Remember why you are here.*

The other doctors stood back. Soldiers stood behind them with long batons. "Ahem." Joseph placed a hand on Patient Zero and shook his shoulder. "Richard. Wake up." When he didn't, Joseph shook him harder.

Richard's eyes cracked open. They were glassy and white as if he had shaken them up like snow globes. His voice was dry and broken. "Dr. Jackowski. Water."

Joseph snatched up a bottle and held it to his lips.

"Thanks," Richard whispered. "Where've you been?"

Joseph gulped and set down the bottle. "I've been attending to Dr. Weinroth."

Richard's eyes shifted to the other doctors.

"She seemed nice. Where is she?"

"She's in another observation room."

"She sick?" Richard asked. His eyebrows limply shifted up.

Joseph looked over at Byrnes. The colonel tapped his wrist impatiently.

"She was infected."

"How?" Richard groaned.

"You don't remember?"

"Remember what?" Richard groaned. He shifted on the table, testing his bindings.

Joseph's brow furrowed. "You, Richard. You ripped off her mask and bit her face."

Richard blinked back tears. His eyes stared straight up at the ceiling. "I didn't. I can't remember anything."

Joseph squeezed his shoulder. "You did. You threw me into the wall. We couldn't stop you."

"I suppose that's why you brought the reinforcements this time." The two soldiers looked ready to let him have it at any moment. Pistols on their hips reminded Joseph that lethal use of force would be authorized, regardless of Patient Zero's importance alive.

"The doctors are here to continue researching you and the virus. They have a series of tests they need to run." He paused. "You understand why we must conduct these experiments, right?"

"Yeah. To create a vaccine for the virus."

"That's correct. Some of the tests we have to conduct may be painful."

Richard bit his lip and tried to nod. "I understand. You know, I didn't ask for any of this." Then quieter, he whispered. "I didn't want this."

"We didn't want this either." *We don't want to do this. I don't want to do this, but my team has overridden me. I must keep it together for the team.* "Will you try to hold it together for us? The American people are depending on you."

Richard tried to nod again, but his head was secured to the table. Joseph turned to the doctors and nodded.

Byrnes walked forward and Joseph stepped back.

"Dr. Nguyen. Let's start with a portion of his liver."

"Partial biopsy?"

"No. I want a sizable portion. Let's get him open."

"You aren't going to sedate him?" Dr. Jackowski questioned.

Byrnes regarded him over his shoulder. "No more than he already is. You of all people saw how that affected him last time. We will use a local."

Joseph's jaw stayed in the dropped position.

"Dr. Jackowski?" Richard yelled. Joseph took a step farther away from them all.

"Dr. Jackowski? Come back," Richard yelled. He squirmed in his restraints. "Don't leave me here alone."

Joseph took another step away from the table.

"Scalpel." The doctor colonel held out his hand.

Dr. Hollis handed the stainless steel cutting tool to Byrnes.

"Dr. Jackowski? What are they doing?" Richard screamed.

"Dr. Nguyen, find something to gag him with. As stimulating as the conversation may be, that's not why we're here." Dr. Nguyen put gauze into his mouth. He unrolled tape and pressed it down onto Richard's cheeks. Richard's yells came out muffled.

"I'll place the incision here," Byrnes said. His free hand massaged near Richard's right side, feeling for the perfect spot.

"There it is," Byrnes said. His hand pressed down and his blade sunk through the layers of Richard's skin, fat, and muscle.

Joseph's back hit the wall as Richard's muffled screams echoed in the operating room.

STEELE
Northern Michigan

The rope creaked in the wind. The body slowly spun, suspended in the air by a thick blackened rope. It was shrunken and charred, skin peeling and cracking in ashy flakes. Its limbs were frozen in a final death spasm, fingers curled near its neck, feet pointed, mouth posed in a scream.

"Looks like Rat-Face," Tess said.

"I wouldn't know one way or another," Steele said. He looked on the ground for any clues. Overturned leaves and footprints littered the forest floor. She walked close, covering her mouth. She tugged on his hand and rubbed his finger. Bits of silver peeked out from his hands beneath the soot.

"It's him. He had a skull ring on each hand."

"Someone's killed them, but why?" Steele said. She didn't answer. He scanned the thick dune woods, peering past trees and shrubs alike. Each tree could hide an enemy human, infected or otherwise.

"We should keep moving. I see tracks here," she said.

"A blind man could follow these. There must be twenty or thirty pairs of feet here."

"Or more." She squeezed her brow together, trying to read him.

Steele took a deep breath, touching his head scar. "That's what I am afraid of," he said.

"Only one way to find out." She walked off following the tracks.

He marched after her deeper into the forest.

They pushed tree branches from their path. Mile after mile they ranged, tracking the mass of people that had gone before them. The people had steamrolled the forest undergrowth without a seeming care in the world. *Brazen or stupid or both and we are walking right down the middle.*

It wasn't long before he passed Tess and took the lead. Long distance races were not his specialty but a low-intensity ruck was well within his wheelhouse. It was just something he could do. It was more of a mindset than actual conditioning that allowed someone to complete feats of endurance but conditioning always helped. *Keep gutting it out one step at a time.*

"Hold up there, Steele. I need a break," Tess said, hands on her hips. "Whew. Haven't had to go this far in a while. I prefer shorter walks to the bar." She gave him a grin.

"Can't keep up?" he said. He knelt down and rested his M4 over his knee. He never really stopped passively listening, looking, or feeling the surrounding environment for things that were out of place. He let all his senses ping. He let his guard down as her lips curled into a mischievous grin.

"I would run you into the ground," Tess said.

Steele couldn't help but feel embarrassed. He knew what she meant and it wasn't a marathon race. She knew what she meant, and yet, he couldn't resist her banter.

"You sure of that?" he said, standing and meeting her eyes. There was something about her eyes. They promised something. A good time. A carefree life. Above all passion. She took a step for him, her hips moving enough to draw his eyes downward across her chest and lower.

Her hand reached up and tugged his beard downward, closer to her face.

"You wouldn't last *five* minutes with me," she whispered. Her lips pursed a bit. Branches cracked and broke in the distance, giving way to intruders. Her eyes went wide and Steele pushed her to the side. He ripped his M4 to his shoulder, eye aiming with his red dot optic. Ugly faces and decrepit decaying bodies filled his optics.

"Infected," he snarled. Dozens of infected marched their way, dead eyes glaring his way, blaming him for his living, breathing life.

"Raaarrr," vibrated in their ears. A tall infected man crashed through the leaves, grabbing them both together. The infected's jawline was stripped clean of all flesh, revealing only ivory bone in its place. Its skin was greenish brown, destroyed by sagging black pus sacks. Gunshot wounds leaking cold black blood lined his chest.

Steele tried to raise his carbine level with the fiend but was unable to get a shot. He instinctually grabbed the infected with his support hand. The infected growled, taking them off the path, its undead strength forcing their feet to backpedal.

Firing his gun point blank, Steele grunted as the gun recoiled hard into the notch of his elbow. Bullets penetrated the thing's leg over and over. Steele pulled the infected hard, forcing the creature to shift its weight to its disintegrated leg. Steele used the torn GVSU t-shirt to topple the creature down onto the ground.

Steele landed on its chest. The creature's mouth opened wide for him, its arms wrapping in a bear hug around him and Tess. The infected's jaws snapped shut and opened further than tendons would allow a normal human's to unhinge and crushed closed again, spittle flying.

The back of Steele's mind screamed. *You don't have time. They're coming. They're coming.* Gritting his teeth, he strained away from its gaping mouth. A gunshot concussed him, and for a moment, he thought he misfired his carbine. The top of the infected's patchy haired skull turned into a volcano of gooey reddish gray matter, quelling its struggle. Tess held her 1911 in, pointing it at them. Steele scrambled upright.

Lining up his sights on the nearest infected, Steele fired and transitioned too quick. He rushed because the dead were almost upon them. Tess shot next to him, her arms extended, elbows almost locked, but open enough to absorb recoil.

"Run!" Steele yelled at her. He pushed her in the direction the infected were not. They sprinted through the forest. Branches scratched their faces. Twigs cut at their arms. Rocks tripped their feet, but they ran. After minutes, he slowed and stopped. Resting on a white pine tree, his gun pointed behind them, he watched and waited for the disorderly pursuit of their enemies. He could hear them. Their movement was easy to identify.

"You okay?" Steele breathed, watching his gun bounce in time to his pounding heartbeat.

"Yeah. I think your five minutes are up," she joked.

He wheezed a few laughs. "Hope you are up for round two. Here they come again."

They weaved through the trees, not with the intention of avoiding detection, but with only the intention of pursuing their prey. His shooting in response was delayed because he spent much more time waiting to get a clear shot than he would have liked. As they grew closer, he stood, not seeing the point of hiding. Tess joined him then, sending rounds into them with efficiency. In minutes, it was over, a smoky cloud hanging in the air.

He released his mag from the mag well and shoved it in his pocket. He replaced the almost empty mag well with a full one. Then he went about reloading his expended magazines. Tess checked her weapon status and joined him, loading bullets into her empty magazines.

"You were made for this," Tess said.

He kept his eyes up while he reloaded. "I was not. I was made for summertime at the beach and a nice glass of rye whiskey on the rocks."

"Deny it all you want, but you were made for it." She shook her head at his apparent stupidity as she loaded her mags.

Steele slipped a loaded 30-round mag into his vest pouch. "I don't want this," he said. He snapped up an empty mag to reload with freshly brassed bullets. "Who would want this disgusting, perverted shithole of a world?"

"Do we ever have a choice of what our world looks like?" she asked.

"We make the world what it is."

"Did you make the world like this?"

"Of course not."

"But the world is like this. Almost everyone is dead. But everyone doesn't need to die. *You* could make this place better. Safer. Habitable."

"I don't see where I fit into this. I keep me and my people in one piece. Nothing more. Nothing less." *Except for all those that have fallen in this futile struggle.*

Tess stopped him by grabbing his sleeve. "Don't bullshit me. The average person can't make this better. Even a man like Pagan can't by himself. Thunder can't. I can't."

"Not my problem," he said.

"Listen, Steele, I can make do. I can hold out, fight, fuck, and barter, but if Pagan is gone…" She stopped and her eyes drifted out into the forest.

He watched her in silence.

"Pagan and I are a team. If he's gone, I don't think I can do it without him."

"We'll find him," Steele uttered.

"Stop." She held up a hand. "You know what world we live in. This search is a courtesy I know he would do for me if I went missing. I have to recognize that he is probably dead like the men that rode with him."

"The chances are high."

She grimaced at his brutally honest words. "I know. Without him, I can survive, but I don't think I can lead Little Sable by myself. Then you arrived. I see you for what you are, and that's somebody that can do this."

"What are you trying to say?" he asked. He felt a headache coming on. One worse than any migraine he'd ever experienced.

"I want you to help me lead Little Sable Point. I want us to be a team. At least until we find Pagan. I will default to you on all security matters."

He released himself from her hand. "I don't want to be your co-leader or whatever it is you want. How would I lead people I don't even know? Why would they follow me?" *And there is no way for me to legitimize my leadership.*

Her eyes pleaded. "Little Sable has some good folk. Men, women, and children. They're scared. They need someone that they can rely on. If we can get Pagan back then you're off the hook. The Red Stripes will help you run security."

"Why don't you ask Thunder? The Red Stripes follow him."

"He doesn't want it. He made that clear in the beginning. He's got his club and he's got a soft spot for Sable, but he doesn't want to lead it."

"And neither do I." Steele moved his carbine low, pointing it toward the ground, and walked ahead. He moved faster than he had before, his boots crunching leaves, creating space between them as if he could outrun her comments.

"Steele, wait." He stopped, more annoyed with her than anything else. "Maybe we could make another arrangement. An open one of course," she smiled coyly and reached out a hand to stroke his cheek.

Steele dodged her, shifting his head out of the way. "I didn't turn you down so we could fuck." He twisted his mouth and scanned the trees.

Tess rolled her eyes as if she didn't believe him. "We're lucky Little Sable Point has gotten as far as it has. I need a man like you by my side. I'm not going anywhere; they trust me and I'm saying that I trust you." She jumped, readjusting her backpack straps. He tried not to notice the perkiness of her breasts. "A good leader knows allies when they appear."

"You don't get it." He jabbed a finger in her direction. "I've lost enough people. I'm the only one left from my counterterrorism team. I've lost friends. I've lost fellow survivors. Now, I've lost my mother. I only have one real thing left and that's Gwen. I…" He stopped, realizing he was yelling and stared at her. "You don't understand."

She nodded knowingly. "That's why you have to do it. You have to do it for her. Little Sable is a good place. She'll thrive there."

His mind wrestled with her words. *Take leadership of a group of people I know nothing about for Gwen? I would do it in a heartbeat if there was any truth to it, but is there any truth to it? I will ultimately be responsible for all their lives.* He clamped his mouth shut instead of responding.

"I see an opportunity here in you. You need us and we need you. Without each other, we won't make it," she said.

Everything seemed so far away except for the ghosts. They lingered behind the trees. They watched him from the shadows. Their dead eyes blamed him for not saving them. They followed him wherever he went. A ragtag band of his fallen people. *The people of Little Sable Point will all haunt you when they are gone. Just like Jarl. And Wheeler. And Lindsay. And Andrea. And Barnes. And Nelson. And Mauser.* The last name made him cringe. *His best friend. Gone rogue. Their friendship dead. If we meet again, I'll have to kill him.*

Tess watched him expectantly as if she already knew the right answer. A look that only women can give men.

He ran a hand over the crest of his healing head wound, a reminder of what this world had to offer. *The list is already so long. Can I add more to it and not break?* "I don't know if I can handle adding any more people to my list." He breathed hard, frowning at this woman. This hearty twig of a woman. Her eyes glowed at him. Wiping her short pointy nose, she smiled a bit.

"This is why you have to do it, because you care."

Can I do this?

Tess reached out for him and he didn't flinch. She tugged his beard a bit. "We need you," she whispered.

He shook his head at her. All the voices in his head screamed for him to run away. His gut told him it was the wrong thing to do. Logic told him he would only suffer for this decision, but something else hid deep down inside him. He drew strength from it like an eternal well within his soul.

"I'm sure I'm going to regret this, but I'll help until we find Pagan."

"Deal. Until we find Pagan."

"When we find him, I will step down as whatever it is I am."

"I will let you go then," she said. Her smile said that he was hers forever.

"I'm going to need your help to make it more organized and structured. Keep people safe. I'll need volunteers to put together some kind of defense force. The Red Stripes are invaluable, but we have to be able to do it on our own."

"I think I can round up some volunteers. But no draft or any kind of martial law. You saw what that got us during the outbreak. A lot of dead people. We're small enough that we respect people's liberties." Her dark eyes stated that she wasn't one to not be trifled with.

"What do you mean?"

"Little Sable thrives because we allow freedom of movement into and out of the camp, respect of personal property, and equal treatment of men, women, and children."

"I'll do my best, but we must set a foundation or we will never be more than a rabble easily destroyed by the infected."

She stuck out her hand close to him. "I hereby appoint you an official representative of Little Sable Point." He shook her hand, locked in by his word and sealed by his handshake.

"What? No secret handshake?" he asked.

"Nope. What you see is what you get." They released hands.

"Come on, partner," he said. He walked ahead of her, wondering if he was being chased or followed.

THE PASTOR

Northern Michigan

The fires from the furnace cast an orange glow upon his followers as if they were burning in hell. They sat complacent in a haphazard set of rows awaiting his guidance, just as they had done before the end of the world. Except they were no longer in his megachurch on the outskirts of Grand Rapids but had taken refuge in the Temple Energy power plant.

Isolated near the lakeshore, the coal power plant had proven a stable, protected base of operations for his followers. A sizable portion of his congregation had followed him out of Grand Rapids to the Lake Michigan shoreline.

When the initial news reports of a deadly virus started spreading, they had congregated inside his giant warehouse-like church. They yearned for direction in the time of uncertainty, fearing their place in the world that God had turned his back on. They fled the city when the government had tried to keep them in place, his decision saving their lives.

After fleeing the city on parish buses, others joined them. People lost and searching, God's purpose shining through them. The others they had found were casualties of Armageddon, scared and alone with no one to help them. No one except God. The pastor accepted them as they accepted God's virtuous light.

"I am the smith of the Lord, and ever his humble servant. He has always known our path for he is omniscient," the pastor said, spreading his arms wide as if he were a graceful crane welcoming his flock. He paced to and fro, letting the people indulge in his holy presence before reaching into his pocket and pulling out a piece of black coal. He rotated it in his fingers, holding it high so they all could see. They gawked as if he held the Hope Diamond, their eyes sucking in its very presence.

"This is one of them. The media in all their corrupted wisdom called them *sick*. People were slaughtered for listening to their lies for they know nothing of God's will. They were blind to what was happening." Shouts of "aye" and "yes" punctuated from his followers.

The pastor tossed the piece of coal into the air and caught it. "This." He twisted it in his fingers. "This is Satan's foot soldier. Some call them infected, but infected with what?"

"Sin," a boy shouted from the front row.

The pastor gingerly bent down in front of the boy. "That's right, Will."

The pastor stood back up, ignoring the pain in his back, and held the piece of coal up. "The government said to restrain them, but we knew better all along. We knew what they were capable of. We knew that they weren't like us anymore. The doctors told us they were sick, but their souls were already gone, replaced with the devil's own ilk. The disciple Mark warned about this in the Bible when Jesus removed the demons and sent them into the swine. They are many and they are Legion."

He held the piece of coal level with his eye. "We know that we are children of God and that the whole world is under the control of the evil one. The host of the dead was chosen by Satan himself to wipe mankind from the earth. They are many. Their sin pollutes everything they touch." A few people shouted nos in the audience. A woman stood pleading, her arms in the air with despair.

He nodded sadly, his thin clean-shaven face gaunt with sorrow. "We live in the most difficult time, but we need not be afraid because when we throw these devils into the holy fire of the Lord-," he said, stopping in front of the large furnace behind him. He tossed the piece of coal into the furnace, and the flames crackled with molten hot fire leaping about. "He rejoices at our blessed acts." His people nodded their heads, murmuring in agreement.

"The more of the Legion you send back to the fires of hell that spawned them, the hotter God's fire will burn in your hearts. It will burn so bright inside you, you will become like molten steel, smoldering with God's love." He locked his hands behind his back and continued his pacing.

"I mold men in the fires of hell and beat them into instruments of God. Instruments of righteousness. This is what you are." He pointed out at them. "*You* wage a holy war against Legion, against those marked by the beast and the unbelievers, against those who refuse to recognize his greatness." His followers stood now, infused with the passion and power of his sermon.

Gesturing for them to be seated, he gave a gentle wave to a man that stood nearby. He was lean and handsome, his wavy blond hair parted and combed over his head.

"Come forward, brother." He waved the man onward with his hand. "Many of you know my disciple, Matthew." Matthew approached, taking his place by the pastor's side, holding his improvised wood-handled flail in his hands.

"When Matthew came to us, he was scared and alone. He knew nothing of God's love." He looked at Matthew. "What was your occupation before Armageddon?"

Matthew smiled at the crowd. He was accustomed to public speaking.

"I was a bank manager at New Heights Bank in Comstock."

"What did you do as a bank manager?"

Matthew's smile faded and he cast his eyes downward. "I gave people bad loans, and when they defaulted on their payments, took their land and homes."

The pastor nodded his head knowingly. He narrowed his eyes, trying to understand. "And why did you do this, Matthew? Those were good people out there, only trying to make ends meet."

Matthew's eyes filled with the tears of regret. "To make more money."

The pastor nodded. "Ah, yes. Greed. Greed is the sin of the many. Money infects all it meets. Yet you are here and one of the highest of God's Chosen people."

Matthew turned toward the pastor. "When you found me, I was starving.

I hadn't eaten in over a week. I was locked inside the bank vault with nothing but a few bottles of water. The devil's own terrified me."

The pastor patted Matthew's shoulder. "You were like a child. A canvas of only needs, but your destiny was not to die."

Everyone's eyes were completely enthralled with the sinful hero's story. Children sat in the front row watching the men, elbows on their knees, hands underneath chins.

"I have sinned. I know what it's like to fall into temptation, but God has shown me the way. He rejoices every time we cleanse one of them from the earth. One club swing. One hammer swing. One bullet at a time." The congregation openly cheered him on, now filled with the fervor of God.

"Your destiny wasn't to sin forever. It was to join the blessed. Tell me, Matthew. How many of Satan's legion have you sent screaming back to hell?

"Two hundred and twenty-six."

"Two hundred and twenty-six of Satan's spawn he has destroyed. He has sent their tormented twisted souls back to hell. For evil hath no place while the righteous stand tall in the eyes of the Lord." People shouted, filled with God's love.

"And how many do you expect to kill in the future?"

Matthew's full smile faded as he humbled himself in front of the congregation.

"So many that the angels will rejoice."

"God wills it!" the pastor shouted, and his people chanted it in return.

He raised his simple carpenter's tool into the air, and they loved him for it.

"Jesus was a carpenter, and therefore, I will use his tool to destroy the wicked. Sleep well tonight, God's Chosen people, for tomorrow our noble crusade continues." He bowed his head in deference to them, holstering his hammer on his belt.

"May you walk in his image, brothers and sisters." He nodded his thanks. He began his walk over to the floor manager's office that he had commandeered as his quarters. His followers, his soldiers of Christ came to shake his hand, and it took him twenty minutes to get inside the small room.

I give them hope where life only gives them despair.

Once inside, he closed the door, sitting down at his desk. *I must keep the fire of the Lord hot or we will lose this battle for his Kingdom is small and the devil's great.*

Shuffling some papers, he glanced over maps of the area. *They're here somewhere.* A group of survivors had been evading him for weeks. They hid somewhere along the coast. He would annex them, and God's Kingdom would grow. Fresh recruits to swell his ranks, or if they were evildoers, they would be purged and their supplies commandeered for his warriors of God. After thirty minutes of outlining the area where he had sent his scouting parties, he let his eyes close for a moment in silent prayer. *Give strength to this old body, O' Lord. Lend me your wisdom. Lend me your power.*

A light rapping on the door forced him to open his eyes. "You may enter."

A broad man with a curly blond hair entered, bowing his head a bit.

"Peter, how can I be of service to you, my son?"

"It's one of the scouting parties." Peter eyed the floor, wringing his hands together as if he were eight years old and caught stealing a cookie.

"Yes. Go on."

"Luke's party found some people." The pastor leaned forward Peter receiving all his attention. *They can't evade me forever.*

Peter's eyes darted back and forth. "Well, actually only one person. The others received *purification.*"

The pastor intertwined his fingers in front of him, considering the information."I see. I do hope Brother Luke remembers my edict regarding the purification of nonbelievers."

Little beads of sweat formed on Peter's forehead. "I believe Brother Luke does. The nonbelievers were hostile. Brother Mathias and Brother John were killed." *Hostile.*

"This is sad news, but God sends us good with the bad. Remember that, Peter. There is always a blessing in bad news." The pastor stood, a black-clad wraith.

"Show me our captive. Then I would like you to give extra rations to Brother Mathias's wife and to Brother John's mother. You will ensure that they are provided for. God cares for all members of his community."

"It will be done." Peter bowed his head.

"Now, take me to the prisoner."

They cut through tents, sleeping bags, and makeshift privacy shelters, flanked on all sides by dull gray piping connecting and curving up and down the walls. They burnt only a small amount of coal, barely turning one of four heavy turbines with the water they heated to steam by the furnace, creating enough electricity for the plant. They would not go cold this winter on the harsh Michigan lakeshore. He had seen to that.

The pastor's shoes scuffed down the corridor with a whisk whisk as he walked. Peter's boots thudded along behind. At the end of the corridor, near the coal fire furnace, was a room. Brothers Luke and Anthony stood outside the room conversing in hushed tones.

"Pastor. I'm pleased that you've come," Luke said with a mean smile.

"You are pleased to present me with one captive that could've been three?" the pastor said, mouth flat.

"The unbelievers were rough, uncouth men. I could see no redemption inside them," Luke said, wiping long strands of black hair out of his face, a thin chin jutting from his jaw.

"That is not for you to decide. Only God knows the true hearts of men."

"But-," Luke said.

"You must exercise some *prudence* in the field, Brother Luke. Show me the captive." Luke physically struggled, holding in his anger. *If he wasn't so devout, I would banish him from God's Kingdom or purify him in God's name.*

The pastor rested a fatherly hand on Luke. "You did well, Brother Luke."

Luke smiled, his canines a few millimeters too long. "Thank you, Pastor," he said, putting a hand on the straight bar handle, lifting the piece of metal upward.

It was dark. A man sat in a lone chair at the center of the room. The captive's head was bowed, and his hands were tied behind his back. The pastor walked into the room, letting his steps fall with authority. The man let his head rise. Blood glistened on his stubbly brown beard, leaking from the corner of his mouth.

"What's your name, child?" the pastor's voice came out hushed.

The man's lips twitched into a smile, blood staining his teeth as if he already bore the hated mark of the beast. The man's smile grew as the pastor stepped closer. *His smile is off-putting; he may be insane. Not the first person who has seen the devil's work and had it break their mind.*

"The pastor asked your name, heathen," Luke spat.

The man's eyes darted toward Luke with disgust, but he kept the smile on his face.

"We will not hurt you anymore, child. Some of our brothers offer less tact than others. Peter bring him water."

Peter brought in a glass, holding it to the man's mouth. He drank greedily.

"What is your name, son? All men have names. Even God's lowest of followers. Speak freely; your soul is at stake." The pastor loomed over him, an angel of judgment in black.

The captive man spit blood on the floor and lifted his head back to the pastor, grinning outrightly now.

"He's broken." *He will not be the last.* The pastor turned toward Luke. "Make an example out of him. He has nothing to offer God's Kingdom," he said with a wave of his hand. Luke loosened a long knife from his belt and licked his lips.

"I'm not broken, Pastor," the man said from behind. His voice was hoarse.

The pastor turned, clasping his hands in front of his body. It was his turn to smile.

"That is good, my son. Perhaps we can help each other. But you must have a name?" The captive's cheek swelled on one side, puffing out like a golf ball.

"My name is Pagan."

The pastor smiled. "Of course it is."

TESS

Northern Michigan

Dark white pine lined the sandy ridge stunted by the barren soil of sand and clay. They followed a white-tailed deer trail that ran along the top of the almost dune. Sticking her thumbs through her pack, she followed behind this broad-backed man she barely knew, a man she had joined forces with on the mere feeling in the back of her spine that she had done the right thing.

He stalked ahead, a leader and protector, putting himself in harm's way first. She had made relations with men like him in the past, but he was different. He carried a weight on his shoulders that would have broken weaker men, and she couldn't tell if it was a general weariness from exhaustion or his thoughts and responsibilities that wore him down. Waving a hand, he silently called her to join him near a short fat pine. *I wonder if he could fit those hands all the way around my waist.*

"What is it?" she asked. He crouched down, gesturing for her to join him.

"How well do you know this area?" he said, voice low.

"Not well, only what we've scouted through. Why?"

"You aren't from here?" he said, eyes bouncing down to her lips if only for a moment.

"Cadillac, Battle Creek, Kalamazoo. Grand Rapids was my latest stomping ground. Then the outbreak forced me here."

He scanned the forest. "I haven't summered up here in years, but I was thinking. If Pentwater is north of here, isn't there a power plant nearby?"

"Do I look like someone who would care about where a polluting energy company resided? Now, if you asked about where a craft brewery is around here, I could definitely point you in the right direction." She let her eyes graze past his, avoiding full contact. "Fetch Brewery is only about twenty-five minutes from here. Damn good place."

"You like beer?" Steele said, bewildered.

"Like it? I used to brew it. I was the brewmaster at First Eagle Brewery," she said.

"No shit. What kind of beer did you brew?"

"I had few favorites. IPAs are my specialty but I also make a mean Dunkel."

"Well, hot damn. You got any back at the camp?" His beard ruffled with the wind, a glimmer of a smile emerging from underneath.

"I wish. If you get me the right ingredients and tools, I could prolly whip up a batch that isn't too far off the original recipe."

"Do the Red Stripes know this? Because I'm sure they would love some fresh brew."

"Never really talked about it, ya know, with the whole dead rising from the grave thing."

"I'm pretty sure you don't understand. Beer is a necessity. Especially in a time like this. They would ride far and wide for ingredients."

"You're preaching to the choir, soldier boy."

"I already told you. I'm not military," he said. "And you don't know anything about a power plant nearby?"

"No. Why do you keep jabbering on about this stupid power plant?" she said, giving him a bit of lip biting. *Can't hurt to keep him interested. It should keep him in my pocket.*

As he talked, he became more and more excited as if he could literally envision his power plant base and the future. "Because what if we can get it running? You know. Have electricity. We could control the supply of power along the lakeshore. We could use it to trade. Not to mention we could secure the facility and not live out in the open because winter is almost here."

"Slow down, cowboy. First, we have to find this mythical power plant.

Second, we have to convince all our people that this is in our best interest."

"What bad could happen?" he asked.

"Are you serious? When you have a resource, people will want it." She folded her hands across her chest. "What about the infected? What if it attracts them?"

His mouth flattened. "Having what other people want brings them to the table."

"Or brings them at night with blood on their minds."

"True. We'll need to provide a common defense or others will take it. That's where those volunteers come into play. Even if I can only get them started, Pagan can train them."

She could practically see the wheels in his head churning out idea after idea. Looking at him, her stomach fluttered a bit. *This is not me. I don't swoon like a school girl over some Neanderthal with a big gun and a scraggly beard.* He had something that made her trust him in a world where trust was hard to come by.

"Let's go, Wyatt Earp. My Pagan won't find himself."

The duo walked over the sandy hills through a sparse forest. The stunted trees struggled to hold on to the sand, roots gripping the loose soil in an effort to stay upright. Green dune grass swished, an army of thin bright green spear points swaying in the waves of the wind.

The tracks, oval-shaped divots, were easy to see in the sand, and it seemed as if a thousand feet had traversed the path. *A blind man could follow these tracks. This is not the action of someone who is in hiding.*

"Hey, Wild Bill," she called up to him.

"What?"

"What if we are only following a huge pack of infected?"

"Then we are going to have a long run back to Red Rhonda."

"Ha," she belted. "What? You aren't going to single-handedly defeat them all? I would have to say I'm a little disappointed."

He glanced over his shoulder, still walking. "Nope. I'm going to run my ass off."

"That doesn't sound like the man I joined forces with."

His head stayed forward. "This is him."

"Geez, you aren't getting all butthurt are you?" she teased.

She could tell by the sound of his voice that he was smiling as he trekked.

"I assure you, my manliness is not determined by whether or not I can defeat a thousand infected at once. In fact, running shows a bit of maturity," he finished, sounding a bit pleased with himself.

"More brains than balls, huh? First man I ever met like that." She laughed loud enough to make sure he heard her.

His shoulders leaned one way and then the other with each step of his feet. His pack groaned, gravity compressing it upon his spine.

"We shall see," he said.

Yes, we shall, Mark Steele.

After thirty minutes of trekking, they struggled up a large ridge. Cresting the top of it, they stopped.

Sprawled out below them lay a large industrial facility sitting next to a canal. Two large smokestacks jutted skyward. The white concrete stacks were encircled by blood red stripes and rose hundreds of feet into the air. A massive pile of black coal sat stacked up near the waterway, a large conveyor belt running from the coal pile to the water. It was as if someone had shoveled a giant pile of snow and dyed it the color of night.

"Wow," she said. "You were right."

She felt his hand on her back shoving her downward to the sand. The miniature gold granules sped for her face, and she barely got her hands underneath her before she was crushed into the ground. The sand gave way beneath her. She squirmed onto her back, and at the same time, her hand instinctively went to her shoulder harness-holstered 1911. Her fingers clawed for her gun, trying to create enough space to release the weapon.

"Get the fuck off me," she growled. His fingers locked around her wrist, pressing it into her body. He held it close, pinning it to her chest. His ironclad fingers dug into her wrist, crushing it. She struggled and tried to wiggle free.

"Shhh. Be quiet," he said. His eyes stared out, scanning the area. She read him, letting her eyes dance back and forth. His eyes weren't wild and frantic like those of a man waging an attack, but calm and concerned, even worried.

He glanced back down at her. Kindness lurked there somewhere.

"There are people down there," he uttered.

"Infected?" she hushed.

"No. People, people." As she relaxed, he gradually let her go and crawled onto his stomach. His elbows dug into the ground as he crawled to the top of the ridge, his long gun laying across his biceps and forearms.

She inched up next to him, peeking over the ridge with hesitant expectation.

Semis, buses, pickups, and cars sat parked near the plant. People walked to and fro, busy with duties and chores that could only be related to the operation of a base camp. Some shoveled coal. Others hauled it away, buckets swaying back and forth as they carried the heavy loads.

"Looks like somebody stole your power plant idea," she said softly.

"Yes, it does. Look at all of them."

"The most live people I've seen since the outbreak," she said.

"Too many people," he said under his breath.

He brought his carbine optic up to his face and carefully scanned the plant and the surroundings.

"I count at least at fifty people working outside. Two snipers there above the entrance. And another two on that corner over there."

Tess squinted, attempting to make out the blurry miniature men sitting still atop the building.

"You aren't worried about them?" she asked, feeling a little nervous about the idea that someone could be lining up their sights on her head as she spoke.

"No. They aren't looking for us necessarily."

"What should we do?"

"There." He pointed to the coal pile. "There's our huckleberry." He handed her his M4 carbine. "The guy digging by the pile with the two guards."

She held the optic close to her eye. Everything zoomed forward. The people were dirty and haggard as if they had trudged along on their mental willpower alone.

A lightly bearded man marched back to the coal power plant, a bucket of coal resting on his shoulder.

"Pagan," she whispered, her heart speeding up. "He's alive."

"Finding him was the easy part," Steele said.

"Breaking him out is going to be a bitch," she replied.

GWEN

Little Sable Point, MI

The ring of vehicles did little to protect her from the wind. Her baggy ACUs did only enough to keep the cool air from biting at her skin. Tracing her footsteps in the sand, she stepped lightly, arms crossed over her body. Her blonde hair whipped back and forth, and she did nothing to stop it from tussling about.

Gwen had passed everything inside the small enclosure at least a half-dozen times. The back of a tractor-trailer sat open, and a fat woman sat on the edge of the trailer with a couple of the Red Stripes. Patrons and visitors of the small community would come and go, presenting something of value for packages of food. Families sat inside their RVs and campers while others camped in blue, red, and green tents outside of cars and hatchbacks. A few kids ran through the tents, playing hide and seek.

On her seventh pass, a man hollered at her from in front of his camper.

"You trying to drill to China, darling?" the older man said. His skin hung off his face, folding over his white turtleneck shirt looking like he lost so much weight that he was trying to keep his skin in tight with his clothes.

Gwen's lips spread in a weak smile. "No, sir. Just thinking." The pills burned in her pocket as if they knew she thought of them. They wanted to be found. They wanted to be taken. They begged her to do it. *If I take enough, it will just go away. How can I do it?*

"My father always told me to avoid a woman when she was thinking too much." He paused and waited for a response. She stared at him with dark eyes.

He wrinkled his nose at her. "I never listened to much he said anyway." He waved her over. "Are you hungry?"

A navy sport coat drooped over his shoulders, the limp fabric searching for a body to fill it out. *Anything to keep my mind off this predicament.* She plodded over to him.

"Cashews?" he asked. He thrust a package of cashews in her direction, shaking them a bit like he was calling a dog with a treat. She cupped her hands and he shook some of the oblong nuts onto her palms.

He grinned, showing yellowish teeth. "Where are my manners?" He put a hand to his chest. "My name is Dr. George Thatcher. Before you ask, I'm not that kind of doctor."

"Gwen Reynolds," she said. She munched a nut, savoring the salty flavor. "What kind of doctor are you?"

"I was a political science professor at Mason College. Small liberal arts university near Midland."

"I'm not familiar with the colleges in this area."

He looked disappointed. "Ah, of course not. Are you in the military? Or should I say, were you in the military?"

"No. These are on loan, but I don't think they're going to ask for them back."

"I suppose not." He looked even more disappointed. "The last I heard about them was the National Guard was protecting the capital building in Lansing. That seems like forever ago. Now, I'm living in a trailer with a bunch of people I only know in passing. And of course, Gordon here. Gordon!" he called out. A fox-colored Pomeranian shot out from beneath his camper. It skipped about at his feet, begging for food.

"Get away, you little devil. Not in front of our guest. Shoo." The small dog continued to scamper about his feet. It danced back and forth, excited at the prospect of being fed. "Fine. Take this," he said, tossing the dog a cashew, which it caught in the air with practiced promptness. The dog did victory circles, chasing its own tail.

"Gordon. Don't be so rude. Here, take this," he said, handing her the cashews. "He loves them." Her lips rose into a genuine smile for the first time in forever.

"It sure looks like it," she said. She held one out, tantalizing the small animal.

"Well, go on. Give him one. Don't be cruel." She threw a nut high in the air and it plopped into the dog's waiting mouth. He crunched the nut once and swallowed, not caring to savor his treat.

"Haha," she half-laughed. She tossed him another and he caught that one too.

Dr. Thatcher looked on like a proud pet father. "Gordon can do more than that."

"Oh can he?" she said amused, her head tilting to the side.

"Sure can. Watch this. Gordon, stand up." The dog stood up on his hind legs. Taking short little steps, the dog did circles for its well-deserved treats.

"Wow, look at him go," she said to the proud owner.

"He's lucky to be here. Before the food truck came, people wanted to eat him. I can't say I wasn't tempted." He patted the dog on the head. Dr. Thatcher stopped, looking up at her. "Where did you come from? I've seen your group. Rough, mean-spirited looking people." He picked Gordon up and held him in his arms.

"Washington, D.C. It went under quick. Nothing anyone did could prevent it. So many people died. Even the emergency bunkers failed."

Dr. Thatcher stroked Gordon's head. "Did you work there?"

"I worked at the National Red Cross Headquarters in D.C." The word *worked* gave her a weird feeling. *I technically never quit, but it's all gone now.*

"Ahh. I see. A bleeding heart."

She didn't answer him. *Am I?*

"Or a heart of stone," he said quietly, petting the head of Gordon. Dr. Thatcher's eyes held a sadness in them. "Don't forget where you came from. The past isn't dead."

High-pitched crying distracted her from the professor. A child stood in the middle of the tents, tears streaming out of her eyes.

"Will you excuse me, professor?"

"Of course," he said with an understanding smile.

Gwen walked over to the crying child. Not more than six years old, the young girl's cheeks were red from sobbing. Gwen crouched down to her level.

"Hi there, young lady. Are you okay?" she said, exaggerating her words in an effort to be comforting.

Unable to get enough air into her lungs, the little girl said with trembling lips, "Dey', day', all lef' me here."

"Who left you here? Your friends?" The small child's head bobbed up and down in agreement.

"My name's Gwen. What's your name?"

"Lacy." The girl sniffled.

"Well, Lacy, I'm going to help you find your friends." She wiped a tear from the girl's cheek, feeling her insides melt. Gwen stood upright. "Do you want me to help you?"

The small girl nodded her head again, and Gwen offered her hand to the little girl. The girl glanced up, unsure about her new friend. Gwen smiled back. After a moment, Lacy decided Gwen was safe enough and grasped Gwen's pinky finger.

With the steps of a child, they circled the inner ring around the lighthouse. Children darted in and out of tents and wheels on the far end of the encampment. They hid beneath trash, scraps, and scattered debris. *Their hearts are still young. Their world will be one filled with only loss and misery, but they don't know it.* It brought her great sadness knowing that they would suffer so much no matter what path their lives took.

Only despair would meet them in the future. A future filled with stomach pains and gut cramps when they had nothing to eat. A future gobbled up in fear of being ripped apart by the undead or being murdered by bandits. A guarantee of psychological damage as they watched their friends, family, and loved ones die around them, victims of violence at the hands of the dead or the guns of the living. Gulping the ball of emotion down her throat, Gwen looked down on little Lacy.

The girl stared up at Gwen, dirt outlining her cherubic small face like apocalyptic cosmetics.

"Are you okay?" Lacy's voice squeaked.

Gwen bent down next to the little girl, wiping a tear from her own face. *Damn hormones.* "Yes, Lacy, everything's fine."

"You don'a look so fine."

Laughing a bit, Gwen wiped her other eye. "Lacy, you go and play with your friends. I see them over there."

"But I don't know where they are."

Gwen stood, peering around the parked vehicles. She spied a child's white shoes sticking out from behind a wheel. She pointed to the feet. "See there? Go get him."

Lacy gushed, looking up at her. "Thanks, lady," she cried out and tagged the other child beneath the rubber tire. They scampered off as the children chased each other. *Let them be young while they can.*

Standing straight, she covered her own stomach as she watched them play. *A few years down the road and one of these kids playing could be mine.* The children brought a sad smile to her lips, making her soul ache just a little less than it had before. For several minutes, she watched them until she noticed a boy, about the age of five, standing away from the rest. His hair was the color of the sun. His eyes were blue but bordered on gray like a smoky ocean wave. His red zip-up sweatshirt hung open shifted to one side as if someone had yanked him around. Beneath the sweater, he wore a blue shirt with a red star emblazoned on the front. She gave him a half wave. Unblinking, he stared back at her as if he expected her to do something.

Uncomfortable, Gwen turned back to the kids now playing tag around a fire pit. Guilt washed over her and she looked back up at the child. He had disappeared. Her maternal instincts went into overdrive.

Rushing, she quickstepped to where the boy had once stood. Using the bumper of a trailer as a brace, she looked underneath. Dune grass lay crushed and limp.

"Hello?" she yelled out. "Boy?" Only the wind and the water answered her. "Come back," she hollered. Dropping to her hands and knees, she crawled to the other side of the trailer. She stood up on the unsecured side of the ring of cars and brushed sand off her clothes. Beach met her feet. Small tracks led away from the vehicular palisade, a little mop of blond hair bouncing over the sand.

"Stop," she called after him. The boy turned toward her, considering her with a half-smile. He let out a high-pitched giggle. She ran after him. The sand ate her feet up, ensuring she made slow progress. The boy topped a sand dune and disappeared. *Goddamn kid, he's going to get himself killed. Along with me.*

After a few moments, she crested the same sand ridge, and the boy stood below playing near the waves. He held a stick in his hand, battling the waves with it. Every time a wave would roll onto the shore, the boy would run inland, laughing at the wild water, swinging his stick wildly at it. He bent his small legs, picked up a rock, and threw it back at the offending waves.

"Come here," she scolded. Her finger pointed to the ground at her side.

The boy turned in her direction, a smile on his lips. The splashing of distress forced her eyes away from him. Her mind instinctually thought of a shark or of somebody drowning, but a man's head and upper torso emerged from the waves.

The infected man's skin sagged low and gray off his face as if it weighed too much for his body, almost as if he were a bloodhound in human form. Wading through the waves, the man was followed by another. And another. They wore hardly recognizable shirts and pants seemingly melted to their waterlogged skin. She drew her knife in a second.

"What are you doing?" a voice shouted behind her. She spun around toward the voice. Ahmed bounded down the dune at her. He held a bat in his hand.

"The boy," she shouted at him. "Help me get him." Ahmed looked over her shoulder, worried.

"Where is he?"

"He's right here," Gwen said, turning back toward the big lake. The boy was gone, only the dead walked in his place.

"He was just here. Help me. Boy! Boy!" she called out.

"I only see infected." Ahmed gripped his bat nervously with both hands.

"Help me." She ran into the water. "Boy! Boy!" she screamed. The ugly faces of the infected struggled for her. She swept the water with her hands. "He was just here," she cried.

Ahmed's bat cracked off the side of an infected head, and it splashed facedown into the water. The torso followed the head, arms spread wide. The body floated on the surface of the waves, tossed around by their force.

Frantic, Gwen spun around in a circle. *Where is he? Where is he?*

"We should go back," Ahmed grunted, as he bashed another skull. Pieces of white cranium splintered and were launched free as pink brains exploded outward.

"He was here," she yelled, wading through the water. Angry sediments floated to the surface of the brown water as she stirred up the lakebed. An arm wrapped around her waist, lifting her up from the shallows.

"Come on," Ahmed's voice reverberated in her ear. As she thrashed in the water, he half-carried, half-dragged her to the beach. "Gwen, please," he muttered, not fighting, but blocking her from going back. More forms came out of the shallows.

"The boy," she breathed, exasperated. Ahmed scowled at the infected in the water.

"I see no boy. If he's smart, he's already back at camp. Come on." They ran back to camp as fast as the sand would allow them. Ahmed snatched up his M4 from their campsite.

"You can't," she breathed. *I'm so tired.* "Go by yourself."

"If only you listened to your own words." He flashed a quick smile at her. "We need to put them down before they reach the perimeter." He raced up a ladder on the backside of a nearby camper.

The slamming of car doors drew their attention. Her bearded agent, deep scar running across his scalp, stepped out of a red Ford Ranger. *Mark. Thank God he is back, and there is that hussy.*

Tess threw a pack on her shoulder, joining Mark as they entered the camp. Her tight black pants revealed her narrow hips, small ass, and petite all-around frame like that of a cat burglar. She turned, saying something to Mark, and he smiled and barked a laugh into the air. *There's no way he finds her funny, that, that pothead.*

Mark made eye contact with Tess as they marched toward her and Tess met his eyes, giving him a soft cradling smile. It may as well have been an invitation back to her camper. When he turned back to Gwen, his eyes quickly darkened as though the sun had eclipsed above them in the sky. *Have I lost you?* Moans rolled up the dunes, and he dropped his pack and ran for them.

JOSEPH

Cheyenne Mountain Complex, CO

The lights from above revealed everything. They shone down unrelentingly from the ceiling, displaying all of the doctors' dirty deeds below. The heart rate monitor beeped. Byrnes and Dr. Nguyen cut away at Patient Zero like he was a thick steak. His body rocked beneath the restraints, still living under their dissecting blades.

Joseph stood in the back watching them take piece after piece off the man. After each piece was taken, whether it was a lobe of lung or a piece of the brain's frontal lobe, they would sew him back up as if they had just completed a successful surgery. Dr. Hollis had been allowed to leave after an hour to assist Dr. Desai in running a gambit of tests, leaving Joseph with the two butchers in blue HAZMAT suits.

Byrnes looked over his shoulder. "Dr. Jackowksi, will you assist Dr. Nguyen with acquiring a biopsy of his heart? That shouldn't be outside your comfort zone." Joseph circled the table. His feet obeyed, his will already overcome by his peers. Dr. Nguyen looked up at Joseph as he stepped up beside him.

Patient Zero's eyes had been taped closed, and his mouth gagged, but beneath the partially open lids, his eyes darted back and forth. Whimpers of pain exited his mouth as if he was exhausted from crying.

"I'm thinking we will make our incision here." Dr. Nguyen's blue-suited finger jabbed Patient Zero in the lower part of his armpit. "Below the swollen lymph node. The node was almost black beneath his pale almost translucent skin like a lump of coal underneath the snow.

"You don't think the groin or stomach?" Joseph asked, referring to other areas to enter into with a catheter in order to reach the heart.

"We had a few difficulties with his gastrointestinal areas." An x of freshly opened and then sewn up again scars crossed Patient Zero's belly.

"I see that," Joseph spat. Richard would probably never be able to relieve himself on his own. Portions of his intestines, stomach, and colon had been snipped away like he was a hairless cat in a middle school science lab.

"But I agree, Dr. Nguyen. Let's try a spot that hasn't been hacked to pieces already." The Asian doctor's eyes narrowed only as far as they could go while still staying open.

"I'll let you guide me then, Doctor." Dr. Nguyen bent close to Patient Zero. His scalpel slid neatly below the blackening lymph node. Dark brown blood seeped from the open wound, and he wiped it away with gauze.

"I am searching for the axillary artery that runs through the upper torso to the heart." A single finger explored the slit he had created. "Ah, there."

"Catheter, please." Joseph picked up a clear tube and handed it to him. The tube was a rigid sheath that would keep the puncture site open for insertion of the flexible thin tube with a camera on one end. Dr. Nguyen threaded the thin tube through the sheath into the artery.

Joseph flipped a switch on a monitor. "Camera's on," Joseph said. A tunnel image came up on the monitor. A round image of the white walls of the artery lined the tunnel. Dr. Nguyen glanced at the screen. "You may begin to feed."

The camera-headed tube drove through the artery, grazing its walls. Dr. Nguyen barely tried to be gentle while feeding the catheter. Joseph glanced at Patient Zero's face. His eyes were only white, rolled up inside his head.

Beep. Beep-beep. Patient Zero's heartbeat slowed. Joseph watched the heart rate monitor closely. "Dr. Nguyen, his blood pressure is dropping. One hundred over fifty. Should we continue?"

"Of course. It's a normal biopsy," Byrnes said from across the table. The man looked angry that they might stop their collection.

Dr. Nguyen nodded and continued to feed the tube. "I've reached the aortic arch. Entering the left ventricle now." The walls of the tunnel on the screen pumped in time with the beating of Patient Zero's heart. The pressure inside the artery slowed, the pushing of blood becoming a drip-drip instead of a thud-thud.

"Dr. Nguyen, get a good sample from there." The colonel pointed on the screen. "Why is that black? I've never seen anything like it."

"Is part of his heart dying? Literally, the tissue appears to be deteriorating," Joseph said. They stared at the screen, ignoring the beeps that crept lower and lower. Until he flatlined. Beeeeeeeep, the heart monitor screamed attention to his predicament.

"He's in cardiac arrest!" Joseph shouted. He placed his hands two inches above the end of the sternum. He let his arms stay straight and began pumping Richard's chest to the beat of a song. After thirty seconds of pounding Richard's chest, he looked at the other doctors. They stood watching.

"Somebody help me," Joseph demanded. Byrnes had the nerve to step back. He held his bloodied hands upright in the air, the backs of his hands to Joseph and Patient Zero. "What are you doing?" Joseph's voice came out in a screech. "He's flatlining."

"We don't really feel the need to resuscitate the patient. In fact, much of this work would be easier if he was already dead."

"Are you kidding me?" Joseph screamed between pumps of his chest. "You are a doctor for Christ's sake. Dr. Nguyen. Help me."

"I'm curious to see the virus after the body expires. It would be interesting to see if he reanimates like the others."

"Get me an AED," Joseph commanded. "I didn't scour this country to find this asshole so I could bring him here and have you hacks kill him." No one moved.

"We only have a paddle defibrillator. We're a research facility, not a surgical center," said Dr. Nguyen. Joseph shoved past Dr. Nguyen, pushing him into a tray that toppled over onto the ground. Joseph ignored his complaints.

Joseph gripped the edges of a metal cart holding the paddle defibrillator. He pulled it toward the flatlining Patient Zero. Byrnes let himself be shouldered to the side. The heart monitor echoed its shrill, dead victory cry over the living.

"Why are you wasting your breath on this creature?" Byrnes hissed. He leaned toward Joseph. Joseph turned away from him. "After what he did to Rebecca?" he whispered.

Joseph flipped a switch on the paddle defibrillator. It warmed up with a high-pitched whine. "Because he's a person. His name is Richard. Now, step aside, asshole." Byrne's eyebrows narrowed, but he took a step back. Joseph rubbed gel on the handled paddles, wires still attaching them to the machine. He swirled them together as the machine warmed up.

"Clear!" he yelled at the other doctors. Joseph stuck the paddles on either end of Richard's heart, and the machine squealed a high-pitched scream as it prepared to put the heart back into rhythm. Bump. Richard's body bounced on the table as far as his restraints would allow.

The heart monitor showed a single flat line. "Again," Joseph said, if only to himself.

Bump. Richard's body leapt off the table. "Again," Joseph screamed. The paddles warmed up, and he placed them around Richard's heart.

"Let him go. He's suffered enough," Byrnes said. He laid a hand on Joseph's shoulder.

"Don't touch me." Joseph shrugged off his hand. He rubbed the paddles together as much to distribute the gel as for good luck. "One more time, you infected bastard," he growled. Patient Zero laid unmoving.

Joseph placed the paddles on the unresponding man's chest. "Clear," he shouted at Byrnes. He made sure to stare the man in his eyes, not caring what he thought.

Bump.

Beep-beep. Beep-beep.

The heart rate monitor clucked away.

"I want you off my project," Byrnes growled into his ear.

Joseph hooked the paddles back on the machine. "I couldn't be happier than to leave a team full of goddamn quacks," he said to Byrnes with a finishing glower for Dr. Nguyen.

***

Hours later, he found himself in Dr. Weinroth's room. Her reclinable hospital bed sat perpendicular with the white wall. A stainless steel sink and a door leading to a bathroom lined the wall. A white dresser sat next to her bed. Her research tablet laid on it. She could make notes and access data files from the doctors on the network.

Joseph pulled up a black metal chair that could be burned or just as easily sprayed down for disease.

He adjusted his surgical mask on his face.

She awoke as he shifted in his chair. Her eyes encrusted with sleep, her head rolled toward him. "You're back," she whispered in a tired voice. Her brown eyes were softer than normal. Their pigment was changing as the disease took hold.

"There's no other place I'd rather be," he said with a smile beneath his mask. He could tell she was smiling beneath hers even if it was faint. The honesty of his words struck him. *Is this true? I would rather be spending my time with a terminally ill patient who will die and rise again and try to kill me?* But he spoke the God's honest truth. Being with her made him feel weird, warm, and fuzzy at the same time. It felt as if he had just discovered the sweet taste of chocolate and craved its sweetness more and more. Chocolate that he would never taste again.

"I was only taking a nap. I've been so tired lately." Her eyes drifted down at her body as if it betrayed her. He reached out and touched her hand. She was still warm. She flinched beneath him but let him hold it. He spun her wrist looking at it.

A thick kevlar band wrapped around her wrist topped off by a plastic brick. "What's that?" he asked.

Her eyes regarded the plastic brick in shame. "It's a sensor that goes off if I try to leave this room. They don't want me wandering around and succumbing to the virus in an area with people." He released her hand. *How dare they? But can I blame them?*

She peered down at her chest. "I have to make sure I keep my heart rate monitors on. If my heartbeat stops, the room locks down."

"I have a feeling you aren't the first one they've done this too," he said.

"No," she said sheepishly.

"Richard flatlined today."

Fear, anger, and pain crossed her eyes. "Did you bring him back?"

"Yes." He rubbed a finger underneath his glasses. "Colonel Byrnes didn't want to. He wanted to pull the plug."

"That man is infuriating. He wasn't like this when I was at Detrick. He has changed, I fear, for the worse."

"He wants me off the team."

She coughed into her hand in exasperation. "He can't. He wouldn't do that."

Joseph flattened his mouth. "Well, he's trying. I will apologize to him so we can carry on, but I don't think it will be long before I need to find a new place of employment, probably outside this mountain fortress."

"Have faith, Joseph. We'll find a way." Her eyes believed every word she said. Blind faith had gotten lesser people through more. Joseph didn't believe her, but he continued to soak in her image as if he would never see her again. She stared back, blinking. They sat in silence. He wanted to rip her mask off and kiss her, even if it meant his own death.

She coughed a bit and reached over, grabbing the tablet. *How can I be falling for a woman that is about to die?*

"When I don't feel like hell, I've been studying these genomes." He could tell she was giving a weak smile underneath her mask. "I'm basically trying to do the work that would take a team of doctors years in about a week. There's so much data. But look here." She turned a tablet toward him and clicked play on a video.

"The monkeypox uses multiple viral ligands and cell surface receptors to fuse to the membrane of healthy cells here. The monkeypox virus is partially absorbed by the healthy cell. The central sheath penetrates the final part of the membrane like a cattle farm compression gun and injects its genetic material with its phage along with the satellite virus here. Once in the cell cytoplasm, the virus unpackages new DNA here, but here, look."

A buckshot of the monkeypox virus DNA sprayed into the cell. The satellite virus released along with the monkeypox DNA, almost floating like a lazy balloon. Monkeypox went to work in the retooling of the host cell.

"Here the human body is attempting to defeat the monkeypox virus, but the satellite is still hiding in all the cells both dead and alive. The body isn't recognizing it. I can't figure it out. It's almost as if the satellite virus didn't do anything. At least not in Patient Zero. It's lysogenic, or lying dormant in his cells, but not active."

"The monkeypox virus is doing all the heavy lifting," Joseph said.

"Correct, but if you look here." She swept to the side and brought up another video. In the corner, it read *Patient Four.* "Look, the satellite virus is raging in this host."

"But that host is dead," he said.

"That's correct. It doesn't make sense but look. The satellite virus has reprogrammed the cells that the monkeypox has commandeered, creating its own new viruses."

"I can't wrap my mind around it either, but I will upload our new data from Patient Zero's biopsies for your review."

"I'll take a look," she said with a sigh. "But I need a nap."

"I'll let you sleep." *Please don't turn. Not yet. Not ever.*

TESS

Little Sable Point, MI

The cracks of gunshots sent an odd tingling down her spine. She watched Steele and Ahmed in action. Witnessing Steele rapid fire from atop the camper gave her a feeling of euphoria. It was as if she watched a human machine that had a systematic successive fire almost like a computer operated semi-automatic rifle.

In one minute it was over, and Garrett and Lenny ran for the perimeter, guns in hand, but the shooting was done. Steele and Ahmed climbed down from their perch, and she watched as he embraced Gwen, both rugged and gentle at the same time. A pang of jealousy stabbed her gut.

"Did you see a boy?" Gwen said into his chest. He pushed her away and held her outward from himself. His eyes read her for answers.

"What boy?" His head jerked toward the beach.

Gwen shrugged his arms away. "He was about four or five. He was out there when they came out of the shallows."

"No," he said quietly.

Tess interrupted. "About this high and black hair?" she said, holding a hand to her chest.

"No, shorter with blond hair," she sniffled.

"No one was there," he said. He looked to her for confirmation.

"I can't think of any children here that look like that, but people come and go. Garrett, can you call everyone together? I have an announcement to make," she said, eying Steele. He stared back and nodded. *Good, he's ready. But what if we don't get Pagan back?*

Garrett's voice boomed like metal scraping over concrete. "Everyone to the semi. Everyone to the food truck." Most people had been hiding in their tents and campers. Blinds shifted in windows. Tents unzipped. Car doors opened, revealing the scared, tired faces of Little Sable Point waiting to die or run.

They were a disorganized herd of sheep with only a pack of wild dogs that could bolt at any time to keep the wolves at bay. Thunder had a good heart, but she also knew that he would do just about anything to survive, and if that meant abandoning Little Sable Point, then so be it. *If any man can do this, Steele can.*

The people gathered around the food trailer. Big Bessie watched from nearby, beady eyes scrutinizing the crowd. No food would leave here without some sort of payment or at least a broken hand. She twirled a tire iron in her meaty paws, ready to lash out if the crowd made a rush for her stash. Tess grabbed a handrail and hauled herself onto the edge of the trailer.

"Is everyone here? Are we missing anyone?" she called out. People turned to one another, shaking their heads.

"Gwen, come up," she commanded. The beautiful blonde stepped up next to her. "This is Gwen. She's worried about a missing child. So please hear her out." *I know why he picked her. Look at her. Her hair is spun from gold. Her cheekbones and nose are regal. She is more of a damn queen than a woman.*

"I'm new to Little Sable Point, so I don't know everyone." People shifted, watching her impatiently.

"I saw a little boy earlier. I don't know his name." Her voice quivered. "He was playing with the other children near the edge of camp. He's about five years old, blond, blue eyes, about this tall."

People glanced at one another. Some rested hands on their own children. Gwen was met with the chirp of crickets. Tess glanced worriedly at the woman. Someone must know whose child it was. "He was wearing a red star shirt and was outside the camp before the dead came."

Gwen peered out, reading the crowd for anything, desperate for something. "Is anyone missing a child?" she called out, her voice rising an octave by itself. The people spoke in low tones to one another.

"Please, he went down to the water. The infected came out of the shallows and we couldn't find him." She was met with silence.

"You think we would know if one of our kids was gone, lady," Jack shouted from the crowd. He was tall, bald, and annoyed the hell out of Tess on multiple occasions.

"Get off the food truck," shouted another. Several other choruses of voices exclaimed their dissatisfaction with Gwen.

Tess lifted her hands off her shoulder harnessed 1911 and raised her hands up, calling for calm. "Now, now. We have to be sure. No one is missing boys, girls, or otherwise." She was met with a chorus of nos. She gave Gwen a sympathetic look.

"I'm sure Gwen was only confused. We're all under a lot of stress here. She's no different." The crowd listened and quieted down. She gave Gwen a pat on the back. The woman's lip trembled a bit, resting into a face of unhappiness. "Go get some rest. It was a misunderstanding." She had empathy for the woman, but Steele looked like he had a mess on his hands with her. *He's probably looking for an easy way out.*

"I know what I saw," Gwen mumbled, stepping down from the back of the trailer.

"I know you did," Tess said, watching her go.

She and Steele argued in hushed tones next to the trailer, Gwen's arms holding her stomach. Steele gestured outward with his hands.

"I'm glad everyone's accounted for," Tess said. The people of Little Sable nodded their agreement.

"The missing child is not the only reason I called you all together today." She stepped from side to side, speaking loud so everyone could hear her.

"As you know, Pagan and I have stood up for Little Sable Point since the beginning. We have kept our doors open. Most stay because it's safer than out there and because of the gracious protection of Thunder and the Red Stripes." She gave Thunder a nod. He smiled back at her, a red bandana holding his long gray hair.

"We found Pagan." People murmured. She nodded and a rumble ran through the ranks.

"Where is he?" shouted Jack, head and shoulders above the rest.

"He's at a power plant about fifteen miles from here. He's a captive of a large group." They talked nervously amongst themselves.

"Let's get him back," shouted Trent. The goateed hunter held up a bolt-action rifle.

"What do they want with us?" asked Joey. She was a young mother with dirty short blonde hair and a scared look on her face at all times.

"I'm not sure. But there are a good number more of them than us." This sent them into a tizzy, all of it related to fear.

"Why would they take him?" yelled Nathan. He was a tall African-American man wearing a dirty white-collared shirt.

"How do we know they won't come here?" shouted Margaret. The older woman's brow creased in concern. She had shown up at the camp two weeks ago, alone with only a shovel in hand.

"We should join them." All their voices talked over one another. Confusion. Chaos. Fear ruled the crowd, threatening to quickly turn them into a mob. Boots hit the metal back of the trailer. She glanced over at Steele, his shoulders wide beneath his tactical vest, gun slung across his chest. She noticed he had put his badge out on top of the vest. *Do you think that holds power over these people still?* Underneath his beard, she could see his jaw tensing.

"Thanks for the great intro," he said out of the side of his mouth.

"I thought I would give you a taste of what is to come." He gave her a dark glare as the people argued amongst themselves.

After a few moments, the crowd settled down, all eyes drawn to the warrior before them. He stood quiet, looking back at them as if he were judging them as much as they were him. The last person quieted down, and he spoke.

"People of Little Sable Point, I'm Mark Steele."

"Yeah. Who cares?" Jack shouted, and the crowd laughed.

Steele pointed at Tess. "Your leader Tess cares. Thunder cares. But to be frank, I don't care if you care."

Jack shut his mouth as others snickered around him.

"I am a former counterterrorism agent with the Division."

"What the hell is that?" said Linda. The short woman had only been there for less than a week and didn't trust a soul.

"We hunt terrorists," he said.

"Where's your little 'Division' now?" Jack piped up.

"As far as I know, gone." The words seemed to almost sting him, but he kept it in. "My entire team is gone." He grimaced while he said that. "I came all the way from Virginia back to Michigan to find a man, Patient Zero, the originator of the virus."

"You find him?" shouted Nathan.

"Yes, and after we found him, we turned him over to the military."

"Where's the military now?" asked a pale man, Jason. He had been a hand at a nearby dairy farm before the outbreak.

"I'm not sure. Maybe Colorado? There's no telling."

"A lotta help you government pukes are. Me and my family were in a FEMA camp near Van Andel Arena when it was overrun. I lost my mother and father because those bastards couldn't keep the dead away. Why should I trust anything you say?" Jack said.

"Well, you'll have to take me at my word. I've lost people too. A lot of people."

Jack snorted. "Then what good are you?"

"I saw him take down twenty infected in thirty seconds earlier today," Tess interjected. All eyes turned to her. "I saw him go out of his way to search for Pagan when he could have stayed here safe." Steele glanced over at her, eyes thanking her. "I've seen what he can do, and I trust him to help keep us going until Pagan returns. Steele will help me lead Little Sable." He nodded thanks to her.

"What do you mean?" Harriet shouted, brown curls bouncing on her shoulders. "What about Pagan?"

"Steele will step in for Pagan until we can get him back," Tess said.

Steele chimed in. "We aren't the only people out there. People took Pagan and killed members of the Red Stripes. We need to prepare for the fact that they might come for us."

The people were quiet.

"I'm allowing Steele to take charge of all security matters at Little Sable. I will assist him and hold him accountable and he will do the same for me. He has given me his word that he will maintain our customs," she called to them.

"We've trusted people like him before, and all it got us was dead. Go fuck yourself," Jack said.

"It's not just the rival group we have to worry about. Do you know how many infected march this way as we speak?"

"No," Jack said.

"The East Coast has been eradicated. The Pentagon has fallen. The only thing coming this way is a wall of dead a hundred miles long."

Children cried. People's eyes went wide. Mouths dropped open.

"Millions of the dead are coming west."

"How can you say that?" Joey said. The young mother clutched a bald baby to her chest.

"It's the truth. We must be honest with what we are dealing with. I don't think they will come this way en masse because Michigan is a peninsula, but thousands will come as people flee ahead of them, and we have to be ready. I will help prepare you for what is to come until Pagan can be released. No one will be left behind, not even Pagan. We'll get him out."

"Why don't we join the other group?" shouted Steve.

"Would you want to join a group that kills our members and holds the other hostage?" he said.

"Well, of course not."

"I agree. It may be a misunderstanding, but we can't give away our position or numbers."

"How will you protect us any better than Pagan?" Jack said. He turned, looking at the people around with his hands out.

"Thunder and his club do a great job." Steele nodded at Thunder. The biker was emotionless. No smile. No frown. He was purely flat. Tess hoped that the plan her and Steele had to train Little Sable Pointers would not push the Red Stripes away. Power shifts from nation-states all the way down to small-town politics never came without a fight.

"I'll train up a group of volunteers to shoot and move like a unit. They will be called upon for defense of Little Sable Point against infected or otherwise."

"There aren't enough of us to put up a fight against the dead," Jack said.

Steele looked down at him. "You're right. But we will hit and move fast against foes that are dead or alive. There are people here who are familiar with this area. We will take the best terrain and fight battles on our terms."

People nodded in agreement. Steele took a deep breath, preparing for his steamroller of a speech.

"We have a choice. We can hide, dreading the day of our demise. Sure, we live for awhile, maybe even in relative peace, but someday the dead will come, or those fools at the power plant will come and put us down like dogs. Worse than that. They'll eat you alive or cut you to pieces." He paused, letting the fear of the situation sink into their brains and guts.

Hackles rose on the back of Tess's neck. Goose pimples replaced hair follicles.

"But we don't have to live in fear. We can stand up. Train up. Expand our reach. Defend ourselves against all enemies, dead or living, and fight. Fight for something greater than ourselves."

"What's that?" someone screamed.

"If the people to your left and your right aren't worth fighting for, maybe you should find a new community. We can fight for each other. We can fight for life."

"Fight for Sable!" Tess shouted next to him. He gave her a sideways glance. She looked back, surprised by her outburst.

He lifted his hand slowly as a fist in the air. "For Sable!" he shouted.

"Fight for Sable," they shouted together. She raised her fist in the air with every shout.

Soon people in the crowd took up the chant.

"Fight for Sable! Fight for freedom! Fight for life!"

For the first time since the outbreak, she felt an odd sense of hope. Her fist pumped in the air alongside this rock of a man. She smiled up at him and he down at her. She grabbed his hand, holding it high in the air. The people of Little Sable Point clapped and cheered.

Gwen stared up at them from below, a twisted look on her face. *Was it anger? Malice? Envy?* It didn't matter because whether Gwen liked it or not, Steele was tied to her now. A man like him never backed out on his word. Tess lifted their hands up higher in the air.

STEELE

Little Sable Point, MI

He looked into the blank faces of the people in front of him. A young orange-haired kid, that couldn't have been more than sixteen shifted on his feet, nervously bouncing.

"This is all of them, out of over two hundred?" Steele asked Tess.

"You said volunteer, not a draft."

Thunder and a few of his Red Stripes stood nearby offering their prior military training but not volunteering for the Little Sable defense unit. *I couldn't have expected club members to quit their brothers and tie themselves in with a bunch of people that would probably get gunned down by more experienced fighters. No, gunned down by more experienced men.*

Volunteer fighters who had a stake in defending their land, family, and the person beside them always fought harder than those conscripted or forced into service. Ancient landowning Greeks had set the foundation of the citizen soldier in western society, a tradition that had lasted through millennia and was imprinted on the souls of all free patriotic men. This tradition had been adopted by the Founding Fathers of the United States and built directly into the Bill of Rights as a fundamental safeguard.

And all that answered the ancient call were ten people. Even after these men and women had been forced to scavenge, fight, and survive on their own, only a few wanted to provide for the common defense.

Seven men stood before him. Three were beyond service age and one appeared to have come from a nursing home. There was a boy who couldn't be more than sixteen and a woman pushing sixty; she looked like she could handle herself better than the lot of them. *What am I going to do with them? Where do you even start with a group like this? Front leaning rest for pushups? No, they'd quit by twelve o'clock noon. The old man will definitely die.*

Steele paced slowly in front of them, thinking of a way to begin. He had kept his badge out on his chest, hoping that it would strengthen his position in their eyes. He eyed Kevin and Ahmed standing nearby. Ahmed raised his eyebrows at him. Kevin stood, lanky arms crossed over his chest. They both were in their ACUs and had their M4s. *They will fight, but it's not enough.*

"Everyone's here for their own reason. Something has lit a fire in your hearts to stand before me, and that's good because I can't fight for you."

He continued walking. "However, I can train you to be more effective in a fight and maybe help you stay alive longer out here."

He stopped in front of the boy. Big ears stuck off of his head. Freckles dotted his nose and cheeks. A mop of wavy orange hair sat atop his head. "Why are you here? What can you provide this unit?"

"You even shave yet?" Garrett hollered over at the boy. The boy gulped, trying to stick out his narrow chest.

Steele gave Garrett a sidelong glance. "Let the boy speak."

"So I can hear about his high score in a video game," Garrett said, with a grin. "This is real life, boy," he yelled at him. "Can't respawn here."

"I said enough, Garrett." Steele outfaced the big biker. Steele's hand itched up his sidearm. Garrett stuck his chin up, towering over Steele.

"I don't care where you been. I bet I been worse," Garrett said, looking down at Steele trying to minimize him. Steele contemplated which way he would strike the man to bring him down. Larger opponents would usually try to overpower their smaller opponents. As the smaller of the two, Steele would distract the man with a kick to his knee and move to disarm him. Then he would have to deal with the responses from Thunder, Half-Barrel, and Bird. If they didn't kill him on the spot, they would certainly beat his face inside out and his great experiment would be over.

"Your little badge don't mean nothin' out here."

Just a piece of metal now, but it symbolizes a layer of trust between the government and the people. "Might not, but I told you to back off." Steele's hand found his tomahawk, eyes never leaving Garrett's. Steele shifted his feet under him, bracing himself. *I'll break his jaw with the flat-ended piece before he can blink.*

Garrett glowered down, fists clenching at his sides, nose flaring out.

"Enough, Garrett," Thunder bellowed. "These are our friends." Garrett let himself shrink an inch.

Steele turned toward Thunder and nodded. Thunder weighed him.

"That's outta respect for Little Sable. If it was just us, I'd let you two fight it out." Steele had no delusions of where he would end up in that brawl with Red Stripe fists raining down on him.

"I understand," Steele said. He turned his back on Garrett. Either he was brave to turn his back, stupid, or confident. He marched back to the boy. His boots swept the sandy soil.

"Who are you and why are you here?" Steele asked the boy, putting his best drill instructor face on.

The boy stuttered. "I...I...I...I'm Max. I'm here alone. My parents." The boy stopped a moment, collecting himself. "My parents are gone and I wanna, wanna learn how to fight." The look on the boy's face made Steele wonder how he had survived this long. Steele almost wished he hadn't asked, feeling a pang of guilt in his gut, but he pushed onward. If the young man couldn't face his reality, he would never be able to kill a man.

"I can teach you to fight, *Max*. But do you have what it takes to win a fight?" Steele put a finger harder than he wanted to on the teenager's chest. "Do you have what it takes inside?" Max's eyes bugged out from his head.

"Ye-ye-yes, sir," he exclaimed. Steele almost had sympathy for what he was about to do. He gave the kid a quick jab to the gut. Not hard, but enough to knock the wind out of his surprised victim. Max coughed and sputtered, dropping to his knees as he regained his breath. His eyes looked betrayed as he tried to breathe in air that eluded his lungs.

"How can I depend on you in a fight when you can't even take a punch to the gut? How can these men and women standing around you depend on you to do what you have to do to win?" He needed soldiers, fighters, at the very least athletes, not teenage boys who didn't have parents. He paced again. Ahmed held him in cold regard.

Kevin leaned forward as he passed. "A little harsh on the kid, don't you think?" His breath reeked of alcohol.

Steele glared at him. Kevin's eyelids were only half-open like he could fall asleep at any minute, a sign that his friend was already well into his drinking for the day. "A little early to be hitting the bottle so hard?"

"Who said I stopped from last night?"

Steele shook his head. "Is he still there?" Kevin looked over his head.

"Yup."

"Then maybe I'm wrong about him," he whispered.

Steele crossed back the way he had come. Eyes followed him back and forth, awaiting the enlightenment that martial prowess gives. It was as if he held the golden ticket to survival that only the misery of military discipline could provide the answer for.

"Do any of you have any prior military or law enforcement experience?"

One of the older men raised his hand. A patchwork beard grew haphazardly over his face. He looked like a man who had shaved on the regular to hide his beard growing deficiencies but hadn't had access to a razor in about five weeks.

"Sir, eight years National Guard."

"What's your name? And do not call me, sir. Jesus."

"Larry Capers, sir?"

"MOS?" Steele demanded.

"I was a 92G, culinary specialist, sir." *His military experience is a goddamn cook.*

"Thank you," Steele said, trying to hide his disappointment. Attitude is a reflection of leadership, and he didn't want them running themselves down at the very beginning.

A man in the middle of the group raised a tired, worn hand. When Steele drew near, he wondered how he had escaped the nursing home and made it to the coast.

"Yes, elder."

"Name is Bengy Sloman, sir." His voice crackled. "Owned a hardware store until recently, and before that, I fought in Korea."

"Korea?" Steele said. *The Forgotten War?* "Like you were stationed in Korea?"

The old man wrinkled his large downward-curved nose. "Nope. Fought there in '52."

This guy can't be serious. "How old are you?"

"I'll be eighty-three in December, sir."

Steele reached out and gently squeezed Bengy's bony shoulder. He leaned close and dropped the level of his voice. "You don't have to be here. You've served enough for your country. Let the younger folk take up the fight. You can rest."

Bengy frowned. His face was lined and worn with speckled skin. "It's a privilege to answer the call. I'd rather fight than have my kids stick me in some nursing home, but I don't think that's likely now." Steele released his shoulder and glanced at Thunder.

"He's a volunteer, ain't he?" Thunder rumbled with a nod.

"Yes, he is. If you get too tired, take a break. I don't want you getting hurt training."

Bengy's mouth twitched, regarding the biker with disdain. The men were the product of two wars in two different times. One war forgotten. One war despised. Bengy had grown up in the shadow of the Greatest Generation while Thunder was a by-product of the counterculture Baby Boomers.

Bengy's hair was still cut short like a fresh recruit, and his face still managed to be cleanly shaven. Thunder's long hair hung down to his shoulders, and his gray beard touched his chest.

"I walked out of Unsan. Not many of us did. I'm not worried about a couple of laps around the compound with you kids."

"Thank you. Feel free to pass along any insights as we train."

Bengy smiled, revealing crooked brown stained teeth. "I'm sure things have changed, but I'll help where I can."

Steele nodded his acknowledgment. *Tough, ancient SOB.*

Retracing his steps, he passed in front of Max. The boy stood erect back in his place.

"You're still here?" Steele addressed him. "Why?"

The boy looked scared like he might try to run. "I-I-I, yes, sir," Max stammered. "I want to fight." Put somebody through enough and they will either quit or be your worst enemy.

"Don't call me sir," Steele said again.

"Yes, sir," Max piped up. He looked down again. His eyes darted between his older peers.

Steele ignored the boy and continued his inspection, stopping in front of the woman. The only woman to answer the call. She had spoken during the meeting the night before. "Why are you here, ma'am?"

Her ear-length hair held more gray streaks through it than her natural auburn color. Her chin was narrow and her mouth wide, making it seem like her face needed more room. She licked her dry lips before she spoke.

"I'm tired of killing those shamblers with a shovel. I want to learn to shoot." Her eyes went downward on the ends making her seem perpetually worried.

"What's your name, ma'am?" he asked.

"Margaret Goodspeed. I lost my husband weeks ago." Even through her downturned eyebrows, her eyes grew cold. "And my kids are at university." Her eyes told him to not ask any more questions about it. Steele nodded, leaving it alone.

"Have you ever used a gun?"

"Never. Anti-gun my whole life," she said, clenching her jaw as if the thought gave her anxiety, however determined she might be.

"Times change. We'll teach you." Steele continued walking. "And you three?"

An average-sized man in his forties with wavy brown hair nodded. "I'm Steve, used to be an engineer." *Should have you planning our fortifications, not manning the barricade with the grunts.* Steele moved on.

A lean black-haired man with pale skin smiled. "I'm Jason."

"Former occupation?"

"Used to be a dairy farmer."

"Good. And you?" Steele looked up at a tall black man with graying hair at the temples.

The man lifted his chin slightly. "I'm Nathan. I was an accountant before all of this."

"And you?" Steele stared at a twenty-something college-aged kid.

"Name's Alex Jones. I was in college in Grand Rapids. Hitched a ride out here with an old couple." The sandy blond young man avoided eye contact with Steele.

"Prior weapons handling experience?" Steele barked at them. Nervous eyes answered.

Their answers came out broken and not even close to being in unison with one another. "No, sir."

Steele sighed. *How many of them will I need to add to my list before the end of the week? You, Steve? You, Larry? All of us?* He wrestled his mind knowing that at some point they would be added to his list.

The last man stood with his bolt-action deer hunting rifle on his shoulder. He had a goatee and longer brown hair with the look of a country boy.

"And you?"

"Name's Trent. Lived up 'bout ten miles that way." He gestured with his head.

"Why aren't you still there? Seems isolated enough up here."

"Those wing nuts burnt my house down. Barely made it out with my family."

"Sorry to hear it. Glad you're here. What do you have there?"

"It's my Winchester XPR .30-06 Springfield. Bagged some big bucks with it."

Trent held it up for Steele to see. Steele took it from him. It weighed about six-and-a-half pounds. Camouflaged synthetic stock. Steele eyed the scope atop the rifle.

"Leupold optics. Good choice." Steele held the rifle to his shoulder and looked through the scope. "Can you shoot?"

Trent nodded. "Yes, sir. Deer hunt every fall. Set me up anywhere and I'll knock 'em dead within at least four hundred yards." He gave Steele a cool look.

Steele smiled. *Finally a shooter.* A glimmer of hope amongst the dim prospects of his volunteers. He turned toward Thunder. "Let's have him help instruct. No use retraining him on a new weapon."

"No problem," Thunder said.

"Glad to have a shooter onboard," Steele said. Trent grinned.

"I tried to get the rest of them knuckleheads to join up, but some folk need more warming up to do. Not too trusting of new folk, especially ones like you claiming they're from the government and going to help." He reached up and touched Steele's bicep. "But I'll say, I believe you. Damn, boss. You work out?"

"Ha. I used to when I had the time."

"Don't look like you stopped."

"Wish I hadn't. Welcome aboard." Steele turned back to Thunder. "The floor is yours. What do we have to train them on?"

Thunder came forward and dropped a large bag in front of Steele. It clanked on the ground. Thunder grunted as he bent low and unzipped the black bag.

Removing the items one by one, he set them back atop the bag.

Two .22s, a 12-gauge shotgun, an M1 Garand, two .30-06 hunting rifles, and an old Colt AR-15. Thunder bent down while unloading the guns and handed them out to the volunteers.

"Make sure Max gets a .22," Steele said under his breath to Thunder.

"Good idea. If he shoots one of us, maybe it won't be so bad," Thunder said.

"Where'd you get that antique?"

Thunder smirked. "I know you're a former agent 'n' all, but let's not get into too much detail about how these guns were acquired."

Steele eyed the man. *He's right. What's it matter now? As long as they work, it doesn't matter.* "Point taken."

Steele surveyed the volunteers. He may as well have given them broomsticks.

Half the group held them as if they were holding an electric eel; the other half hugged them tight as if they never wanted to let them go.

"Which one, old-timer?" Thunder boomed.

"Nothing better than an M1 Garand," Bengy said, holding his wood stocked gun out for his own inspection. "Like an old friend she is," the old man said to himself.

"Is this a machine gun?" Steve asked, holding the AR-15.

Steele took a deep breath. *This is going to be a long day.*

KINNICK
Golden Triangle, CO

A green little airplane inched its way up a giant flat flight screen over twenty feet high. The number US 19 was tagged on it. Only a few planes floated on the black radar screen like a 1980's video game. Kinnick watched the NORAD operations center work as he waited for the vice president. For hours, he sat with the operations staff, staring at the green planes that ticked across the screen from Alaska to Peterson Airfield. Blips of helicopters shot in and out of Peterson's airspace. *Combat runs.*

"You got any fast movers going?" Kinnick asked a female captain sitting at a computer. The woman glanced at Kinnick, removing strands of blonde hair from behind her ear, and gave him a flash of white teeth.

"A few, but most of the airfields where they're stationed are offline. A squadron of F-16s ended up here, but not many of them to go around. Peterson is a slow mover airfield and a large portion of Air Force Space Command. We mostly do resupply with the option to intercept from other airfields around the nation. We don't really have an air-to-air threat so most of our resources like fuel are going to close air support. Apaches, Cobras and a squadron of A-10s up from Davis-Monthan."

"How are the space boys doing?"

"They've been scrambling since we started losing satellites."

She looked at his Army Combat Uniform. "You an Army flyer?"

"Air Force, actually. C-130 Hercules. Spent a little bit of time here, but that seems like a lifetime ago."

She glanced at his uniform, raising an eyebrow. "What's with the Army uniform?"

He chuckled, looking down at his uniform. He pulled on the jacket sleeve. "You could say that I've been adopted. Always a flyer, no matter what uniform I wear."

"We've been looking for more pilots. Our crews have been running ragged on only a few hours of sleep a night." They flew high in the sky above the ruined earth. Miles away from the dead bodies and their rotting stench. Miles away from the cries for help. Thousands of meters from the infected, marching unknown below him. Easy to forget the reality when you were in the clouds.

Kinnick gave her a grim smile. "I think my fight is going to be on the ground for this war. A friend once told me that boots on the ground was the only way to really win a war, and I think he's got the right idea on this one."

The captain looked nervous as if he were asking her to get on the frontline.

"You been off this base? You seen any of them?" Kinnick asked.

"No, not after the lockdown. All I hear are the horror stories." She looked down at her keyboard as if the keys were the only thing keeping her alive.

A man in a blue uniform with stars on his shoulders entered the floor from the vice president's War Room. He marched for Kinnick with purpose in his step.

"Maybe when your shift is done we can grab a coffee? Talk about better days."

She covered her microphone with her hand, glancing down at his full bird on the front of his uniform. "Is that an order, sir?"

"No, ma'am, and I'm retired."

She gave him a soft smile with her slightly pursed rose lips. "Sure."

"I'm not even sure I know your name, Captain."

"It's Gallagher, sir."

"You can call me, Mike."

"Okay, Mike." She smiled a bit and her eyes darted behind him. Kinnick could feel the general's presence.

"Colonel Kinnick?"

"Yes, sir." Kinnick stood at attention.

The three-star general in a blue army dress uniform nodded. "I'm General Monroe. Stand easy."

Kinnick relaxed. Old habits died hard.

"You may come with me. The vice president is ready for you."

The general's eyes fell upon the captain, now trying to look busy at her computer screen.

"I see Captain Gallagher has been taking care of you while you were waiting," the broad-shouldered general said to him.

Kinnick's mouth quivered, thinking about smiling. "Yes, sir. She has been very accommodating. Gave me a chance to catch up on the ongoing aviation operations."

"She's a good airman. We all have a part to play in this war," Monroe said.

"That's correct, sir."

"Follow me." The general waved him forward. "I read your after-action report on the search and rescue mission. That's some damn good work. I'm thinking about recruiting you for my division. You set the bar high. By the time this is done, you may have a promotion lined up."

I'm not doing this for promotion. This is survival. "With all due respect, I'm retired, sir."

The general opened the door, holding it into the War Room.

"No one's retired anymore."

Kinnick entered the room. The vice president sat at the head of his War Room conference table. A four-star general with glasses sat on his right in a blue uniform. *Must be NORAD's base commander, an Air Force general.* An Air Force one-star general sat on the four-star's right. Monroe took a seat on the vice president's left. A collection of colonels, lieutenant colonels, and majors sat on either side of the filled table. The vice president smiled at something the four-star said and nodded to Kinnick.

"Colonel Kinnick. It's good to see you again," the vice president said. He wore the same stained shirt and loose tie he had worn the day before. "I see you met General Monroe, commanding officer of Fort Carson. He has adopted all ground forces for continuing operations, and this is General

Daugherty, highest ranking general in our armed forces as we speak. He is developing the strategy to take back America." The blue-uniformed Air Force general nodded to Kinnick, looking over his glasses.

General Daugherty pointed. "Why don't you take a seat, and we will get started."

Eyes turned toward Kinnick. A single empty seat sat at the opposing side of the table across from Vice President Brady. Kinnick took the leather armrests in his hands and settled in, not finding the seat comfortable.

Vice President Brady looked like a mess instead of the Leader of the Free World. His American flag pin on his lapel was tilted a bit to the left. The military men around him looked clean and well-kempt, the stress of war not showing real strain on their physical appearance. Vice President Brady treated his appearance with the air of a divorced bachelor. Unshaven. Messy hair. Dirty clothes. He folded his hands together on the table.

"Everyone here knows the gravity of the situation. General Daugherty has put forth a plan to eliminate the infected that will quickly gain us the upper hand in this conflict. Tactical nuclear strikes along the West Coast. Please elaborate, General."

"Yes, sir," Daugherty stood. He clicked a button on his remote control and a giant map of the United States lit up at the back of the room.

"Gentlemen, our nation hangs by a thread. The enemy has taken strangleholds of both our coastlines, driving us inland and pinching us in the middle of the nation. We're estimating a ninety-three percent infection rate. Most of our seven percent is sitting in-between the Rockies and the Mississippi which means we are effectively surrounded. We cannot fight on two fronts in this battle. With limited forces at our disposal, we must free up one of our flanks in order to concentrate our forces on the other. As we speak, millions of infected march from cities along the West Coast toward the interior. Countless more reside in the cities themselves and will eventually make their way here. They will not stop." He glanced down at his notes. "Has everyone been briefed on Operation Just Resolve?"

The officers around the room nodded their heads, affirming yes.

"Good. Let me be brief. Just Resolve is a multitiered approach. We still have access to considerable nuclear assets within our strategic triad. The USS Kentucky and the USS Louisiana are Ohio-class submarines and sitting off the coast of California as we speak, carrying twenty-four thermonuclear warheads each. They are currently eighty-seven days into a ninety-day patrol. They are reaching their capacity to function without resupply. We can hold them for probably an extra week off the coast, but they will be ineffective after that."

"They can't resupply in Alaska?" Kinnick asked. Daugherty looked irritated by the interruption. He glared over his glasses but answered the question.

"The USS Kentucky and USS Louisiana will travel to Anchorage after their mission is complete. If we send them now, that puts us over a week behind for any offensive strikes. A week we do not have. We could have millions of infected on our doorstep in a week. Worse yet, we could have them on the move, too spread out for an effective response." He glared around the table.

"May I continue?" Daugherty asked the group. "Those aren't our only assets. We have two B2 bomber squadrons able to fly from Peterson as well as a squadron of F-16s that can be outfitted if need be. The problem is our GPS systems. All of our GPS stations, except the one here in Colorado Springs, are offline. As we know, our systems must recalibrate to stay accurate. There hasn't been recalibration in over a month. Lack of appropriate navigation capabilities will hamper our efforts severely. However, I have faith in my squadrons here that they will find their targets if asked to do it the old fashion way."

A lieutenant colonel with short brown hair smiled broadly. "My boys are up to the challenge."

"That's good, Colonel Hicks. We need them on their A-game for this operation," Daugherty said.

"We will move the USS Kentucky and the USS Louisiana north and use them to strike San Francisco and San Jose, Seattle, Portland, Sacramento, and Spokane. This will allow them the opportunity to get a head start on their resupply run.

Vice President Brady looked miserable at the end of the table. Kinnick saw him burp under this breath and blow it to the side.

Vice President Brady placed his hands on the edge of the table. "Anybody want a drink?" Vice President Brady said. He looked around at the officers and abruptly stood up. He walked over to the cabinet holding his scotch decanter near the head of the room. "I feel like we could all use one. Can't have a good 'let's nuke the United States,' conversation without one." Daugherty watched the vice president with apparent disgust behind his back. The vice president fumbled with the crystal top of the decanter. "I think that was Churchill who said that."

"No, sir. May I continue the briefing?"

The vice president didn't say anything but ripped the top off the decanter. The crystal on crystal friction rang around the room.

Daugherty punched a button on his remote and the subs' attack routes lit up. He clicked another button, bringing up mini-airplanes headed west.

"Colonel Hicks, we will need your squadrons to hit Los Angeles, Phoenix, San Diego, Las Vegas, Tucson, and if we can get it done, Albuquerque and Salt Lake City. I have half a mind to have you hit some targets below the border. General Urban has been screaming about proper air support for weeks. Hitting some targets below Texas may alleviate some pressure on his command, but I'm not sure we're going to get the go-ahead on that."

"General Daugherty," the vice president interrupted. He spoke over his shoulder. The general's chin lowered to his chest.

"Yes, sir."

Brady's words slurred a bit as he spoke. "Can somebody get me some ice?"

General Daugherty glared at a major. "Major Day, can you oblige the Vice President?" The major stood and hurried from the room.

The vice president watched him go. "Wait, Major." Day stopped looking admonished. The vice president handed him the ice bucket. "Can't forget this." Day took the ice bucket and fled the War Room.

The vice president turned back to the table. "You're sure this is the best plan? What about the 'Mother of All Bombs' bomb?" He waved a hand to his side as he spoke. "Wouldn't that negate any fallout concerns?"

"I'm not sure of any other way to put this clearly. We're on the brink. Infection rates are through the roof. Here." Daugherty clicked the map off and pulled up another.

The vice president raised a hand in the air. "I've seen it plenty of times."

Daugherty licked his lips. "The GBU-43/B Massive Ordnance Air Blast bombs are off the table. We have fifteen in our arsenal and they only have the explosive yield of a small tactical nuclear weapon. We need these infected hotbeds off the table with a certainty that only nuclear weapons can give us."

The vice president nodded. The door clicked quietly open and Day tried to sneak back into the room, carrying the bucket of ice.

The vice president stared his way and waved him forward. "Hurry up, now," he said. Day handed it to the vice president, keeping his head low.

"Thanks, Champ." The major hurried to go take his seat.

"Let's continue with the brief. Our-," Daugherty's voice stopped.

The vice president dug his hand into the ice. The ice loudly crunched and broke, the sound magnified by the bucket. "We are talking about destroying every major city center on the West Coast. I need assurances." He clinked ice cubes into his crystal glass. He dropped them one at a time, waiting for General Daugherty's response.

The general frowned as he thought. His nostrils flared. "I will elaborate again. The state of your armed forces is abysmal. We've been over the contingency plans. We have only a small fraction of our armed forces operational, and we must stem the tide of the infected. The only radical change to this trend is our nuclear arsenal. I don't want to do it. By God, it is not what these missiles were made for, but I believe it will get the job done."

"Mr. Vice President, what if I told you that you didn't have to drop any nukes?" Kinnick said, calling out across the room.

Vice President Brady spun around. His eyebrows rose on his forehead in attention, and he brought his drink up to the center of his chest. "Colonel Kinnick. I was wondering when you would speak up." The vice president smiled at him.

Daugherty shot daggers with his eyes at Kinnick. *Don't jump the chain of command if you want to keep your job.* Kinnick ignored him. *Fuck it. We'll all be dead soon anyway.*

Brady slurped the liquor from his glass as he took his seat again. "Well, what do you have for me? I trust it is a better plan than General Daugherty put forth." Daugherty chewed his lip barely able to restrain his anger. The general's eyes blinked rapidly behind his glasses.

The vice president dared him with unafraid eyes. "General, do we have an issue?"

Daugherty's face turned red and he glared at Kinnick.

"I gave the colonel twenty-four hours to come up with an alternative plan. Now, let's hear it."

"Thank you, sir," Kinnick said.

Brady nodded and spread his arms out wide.

"No one will say I didn't exhaust all my options. All of you men can attest to that." He pointed at a few of his officers.

Kinnick stood up, clutching his paper map. He rolled the large map of Colorado out across the table. The state was a basic rectangle. Highway arteries stretched across the state in the shape of a cross, spread up and down, left and right, following the edge of the Rocky Mountains. He waved at a Day. "Can you hold that down?"

Day stood and held down a corner of the map.

"Thank you. All right." Licking his lips, Kinnick started, leaning on the table. "The Rocky Mountains provide a natural barrier between us and the Western cities."

"That's exactly why it makes sense for us to nuke them. The fallout will be trapped on the other side of the mountains," Lieutenant Colonel Gaines said with a reassuring look to Daugherty.

I'm not going to get support from former colleagues here. Kinnick pulled a marker from his pocket and held it up like a professor in class. "You are correct, Colonel, but what if we didn't need to drop the nukes at all. If we can secure and hold these few passes through the Rockies," he said, as he circled each pass on the map, "we will be able to stop any large hordes of infected from attacking our rear, buying us time."

"I would say you are trying to do this the really, really hard way. We would bleed our remaining forces dry trying to hold the passes. How many soldiers would we need to hold those passes? Ten thousand?" said Daugherty.

Dark-blue uniformed General Monroe shifted in his seat. "Without the majority of Fort Carson here, it would be very difficult. I have to agree the drain on manpower will stretch us thin."

"It won't. I assure you. Watch." Kinnick continued to circle the passes. "I have narrowed it down to the major roadways through Colorado." He drew a large X north and a bit west of the center of Colorado. "We start with the Eisenhower Tunnel. We will need to block that first. This should divert the main body of the infected outwards, pinning them within the canyons of the mountain range. They will eventually funnel toward Dunluce Pass. Here." He dragged the marker over the map a few inches and tapped the pass with it. Black dots blotted the paper. "I would say a company of men could hold that against tens of thousands of infected for a period of time. A couple of platoons or even a single platoon at South Fork, Mosquito, and Independence Passes. Combined with your combat aviation brigades and A-10s, even the F-16s, we should be able to hold. Give me a battalion, and I will hold Colorado."

Daugherty shook his head in disbelief. "You're telling me that you can fend off roughly sixty million infected with five hundred soldiers? You're insane. We've had entire brigade combat teams and divisions decimated by these things."

Kinnick looked at the General Daugherty. *What will you do? Try to ruin my career? I'm retired. No place to go. No asses to kiss. Only an opportunity to get eaten alive on a mountaintop in the middle of nowhere.* Kinnick looked at Daugherty and leaned into the table. "I only need to hold until it snows. We're guaranteed snow by mid-November, which means I only need to hold for about a month. I can do it."

"This guy has got some big fucking balls," Monroe said with a laugh.

"Or a death wish," Daugherty snapped.

Brady laughed, making sure to get some alcohol in his mouth between laughs. His laugh was loud and boisterous as if he were at a college bar instead of the War Room of an acting president.

Daugherty squeezed an eyebrow in-between his fingers. "Strategically, this plan doesn't make sense."

"Hold on, Chuck. He's an amusing fella. I mean *this* is the colonel who found goddamn Patient Zero." The vice president drank some more booze, shaking his head. "You have to be a little crazy if you undertook that mission and came out alive. Clever plan, but the answer is, no."

Kinnick blinked rapidly, digesting his rejection. *What? Not even a shot?*

"Sir, with all due respect. Give me a battalion and I will protect your flank." Kinnick stood erect, hands at his sides, chin up, chest out, eyes forward.

"The vice president's right. It's too much to risk on the backs of men. We will conduct our nuclear strike and be assured our flank is protected. We will not hope that your plan works. We will rain fire from above and know we are secure," Daugherty said.

The vice president smiled at Kinnick, who felt like the man might outright laugh at him. The vice president shrugged his shoulders as if he didn't care anymore. "I'm leaning toward General Daugherty's plan. Eliminating the cities where most of our population is concentrated will greatly relieve pressure from our battle plan."

Kinnick put his hands on the table, leaning in. "Give me two hundred soldiers and I will protect your flank. If I can't hold the flank, you can unleash a hell on our country that has never before been seen in the history of mankind. Let me try. Let me give you the opportunity to say we did everything we could in our darkest hour to prevent a holocaust beyond imagination."

General Monroe watched him, taking in his words, his chin nodding. He turned to the vice president. "Sir, Colonel Kinnick has a point. We still have options on the table. Hold the nukes in reserve. Let's see what he can do."

"You want to waste more lives on this *fool's* errand? Those are our boys he's leading to the slaughter when we've already lost so many," Daugherty said.

"What will happen when you have to look your children in the face and tell them what you've done?" Kinnick said, his voice rising.

Daugherty's mouth clamped shut. An ashamed anger settled over his features. "I will tell them that I helped win an unwinnable war so they could have a future."

"A future where they will scrape a life out of the ashes. Will you leave out the part where you incinerated half of the country?"

"I will tell them that what was done needed to be done."

The vice president swirled the ice around in his glass. He lifted a hand partially in the air, calling the debate to a stop.

"Kinnick, you're crazy, and I like you. General Daugherty, you're a strategic mastermind, but I would love to have some plausible deniability on this one. Eventually, when this is over, there will be questions," he said. His eyes stared through Kinnick. "I'm inclined to see if you can work a miracle. I'll give you four days to secure and close off the routes into Colorado, but General Monroe, do not weaken our perimeter here."

Kinnick smiled, knowing that he had probably signed his own death warrant, but it gave the nation a chance to hold onto some of its purity.

"Thank you, sir." He turned to the broad Army general. "General Monroe, would you be willing to donate your 2nd Special Forces battalion? Perhaps a Stryker company." Visions of the large personnel carriers plowing over infected danced in his mind followed by attack helicopters rocketing the infected into fiery pieces. "We will need to get the attack choppers to loosen them up before we go in." Kinnick grabbed his map and started to roll it up.

Monroe grimaced. "I would give you an entire division if I could, but I can't. The most I can spare is a single company of men."

Kinnick's heart sank. He would need more than that to stand a chance. He turned to Daugherty.

"We will be hard-pressed, but with heavy air support we will hold." Kinnick gulped. The look on the general's face was one of disgust.

"Air support will remain concentrated in the Colorado Springs area. Our resources are not infinite, and we must maintain the integrity of this operating base."

Kinnick looked back at Monroe, his only real advocate in the room. "Only a hundred and fifty men, sir?" *Without air support, we'll die.*

Monroe nodded, thick jaw clenching. "Less. Most of our units have been pieced together and reorganized. You will make due, of that I have no doubt. Or the vice president will order the destruction of the entire Western seaboard."

STEELE

Little Sable Point, MI

Thunder had instructed the volunteers all morning. He cursed and pointed and explained in detail everything he could about firearms. The sun had made an appearance but only enough to dull the chill in the brisk air. The pale yellow circle traveled to the middle of the sky above them.

Steele had listened as Thunder spent hours going over the nomenclature of the weapons. He explained the merits of weapons safety with repetitious focus on not pointing the weapons at one another. It was a foundational rule of gun safety, and people needed a constant reminder. The recruits took apart their weapons piece by piece and put them back together again as Thunder instructed them on familiarization.

In the afternoon, Steele took over. A mild breeze traveled down the beach and through the dunes.

"Leave the weapons and follow me," Steele instructed. A couple of volunteers set their weapons down. Others looked at him, confused.

"We can't take them?" Alex asked. The college student had picked up the weapon with some aptitude, enough aptitude for Steele to hope that he may become an asset to the group someday.

"Won't need them," Steele said.

"What if infected come around?"

"You can run back. We won't need to go far."

"What's the point in training on these things if we don't get to use them?"

Steele walked closer to the young man.

"Not until you get more training. I don't want you shooting me by mistake. Now, let's move!" Steele shouted. Alex set his gun down slower than Steele would have liked, but they all followed him into the dunes leading to the beach. They lazily made a single file line. Nervous chatter sounded off between them.

Steele drew them to a halt near the washed up bodies of the slain infected. The small waves tossed and rolled them like the carcasses of dead fish. Max looked at him questioningly as they approached the stinking bodies, covering his nose and mouth with the sleeve of his sweatshirt.

"They smell terrible," Max said from underneath his sleeve. The stench releasing from the bodies was compounded by the water lapping and tussling them. Steele poked at one with the tip of his boot and flies burst into a black rain cloud.

Steele faced them and gave him a smile. "Yes, they do, Max. Everybody grab a body. You want to shoot. Well, here's your target."

The line of volunteers didn't move. They shifted in the sand, staring at their disgusting task.

"I feel like that was pretty clear," Steele said to them.

"We can't use cardboard or something?" Hank said. He was an overweight, retired factory worker from a furniture company in Grand Rapids with thinning hair.

"Not as good as the real thing."

"What about the bodies by the campers?" Max asked.

"Because they don't have heads," Steele responded. To everyone else, he said, "I wasn't joking. Grab a body or you're done here."

Margaret tied a red handkerchief around her head like a Wild West bandit and marched forward. Larry trailed behind her, his beer belly jiggling as he walked down the beach.

"What are you waiting for?" Steele commanded. "Steve and Max, grab this one," he said, waving at them. "Alex and Hank, grab that one. And you two grab that one over there. Try and get the ones with the most head still remaining." He put his hands on his hips and watched his volunteers struggle.

A limp body is difficult to pick up and carry. A waterlogged, dead, limp body was even worse. Steele watched as Max puked onto the sand. Nathan struggled but held it in, the black man gritting his teeth to hoist his body. Hank heaved, breathing hard, and Trent dragged a body by himself like he had bagged a prize buck.

Steele held his stomach contents in and made sure that they didn't see that it made him feel equally as ill. *Never show them weakness during turmoil, and they will follow you for it*, said one voice in his head. *Never make them do something you wouldn't do*, said the other.

"Damn it," he said under his breath. He marched down to the water. A body lay in the surf, rocking with the charge and retreat of the waves. The dead man's head lay twisted on its side, mouth open as if during his last breath he had called for help, but Steele knew it only called for the flesh of the living.

Steele covered his face with a green and black shemagh. Tess had given it to him out of a stash of Pagan's clothes, saying that he had used it during his military deployments. Steele was grateful. The shemagh was an amazingly versatile piece of clothing. Originally used throughout the Arab world, it had been adopted by Westerners frequenting or fighting in the region. It could be wrapped in dozens of different styles to protect one from the heat, wind, cold. It could be used as a tourniquet, sling, pillow, or a bag. In Steele's case, he used it for protecting his nose from the onslaught of rotting flesh.

Steele unsheathed his dagger and crouched into a squat. Slipping his dagger into the soft spot between the spine and head, he made sure he wasn't picking up a yet functioning infected. Getting his heels under him, he hefted the body. The torso and head flopped to the side, but he managed to get a shoulder underneath it. Sickening pops and noises rippled inside the dead infected. A scattering of black and orange beetles, ticks, and bugs scrambled for safety after being exposed to the light.

"Heavy fuck, aren't ya," he said to himself. Readjusting the dead man's weight, he double-timed back to the camp. He made sure to beat the volunteers, tossing his body down into the dune grass before the others. *Lead by example. Show them the correct actions to take. You are a leader, not an office manager.*

His volunteers straggled in gagging and complaining.

"Alright. Grab those logs and prop these bastards up. I want their heads leaning upright. Spaced out every five yards."

When they were finished prepping their targets, he surveyed their work. Dead bodies stood upright, tongues out, eyes white, horrific gore-covered mouths hanging open.

"Good. Now, for some fun stuff. Everyone to the camper." Their speed was agonizingly slow as they made their way to the camper roof. Steele joined them, dropping a box of .22 ammunition at their feet.

"Two at a time, we are going to shoot the bodies out there. Some of you may be wondering why we are using the dead bodies. It is scientifically proven that when people shoot things that look like other people, they are much more likely to get the job done in real life. With round bullseye targets, the results are significantly lower. This is a form of conditioning. If you don't think you can handle it, no one will think less of you, but this isn't the right place for you." He stopped, waiting for any of them to leave. They stayed, eagerly waiting for more instruction.

"I don't care about body shots. That training is obsolete now. I want everyone to aim for the head. A head shot will kill both people and the infected, body shots only people." His volunteers nodded. Having a blank slate with the trainees made them much easier to train. He wouldn't have to retrain the commonly taught "center mass" shooting technique. The rules had changed and he was adapting with them.

"Larry and Margaret, would you like to go first?" he asked. Larry took the gun in his hands. Margaret shook her head no. She looked down toward the ground, unable to meet his eyes.

"What's the matter?" he asked her.

"I'm nervous," she complained.

"You came to me because you wanted to learn to fight. Now, I'm offering you the opportunity and you say no?" He gave her an incredulous look. "Please don't waste my time."

Her eyebrows dipped on the sides making her look scared. "I want to learn, I really do, but can I shoot something else?" She pointed at the propped up bodies. "You know, something other than them."

"No, you shoot the dead. This is a proven form of firearms training. You will see how the bullet affects the human body. It will lessen the shock when it happens for real. And it will happen. You will kill the infected or somebody else, but in this world, you will kill. This training will give you the edge to do the things that need done and worry about the effects later. Do you understand?"

"Yes, but…" she trailed off.

"You can go back to using a shovel, in which case you are useless to me, or you can learn how to shoot a gun and protect yourself and your family."

She stared down at the infected bodies. The bodies sagged onto their stakes.

"My family's gone," she whispered. He held the gun out near her body. "I couldn't fire Brian's gun. I hated that thing in the house. He was always harping about self-defense and the like, but we both knew we could never use it. Then the infected broke inside and massacred him while I watched. I haven't heard from my kids since the end of August. They were up at university for welcome week. I'm not stupid. I know what that means."

Steele sighed, pushing his bottom lip into his mustache, sealing his mouth. "No one can replace them, but you have a family all around you. You've survived, and these people need you to learn how to fight. So the same things that happened to Brian won't happen to Larry. Or Max. Or Nathan. As hard as it is, this is your family now." She looked around him at the faces of the other volunteers.

"Take the gun, Margaret," Steele said, pushing it further into her hands.

Her hands hovered around the stock of the gun. "I'm not sure." Her eyes darted up at him. "You can call me Margie. Only Brian called me Margaret."

"I'm sure." He nodded his affirmation. He looked across at Larry. "Larry, you sure?"

Larry's bald head bobbed up and down.

"Steve, you want Margie here?"

Steve gave a slight nod. "Yes, I do."

Steele leaned closer to her. "We all need you. You're here for a reason. I'm giving you a second chance to save your people."

Her hands wavered as she accepted the weapon and magazine.

"You made the right choice," he said to her. He moved on, looking at the rest of their faces. "Now. Let's go over some of the basics. From far away, it is easier to shoot from a more steady kneeling position. It will allow you to support your off arm while you shoot. Kneel first." Margie and Larry kneeled. "And sit back on your foot."

"Load your weapons and keep them pointed downrange." Magazines tentatively inched their way into weapons.

"You ain't going to break them. Slam those mags in," Steele yelled.

Magazines clanked as they were forced into place.

Steele knelt in-between them. He sat back on his strong-side leg with his support-side leg upright. "Now, watch the way I do this." He brought the butt of his M4 up to his shoulder and kept it tight to his shoulder pocket, the place between your shoulder and the edge of the pectoral muscle. His pressure was firm yet relaxed enough to allow his shoulder to absorb recoil. He let his support arm tricep rest not on his knee, but into the meat of his leg next to his knee. "Depending on how high or low your optic is will determine where the butt is going to sit in your shoulder pocket. I don't want you moving your neck all funny to get a sight picture." He looked up at the others, gauging whether or not they understood. Completely enthralled eyes watched his every move as he taught a beginning shooter's course.

"I don't care that the gun wavers a bit as I aim. I care that the crosshairs are hovering near where I would like them to be. A trigger press is never fast. Remember slow is smooth, smooth is fast. Only as fast as you can be accurate. As I pull the trigger, the weapon will fire. After it fires, the trigger resets. I want to take the slack out of the trigger after every shot because this shortens the amount of time between shots. I don't care that the head is fuzzy in my sights. I will not anticipate the carbine firing but will know that it is going to fire only when I am pressing the trigger."

Bang. The carbine went off and a dead infected man's chin disintegrated into his neck revealing white bone beneath.

"Does everyone understand?" he asked, lowering his M4. Wide eyes stared back at him and they nodded vigorously.

"Good." He stood back up in the middle of the shooters.

"Everyone. The line is hot. You may begin firing." He stood between them, ensuring their safety as well as watching their shots.

Bang. Larry fired first. Sand waved up at them from behind the bodies in a shameful hello. *Not comforting.* Bang. More sand sprang up. Bang. The infected man's shoulder twitched. A leg wiggled. A few bodies jerked, but mostly the sand took the brunt of the punishment.

Margie knelt, still holding her gun. Her eyes were drawn down to it. She was mesmerized by it. Steele stood near her, shadowing her with his frame.

"Margie, you may fire your weapon," he said, loud enough to make sure she heard him clearly.

She jerked as if she had been shot. Her eyes drifted up to him and her shoulders slumped. Her crow's-feet deepened on her face in a grimace that settled into a sad smile.

He tilted his head at the bodies in the sand. "Margie, you may fire."

She sighed as if his persistence had finally broken her down and hefted the weapon near her shoulder.

"Hold it tighter. Now, keep your sight picture level." He held out his hand in a level straight line. "Put it right on that ugly SOB's head and gently pull the trigger."

She let the gun sights lower a bit. "I don't know."

"You wanted to be here. Protect your family and friends. Pick the sights up and fire your weapon."

She gave him a terse nod and hammered on the trigger. The shot went wide, sending sand in the air.

"Treat the trigger like a handshake with an old friend. Firm but gentle. No tension in your firing hand," he said. He stepped down the line providing Larry with instruction before they switched shooters.

***

Three hours later, he could see their patience waning and fatigue setting in.

"Okay, Gregor. Hold." The large long-haired man let his gun drop. The big welder gave off the impression he could play a bad guy in a horror film, but in actuality, was a gentle soul.

"Who's the best shot out here today?" All eyes ran to Margie. Steele was only a little surprised. After she had gotten over her fear of the weapon, she picked up its usage with some easy instruction.

"Now, Margie. Do what you've been doing all day." She gave him a half-smile and held the .22 to her shoulder. *A few hours ago you were afraid; now you stand with some confidence.*

"Nice and easy now. Slow is smooth," he whispered behind her. Seconds ticked by as she zeroed in on her shot. Long moments later, the gun's barrel exploded. The closest infected's head smacked against the stake, a dime-sized hole appearing in its forehead.

"That's a direct hit," Steele exclaimed. She lowered the .22, looking down at the body in satisfaction. "Everybody give Margie a round of applause." The volunteers clapped for a few seconds for her. She smiled over her shoulder at him. "Again," he commanded, his voice stern. She took aim, slowly depressing the trigger. Boom. The infected's head lolled to the other side. A red hole appeared through its cheek.

Her brown eyes darted to him for approval.

"Again," he commanded, neither giving her a smile or any praise. She lined up her sights, taking her time.

Steele leaned close to her gray-streaked hair. "Again," he yelled in her ear. Fearful eyes darted back at him, nervousness dancing across her. "Why are you looking at me? Shoot the damn infected," he yelled. He thrust his arm outward pointing a finger.

Resting her cheek on the stock, she lined up her sights. Her right eye squinted.

"I said again, volunteer." His words seemed to whip her, but he continued on anyway. "In the time you took to line up your shots, they've butchered Larry because he couldn't hit a fucking thing." He gave Larry a sidelong glance. Larry's eyes blinked with shame. He went back to Margie to break her down. "And now they're coming for you. I said fire again."

The gun shook in her hands.

"I said fire, goddamnit. They're in your house murdering Brian. Save your husband. Shoot."

She jerked the trigger and the shot went wide, spraying beach sand in the air. She laid the weapon on the ground, looking abashed as color rose in her cheeks.

He clenched his jaw. "Why are you looking at me? Why did you drop your weapon? Are you a hand-to-hand combat expert? Can you wield a knife like a Kali master? They are going to kill you. Keep shooting. Keep shooting!" he screamed, in his best drill instructor voice.

She hesitantly picked up the gun and fired. Her shots went wide, high, and short. A few hit the bodies. Her magazine went dry. She looked at him from the corner of her eye, awaiting his reprimand.

He put a hand on her back. She flinched under his touch. "To have died once is enough. Make sure your weapon is safe."

She slid the bolt backward and inspected the extraction port. He looked over her shoulder. "The weapon is safe. You may return to the line." She hurriedly joined the other volunteers.

Steele paced in front of them. He spoke in a calm voice. "I need you to be able to do that under pressure." Margie nodded her head and gave a short smile.

He addressed everyone. "That was only a taste of stress inoculation training. We must be able to fire under pressure. Your mechanics aren't bad, but you all need work. Same time tomorrow. Unfortunately, we don't have enough ammo to do this every day. So tomorrow is dry fire practice and tactical movement drills." They all nodded and climbed back down from the trailer, walking back to their abodes. Steele watched them walk away. Alex and Jason talked excitedly to one another. *Can they handle this?*

He was tired from the instruction. Shouldering the sling of his M4, he went back to his tent.

Gwen looked up when he unzipped the front flap. He plopped down next to her with a grunt, his body finally allowed to rest. She watched him for a moment. "How'd they do?" she asked.

He set his M4 near the side of his sleeping bag, its barrel pointed toward the door, and laid back.

"There's always tomorrow."

TESS

Little Sable Point, MI

Yells broke her sleep in the night like twigs snapping beneath the heavy tread of a combat boot. She sat up in her futon bed, reaching for Pagan's side. A handful of blanket made her painfully aware that she was alone. His corner of the bed was a mess of blankets as if she had created a blanket Pagan to hold in the night. She kicked her feet free of them and threw on her harness, the weight of the 1911 weighing on her shoulders.

Draping her silk robe over her naked shoulders, she shoved open the door to her camper. She hopped out into the darkness. The voices sounded off, trapped inside the ring of vehicles. Steele's angry voice joined the fray, making her run faster. Her robe flapped around her as she raced past the lighthouse for the vehicle-made entrance of Little Sable Point.

As she grew closer to the shouting, Steele stood out in his blue boxer briefs, pointing his M4 at a man in a pickup. Jack sat behind the wheel of his pickup, hands in the air. His wife, Julie, cried in the passenger side, holding their youngest in her arms. In the backseat, their oldest bawled.

Julie looked out her window and saw Tess coming. "Please, Tess. You promised," she cried. She held her child's crying face to her chest.

"What's going on? What are you doing?" she asked. Jack was one of the few who didn't seem enthusiastic about Steele's new job title. She had taken note when she announced she was bringing him into the fold. His departure didn't surprise her. Steele's actions did.

Steele spoke out without looking at her. His eyes never left Jack. "The Red Stripes caught Jack trying to steal from us and then leave in the cover of darkness."

Jack shook his head no. "It's a lie." He pointed at Tess. "You said we could leave anytime we wanted. It was one of your guarantees. Tell your fascist lapdog to stop pointing his gun at my family." *This shady bastard is right.*

She looked over the roof of the pickup at Steele. "He's right, Steele. We agreed that people can come and go as they see fit."

Steele sidestepped to his left so he had a better angle to see her while keeping an eye on Jack.

"We never agreed people could rob us. Let me search his car. Anything that's ours stays and then he can go," he said.

People emerged from their shelters like curious lemurs, and a crowd was starting to gather to get a view of the dispute.

"Jack has been here for a long time. He wouldn't rob us," Tess said. Her next words were directed at Jack. "Why are you leaving now?"

"I think his actions speak for themselves. There's a group out there that is safer than here. Why wouldn't we all go?" Jack said.

"Because they're crazy. They're holding Pagan hostage for Christ's sake."

Jack faced her with a side glance at Steele. "In a few weeks, we could have snow on the ground. They got a real roof over their head, food, and power. How crazy can they be? You ever think that maybe we're the crazy ones out here, slumming it in the shadow of an antique lighthouse?"

"No one said you had to stay."

"Then let me and my family go," Jack hissed, his lip curling.

More people were showing up, including some of Steele's volunteers. Steele leaned, looking into the backseat of the pickup. He closed in on the driver's side door. One hand on his weapon and the other on the door handle, he yanked the door open. He forced Jack from the car amidst the screams of his children. Pushing Jack's hands on the back of the truck bed, he searched his pockets.

"My gun's wedged between the console and the seat," Jack said.

Steele called over to Trent. "Check it." The hunter dug into the driver's seat removing a Glock 22 from the car.

Steele turned back to Jack. "You got anything in your pockets?" he asked. He frisked Jack from his waistband to his pockets and then Jack's pockets all the way down to his boots.

Tess circled the vehicle. Black plastic bags sat in the pickup truck bed. She inched one open with the muzzle of her .45 1911. A can clanked to the truck bed and rolled end over end away from her all the way to the tailgate.

"That's my food," Jack said to her. His eyes were angry and dark in the night.

"All of it?" she asked. He had three large trash bags filled with canned goods.

"Where did you get all of this?"

"Tess, it was selfish, but I had to keep some stockpiled in case we had to get out of here. And now that you've handed the camp over to Mr. Gestapo, I'm leaving." Steele had finished searching the man and picked up one of the bags.

"This is a lot of food. Our camp could use it."

Steele's eyes met Tess's. She shook her head no. She could read his mind. He would take Jack's food and leave him hungry to feed the group for another week. Sacrifice the small for the group's greater good.

"Steele. You said you would hold to the rules. No one is a hostage here. They're free to go."

He set the bag back in the bed of Jack's truck. His brow crisscrossed in fury.

"You're right. But when we run low on food because this selfish bastard has been thieving, you can be the one to look the kids in the eyes and tell them to stop crying." His words stung her like barbed arrows. But he had made a promise.

"We will find a way. We always do." Her words felt as hollow as an empty theater.

"Sure you will, sweetheart." Jack sneered. "You hear me, Little Sable. This place is going to burn. And your two fearless leaders here are to blame. Do yourself a favor and leave as soon as you can," Jack yelled out to all the people.

Steele glared at the man. Tess thought he was going to pull the trigger on him. "Get out of here," he growled.

Jack hopped into the driver's seat. "My gun?" Jack asked, holding out an arm.

Trent stepped up, handing it to Steele. Steele looked at the gun for a moment and then held it at his side, glaring at Jack. He dropped the magazine and racked the slide back, catching the round. He placed the pieces back into Jack's hand. His eyes flashed into the backseat. "If you didn't have the kids, you wouldn't be getting this back."

Jack snatched the pieces away and shoved it in the seat.

Steele waved his arm at the Red Stripes to pull back the pickups blocking the entrance. The trucks rolled back, and Jack gunned it through the opening, spinning his tires in an effort to escape.

They all stood watching the red taillights of his pickup grow smaller and smaller and finally disappear into the forest.

"We should have stopped him from leaving," Steele said.

"It's not our right to prevent him from going."

"Maybe it should have been. What if he tells them where we are? Now, I don't have the element of surprise if we are going to rescue Pagan. What if he leads them here? We have a motorcycle gang who is here on charity and a ten-person neighborhood watch who can't handle a gun without shooting themselves in the foot."

"Hey now," Trent said.

Steele glanced back at the deer hunter. "No offense."

We cannot compromise the integrity of this place. I won't. "If we don't adhere to the things that make this place unique, then we are no better than those people out there."

Steele took a hand and rubbed his forehead. "I know what I promised." He looked at the ground. "We're vulnerable. Our position is weak and we are entirely dependent on the Red Stripes."

She glanced over at Half-Barrel and Bedford. They smoked cigarettes, leaning on a pickup blocking the entrance.

The coolness of the night made her pull her robe tighter around her body.

"I know," she whispered. His body shivered a bit, but she could tell he was trying to hide it.

"Shit, it's cold," he said. He wrapped an arm around his torso.

She gave him a little smile. "Say, you want to come back for a nightcap? Warm up a bit. Pagan's got a half-gallon of Lord Calvert sitting in the camper."

He scratched his head, looking back toward his tent.

"Isn't it bad luck to drink another man's liquor while he's being held hostage?"

"Old wives' tale." She watched him squirm a bit under her gaze.

His tone grew strict. "I'm only going to do one. I've got another long day of 'don't shoot yourself' tomorrow with the volunteers."

They walked back to her camper and she flicked on an electric lantern. She set it on the camper table. A dim glow filled the musty inside.

"Don't look," she commanded over her shoulder.

"What?" he said.

She let her thin black robe drop to the ground and removed her gun harness. Her body was bare aside from her thong. It sounded like someone had choked the words from his mouth. She could feel his eyes on her flesh. Grabbing a sweatshirt from a pile in the corner, she threw it on. Turning, she caught his eye. Hairy chested, big bearded, he stood there in his boxer briefs, nearly naked as well. His eyes were large and he looked like he was trying not to stare at her legs.

"I'm a terrible host. Grab a blanket or something." She waved a finger to a cupboard on the wall. *But I wouldn't mind if you stayed that way.* "Unless you wanted to stay warm the old-fashioned way?" She smirked at him.

His eyes ran down to her lips and she full-on smiled. "I'll take a blanket," he gargled out after a moment. He went into a cupboard, using it to block his view of her. He found one and wrapped it around his shoulders.

She snatched a blanket off her bed and covered herself with it. "Don't get your panties in a bunch. I covered up."

He closed the cupboard slowly.

Opening up her futon bed, she pulled out the half gallon bottle of whiskey and snagged a couple of shot glasses from the table. Clanking them upright, she poured the honey-colored booze into the glasses. She held one out and he took it from her. He eyed the alcohol with a small smile under his beard.

"Been awhile since I had some of this," he said with a smile. He hefted the alcohol to his lips.

"Wait," she commanded, and his hand stayed hovering near his lips. "You can't crush the shot without saying cheers to something."

"Haha. Forgive me," he said with a slight turn of his head.

"To Little Sable Point. May it be a beacon of light for those in need."

"To Little Sable Point. May it be strong enough to weather the storm," he added, throwing his head back and downing his shot. "Woo, that'll wake you up in the morning." He shook his head out.

She smiled at him, her eyes filling with mirth. "How about another?"

"How about it," he said with a smile.

JOSEPH

Cheyenne Mountain Complex, CO

Joseph rubbed his eyes beneath his glasses. His mind was foggy and his body weary. He had spent two days with Rebecca trying to pour over the samples from Patient Zero, countless infected, and his samples from Africa, all having been digitalized for mass research.

He hadn't left her side in over twenty-four hours. A ball of tension and tired muscle had formed in the base of his neck from hunching over his laptop. The spot right below where the cranium connects with the spinal column. The spot that one could take out to stop the infected permanently.

Rebecca drifted in and out of sleep. He felt guilty picking her brain when she was awake, knowing that she needed her strength to fight her losing battle against the pathogen.

It broke his heart to have a front row seat as she degraded. She struggled to stay awake and help him, and she grew weaker by the hour. Pockmarks had appeared and begun to polka-dot her face like severe acne. They were eraser-sized bumps underneath her skin. Some of her lymph nodes had enlarged to the size of cherries, pushing out from beneath her skin. The swelling was due to the monkeypox virus, the gateway virus for their mystery satellite virus.

New data popped up on the shared server from Byrnes's experiments on Patient Zero. Joseph double-clicked the file, a yellow folder that read "Liver Samples." Joseph skipped through dozens of videos of the virus as it infected live cells.

Like a doorway, the monkeypox would latch onto the clean cell using tentacle-like receptors to hook in. A hose-like apparatus would punch into the host cell and the transfer of DNA would begin. It was a disgustingly simple process and fast.

The injection took place and the virus shot its genetic material inside the host cell. The monkeypox virus moved its own genetic material inside. Close behind it, the satellite cell tailed behind like a little brother into the host cell. The monkeypox virus would disengage and float to its next cellular victim. Later, the satellite dealt out its own version of viral reprogramming of the host virus and host cell.

He scrolled down to another video. *There has to be a way to work through this.* He covered his mouth over his surgical mask as he yawned.

Rebecca coughed herself awake. "Hi, Joseph," she said through her mask. A fleck of blood dotted her surgical mask. *The virus is in her lungs*, he thought. He inched backward in his chair.

"There's something I want to show you," she said. Her voice sounded raw as if she had been out all night at a concert. "I saw it the other day but couldn't wrap my mind around it."

"What's that?" he asked, setting down his laptop. She grabbed her tablet from the side table. He moved closer to her and tried to ignore the blood on her mask. She swiped on her tablet, searching for an image.

"Look here." She flipped her tablet around his way. Joseph studied the image for a moment. The patient's name read Weinroth along the top.

"This is your blood work," he mumbled. *Eventually, she will be just that. A data file.* He gulped down his sadness.

Her lighter brown eyes watched him. "Yes, it is. Now watch." She clicked a sideways triangle on the screen and the video began.

A monkeypox viral cell attached to a healthy cell as he had seen before. Satellite virus tagged along and injected itself into the cell.

"It's as we've seen before. The healthy cell has the satellite DNA inside it along with monkeypox." She dragged her finger along the bottom, fast-forwarding the video.

"But what about there?" The cell moved to the bottom of the blood vessel and lay still.

"The cell is lysogenic, in its dormant phase. That's the virus taking over," Joseph said.

"But is it?"

Joseph stared at the video. The cell lay dormant as if it hibernated at the bottom of a blood vessel. She dragged her finger along the time bar. The video skipped hours.

"Here," she said. "Now watch." The still cell twitched and began to move. It caught another cell on the way by and the satellite virus injected its DNA into it.

"Wait. It has a new receptor?" he asked.

"Yes, but continue watching," she said.

The newly infected cell floated away and seemingly went dormant until it too rose up again to propagate itself onward.

"We all know that a virus needs a live cell to propagate itself. The only possible explanation is that the cell becomes dormant while the virus changes the DNA within the cell." His head felt like it weighed thirty pounds and his neck could only support a paltry seven.

"And people are supposed to stay dead when they die," she finished. He stared at her.

He blinked, trying to focus on what she was saying. "What are you trying to say?"

She swiped to another video. "Look at this sample from an infected person who had already expired."

Cells danced inside the veins. A pile of cells twitched and quivered. The cells swam inside, latching onto any cell not infected.

"This subject is dead?" He rubbed his neck now, trying to work out the knot that formed at its base.

"Yes. It was taken from a man outside Atlanta who had been dead for four days."

"Theoretically, this is not possible. It's not possible that his cells are still operating after four days." His mind raced as he tried to comprehend the information. He knew the host died after infection. He knew the dead still operated physically after death. He knew the satellite virus was to blame.

"Yes, Joseph. Four days is a long time, but theoretically, it's not possible for those cells to behave in that fashion after so long. But. Let me go out on a long limb here. What if the cell had to be dead for the virus to take over?"

Joseph squeezed his eyes shut. "No, no. Every study known to man states the same thing: a virus needs a live cell to spread."

She coughed again and closed her eyes in pain. Her forehead squeezed and lines creased it. She laid there in obvious pain. His heart leapt for her in his chest. *There has to be something I can do.*

"Entertain the thought, Joseph. This is a game changer. Something that has turned the world upside down. The dead have risen. It's unbelievable enough in itself. We have to entertain the idea that this virus operates outside the normal conventions of virology," she whispered, her voice raspy.

Joseph stared at the video. He whispered it to himself out loud. "What if the virus required the host cell to be dead? What if it was hiding in the monkeypox infected cells, waiting for the host cells to die to activate itself?" He ran a hand through his hair. "It explains the speed at which the virus has mutated. Going from days for the patient to die, to minutes, to seconds. It initially needed the monkeypox, but now, as more and more people die, it only needs itself to propagate itself." He glanced up at her over the tablet.

"It also explains why the dead rise up. The virus is controlling them at a cellular level but needs the infected dead to do so," she said softly.

"Dear God," he whispered. His hand covered his masked mouth.

She looked like she wanted to cry. "I know."

He felt dizzy like he couldn't get enough oxygen. "This is an extinction event. Dinosaur killer. The epoch ends here. We aren't biologically equipped to fight this off. The body won't recognize the dead cells as a threat. It allows the virus free reign, unhindered by the body's defenses."

"If we can develop a vaccine, we at least have a fighting chance," she whispered.

"How? We are dealing with something that has turned our understanding of science on its head. How do I make a vaccine for something that doesn't follow the rules?" Joseph said. He put his head in his hands. "We are all going to die."

She coughed. It sounded like fluid was building up in her lungs. "You are going to stop this," she said.

He shook his head in dismay. "Rebecca, you are dying of a disease I can't fix. In a few days, you'll be dead and I will be alone in this fight. I can't possibly do this by myself."

Tears formed at the corners of her eyes. "I know that, Joseph, but who are you if you don't try?"

"I'm a nobody who failed the world when it needed him the most."

Her hand reached for his and she squeezed it tight. Her hand was cool on his. "You don't have a choice. Find it in yourself to do this. You have what it takes. Now go do it."

He bit his lip. He stretched his neck. The knot was still in place, making the rest of his back hurt down through his shoulder blades.

"Rebecca, please don't patronize me."

"I believe in you." Her eyes crinkled as she smiled.

I wish I did. He gave her a determined gaze.

"I'll need your help because you know Byrnes won't help me."

"I know he won't. He used to be such a different man, difficult but in an ingenious kind of way," she trailed off thinking about the past, her life now only judged by days and hours.

"Where do we start?" Joseph said. A clock ticked in the back of his mind.

"I've got an idea." She held up her tablet. "Take a look here."

Joseph couldn't hold himself back. "Rebecca," was all he could utter. Her eyes darted from the tablet back to him. His mouth dropped open a little as he grappled with the words to say to her. "I. Never mind."

She looked away, uncomfortable, but her sad eyes drifted back to him. Her eyes saddened.

"I know, Joseph. I felt it too. But we can't think like this. Soon I'll be gone."

Joseph's head wavered. "I know." He wiped a tear from the corner of his eye. His mouth formed a sad smile. "We make a good team, you know." He sniffled.

"Yes, Joseph. We do." She paused a moment, her eyes blinking rapidly as they whispered a life that they would never have together. A flash of a future that would never exist in this world. An echo of unspoken love. "Back to the data," she said, looking back down at the tablet.

He watched her as she scrolled through. *If only we had more time together.*

They worked for hours until Rebecca fell asleep. Rubbing his eyes, Joseph stood. Her skin was pale. The pockmarks poked out all over her face and arms, and her hair was a sweet sugarplum auburn.

He bent down close and let his covered lips graze her forehead.

"I'll see you soon," he whispered and silently closed the door behind him.

GWEN

Little Sable Point, Michigan

She awoke with the sun illuminating the blue nylon top of her tent. Stretching her arms above her head, she rolled over, staring at the ceiling, not remembering a recent time she had slept that well. The sunlight filtered through the nylon, softening the color to an almost baby blue. The sandy ground beneath her tent had formed a mold to her body from where she had laid all night. *I'm not even feeling nauseous this morning.*

Not bothering to turn his way, her hand felt for Mark, patting his side of the tent. She expected a broad hairy shoulder, but instead, a cool sleeping bag met her fingertips. She glanced over. Picking up his sleeping bag, she flung it open, revealing no Mark Steele underneath.

"Mark?" she said softly. But he wasn't there to respond. *Last thing I remember are people yelling and him leaving, but I just couldn't stay awake.* Fear stabbed her gut. *What if he was hurt? Or needed my help? And my pregnant ass just fell asleep in the tent.*

She grabbed her camouflage pants and slipped them over her legs. She wrapped the jacket around her torso. It was loose and baggy at best. Good for covering up her pregnancy and not the least bit flattering. She tied up her hair in a ponytail and went outside. The morning was brisk with a wind blowing off the beach. It sent a low whistle around the vehicles parked in a circle like covered wagons. She casually slung her M4 over her shoulder. The tall and slender lighthouse, built with reddish-brown bricks, loomed over them all. Its lantern room was capped with a black top.

A few people stoked campfires near their respective vehicles. She walked past a couple of kids that played in the sand under the watchful guise of their father. She gave him a smile as she walked by. His gaze was openly hostile.

"Why don't you go play inside," he yelled at the children.

"Ah, come on, Dad," squeaked a little girl.

"Yeah, why, Dad?"

"Just do as you're told," he said. The kids ran for their camper. He patted their heads on the way by as a form of encouragement for obeying. Gwen kept walking under the father's mistrusting gaze. *He couldn't possibly think that I would pose a threat to his kids. Impossible. I love children. Hell, I am pregnant with one. And I lost a kid which was apparently not real and now everyone thinks I'm a loon. But it was real. I saw the child. I heard him laugh.*

She walked past Dr. Thatcher's camper. He wasn't outside, but she thought she saw his blinds move as she passed. *Now the poor child is probably in some infected's belly because I couldn't save him. Or I'm actually crazy.*

Ahead she saw them. They moved as if they were trying to move in sync but could only manage a off-beat effort. Mark was in the center calling out orders.

"Margie, quit crossing forward. Your responsibility is the left side. Don't look back at me. Look outward left." The small circle of people continued their haphazard progress.

Mark looked back behind him. The volunteer pointed a gun into Mark's back. "Steve, why are you flagging me? You need to be looking backward at least a part of the time. You're covering our six."

The man stopped. "What do you mean? I thought I had the right," Steve said.

Mark held up a fist. Half the group kept going; the other half ran into him. If he wasn't so serious, she would have laughed at them.

"Everyone bring it in." The rest of the group fell in around him. He saw her and made eye contact.

"Okay. That was rough. We're going to keep working on tactical movement later, but in the meantime, meet with Thunder and go over some dry firing. We will get back up this afternoon to go over room stacking."

A mishmash of wannabe warriors, they trailed off talking to one another. A mop of waist-high blond hair ran along their side. *Was that the boy among them?* She stood on her tiptoes trying to see into the group, looking for the little blond haired boy.

"Hey, babe," he said, approaching her. "You see something?" he asked, turning sideways to look at his retreating volunteers.

The people moved on and she lost sight of anything resembling the marching phantom child.

"Uh, no. Just looking for you."

He ran a finger over his scar and winced, rubbing the edge of it with his fingertip as though it caused him to have a headache.

"Yeah, I, uh," he said, wafting a fiery breath of booze on her. His eyes were bloodshot, and he looked more disheveled than normal.

"Oh my God, Mark. You reek like booze. What happened last night?"

He avoided her eyes, still rubbing his scar.

"We had a few drinks after we let Jack and his family go."

"Why did he leave?"

"I'm not sure. Apparently, he thinks he's better off somewhere else since my appearance. I wanted to commandeer his food but thought better of it."

"Did you and the volunteers have drinks?"

"I'm pretty hungover. Can we talk about this later?" he pleaded, his eyes guilty.

Her eyes narrowed, gleaning the truth from him every moment. "Who did you drink with?" she said. *It better not be that skinny little thing.*

"Gwen, I had a few drinks with Tess. We were really stressed out from the altercation with Jack and needed to blow off some steam. You know?" His eyes begged to be believed.

Oh really.

"No, I don't know. I can presume that's where you slept last night from your generally hungover appearance."

"I passed out in the camper. Nothing happened. She's like one of the guys. You know, no big deal," he said. He put a hand on his head. "My head. I would kill for some ibuprofen right now."

She slapped his arm. "Serves you right. What do you mean nothing happened?" She made sure to not allow him any kind of response. "Nothing happened? Are you an idiot? You slept over in another woman's house."

"Camper."

"Whatever! After a night of drinking, and you think it's no big deal?" she yelled at him.

"It's not like that," he pleaded.

Her anger boiled inside of her. *How dare he do this to me? Especially after he got me pregnant, he went out on the town with some cupcake, having drinks like it's fucking New Year's Eve.*

"That's no way for a father to behave. You have responsibilities," she shouted. Her jaw dropped after she said it. She hadn't meant to tell him this way. She hadn't meant for any of this. It dribbled on out, and now it sat there like a twenty-ton elephant in the room.

He stopped rubbing his scar. His hand fell to his side. "Excuse me. What did you say?" he said, his eyes growing wide. Her mouth clamped closed as if she were forbidding herself to say it again.

"What did you say?" he prodded.

She looked away from him. "I. Said. You are going to be a *father*. So you better start acting like one."

His hand ran over the top of his skull repeatedly then moved down to his mustache as he smoothed that down with his fingers.

"Since when? The pills didn't work?" he asked.

She could feel the fire in her cheeks. "Excuse me?"

He gulped, the fear only a woman's anger could bring appearing in his eyes. "I don't understand."

"You're an idiot. Do I have to spell this out for you? I didn't take the pills because I was already pregnant."

"How do you know?" he said, a dumb expression on his face. He blinked repeatedly.

"You are dense, aren't you?" she said. She crossed her arms over her breasts and winced. *Tender ladies.* "I took the test over a week ago. I took the test three or four times to be sure." Her eyes darted up to his to see if his reaction was legitimate or if he was trying to fake some sort of emotion.

His mouth turned into a smile. "Oh my God." His eyes grew distant. "We're going to be parents." He blinked rapidly. "I'm going to be a father. Oh, my God, I'm going to be a dad," he said louder and louder. He turned away from her and called over to Half-Barrel, who was sitting guard at the entrance.

"Half-Barrel, I'm gonna be a dad!" he shouted. The man made of kegs gave him a thumbs up.

"Good stuff," his gruff voice shouted in return.

He looked back at her, grabbing her by her shoulders.

"We are going to be parents," he shouted in her ears, as he yanked her into the air, twirling her around.

He set her down laughing. Then his laughter died in his throat. He looked past her. "Oh my God. We're going to be parents in this mess."

"I know," she sniffled. She rested her arms over her stomach. "Don't you see why I've been so upset? How can we bring a child into this? A ring of cars is the only thing between us and being eaten alive. We don't have food. Most of these vehicles don't have enough fuel to leave. We don't even know where your mother is." She looked at him. *What do I expect for a friggin' answer?*

His features settled in worry and he gripped her by the arms. "We will make do and I will find her."

She looked away. "I'm scared. There are no doctors. No help. And the infected are all over."

He leaned in close, putting a finger gently underneath her chin so she could see him. His blond-bearded face loomed near hers. His ocean storm blue eyes held every word true. "I promise you; nothing will happen to you or our baby. We will make this work."

She met his eyes and nodded her head.

He wrapped his arms around her and squeezed tight. That's when her tears started to flow. Tears she didn't think she had in her anymore. She didn't want them to, but they did. She promised herself she wouldn't cry for this world, but how could she not cry for her unborn baby? *Damn hormones.*

"Don't squeeze too much. Today is the first day in a long time I haven't felt sick, so let's try and keep it that way." She let her emotions calm.

"I don't want to hurt the baby." He bent down close to her stomach, his hands hovering over her non-existent belly.

His hands ran over her and he stopped them over her navel. He waited a moment, smiling. "I can't feel anything." He grew worried and looked at her. "Is that bad?"

She placed his hands inside hers. "That's cause it's only the size of a cherry right now."

He laughed and smiled at her, moving his hand across her stomach. "Wait, what was that?"

She swatted at him. "That was my stomach, dummy."

"You sure? Felt something there."

She pulled away from him with an amused dirty look. Then she remembered what prompted this conversation. "You promise me nothing happened between you and that woman?"

"Gwen, please. Nothing happened. We had a few drinks. She and I are a team." She held her head back, judging his truthfulness. His face looked innocent and she knew he didn't have the wherewithal to lie to her that well.

"I believe you," she said, burying herself in his chest. His warmth and body made her feel secure. A rock that she knew would be there for her, and now, her child as well.

"Steele," shouted a man from across the way. The shouting ruptured their moment. Mark tensed as if he were about to fight. His arms went tight around her as if he feared he may never hold her again.

"Right here," he called back. The words echoed in his chest. Bedford came running up, his black leather MC vest blowing out as he ran. The short gray-haired man stopped. Mark kept her close to his body but loosened his grip.

"I'm going to be a dad," Mark said to him, but his smile faded as he saw the look on Bedford's face.

"That's great, man, but we have a problem," he said. Bedford nodded a black and gray goatee to her. "Congrats, ma'am," he said in hurried respect.

"Thanks," Gwen said. She held Mark's waist with both her arms.

"Thunder can't handle it? I need some time alone with Gwen. We're going to have a baby!" Mark exclaimed.

Bedford shook his head vigorously. "Nah. He wants you there."

"Come on. It can't be that bad?"

Bedford leaned in closer and whispered. "Armed men are at the gate, and they are asking for you by name."

Mark exhaled loudly. "Damn." He stared at the ground for a second. "I'm sorry, babe. We'll celebrate later. Can you get Ahmed to the lighthouse? I don't know who the fuck is up there, but they should have warned us. Send Kevin to me."

She nodded. "I will." Turning to leave, he stopped her and laid an alcohol-tinged kiss right on her lips.

"Love you." He grinned and took off with Bedford.

"You need to brush your teeth, and I love you too," she yelled after him. She ran for the tents.

"Ahmed. Kevin," she shouted. Ahmed was out of the tent in seconds, gun in hand. Kevin was a few seconds behind him.

"What's up?" Ahmed asked. He scratched his fuzzy-haired skull, scanning the ring of cars.

"Men have come to the camp. Mark wants you in the lighthouse to cover him." Kevin's features relaxed, relieved to not have been the one selected to run up dozens of stairs to the top.

"Kevin, come with me to the gate," she said. She moved fast over the enclosure for the entrance. The tall man jogged to keep up.

She looked up at him. "I told him."

Kevin smiled back at her. "He was happy, wasn't he?"

"Yes, but," she stopped herself.

"But what?" he asked as they ran.

"Nothing." *But what if I am not ready for this?*

STEELE

Little Sable Point, MI

Members of the leather-clad Red Stripes lined the backs of the pickups that sealed off the de facto entrance of Little Sable Point to the rest of the world. Interspersed among them were Steele's Little Sable volunteers. Margie knelt next to orange-headed Max, who looked like he had already peed his pants. Bald Larry and fat Hank were down the line. Trent's eye was behind his scope, mossy oak camouflage ball cap on his skull, and Old Bengy used a tailgate to line up his shot with his M1 Garand. *Would they even fight if it came to it?* Steele pushed the thought from his mind. *I may have to do all the shooting.*

Thunder crouched low, his gut hanging between his legs, walking behind them, trying to keep his girth from being exposed to potential gunfire.

Steele ran bent at the waist and took cover behind the engine block of a white pickup truck next to Thunder. *Engine blocks and wheel wells would stop most rounds. Most rounds.*

The heavyset gray-bearded man struggled to kneel on his left leg. When he finally got himself lowered to the ground, he grimaced at Steele. "Don't bend like they used to."

"I know what you mean," Steele said. He had suffered his fair share of injury in his lifetime. Between high-school and college sports to training injuries he had received while with the Division, he was no novice to parts of his body not functioning like they used to. Even when injuries to your knees, shoulders, or back healed, they were a little less functional than they used to be, and it took a little bit longer to recover each time.

Thunder laughed. "You better enjoy it while you got it because before you know it, you're old and fat like me."

Steele smiled. "I'll remember that. What we got?" Steele whispered. He didn't know why he was whispering. The outsiders would never hear them.

"Looks like two trucks, about eight or nine men. There are two in the beds of each truck with high-powered rifles pointed our way."

Steele flexed his scar-tissued scalp. "You think they know how to use them?"

The older man glanced behind him. "Wouldn't want to risk it. Even pieces of shit get lucky sometimes."

"I'd prefer not taking another shot to the head either." He gave Thunder a smile while his gut churned at the nauseating thought.

Steele nodded to Trent. "You wanna get up in the lighthouse with Ahmed. I want you focused on the guys in the pickup truck beds. They're the biggest threat."

Trent nodded. "That won't be a problem." He hustled away with a bend in his back and a deer hunting rifle in one hand.

"Mark Steele," came a shout from the other side.

Steele looked up at the lighthouse, giving Trent a minute to join Ahmed at the top. *They better be in place or I may as well be naked out there.*

"Mark Steele," boomed the voice again. Steele ignored the man, letting him holler longer.

He tried to see Trent above but had no vantage. His gut feeling told him that they were ready though. He looked down the line. His volunteers that could hardly hit an unmoving target hid crouched down, an assortment of guns pointed outward. *Trust. Can you trust the greenest of the green?*

Steele grabbed Thunder's shoulder, getting close to the big biker.

"If this doesn't go right, make sure to put them all down. No one can escape."

Thunder's eyes sparkled beneath his red bandana and bushy gray eyebrows. "Won't be a problem. If they run, we'll mount up and ride them down."

Steele nodded. "Oh, and did I tell you? I'm going to be a dad." Before Thunder could respond, Steele rose up, slinging his carbine downward before standing fully upright.

On the sand swept sidewalk that led to the lighthouse stood a man about thirty yards from where Steele stood. From a distance, he appeared to be Steele's beefier cousin with one distinction: he had curly hair. This man had the same darkish blond hair, brownish-blond beard, large frame, and a strong stance. He looked about the same age as Steele.

For a moment, Steele thought he recognized the man. *Where do I know you? Not from home. Not from town.* His mind zipped over how he might know people still in Michigan after he hadn't lived there for years. *High-school football?* He vaguely remembered going toe to toe with a vicious offensive guard twelve years back in the state finals of the high-school football championship. The opposing team had been full of Dutch giants. Their names were too long for the backs of their jerseys, and they were tough as nails.

"I'm Steele," he said loud enough for the man to hear.

"I'm Peter," the man shouted. "We can meet in the middle. All the shouting gets on my nerves."

Steele looked down at Thunder. The older man nodded. "Make sure none of our shooters hit me if things go south."

Thunder snorted. "Why ask me to do the impossible?"

Steele hopped the hood of the pickup, sliding across and landing on his feet. He trekked downrange feeling that someone, anyone, was going to put a bullet in his front or back or both. It was as if he walked into a two-sided firing range and all sights were on him.

The two men closed in on one another like they were about to drawdown in a Old West gunfight at high noon. They stopped, giving each other a good five yards. *Definitely could be my cousin. I'm going to feel bad if I have to kill him. If things get dicey, I'll quick draw the Beretta and fire from the hip. Three rounds to the chest and I'll rush him. Get in close and use his body as cover. I'll take him to the ground and hope that nobody from his side can shoot worth a damn.*

Peter wore dirty jeans, tan boots, and a heavy navy-colored fleece that was probably hiding even more size underneath. His eyes weighed Steele up and down. Steele hadn't had time to throw on his vest and felt bare without his other gear. He let his M4 lay across his chest diagonally with his hand resting on the stock and his index finger laying flat above the trigger.

Peter's features were calm or perhaps unimpressed by the man before him. He looked as if he had already known everything about Steele down to the scar on his head. Scoped rifles pointed in their direction from the beds of the pickups. Men knelt on the ground next to open doors, using them as concealment.

"You Mark Steele?" Peter kept his chin upright as if he held some sort of high rank. Taking the initiative in a negotiation had its advantages and disadvantages. Steele was learning what type of man Peter was as he spoke. Steele tilted his head, half-considering the people behind him.

"Some call me that."

Peter's brow creased a bit. "I came here to speak with this man. So if you aren't him, I'd prefer not to waste my time," Peter said, looking at the encampment over Steele's shoulder.

"You can speak to me," Steele said with a nod.

"So this is it? We've been looking for you, but now that we've found you, I'll say I expected more."

Steele was silent, not taking the bait for conflict.

Peter eyed him for a moment. "I come on the behalf of the pastor, the blessed leader of the Chosen people. He wishes to meet with you and discuss terms for our communities." *The pastor is the leader of the Chosen.*

"This pastor guy, why didn't he come himself? We could have made our *terms* here and now."

Peter didn't hesitate. "The pastor will have you meet him on his terms." *A command?*

"Why should I?" Steele said. He knew why, but he wanted the man to spell it out.

"We have a man that belongs to your group. He goes by the name Pagan." Peter's face twisted with the word Pagan as if it soured in his mouth as he said it. "He's our hostage to ensure you act in good faith."

Steele adjusted his weight through his legs. The act of setting himself up nonchalantly for a strike gave him confidence. He knew Peter had the edge. It was time to chip away at it. "Show me good faith. Give me proof of life or he's as good as dead to us."

Peter, a man that was used to having his commands followed, grew agitated by Steele's demand. He clenched a fist before he spoke. "He's safe at our facility."

"Let me see him. Take me to your facility."

Peter shook his head. "I can't do that."

Steele cocked his head to the side curious. "Peter, you came here talking about good faith. Where's yours? Bring Pagan back here and show him to me."

Peter snorted. "So you can ambush us and take him back? I wouldn't trust you as far as I could throw ya."

Then you're smarter than you look. "Why should I trust you?"

"Because you don't have a choice if you want him back." He nodded at Little Sable Point. "I can tell right now by the look of your *camp*, you won't stand a chance against us," Peter said, his face growing red in anger.

Steele knew they had the men to annihilate his group. The Chosen knew where Steele's group resided. The Chosen could be down the road in less than an hour with God knows how many men. Steele's ten and Thunder's thirty-three, if Thunder decided to stick around, wouldn't have a chance.

Steele squinted his eyes. "You know you look familiar," he said, scratching his beard with his support hand.

"I didn't come here to play games," Peter said. "Will you meet our terms?"

"You play ball for Hudsonville Reformed?" Steele asked.

Confusion settled on Peter's face. "Um." He paused, uncomfortable with the situation. He looked back over his shoulder at his men. "Yeah. How'd you know that?"

"State Finals, 2003?" Steele inquired.

"Yeah, we lost in overtime. I played pulling guard."

Steele smiled. "I was a middle linebacker on Bloomfield."

A grin slowly crawled onto Peter's face. He snorted a laugh. "Well, I'll be damned. You played ball for Bloomfield?" He shook his head in disbelief. "You had that running back that ran all over us for four quarters, and we still took you to overtime."

"You remember that goal-line stand?" Steele asked, letting himself smile.

"How could I forget? We ran a double trap to the right. I pulled along with our center, Danny Vanholden. He kicked the corner out. But when I hit the hole, this tough bastard was already there, and that bastard was you."

"I think you gave me a concussion on the hit," Steele laughed.

Peter grinned. "It was a trench war. We dug our feet through the turf, but it seemed that you kept getting more and more help, and by the time the whistle was blown, the pile was on the ground and we were short. One more inch."

"I'll never forget it," Steele said.

"How could you? Overtime. Final seconds. An inch and the game was ours."

"But the inch was ours," Steele said with a sad smile.

"Yeah." Peter's eyes drooped downcast. Those days seemed like ages ago, where young men could battle on a football field and live instead of warring against one another on the battlefield to survive. No one would play that again. Not their kids. Not anyone.

Steele stuck out his hand. "I'll meet with the pastor. If he has hard-nosed guys like you on his side, I'm sure we can work this thing out."

Steele slung his carbine to his back and Peter grinned. Relief crossed his features. "I'm sure we can." He took Steele's hand in his. His palms were like steaks. Both groups let themselves relax.

One of Peter's men stood up from behind cover and brought his shotgun upright against his shoulder, the muzzle pointed in the air and a smile on his lips.

A crack echoed through the air. It shattered the peaceful sound of the lake and trees. Everything stopped. Gunfire will freeze some men; it will cause others to take cover. If a man's training is right, it will throw him into action. It took fractions of a second before anyone recognized what had happened.

After a second, Peter's eyes went wide and he tensed. Neurons fired in each man's brain to the stimulus of danger. Steele's reaction to the boom was a fraction of a second faster like he was hot off the line in the championship game.

Steele crushed Peter's hand and yanked Peter's arm past him. He offset himself at the same time. He chopped the side of his hand into the back of Peter's neck as he brought the bigger man to the ground. The shock of the strike to Peter's neck stunned him, making his body go limp. Steele landed on top of the motionless man.

Bullets whizzed overhead and Steele used his body to cover Peter's. Peter's head rolled to the side, unresponsive.

"What the fuck!" Steele screamed at the top his lungs. The ting of bullets entering and exiting the vehicles combined with the whistle of bullets sailing overhead. Everyone shot. He crawled in the middle, wrestling his M4 off his back while trying to stay low enough to not catch a round through his elbow as he reached.

A lone young Chosen man crouched behind a door. This barely mustached man struggled with his magazine, unable to reload his gun. Steele lined up his red dot on the man's hip. He squeezed a round through his pelvic girdle. The man collapsed back on his side. He turned his head away and screamed in pain. It was high-pitched and an awful mix when combined with the gunshots. The Chosen leaned on a single elbow, crying in pain while trying to seat his magazine. Steele put three rounds into this torso. Tap. Tap. Tap. The man laid down as if he had grown tired and was ready for bed and stopped moving. Steele scanned their vehicles. Not one of the Chosen was upright, but the bullets kept flying.

"Cease fire," he yelled behind him. After a minute, the firing slowed and stopped.

Thunder's angry voice rose roughly above. "Cease fire," he screamed repeatedly.

Should I even stand up? A woman broke from the barricaded entrance and sprinted for him.

Using his gun as a crutch, Steele stood up. "Mark, Jesus," Gwen yelled at him. She wrapped her arms around his neck.

"What are you doing here?" he yelled.

Her hands searched his body for wounds.

"I'm fine," he said gruffer than he wanted. "What the hell just happened?" he shouted over her head at the barricade.

"I don't know. All of a sudden, everyone was shooting. I told them to stop, but no one could hear me over the gunfire," Gwen said.

Steele surveyed the pastor's men dying in bubbling puddles of their own blood. The Red Stripes and volunteers from Little Sable Point came out from their barricade. A quiet murmur leaked from their ranks. It was like a car accident they couldn't take their eyes from, except they were the ones that had caused it. Larry looked sorry. Margie could only stare, an arm wrapped around Max. Max's eyes were almost as wide as his head. Hank looked away and Gregor's face lacked remorse. People covered their mouths and shook their heads in disgust.

Steele watched blood pump out of the nearest Chosen man's body with the last beats of his heart. Anger welled up inside him.

"Little Sable, you shot first, so now we have to deal with the consequences. Roll those trucks inside. Gather their weapons and anything of value." Steele walked over to one of the bodies and pulled out his tomahawk. He twirled it once in anger, looking down at the man.

The Chosen soldier lay on the ground broken and gasping for breath. His brown hair was stuck to his head with sweat and fresh blood. Blood flowed from the side of his mouth. His flesh had been jaggedly ripped apart by no fewer than three bullets. The fact that he hadn't bled out yet was a miracle in itself. The man knew he was dead yet still fought it. Steele bent down. The man grabbed his hand, blood squishing in-between their fingers.

Steele waited a moment. The man gulped his own blood down his throat and rapidly blinked his eyes open as wide as he could manage. It was as if he were trying to see as much as possible before he expired. His existence ended a second later with a swing of Steele's tomahawk into the side of his neck. The last bit of blood inside the mangled man sprayed onto the ground. Steele bent down and wiped his tomahawk blade on his long green sleeve and wedged his axe back into his belt.

The people of Sable Point stared at him blankly, equally amazed and shocked. They were afraid. They had finally seen violence up-close by their own hands and were shocked at what they had been a part of.

Steele pointed a finger at Peter's body.

"Somebody pick him up," he said then stormed back to Little Sable Point. On the way by, he shouted at Thunder. "Come with me." Thunder adjusted his colors, a frown on his face. "We're going to war."

KINNICK

Golden Triangle, CO

The hangar was dark in the early morning. Boxes of ammunition and supplies had taken the place of the huge aircraft that normally resided there. He could make out the camouflaged, armed men inside. Guns rattled on magazines, grenades clanked on flashlights, and bullets clicked as they were prepped inside magazines. Soldiers in full combat kit or battle rattle milled about the tall and wide-entranced hangar. They checked each other's gear, making small talk to calm their nerves. The soldiers hadn't noticed their new commanding officer observing them from afar.

"They're young," Hunter said behind him. A C-130 growled as it lifted off in the distance, slowly rising in the air like a fat but determined pigeon.

"You were young once and went to war."

"Not like this. We had the whole of America's military might at our backs. These men have only a fraction of that and each other."

"Then we'll have to rely heavily on the senior non-coms to keep them on the right track," Kinnick said in response, turning his back to the man. He felt every year of his age and then some. *I am literally getting too old for this.*

"Yes, we will," Hunter said. He ran a hand through his beard. "Be wary of old men in a profession where men die young."

Kinnick laughed. "Sometimes I think it's only luck that's keeping me on this planet."

Hunter looped his fingers through his vest. "Luck or a curse."

"Hard to tell the difference, isn't it." Kinnick watched them.

A nearby group of young soldiers talked loud, covering up their nervousness with male bravado. Another cluster laughed together. One man danced in the middle of the group like he was on a dance floor at a club. *Even after all this, there is still some life left in the youth. Perhaps we can survive. They're young but all are veterans now.*

The senior soldiers looked on, checking gear. A few smiled as they listened to the stories the younger men bragged about. The veterans were his go-to soldiers. This mission would crutch on them. If any of them hadn't been in the fight yet, soon they would have their baptism by tooth and nail.

"I wonder what they've been told about this mission?" Kinnick said to his senior NCO. He hesitated to call Hunter his friend, but if surviving together made men friends then they were best buddies.

"What does it matter? They still have to embrace the suck because that's their job," Hunter said. He spit chew from a ball in the side of his mouth. The brown liquid splatted on the ground. Kinnick knew the man had stocked up on little brown tins of chewing tobacco from the post exchange on the base.

"It matters," Kinnick said. *Men fight better if they know what's at stake.*

Turmelle and Hawkins joined them. They had huge packs filled with every known piece of gear, and they looked like they were going into the field forever.

"This is it?" Turmelle said. The curly haired soldier ran his finger along the hilt of his kukri as if it soothed his nerves.

"This is it, Sergeant," Kinnick said. *This is it. All that stands between us and nuclear holocaust.*

"This is not enough men. This is not even an entire company," Hawkins said. His voice was methodical. His ever analyzing mind had done the math, and they had come up on the less-than-winning side of the equation.

Kinnick eyed the man from the corner of his eyes. *He's right and you know it.* "It will be enough. Come on." He gave a terse wave of his hand to be followed.

Kinnick approached the reorganized company of soldiers followed by the remaining ODA 51 "Skins." He had 102 men in his command given to him by General Monroe. The other soldiers and Marines from his search and rescue team had been reappropriated by their parent services. Their administrative skills would keep them out of the field.

One hundred and two plus three Special Forces Green Berets. The only superior who had any faith in the mission they were about to undertake was Monroe, yet he didn't have enough faith to give him a battalion of men, let alone a full company or any air support. *Am I the blind one here?*

His four platoon leaders met him, all men in their twenties. They stood by a folding table sitting near the entrance of the hangar.

"Gentlemen, I am Colonel Kinnick. Captain Wilkes has been reassigned. I'm your CO for this operation. I understand all of you men are from the same brigade but have been reorganized into a new company." The men nodded the affirmative. "That will be sufficient. I'm going to need men who work well together. I also understand that your platoons have been cut down by two squads apiece in your reorganization. Unfortunate, but we will make do." Kinnick eyed them fiercely. *We have determination on our side.* "Now, who are you?" He pointed to a short man on the left.

"Lieutenant Wyman, sir." Wyman was short with the build of a wrestler and had scrunched misshapen cauliflower ears to match. He continued, "1st Platoon, the "Minute Men", C Company, 2nd Battalion, 21st Infantry. We are the Bunker Hill Brigade. Always Steadfast is our motto."

"Let's hope that remains true," Kinnick said to the man.

Next to him stood a man with the build of a linebacker. Kinnick gave him a nod. "Second Platoon Leader Lieutenant Stark. The 2nd Platoon are the Regulators, sir." His eyes were fierce as if he were already in the fight.

A soldier with a slight hunch in his posture, like he was carrying too heavy of a backpack, stood next to Stark. "Lieutenant Elwood, 3rd Platoon, we go by the Heartbreakers." Elwood's look was anything but. He looked like he belonged in his mother's basement playing a role-playing game with four of his closest virgin friends. Kinnick nodded to him.

The last platoon leader was tall. If he hadn't played basketball in college, he should have. "Lieutenant Dearborn, 4th Platoon, we are the Associators, sir.

Kinnick eyed his officers. "Your men look good. I trust you are prepped for an extended patrol into the field?"

"Yes, sir," they said in unison. Kinnick turned to Hunter.

"You hear that, Master Sergeant? We got a real group of hard chargers here. I like that."

Hunter gave him a fake smile and swapped the chew around in his mouth. "Hope they can scrap as good as they holler."

Kinnick stretched a large map of Colorado on a table. "Please take a look at this map." He waited for the officers to move closer. "First Platoon, you're going to put down here." Kinnick pointed to the pass farthest south. "South Fork. The helos will drop you here. It's flat and above the pass that you must defend. I would recommend deployment on either side of the pass. Worst comes to worst, you can throw rocks at them." His officers gave him a pity laugh, not knowing that he was dead serious.

Kinnick's thumb tapped the map. "I don't expect much added pressure your way after we block the tunnel."

Wyman nodded, his thick wrestler's neck relinquishing his head for a moment.

"Lieutenant Dearborn, you're going to be in a difficult position." He looked up at the man. Dearborn's look was cool as if he were at the free-throw line and the game was at stake. "I don't like it, but we're going to split your platoon. Your 1st squad will be at Mosquito Pass." Kinnick tapped the map, tap-tap-tap with his fingertip. "Now, the land around this pass is very rocky. They're going to put you down here." He dragged his finger across the map a bit. "It's about two miles away and you will have to ruck in. Our pilots assure us there is no alternative because of the terrain." He let his finger run along a thin gray line on his map. "You're going to have to follow the road up the pass and climb to defensible firing positions." He looked back up at the towering lieutenant. "Second squad, 4th Platoon, will be headed to Independence Pass. Those lakes around the road provide a nice funnel for the Zulus." He let his orders percolate into their minds. "Questions?"

Dearborn nodded slowly, his eyes frigid. "Yes, sir. Can they swim?"

Kinnick blinked. The question was simple yet caught him off guard. *People could swim. Why not these disgusting bastards?*

"From everything I've read and seen, no, they cannot. Master Sergeant, have you seen any aptitude in them for swimming or anything out of the ordinary?"

"Nah. They're about as useless as tits on a hog in the water. Doesn't mean they can't float their dead ass across by accident though."

Kinnick nodded. "Lieutenant, your flanks will be relatively secure at Independence but do not neglect them."

Dearborn ducked his chin in acknowledgment.

Kinnick made eye contact with Stark and Elwood. Stark's eyes were the color of ice and Elwood's the top of a buttermilk biscuit. "Second and 3rd Platoons will be putting down at Eisenhower Tunnel. Here we will clear the tunnel, seal it. This is pivotal to the plan. If we cannot get the tunnel sealed, the dead will continue on into Colorado unimpeded and all of this is for nothing."

He put both his hands on the table, leaning in over the map. He made sure to lock eyes with the two lieutenants so they understood the importance of that part of the mission.

"After the tunnel is sealed, we will move by foot about three miles to Dunluce Pass." His finger jumped a bit on the map.

"This will be the focal point. Dunluce is where we expect to meet the main body of the enemy. When we close off the tunnel, the natural flow of the land will push the Zulus to Dunluce, and to a lesser extent, Mosquito and Independence passes."

"What air assets will we have available to us?" Stark asked. He rested his arm on the butt stock of his black M4A1 carbine.

Kinnick shook his head no. "None. We haven't been allocated any air assets aside from a drop-off."

"No medevac or close air support?" Dearborn said asked in disbelief. The tall soldier looked down on them all.

"You heard the colonel. Just a drop off, and no love after that," Hunter said.

"What about armor or Stryker support, sir?" Stark asked, fire hidden behind his eyes. He was beginning to see the mission for what it was: a swift and certain execution. Boots shuffled on the concrete hangar floor.

"I would love a battalion of Strykers or Bradleys, really anything that could put some hurt out there, but that was not my decision," Kinnick said.

"What support are we going to have out there?" Elwood questioned with a look at his peers for approval.

"The terrain," Hunter paused and spit on the concrete, "should be in our favor. The Zulus don't climb well. Use it to your advantage."

"Is that confirmed, sir? That they don't climb. I've never seen it, but that doesn't mean they don't do it," Wyman said.

"It's not confirmed. There is much we still don't know about them, but I know headshots do the trick. Remind your soldiers of that. Avoid body shots." The lieutenants nodded.

"Remember, gentlemen, we need only to hold until it snows. It could be a week from now or a month, but we will hold. The alternative is that the vice president will launch thermonuclear weapons against the West Coast."

The young platoon leaders' eyes widened even as they tried to take it in stride.

Elwood blinked rapidly. "Sir, they are going to nuke the United States?" he asked.

"That's correct, Lieutenant. If we fail to hold the passes, they will launch against *our* cities."

"Jesus Christ," Wyman cursed, his mouth dropping open.

Kinnick had debated whether or not to throw in that beautiful prospect of what happened if they failed. He would want his superiors to be forward with him about what was at stake. His men deserved to know the reason why they fought was so much greater than survival.

"You're not some speed bump in the way of the Zulus: you're a wall they must never get over. You're a line they must never penetrate. We must hold at all costs. Millions of living Americans are depending on you." *Definitely not millions.*

"We're going to be working in the mountains. Our communications will be disrupted until we can get some high-frequency radios up and running.

Our GPS will be spotty and unreliable at best. I hope you paid attention in land navigation. Do what you can to keep me posted on your situation. That's all, men. Best of luck, remember your motto: Always Steadfast."

"Hooah!" they shouted. His officers walked back with their respective depleted platoons.

Hunter shuffled up next to Kinnick. "It's going to be tough out there with no support. They'll be on an island. Alone," Hunter said, holding his tan LW SCAR. Strapped to his back was a scoped Mk 12 Special Purpose Rifle, and on his hip, a Beretta M9A1. His vest and battle belt held at least fifteen magazines.

"I would take a group of boy scouts up there if that's all we had. We simply have to try."

"I understand, sir. I was thinking." He rolled a tin of chewing tobacco out of his pocket and slapped his index finger on the top. "We could attach myself and the others from ODA 51 to each of the platoons. I know the platoons have their own NCOs, but it might stiffen them up a bit. Ya know, give them a bit more confidence when they are alone, staring down the barrel of a gun." He shoved a wad of dark brown chew in his lower lip.

"Or a horde of ravenous cannibals." Kinnick tried to figure out what was the best use of his tiny forces. "I've considered that. I would rather have all of you with me, but you may be right. I'll have about fifty men with me to address the brunt of the infected force." *The SF guys would be a nice thing to keep in my back pocket for when things get hairy. They would also ensure the success of the units they were attached too.*

Hunter shrugged. "It's up to you. We are your instruments of death." He gave Kinnick a fake bow.

"If only I had a couple thousand clones of you."

"The world would tremble," Hunter said with a grin, squeezing his chew-filled lip back into his gums.

"I don't want to do it, but let's put Sergeant Turmelle with Wyman's 1st Platoon, and Sergeant Hawkins can take Dearborn's 1st squad. You, however, are with me. Will you let the LTs know?" Kinnick said. Hunter walked off to give the news. Kinnick turned to Turmelle. Turmelle's eyes said he was ready for anything, including giving his life.

"Thank you for everything. Keep them in one piece out there."

"I would say it's been fun, sir. But this has been a real bag of dicks. See you in a few weeks," Turmelle said. Turmelle slapped hands with Hawkins. "Sins and skins," they said to one another. He hefted his pack and walked off.

"Sergeant Hawkins, we couldn't have done it without you. I'll see you when this is over," Kinnick said. He stuck out a hand and the half-Asian man took it. He said goodbye with his eyes.

"When this is over," was all Hawkins said, and he walked off to join his new platoon.

Hunter returned to Kinnick. "The men are ready, sir."

All of his company stood in a loose line of helmeted, camouflaged soldiers. Kinnick unslung his M4 carbine. He eyed the soldiers staring back him. They looked to him for inspiration. He was responsible for each and every one of their lives. *If they die, it was because I led them to their deaths.*

Young, bright eyes stared back. Scared eyes hid next to them. Eager eyes were next to those. Every soldier wanted to get some.

"We are with you, sir," a soldier shouted in front. Kinnick licked his lips, for the first time realizing how dry they were and how nervous he was.

"Gentlemen, let's get this done," he barked. Kinnick held his carbine in the air. The men surged for their helicopters, yelling at the top of their lungs.

STEELE

Little Sable Point, MI

He leaned on the built-in fake plastic table inside Tess's camper. Despite the coolness outside, the camper was hot and stuffy from the body heat of all the people crammed in. The wind whistled outside and the camper shuddered under the assault of the strong gusts of air.

Storm clouds brewed over the huge lake like a collecting army of darkness in the sky. In the clouds' shadow, the volunteers of Little Sable Point buried their folly in a shallow ditch outside the camp, a task that Steele had set them to with no discussion. The murder of the Chosen men very well could be their death sentence. Little Sable Point had dug their own grave six-feet down, and now it was Steele's responsibility to drag them out.

Thunder sat crushed in a corner, his belly pressed uncomfortably against the table. Next to him was Kevin, who was sandwiched between Thunder and Ahmed. Ahmed sat on the very edge of the table, leaning with his knees spread wide. Tess presided from her futon-style bed, her knees pulled up to her chest in an effort to separate herself from them. Gwen sat across from Thunder, her arms folded below her chest, a dour look scrawled over her face. Garret and Half-Barrel stood in the kitchenette, spanning wall to wall.

Steele stood in the middle of the narrow aisle. His arms were folded tightly over his chest. "What happened?" Steele asked. He eyed them all in turn. Someone had to have known who shot first. Everyone sat silent, knowing that no matter the perpetrator the results were dire for all.

"I'm standing in the middle shaking hands with Peter, and some lackwit fucking shoots one of the Chosen. If that isn't bad enough, the whole motley crew jumps in and a gun battle starts. How the fuck am I going to get these fools to come to the table again with that breach of trust?"

"They're crackpots anyway," Tess said from her corner.

Steele pointed a finger at her, shaking his head. "No, Tess. You saw their camp. The crackpots are the majority, and we just killed eight of their men. How do I bring that to the table? Of all people, you should want to negotiate. Pagan's life is at stake, and they have no reason to not kill him now." She put her chin back down on her knees, admonished by him. He turned toward Thunder.

"I thought you had them thoroughly scared enough to not shoot."

Thunder coughed into his fist. "It was their first fight. Everyone was jumpy."

Steele clenched his jaw. "It's their second fight I'm worried about. Can we still count on your men?"

Thunder's eyebrows tickled one another like two caterpillars mating.

"I don't like the way you're talkin' to me. But I like you, so I won't lie to you. My club is tied to this place. A few of the boys have girlfriends and the like in the camp, but if it's time to leave then we won't hesitate to go."

And I have no choice but to let you, even if I wanted to stop you. Our fragile experiment is unraveling.

Tess didn't look pleased, and why would she? The community she had started was now at war with one that was vastly larger. Now, the men responsible for its security were discussing the option of leaving.

Steele ran his fingers through his beard. The situation couldn't get any worse.

"Well, I'm open to suggestions. What do we do?"

Silence met him. "Kevin? Ideas? Some historical plan that worked for an ancient hero or general?" The lanky man shook his head no. "You mean in the history of the world, there is no nation, state, or city that has had to deal with anything like this?"

Kevin shrugged. "Well, of course, there's plenty of examples of smaller forces defeating larger opponents. Roger I at Cerami in 1063. Aussies at Long Tan in Vietnam. But those were trained armies. For us, I got nothing."

"Of course. Now you're quiet."

"I mean there were the Hussites led by the famous Jan Žižka at Viktov Hill?" Nobody said anything and they sat in silence trying to decide if Kevin had fabricated the man and battle.

"Please, enlighten us." Steele demanded.

"A poor Protestant peasant army withstood an attack by crusading knights in the 1420s."

"That sounds closer. How'd they do it?"

"Scholars debate. But the untrained peasants held fortifications of battle-wagons, and a host of town militia surprised and flanked the attacking knights in a vineyard. Not sure what we can do with that."

"I'll keep it in mind for what it's worth."

He looked at Ahmed. "Any tricks up your sleeve?"

"No," he said flatly.

"Gwen?"

"We could give our captive back and tell them it was a misunderstanding."

Steele turned his lips down. "You want me to walk into their camp, tell them it was an accident, and give their man back. Sorry, Pastor. I killed eight of your men, but you can have this one back."

Her mouth closed. Her lips were pensive. "I didn't say it was great, but it's something."

"Any other ideas? This is supposed to be a debate. A meeting of the minds. I would appreciate an idea that doesn't get me and you all killed in the process."

"We could kill the captive, ditch their gear, and if any more of them come a knocking, tell them we never heard of 'em," Thunder said.

"They asked for me by name. They know we're here," Steele retorted. He sighed.

"I'll leave you to it, but I'm going to talk to Peter. See what intel I can gather from him. Numbers, strategy, anything that will give us an edge. Please try and figure something out. Double the guards at the gates. Ahmed and

Kevin, grab Margie and Trent and take turns in the lighthouse."

"I'll do it," Gwen said.

"Babe, please. It's cold and windy, no place for someone in your condition."

She rolled her eyes. "It's not a condition. I'm pregnant. I'm a good shot, just as good as Ahmed, and I want to help."

Ahmed smiled in defeat. "She has a point."

"Then be my guest," Steele said in a short manner. "What would I know?"

He let the screen door bang closed behind him as he left the camper. *I guess this is the new definition of shit creek.* The wind whipped his borrowed Army Combat Uniform, stinging his cheeks red as he walked. He shuffled past the red-brick lighthouse, making his way to an abandoned semi-trailer at the farthest end of the enclosure. A small number of tents and cars sat parked there. Only a few people would be close enough to hear this.

Max stood guard like a goofy child's doll with a gun. He stood at attention as Steele approached, puffing his chest out as far as he could. He threw a hand up in a terrible mock salute almost dropping his gun in the process.

Steele inspected him and gave him a once-over. "No need to salute, Max. We aren't in the military," he said.

Max's knuckles half-hovered near his forehead, blinking, trying to decide if Steele was testing him or not. After a moment, he finally let his hand rest at his side.

"The d-d-door has been locked the entire time, s-sir."

Should I fight the 'sir' battle again? Or leave him be?

"Good work, volunteer." Steele jangled the key in his pocket, wrapping his hands around the silver lock. Max watched him with renewed interest. His eyes leapt from the lock to Steele's face. Steele tried to ignore him.

"I shot one of them today. I pulled the trigger and I saw him grab his chest," Max said half to himself and half to Steele. It sounded like he was searching for validation for his actions. It was as if he were asking Steele to explain the cascading emotions roiling inside him.

Steele stopped and set the opened lock down. *He's not ready for this. This is as much my failure as it is his emotional immaturity.*

Steele looked down into the young man's eyes. "A lot of people were shooting out there today. It probably wasn't you." Max hung onto his every word as if he spoke the gospel.

Volunteering had put them on a collision course to change their lives. *How could I have prepared them for the psychological battle for their humanity? How many teenage men had suffered the trauma of killing another human being, and not the dead, but the living during wars throughout the ages? How did the men who had been through it counsel them? How did they bring them to the acceptance of what they had done? How did they help them digest what they had done in the name of the greater good? How will you digest it, Mark?*

Max's eyes stared out past Steele into nothing as he relived the incident. "He look-looked right at me as if he knew it was-was me. I-I-I'm sure of it. Like he blamed me for killing him," Max said, the side of his mouth twitching.

Steele gripped Max by the shoulder, giving it a squeeze. "Max, those men could have lived through today, but fate was not on their side. Things went wrong, and we had to kill them so they wouldn't harm us." *As much as I'm pissed about that entire situation.*

Max nodded feverishly, seeking any sort of relief from his internal anguish. "How'd you do it? I mean. How do you make it so it's not always on your mind?" The boy blinked rapidly.

By listing out their names in my mind and making sure their memory goes on. Jarl. He touched the chain around his neck carrying his hammer necklace. *Having the lives of the fallen haunt me until I join them.* Steele released Max's shoulder. "As we continue to train, you will build a camaraderie with the other men and women within your unit. You will deal with the enemy's death by making sure your unit lives. You will learn to do anything for your brothers and sisters in arms. It isn't about the enemy because the enemy will always be there. It's about the people to your left and to your right. Bring them home safe and you'll bring yourself home safe." *Just like my team, Jarl, Andrea, Wheeler. Just like Mauser. All gone.*

Steele set the padlock down. "It's not about them. It's about us. Remember that. Always." Heaving, he pulled on the heavy semi-trailer door.

It creaked as it swung open. Max moved to the side, still watching Steele like a puppy.

Steele glanced back at him over his shoulder. "How about you take a break? I can watch this guy for awhile." Max looked up into his eyes, excited to be relieved of duty, distraught that he couldn't spend more time with Steele.

"Are you sure, sir?"

Steele nodded. "I am. Get on out of here."

Max hustled off like he had been let out for recess for the day. *I have to try to keep the idea alive. Enough innocence was lost today.*

Steele grabbed a handrail and hoisted himself inside the dark trailer. He could hear the other man breathing at the far end. Steele gave one glance through the opening before closing the doors with a clank.

Steele's feet echoed between the hollow walls of the trailer. Peter's frame appeared first, kneeling, hands chained to a hook on the floor as if he were kneeling in prayer. Steele flicked his flashlight on, shining it in Peter's eyes. He turned his head and shied away from the light.

Bottled water sat in the corner out of Peter's reach. Grabbing one, Steele handed it to Peter, removing the light from his eyes. Holding the water in his chained hands, Peter let his head fall back then poured the water into his mouth, never taking his shadowed eyes off of Steele.

"Where are the rest of my brothers?" Peter croaked, setting the water down.

Steele waited a moment. "There's no way to put this delicately. They're dead." Steele watched the man absorb the bad news. Peter gradually shook his head, acknowledging that his friends, comrades, and men had been murdered.

"May their souls rest in peace," Peter said aloud. He mumbled more prayers inaudibly under his breath.

"That was a mistake," Steele said down to him. He let his flashlight drift down, pointing it at the ground.

Peter didn't acknowledge him, his head bowed in prayer.

"We never planned to kill your men. Hell, they almost shot me." Steele showed a quick smile, but Peter's curly head stayed down, hands chained together, fingers locked in prayer. Steele sighed. *It was a mistake.* Peter's prayers grew quieter, his lips hardly moving.

"I hope your neck isn't hurt too bad. I had to react fast when the shooting started. Probably saved your life," Steele let out a short laugh. "Can we talk?"

Peter's head bowed lower. "Peter, man. Come on, let's talk. This world is crazy. Mistakes happened. The dead have risen. I need you to talk to me." Steele's voice turned stern toward the end, his request becoming a command. Peter raised his chin up, meeting Steele's eyes. His eyes lacked fear. His lids dipped low in meditation, and his mouth continued to move.

"How many people are in your camp?" Steele watched the man as he continued to pray, ignoring his request. He crouched down in front of him. "We have to talk, one way or another." *I'm glad I sent Max away. He shouldn't have to hear this.* "I want this to be easy, and it can be, but we have to have a conversation. Who's the pastor? What does he want?"

Peter's eyes had a sad, tired look to them as if he was generally worn out. Steele set his flashlight on the floor, letting it partially light up his captive.

"I don't have time for this God patty-cake game. Talk to me." Peter breathed in heavily and continued praying.

I didn't want this. I don't want this. But if I don't do this, I'll be blind in a fight that is already out of hand. Steele balled up a fist and swung hard into Peter's cheek. The sound was like the slap of raw steak on a plate. Peter crashed onto his side, his shoulder banging into the floor.

Shaking his hand, Steele stared down at the man. *Damn that hurt.* "How many fighters are in your camp?"

Peter's voice grew louder. "Though I walk through the valley of the shadow of death," he said up at him.

Steele walked closer, grabbing Peter by the scruff of his shirt.

Peter stared defiantly up at him. Steele's fist rocketed into the man's eye and his head bounced off the metal floor. *I don't want to do this.*

"How many fighters?" Peter looked up at him, seeing stars, his eyes almost crossed.

"I fear no evil for he is with me," Peter said louder.

"Stop with that mumbo jumbo. Give me a number and I'll get you some water." Steele lifted Peter by his shirt off the floor, raising his fist high in the air. *This hurts me too.*

Peter's eyes were those of an unrepentant man. "The Army of the Lord is guided by angels. Our numbers matter not for our cause is just in the eyes of God."

"Peter, please. Don't make me do this." He meant every word. "We can still come out of this as allies."

Peter spit blood on the ground. "Your actions are those of a true unbeliever, Mark Steele, corrupted and misguided by the devil." Steele's fist connected with Peter's mouth. Pain shot through his hand and into his wrist, so he knew it must have hurt Peter. Peter lay on the ground, coughing up blood in painful hacks. He spit and two little white teeth tinkled onto the container floor.

"This is me being nice about it. You don't want to see me get mean." Peter kept his head low.

"While the devil roars and looks for someone to devour, you must stand to resist him in faith."

Steele stood upright, shaking his hand. "Well, I'm tired of hurting my own hand."

Steele turned around fetching a bucket of water and some rags. He wished it had been the first time he had utilized such advanced methods, but it wasn't. The rags would muffle the screams, and hopefully, no one would hear. "This isn't going to be fun."

JOSEPH

Cheyenne Mountain Complex, CO

Joseph's knuckles rapped on a white door that sounded like it was made of synthetic material, not wood, a more plastic substance than anything else. The inside of the Cheyenne Mountain Complex was covered in synthetic material. In particular, the BLS-4 lab was covered in clean white material almost as if they were in a spaceship rather than a mountain.

"Who is it?" responded Byrnes from inside. Even his muffled voice sounded morose through the door.

"It's Dr. Jackowski," he said into the crack of the door. *Stay calm. We are on the same team. But are we?* His mind battered away at any confidence he had.

"You may enter."

Joseph pressed down on the flat-handled doorknob and entered Byrnes's office. The ceiling lights were off and soft lamplight illuminated his desk. The colonel peered over spectacles, holding papers he had been reading. He set the papers down and leaned back in his chair. He wore combat ACUs as if he were ready to go into the field at a moment's notice. The center of his chest was decorated with an eagle with spread wings.

"To what do I owe this pleasure?" he said. His words dripped with sarcasm

Joseph shook angry thoughts from his mind. He gestured to a metal chair. "May I take a seat?"

Byrnes waved a finger like he swiped Joseph. "Yes."

Joseph hastily sat down. He exhaled sharply and adjusted his glasses. "I'm going to put this bluntly."

"I appreciate you valuing our time," Byrnes said quickly.

Joseph adjusted himself in his seat, caught off guard.

"How's Rebecca?" Byrnes asked. His mouth settled into a frown.

Joseph eyed him, trying to see if the man had any actual concern for her. "She's hanging on."

The colonel met his eyes. "She'll be missed. Never met a smarter doctor." He folded his hands in front of him.

Joseph rubbed his thumbnail with his other hand. The colonel unnerved him, sitting there almost smug in a depressed kind of way. The man even managed to look sullen while clearly happy with himself.

Joseph swallowed his pride. "I know we may have a difference of opinion on our methods of discovery, but we work better as a team than rivals."

Byrnes looked away at the wall and back to Joseph. "That may be true, but I need people that are on board with our mission. Dr. Nguyen has already made some great progress. He has isolated the monkeypox gene. In time, we will be able to block it from transmission. With some slight modifications of the smallpox vaccine, we believe that we can prevent up to ninety-five percent of monkeypox infections from taking place. We'll have a sustainable supply to be distributed." He finished with a bit of a sulky smirk. "We never would have been able to accomplish this without massive tissue harvesting."

"What kind of testing have you done on the satellite virus? Have you isolated it?" Joseph said. His mind quickly brushed over the thought of social amends.

Byrnes's frown deepened. "The satellite virus needs the monkeypox virus to survive. It's a parasite on the host virus," he said.

"You haven't seen it operate on its own?"

Byrnes licked his lips, uncertainty settling into his words. "Yes, only after the monkeypox virus has begun its gene transfer process."

"Have you watched what the satellite virus does after the monkeypox virus moves on?" Joseph leaned in. He knew the bomb he was about to drop on the colonel would blow his mind. He put his hands on the desk, closing the gap between them.

"It activates, causing some severe symptoms. Not possible without monkeypox." Byrnes sighed. "Have you come to amaze me with information we already know?"

Joseph took his tablet and handed it to the colonel. "Watch this," Joseph said. The colonel took the tablet and tapped the screen. He watched, looking over his glasses.

The clip ran. Joseph had memorized the entire thing. "At 1:34, pay close attention. Watch the cell with the parasite virus," Joseph instructed.

The glare from the video reflected in the colonel's eyes. His eyes narrowed as he watched the nightmare virus at work modifying the healthy cells genetic material into its own twisted genetic concoction like dark cellular machinery. The man was silent as he watched.

"The infected cell died," Joseph said. Byrnes's eyes went from the video to Joseph and back again. He scrolled his finger over the play bar, rewinding the clip, his mouth settling in a frown.

"The cell can't be dead," Byrnes said. He rewound the clip again. "It must go into a dormant state."

"No, see there. The cell has died, but the virus doesn't become active until after the cell begins to deteriorate."

"That's not possible. Viruses require a live organism to reproduce. This is Biology 101."

"I know, Byrnes, but look at the satellite virus. It only becomes active after death. Monkeypox was only a vector where the satellite virus could only be successful if the patients expired."

Byrnes took his glasses off and rubbed his eyes. "This cannot be possible. I…I can't believe this. This goes against everything we know." Doubt etched his long face.

Joseph shook his head. "I know. I feel the same way, but we're witnessing a new phase of evolution."

Byrnes shook his head no and took up the video again. "Has to be an anomaly," he said under his breath.

"Think about it, Colonel. What is the fastest way to create more dead cells?"

"Hemorrhage."

"What is the fastest way to get someone to hemorrhage?"

Byrnes locked eyes with Joseph. "Massive trauma. Jesus Christ. The virus is programming dead cellular DNA to rip people apart and in the process spread itself. The hastening of biological death speeds up the spread of infection." He blinked as his mind attempted to comprehend the information. "This is the first of its kind. Do you realize what this means?"

Joseph knew already. He could hardly accept it. It went against all convention, but now it was reality.

"This is the dawn of a new age in evolution. The discovery of the first dead virus. The rise of the Primus Necrovirus."

STEELE

Little Sable Point, MI

Wiping his hands on a rag, he walked to the other end of the semi-trailer. He scrubbed blood and vomit off his hands and stuffed a silver cross into his pocket. It hadn't taken more than an hour after he started, most of the time dedicated to preparing the individual to be psychologically broken.

He pushed the heavy metal door and it creaked open. He peered out to see if anyone had heard what had happened. The calls for help. The cries to stop. Mostly the gasps for air as Peter struggled to breathe. People in the community went about their normal business. Men stood watch atop the lighthouse. A woman stoked a fire. Water was being brought in from the lake in buckets to be purified.

No crowd had gathered to reprimand him or administer vigilante justice for his shadowy actions.

Tossing the blood-soaked rag in the back, he hopped down to the ground. He closed the doors up and latched them closed, looping the padlock back in place and cinching it together.

Gwen's voice startled him. "What were you doing in there?"

He turned around gathering himself and rested on the trailer away from her. "I thought you were in the lighthouse?" He rubbed his scratched and swelling knuckles. *Peter's face was hard.* He supposed everyone's face was hard but never as hard as when you crushed it with your fist. *His head is harder.*

"I was, but I saw you go in there awhile ago." Her eyes weighed him up and down. "How's the captive?"

He's lucky to still have most of his teeth. "I don't want to talk about it." Her face clouded at the words, and her eyes grew accusing.

"So he didn't say anything?" she said. She would dig and dig and dig until she uncovered what she wanted.

"He talked, but I don't want to talk about it."

"Well, that's nice. So, you walked in there and he told you everything he knows." Her eyebrows stayed at the top of her head. "How'd you make him talk?" she said.

"So I guess it's my turn for interrogation." He furrowed his brow in defiance. "I don't have time for this."

"Make time for me," she said, her eyes trying to read him. She crossed her hands over her stomach and let her cool eyes judge him. He avoided eye contact with her, focusing on the lighthouse instead.

He put his bruised hands in his pockets. "I made him talk."

"I asked, how?" she said, looking up at him. Her eyes glistened, afraid of his answer.

She must know deep down that this was necessary. "I used enhanced interrogation methods on him until he told me what I wanted to know." He looked at her green eyes, watching as salty tears continued to form.

"So you tortured him?" She looked away as she said it, biting her lip as if she couldn't stand to associate him and that word together.

"Not exactly." *They call it enhanced interrogation for a reason. It's terrifying and in some instances works. In other instances, it produces a result. That result is more hazy.*

"What exactly happened then?"

"What the hell else am I supposed to do? The die is cast. We have a fight on our hands, and it's win or die, and that includes you and *our baby*," he growled and said the last two words as a whisper. He wanted to scream. This mess they put him in. All their lives on his shoulders. "I'm going to do what it takes to win. You don't know about these people. If half of what Peter said is true, it's as bad as it gets."

"It's always been a mess since the beginning, but there's one thing that drives you. Your duty. What happened to your duty? What happened to the promise you made yourself in the townhouse in Virginia?" A tear fell down her face as she said it, a tear for his soul that he ignored.

"This is my goddamn duty," he growled at her. She took a step back from him as if his words had formed a hand and struck her face.

"My *duty* is to protect you and that baby first. Lead and protect these people, second."

"Was what you did right?" she asked. Her eyes quizzed him.

He pointed out at the community. "Was it right that we gunned down the pastor's men? No, but it happened, and now we have a fight on our hands. You have a choice in this Gwen. I give you that choice because I do what needs to be done." He wouldn't say evil. It wasn't evil. He knew it wasn't good, but he knew it couldn't be evil if the good guys won.

"I don't have the luxury of time, manpower, money, technology, fucking anything. Do you want to know what I found out?"

She shook her head no, her chin lowering to her chest, but he told her anyway. If people knew what evil was at work in the world, they would barricade their houses and never come out or steel themselves for the fight.

"This pastor is a nasty dude." He stopped himself. She needed to know. People can't live blind to the forces of darkness arrayed against them. They must brace themselves for the upcoming battle. They must see the enemy for what they are. They must build their fortitude for the fight ahead.

"The pastor is insane. Some sort of religious zealot screwhead." Steele shook his head. "I didn't understand half the religious bullshit Peter was saying. He kept mentioning the Kingdom of God and his Chosen people. I don't know what that means, but I understand the numbers. He has over five hundred armed men under his command. Five hundred. I have ten." Her eyes widened.

"He has a safe place. A fortress. Hell, he could sit back and wait for us to starve and then kill us, or he could wait for us to go to him and then he can really torture us, finishing us off with a slow roasting barbecue. They've been 'purifying' people with fire and I don't mean singeing a little hair. I mean burning people while they are still alive."

"How do you know?" She was closed off from him but listening.

"Peter confirmed what I had already seen. Rat-Face had been hung from a tree, doused in gasoline, and burned alive. His mouth was hanging open in a final scream."

Gwen's eyes went wide.

"I'm not the bad guy here, far from it. Peter will live. But what options do I have? I either get the intelligence and we have a small chance, or I talk to a fanatic all day, get nothing for it, and our odds of surviving grow even dimmer by the hour."

"There has to be a better way than this," she said, spreading her arms quickly and letting them fall back across her stomach, protecting herself from either the wind or his presence.

"There is. I sit and befriend him over a period of months. Give him things. Feed him. Talk to him. Gain his trust. But I don't have enough time. This is a ticking time-bomb scenario." He looked down. *Peter and I could have been friends. He may even have become an ally over time.*

"How do you know these things?" she asked softly, her voice fearing the answer to her question.

"I've done this before." He watched her for a moment and quickly started again. "In the Division."

"Oh." Her face grew sad as she read into his eyes.

He looked past her. "It's more to scare the prisoner than anything else. Aside from some bruises, he won't be permanently damaged. I'm sure he hates me, but I can live with that."

"It doesn't hurt *you*?"

He wobbled his head, no.

"No, I kind of turn it off. Separate myself from the situation. Kind of the same as when I shoot someone. There is a 'work me' and the Mark you know."

"Sometimes I feel like I don't even know either of you." She reached up, touching his face with a gentle hand. It almost felt foreign to him, like he had only ever known the violence of touch. "And who will save you?"

He felt the lump in his throat. *Am I doing the right thing? How long before I can't come back? Have I already gone too far?*

"What's done is done. We can't look back now." He took her hand off of his face. "Just accept me."

She nodded vigorously. "I accept all of you," she whispered. He stuck out his hand, and she took his fingers into hers. They walked back to their tent hand-in-hand.

THE PASTOR

Temple Energy Plant, MI

The pastor smashed his glass into the wall. It shattered below a bulletin board he was using to pin up maps of the area. Matthew peered at his own feet, brushing his flawless hair back into place with a nervous hand. Paul rubbed his hands together in front of his body as if he couldn't get whichever sin he was wrestling with off his skin. Even Luke with his greasy long black hair appeared somewhat uncomfortable.

"They haven't returned? I thought this place was only fifteen miles away," he said, looking back at his maps as if he didn't believe anything they would say anyway.

"Maybe they're running behind?" Paul said, his voice meek from inside his long-limbed frame.

"Peter is not one to be late. He knows better. He had strict instructions to deliver the message and return. No supply runs. No fighting. Straight there and back." He drummed his fingers on his fake tan wood desk. *Peter would not deviate from his task. I shouldn't have shown such anger in front of my disciples.* He took a deep breath. *Even Christ showed his anger when the people used his temple as a market.* Smoothing his black shirt, he stared at the map on the wall. Faded light blue water pushed up against a jagged lime green coastline. A black marker circle enveloped a single half-inch pink lighthouse near the shore of Lake Michigan.

"I could take a larger group to their camp and *purify* them if my father wills it," Luke said, licking his lips. Luke wasn't a member of his parish before the outbreak. He came upon them, eagerly adopting their ideology and methods.

"No." The pastor met his disciple's eyes. Luke was unwavering like an unafraid dog. "You are too eager, Luke." *Your eagerness may be rewarded yet. But I must be patient. I will hold him in reserve.*

Luke's lips twitched. "Your wish is my command." Luke bowed his head in deference.

Rabid dogs always turn on their masters. Who will watch him now that Peter is gone? Paul? No, he is too timid. Matthew may be sufficient.

The handsome blond man stared right at him as if he could read his mind.

"You may go and bring in our new brother," the pastor said, waving a hand at them. Luke left the room and returned a moment later followed by a bald-headed man.

"Come in," the pastor said. The man stood as if he were in the vice principal's office.

"How are you and your family enjoying our accommodations, Brother Jack?" he said, folding his hands on his desk.

"Very good, pastor. The food has been wonderful. Thank you for accepting us." The new member towered over the others in the room.

"God's Kingdom is open to all who are his sons and daughters," he said.

"Amen," Jack said, eyes searching the floor for inspiration.

"I need you to deliver a message for me to your-," the pastor said, stopping to consider his words, "former camp."

"I don't know. They weren't happy about my family leaving. That bastard Steele tried to stop me. Threatened to hurt me and my family."

"God has no mercy for such roguish men. Fire may purify him of his sins."

"I…" Jack's eyes widened. "You would burn him?" His face twisted at the words.

The pastor spread his hands. "Alas, it is not up to me. I am but a vessel of the greater good. It's apparent that this Steele doesn't take kindly to my followers, so I will send you instead."

"But I'm one of your followers now."

"God has brought you to me for a reason. His will is seen clearly," the pastor said, raising an eyebrow at the men.

"But I don't-," Jack said.

The pastor cut him off. "Your family will be safe. I assure you." He let his eyes rest on Jack's ruddy face. Jack gulped.

"Luke," the Pastor said.

A slick stringy-black-haired man stepped up. "Yes, Pastor," he said.

"I would like you to put Jack's family under special watch while he delivers a message for me. I want you to make sure they never leave your sight." Luke licked his lips.

"As you command," Luke said with a bow of his head. Luke gave Jack a cruel smile. The pastor waved him out. Luke turned and left the room. Jack watched the twisted man leave, visibly shaken.

The pastor eyed Jack's troubled face. "You see, they will be safe the entire time. I give you my word."

KINNICK

Eisenhower Tunnel, CO

The brown land surrounding the highway tunnel entrance was covered with rocks and thin straight pines that covered the mountainous terrain. It looked like a boxy two-lane storage warehouse built into the side of the mountain. A brown base of concrete led up to a block of beige concrete with small windows facing the highway.

The helicopter hovered, the roadway growing closer and closer beneath them. Within moments, the chopper touched the concrete with a bump. Soldiers jumped out. Thick boot treads thudded onto the highway. They dodged chunks of debris and worked around abandoned vehicles.

Kinnick hopped off the helo following Hunter. He kept the back of his senior NCO close.

"I want three-hundred-and sixty-degree coverage," Hunter called out to the men. First squad, 2nd Platoon spread out in every direction. They weaved into and behind abandoned vehicles. They used the cars as cover. They were the first boots on the ground for Kinnick's desperate operation.

They held their positions as the helicopter ascended and disappeared. The thundering of rotors announced more of their comrades. In one minute, another helicopter set down. Boots pounded the concrete as they raced to fill in gaps within their sectors. This happened four more times until the entirety of the 2nd and 3rd Platoons were on the ground in a circular defensive position. A cache of supplies was set down in the middle.

"That's all of them," Hunter said, watching the last helicopter fly away. He spit on the ground. Brown stained the concrete.

"It'll have to do," Kinnick said. Hunter nodded his affirmation.

Hunter gestured with his head. "So that's the fucker we gotta take down?"

Four hundred yards ahead, the Eisenhower Tunnel loomed like a German World War II bunker and Kinnick's men were the first onto the sandy beaches of Normandy.

"That ugly behemoth is it." The task of taking it down daunted Kinnick, and dread filled the air as if his men expected to be shredded by bullets at any minute. *Not bullets but teeth.* Gunfire rattled from its direction.

"Lieutenant Stark, give me a sitrep," Kinnick shouted. The linebacker of an officer knelt behind a red Ford Taurus.

Stark turned his head to the side as if he were calling a shift in his defensive set. "Sir, we got infected coming out of the tunnel."

"Leave your 2nd squad in place covering the tunnel. Move 1st squad to our right flank, and you go with them. I want you to take them to the other side of that ridge. I want to know what we are dealing with. Report back as soon as you get eyes on," Kinnick shouted. The thick-necked man ran to his 1st squad, leading them through the cars. Gunfire popped off from the squad as they moved.

Kinnick turned to his left. Elwood's 3rd Platoon took cover next to him. "Lieutenant Elwood, I need your 2nd squad to cover our left flank. Leave your 1st squad with me." The hunched lieutenant nodded his head vigorously as if he just had a winning roll in D&D.

"Sergeant Matthews, stay with the colonel. You are covering the tunnel. Sergeant Putnam, bring 2nd squad up the hill with me," he shouted. Fourteen men ran for the sides of a hill. Slowly, they scrambled up the hill, taking a flanking position.

Kinnick pointed. "Hunter, concentrate fire on the tunnel entrance. After they are thinned out, I want 2nd squad, 2nd Platoon to move up. Bounding overwatch with 1st squad, 3rd Platoon. In the meantime, we have to figure out a way to seal the tunnel."

The master sergeant stood, staring. He pointed his gun at Kinnick. Fire exploded outward from the barrel. His SCAR boomed, fast and furious. Kinnick flinched and adrenaline spiked in his gut. An infected woman with gray skin and tangled black hair dropped behind him.

"We got a hot zone," Hunter yelled. "We should get elevated."

"I want that tunnel sealed," Kinnick yelled over the gunfire.

Camouflaged soldiers of Stark's 2nd squad bounded forward under the watchful eye of Matthews and 1st squad. Stark's 2nd squad took positions behind cars, weapons pointed at the tunnel entrance. Gunfire pumped out of M4 carbines; M249 light machine guns and M240 machine guns unloaded into the tunnel entrance.

Kinnick and Hunter followed Matthews and 1st squad forward through cars and infected bodies alike. Kinnick tried to keep up, feeling every minute of his age. Open luggage, empty water bottles, metal and plastic pieces of crashed cars littered the ground. Then there were the bodies. Bullet holes riddled their torsos and extremities. Kinnick knew those wounds were ineffective, but at some point, a round had destroyed their heads because the infected no longer sought the living.

Kinnick lunged over a man split in half, his guts strewn about like roadkill. Kinnick's feet were heavy. Hounding Matthews and 1st squad, they passed Stark's 2nd squad and took up firing positions behind cars and trucks alike. Kinnick leaned over the back of a pickup. Ping-ping. Ping. His carbine sounded off and an infected fell. He tried to focus more on catching his breath because within a minute he would be back on the move again.

The squads repeated the bounding action. The soldiers from 2nd squad surged past Kinnick and Hunter. Closer and closer they moved to the tunnel entrance, guns blazing as they moved. The tunnel entrance grew larger and larger, like a giant mouth getting ready to devour them. The sheer magnitude of the mountains towered even higher around them.

They slowed down as more infected stumbled from the darkness of the tunnels, a horde of rats from the bowels of the earth. They hobbled out, white eyes penetrating the living soldiers. His men held a continued rate of fire, dropping the dead as effectively as could be deemed possible. Fifteen minutes of continuous roaring gunfire passed, round after round. Calls for reloads were shouted, but the men laid down enough firepower to stem the tide of the infected. Kinnick glanced up the ridge. He could see the tiny members of Stark's 1st squad disappearing over the ridge top that was more of a ski slope than a hill.

"Keep it up," Kinnick shouted down the line. He had no idea if the soldiers could hear him over the rippling clamor of gunfire.

Kinnick inched closer to Hunter. The master sergeant fired his SCAR in controlled bursts. "How are we going to get this tunnel blocked? Our plan was to blow the tunnel. Now, I'm not even sure we can get inside." Kinnick said to him.

Hunter's shoulder rocked as he finished a magazine.

"Reloading," he yelled. His fingers slammed a full magazine back into his SCAR. "Not sure, but we can't keep this up. Look," Hunter said. He pointed. Walls of flesh and bone grew larger as more came into the light. Hundreds milled shoulder to shoulder, turning into thousands.

"Pull 2nd squad back. We are moving to Plan B," Kinnick said into his radio. The soldiers of 2nd squad were about ten yards farther ahead and offset from 1st squad.

"Second, rally on, First," Hunter said into his radio. The soldiers turned back and gave up their ground.

Hunter waved his arm at Elwood, on their left flank, then gave three pumps of his hand at the tunnel.

"Elwood, hit 'em with the rockets. Then we will block up the entrance with vehicles," Kinnick said into his radio.

Seconds later, white smoke streaked into the air diagonally from above, and the entrance of Eisenhower Tunnel erupted into an orange ball of flame. The dead that weren't annihilated on impact were launched into the air. Others walked into the flames. Fire caught their clothes and hair, engulfing their bodies in a red-licking blaze. They collapsed onto the pavement as they were cooked by the fire.

Another rocket streaked inside the tunnel. It exploded and a series of booms rocked the ground as cars blew apart. His men cheered. A third rocket penetrated the tunnel entrance. The ground shook upon impact.

"If the bastards didn't know we're here, they do now," Hunter growled, looking over the top of his rifle.

Kinnick watched the flames and black smoke billow out from the tunnel.

"Cease fire, Elwood," Kinnick said into his radio. The rockets stopped. Only the soft sound of crackling flames was in the air. Kinnick snatched up his binoculars. Zooming in, he scanned the inferno and black smoke. A man crawled on the ground. Others struggled upright, but most were pieces of charred flesh strewn about the ground.

"I'm not seeing many Zulus," Kinnick said. "Stay alert," he shouted. *No sound of the dead.* His ears still rang from the gunfire and rockets. *Would you hear them even if they were coming?*

He dropped the binoculars. A sudden explosion sounded off in the tunnel, causing him to flinch. A man staggered out of the tunnel. A soldier in the front row fired rounds into his chest, slowing it down. When the top of the infected's skull flew off, his body collapsed.

"Looks clear," Kinnick said.

"Don't count your chickens," Hunter said. His gaze settled hard on the burning vehicles as if he didn't trust them for even a second.

Movement caught Kinnick's eye out of his peripheral vision. He put the binoculars back up to his eyes. A man topped the ridge above the tunnel. He carried another man. Other forms turned into more men. Gunfire sounded like firecrackers from atop the mountain as men shot rearward. Kinnick raised the binoculars back up to his face. Stark carried a bloodied man, his arm wrapped around his waist. They stumbled down the mountainside followed by the rest of his squad.

"Lieutenant Stark, what's your status?" Kinnick said into his radio.

"They're coming," Stark panted. The microphone cracked and popped. "They're coming," he breathed heavily into the radio.

Hunter looked at Kinnick, brown beard twitching as he tongued the wad of chew in his mouth. Kinnick looked up at Lieutenant Elwood's men on the other ridge. He could tell the man was staring back in his direction.

"That's not enough men," Kinnick groaned.

Stark hoisted his comrade up onto his shoulder and leapt down the mountain, jumping from rock to rock. As he neared the bottom he stopped. He cupped his hands to mouth and screamed.

"We have to move!"

GWEN

Little Sable Point, MI

Gwen lounged in the corner of the fold-out bench table in Tess's camper, sipping some very thin tea. It tasted like she was drinking water out of a cup she had used for tea the day before. The only good part about it was that it was hot. The reused tea bags made them last longer, providing her with a touch of respite from her nausea that came and went, seemingly with the wind.

Steele sat across from her, hands wrapped around a hot mug of instant coffee. He gave her a weak smile, only showing her a fraction of his uncertainty. His hair had started to fill in along his hair-part scar, making him look less like a committed patient.

Jack had shown up in the night, throwing the camp into an uproar. The message he carried had only made it worse. He sat outside their camper under the guard of Margie while they debated the plan to move forward.

Tess sat, legs crossed on her futon-style bed, a blanket wrapped around her shoulders making her look like a little boy with her slender features and short hair. Thunder stood in the corner, arms across his barrel chest.

"So, that dick, Jack, claims the pastor wants a truce. Do we believe him?" Thunder said, his bushy eyebrows pressed together.

"If we don't, we're most certainly at war. Meeting gives us a shot," Steele said.

"As much as I'd rather tell them to fuck off, I agree," Thunder said.

"You want to meet with this nut job?" Tess said. She gave him a questioning look.

"I will if it prevents further bloodshed."

"Fine. Let's say we do meet with this *pastor*. Do we bring Peter and try and to make a trade for Pagan?" Tess wiped her nose with a hand beneath her blanket.

Steele scratched at his scar. "He was alive a few days ago, although there's no guarantee he is now. If he's not and we show up with Peter, there's not much to stop the Chosen from gunning us down and taking Peter back."

"We could go in force. Show them we aren't afraid," Tess said.

Steele shook his head. "As your partner in command, I would strongly advise against that. It would look like an open declaration of war. We are supposed to be calling a truce," Steele said. He tried to unsnarl his beard, his fingers working through it slowly.

"I'm with Steele. It will only confirm the worst in their eyes," Thunder said.

"What's to prevent them from shooting us either way and taking Peter back?" Tess asked.

"Nothing. But I don't think their leader would invite us to their camp and gun us down for no reason." Steele pulled the end of his beard.

"No reason other than you did the exact same thing to them," Gwen said, piping up. Steele glared at her.

"Okay, any ideas then?" he said.

"You could show up unarmed aside from melee weapons," Gwen said.

Steele's eyes narrowed. "I'm not going unarmed."

"Who said you had to go?" Gwen said. Steele looked uncomfortable as he shifted his weight in his seat. He wasn't used to being asked to stay behind. His eyes darted at Tess.

Possessiveness rose up in Gwen when she noticed who Mark was looking to for support. *Don't you look at her. Look at me. I am yours. Not her. She doesn't get to have you. I do.*

"I feel like I should be the one to go. I'm responsible for this community's security, and as a leader, I should be the one at the negotiating table. I don't really feel like I have a choice."

"But-," Gwen squeaked.

"And I won't go without him," Tess said.

And who said you were going, bitch? Don't think I don't know what you are doing, taking his side on anything we disagree on. She let her eyes talk for her.

"I don't see why you and Thunder couldn't go?" Gwen asked as sweetly as she could. She let her eyes fall on the big biker, testing his mettle with her look.

Thunder coughed in his hand. She could tell he was flustered by her words. "It ain't my fight."

"But it will be if they come here again," she said.

"Then maybe it's best if me and my boys head north. We all could. Leave this mess behind us. We could *dispose* of Jack along the way. My boys wouldn't have a problem with that. He's a whiny jackass who clearly has no loyalty."

"No." Steele shook his head. He waved a hand at Thunder. "I won't have more innocent blood on my hands, no matter how much I dislike the man."

Peter's blood coats your hands, Mark.

The older man nodded his acceptance.

"Best case scenario, we hold Peter as collateral to trade for Pagan. Tess and I have to meet with this pastor and see if we can smooth everything over. Make a deal with the man. Thunder, will you provide escort?"

Thunder tightened his bandana. "Me and the Red Stripes will give you a lift."

"Good, then it's settled." Steele rose out of his seat. "Thank you for the coffee, Tess. Tomorrow after daybreak?" he said.

"I can't wait," she said, sarcasm riddling her voice.

Gwen stood up, making sure to give Tess a cold gaze before she followed Mark out of the camper. After they were out of earshot, she grabbed his sleeve, making him stop.

"Why were you blowing me off in there? We talked about discussing our decisions," she said.

"We did discuss it with everyone. I made a promise to protect these people in Pagan's absence and I won't back down now."

"They got along fine before you came around. And what about me? I'm fucking pregnant. What if something happens? You're going to risk leaving me pregnant and alone in the middle of this hell?"

"Every move we make is a risk," he exclaimed. His eyes turned empathetic. "I know you're worried. I wouldn't take a risk if I didn't think I had to. The alternative is they come here in force and murder us. If not today, tomorrow, if not tomorrow, the next day. Staying would buy you a day with me. I'm trying to buy us a life."

She looked down. Sand. Rocks. The wind took a piece of trash, spiraling through the camp. Smoking fires burnt in pits. Tarps on makeshift shelters ruffled in the wind. "I deserve better than this." She waved her arms wide. "Better than this *camp*."

Margie and Jack looked up from the other end of the camper. Margie loosely held a hunting rifle in her hands next to Jack, who sat in a folding chair, hands clasped in front of him.

Gwen went to leave and he grabbed her by the shoulders. She wanted to cry. *Goddamn hormones. Is it the hormones?*

"You don't want to be with me. You want a new one," she uttered.

His eyes were hurt as he read her. "What do you mean?"

He knows exactly what I mean. She wiped her nose. "I see the way you look at her. She's fun and pretty with a skinny little body. I'm getting all swollen and pregnant. Disgusting."

"Babe, no." He reached a hand up to her face, wiping a thumb near the corner of her eye. She crossed her arms, uncomfortably looking away.

"I do these things for you. Trust me when I say I will come back to you. No one can keep us apart." She knew he lied, but it made her feel like she was back in Virginia saying goodbye to him before he deployed across the planet on the hunt for evil men in even darker places. It made her feel as if everything was almost back to normal even in their disjointed life dominated by Counterterrorism Division demands.

"I need you here," she mumbled. He pulled her chin up with a rough finger.

"I can't be," he said softly. His blue eyes were almost cold steel.

"I know," she said, turning away. *I know you have chosen your duty, but when will you choose me? When do you choose us? At what point do we become your duty?*

STEELE

Temple Energy Plant, MI

The sun sat low in the sky, beginning its lazy daily ascent.

A dozen guns pointed in their direction. Three Chosen men stood behind the chain-link gate, guns held in the low ready. Each man wore something different showing no uniformity. One blue jacket, one black jacket, and one camouflage jacket. Others were behind them in front of the power plant. They laid out prone or knelt in cover behind piles of coal. On the roof of the power plant, Steele could barely make out the small forms of men with sniper rifles zeroed in on them.

Steele and Tess stood in the middle of a sand-swept road, waiting to be acknowledged with bullets or otherwise. Jack stood wisely back a few yards away from them.

Out of the corner of her eye, he watched Tess. Her short hair was slicked back like a 1950's greaser. She visibly gulped.

"They would have shot us already if they were going to," he whispered to her under his breath. Nodding her head little by little, she acknowledged him.

"Still not comforted," she whispered back.

"It never gets any easier," Steele said, making sure his Thor's hammer medallion, Mjolnir, was tucked inside his shirt. *The last thing I need is somebody getting the wrong idea.* He raised his hands in the air, holding them up for everyone to see. Tess did the same. Jack stood behind them, hands up.

"We're here to meet with the pastor. We brought your man, *Jack*," Steele shouted.

The man in the black jacket with a light brown beard got closer to the fence.

"And who the fuck are you?" he shouted through the fence.

Steele kept his hands in the air. "You know who we are."

The man's eyes widened and then narrowed. "Must be Steele, huh? We've been waiting for you. Leave your weapons on the ground."

Steele laid his M4 carbine and M9 Beretta on the ground. Tess set her Colt 1911 next to his guns. They both stood back up straight, hands high.

"Don't forget your hatchet," the man shouted at Steele. Steele ripped it from his belt, flipped it in his hand, and set it on the ground. The man behind the gate snorted. "Open it up."

The chain-link fence shuddered as the other men pushed it open.

Steele walked forward and one of the Chosen raced out to collect their weapons. A goateed man slapped hands with Jack and smiled.

"Good to have you back, Brother Jack." Jack gave him an awkward pat on the back. Steele watched them.

So Jack made some new friends, sneaky rat, and has already gave them all the information they needed to infiltrate, assault, and destroy Little Sable.

With a clunk, a wheeled chain-link fence gate rolled closed behind them, effectively shutting them in. The rumble of motorcycles fired up in the distance. Their engines roared like lions. *We are still free* they seemed to shout. Chosen men twisted, leveling their guns in the direction of the sound.

The man with the soft beard leveled his shotgun at them from the hip. "Got some friends out there, don't ya?" he said. He eyed the treelined road leading away from the plant.

Steele gave a glance backward. He leveled with the man eye to eye. "We have plenty of friends."

"So do we," the man rebutted with a smile. His glance was off-putting, like that of a sober madman. The way he uttered the words made Steele wonder what he meant. *Did the Red Stripes just deliver us to the pastor's men as allies or as prisoners? Was this the deal the entire time? Get rid of the troublemakers? No. Not Thunder. He loves his freedom just as much as we do. Maybe he just guaranteed it.* Steele swallowed his doubt.

A handsome man emerged from the power plant's double-metal door entrance. He wore khaki pants and a nice zip-up sweater. A wooden flail hung from his belt and Steele wondered if it ever swung into his legs while he walked, banging his knees and shins. He waved them forward.

The man gave them a smile. His wavy blond hair was combed all to one side with a nice part. "Seth, bring them on in. The pastor is waiting."

Who is this guy? Some sort of used car salesman?

"We're coming, Brother Matthew," Seth said. He turned to them. "Come on, Steele, and oh yeah, who are you?"

"I'm Tess," she spat with venom.

"Spunky. Thought you were a boy," he said with a laugh.

"More of a man than you'll ever be," she said.

Seth's eyes darkened. "If you lived here, you'd know better than to speak to a man like that."

"That's why I don't live in this penitentiary."

Steele gave Tess a fake smile. "I believe our *host*, Seth, was going to take us inside to our meeting."

"Come on," Seth grunted. He walked them past Matthew inside the metal doors.

They stepped inside and were immediately buffeted by the smell of cooking food and laughter. Kids pushed their way by chasing one another.

"You're it," one screeched.

They ducked in and out of dormant machinery surrounded by metal piping. Women sat in circles preparing food to be cooked. Women and children peered out from behind tents and dividers watching the newcomers. Men chatted here and there. None seemed starved or suffering from malnutrition or apparent abuse. Guns were abundant among them. A few regarded them as they walked by.

Seth led them through the large open floor; each room they passed was filled with more people. *There must be at least a thousand people living here. So Peter told the truth. A power plant fortress with over a thousand people. I was skeptical based on my method of elicitation, but he told the truth.*

They crossed the entire plant. On the far side of the plant, Seth lifted a lever and opened a barred door. Bright morning light hit them again. *Why are they leading us back outside?* Coal piles loomed over two stories high on flat open ground.

Seth ushered them forward and brought them down the middle of a gravel-filled path. The path led them in-between giant black rocky piles. The land gradually sloped downward, leading them to water. A narrow canal widened into a lake. Seth stopped them. A tall, slightly hunched old man stood in the water, his back to them.

His dark pants were cuffed up to his thin calves. His bare feet were submerged in the water. Long-fingered hands were clasped behind his back. It was as if he were going to issue commands to the far-reaching body of water. A faded, worn wood carpenter's hammer was stuck through his belt.

Seth stopped and cleared his throat. "Pastor. Mr. Steele and Miss Tess are here."

The man didn't turn around. He continued to look out over the water as if it were telling him a story.

After a moment, the man spoke softly. "Seth, you may go." He didn't look at them. He waved two fingers with his right hand. Seth hesitated. He gave Steele a wary glance, untrusting of him.

"Pastor, you shouldn't be left alone with these Gentiles," Seth hissed.

"You may go, Brother." The Pastor waved his two fingers in the air. "God will protect me."

"As you command." Seth bent his head downward toward the ground in obedience. He gave Steele a threatening look and walked back to the plant, feet crunching in the gravel.

They all stood in silence and moments floated by, evaporating into the morning air. *Bold move meeting us by yourself. In two seconds, I could have my hands around his neck. Will your God protect you when I hold you under that water until you stop moving?*

Tess gave Steele a questioning look. She mouthed, "Do we say something?"

Steele shrugged his shoulders. They were at his mercy. The silence was awkward, long, and almost peaceful.

"The water is warmer here," the pastor said. His back held a slight hunch as if it were permanently sore. “Not as warm as if the power plant was running at full capacity. But even the little we use heats the water somewhat,” he said, bringing a foot out and shaking it off.

Steele held his tongue. He didn’t want to walk into some sort of mind game with the man.

The pastor dried his feet with a small hand towel. He looked up at them between wiping his feet. “Water is the symbol of life. It brings us rebirth in God’s eyes. It washes away our sins. It brings us new life. It is the harbinger of good.” A smile stretched across his long, weathered face. “And it helps my swelling feet.”

The pastor slipped his feet back into a pair of black shoes. “You look familiar to me, son.” He blinked as if trying to bring up a photograph of Steele in his mind. “I don’t recall. An old mind is filled with ages of knowledge but won’t be able to remember where you placed your keys.”

Steele said nothing in response. He let his eyes remain fierce.

The pastor smiled with tight-lips. “So they call you Steele.” He looked Steele up and down. “A fitting name for a man forged by conflict.” He turned to Tess. “And you must be Tess, an expert on our civil freedoms if what I’m told is true. In another time, I would like to speak with you of moral topics, maybe even have a debate. The church has moved away from debating nonbelievers, something that I never understood. For with righteous purpose on one’s side, victory is all but assured.” Tess gave Steele a sidelong glance, her eyes asking if this guy was a loon. Steele gave her a grim smile in response.

“We came to discuss terms,” Steele said, keeping his tone flat and his voice calm.

The pastor grinned a smile of old understanding. “A direct man as well. It’s funny. Before this pestilence gripped our nation, I yearned for quieter days of no cell phones buzzing or the youth being distracted by social media. The days where you could go outside and hear the sound of silence. A slower time. And now that we have this, everything still seems so rushed.”

The pastor stood watching Steele. His eyes were judging Steele, watching him for anything that indicated his character or the depth of his soul. Steele felt like he might clench his teeth so tightly that he would bite through his jaw, but held himself in check.

"I hope that Peter is unharmed," the pastor continued.

"He is." Steele produced a small silver cross necklace. He reached out his hand and gave it to the pastor. The pastor inspected the cross and placed it in his pocket. His eyes narrowed to slits, weighing Steele's truthfulness.

"It would be a shame if you took this from his corpse and lied to me." His eyes looked into Steele. Steele met him eye for eye.

"He's safe. You have my word."

"Your word? A word from a man today means little. How can we trust a man's word when men beat each other to death over a piece of bread? Only the word of God is something you can trust," the pastor said.

"I am a man of my word. I swore an oath to my country, an oath that I've kept."

"Ah, a military man? No. Not military. Your look is too uncouth. Unorthodox." He pursed his lips. "Something more covert. An undercover agent? DEA or something?"

"I worked for the government."

The pastor nodded, a seemingly comprehending head maneuver.

"Pay unto Caesar what is his, but Steele, you've forgotten to pay unto God what is his as is written in the Bible," the pastor lectured. His chin rose slightly as if Tess and Steele were his parish.

"We aren't here to banter fucking gospel, preacher. What about Pagan?" Tess said, piping up from Steele's side. Steele could feel the angry energy ebbing off of her tiny frame.

"Yes. Mr. Pagan. He is serving a penance through manual labor."

"Penance?! For what?" she said, exasperated.

"For his sins. He was such a misguided man, but I have faith God will yet touch his soul."

"He doesn't *need* penance," she said.

The pastor smiled, lips pressed together. "Everyone needs penance. Follow me."

The pastor passed through the middle of them, walking out in front. He marched through the heaping piles of coal.

"Plenty of coal here. We could supply this plant for years if not longer. If we could get a good enough presence, we could supply entire communities with power. God willing, we could supply hundreds, if not thousands, of people with power. We would need them to be in the local area, but my men assure me we could fix the transformers and scrap the rest of them for parts." Steele didn't know if he spoke the truth, but there was a ton of coal piled up. Coal was a resource they could still use, power plant or not.

The old man had long strides. He quickly brought them back around the coal plant. Hundreds of cars, trucks, and semis sat in the plant parking lot. "We have enough vehicles to keep up constant supply lines between communities. We can send out scouting parties. Bus people without a place to our communities. We could set up new settlements. My people already travel far and wide eradicating those who've come back to our realm as Satan's Legion."

Steele breathed hard looking at all the cars. *They have so many more than we do.* "A worthy cause," Steele said to him. The more dead they slew the less Steele may have to face.

The pastor nodded. "Yes. It is the most important of causes. Jesus crusaded against death, and now, we do as well."

Steele bent to Tess. She turned her ear. "We cannot win a war against these people," he whispered to Tess. She frowned, eying all the cars.

"Keep following me," the pastor said with a friendly wave. They tailed him. People from the power plant watched them as they walked by. They bowed their heads to the pastor in reverence.

He stopped in an open field that once looked like it was used to set trailer beds. Weeds grew in the gray gravel-covered grounds. Armed men stood about talking as if they awaited them. An eight-foot beam stood straight out of the ground, dark and charred ashes mounding at the base. Steele's gut spiked adrenaline. *This does not look good.*

"Steele and Tess. I have shown you what this place can be. I have given you a glimpse of the Kingdom of God on Earth. We have the opportunity to shed God's light along this entire west coast of Michigan. We have the opportunity to share this with everyone. To rebuild *life*. To save people's souls and destroy the devil where his ugly head shows itself." The pastor squeezed his fist together in a ball.

"What do you want from us?" Steele said.

The pastor let his hand fall to his side and he looked up at the sky. "It's not what I want. It's what he wants. I can only fight for your souls."

"So you're taking your orders from a magical gray-bearded man in the sky?" Tess interjected.

The pastor did not smile at her. The look in his eyes said his tolerance was wearing thin.

"That isn't helping," Steele said to her with a terse look.

She turned on him. "So what, muscle brain? You take your orders from a person who lives on a cloud too?"

"No, I didn't say that, but we're trying to come to terms, not insult our host."

"He's right. You can do whatever you want, Pastor," she groaned.

"Thank you, my daughter."

"I'm not your daughter."

His long face nodded in acknowledgment of her wishes. "If only I could have found you sooner."

"Pastor, I'm impressed with your operation. You're capable of good force projection." Steele eyed the armed men standing around. Confidence hung about them, not a military confidence, but one of men that held a certain righteousness in their favor. A fervor of a gang of like-minded men. *Not a fight I want today.* "What are your terms?"

The Chosen men shuffled on their feet, guns gripped in hands. They all watched Steele and Tess with fervent eyes as if they waited to administer their religious justice upon the two unarmed people at any moment.

The pastor clasped his hands in front of him. "It's clear that at the very least some of my followers have been slain. I will not ask why. Peter is level-headed, and I wouldn't expect it to be his fault," he stopped, giving Tess a dirty look.

"Mistakes were made. I regret that, but Peter is alive," Steele said.

The pastor nodded his head. "Sometimes God takes our sons and daughters before their time, but this was a part of his plan. I will not claim to understand why he does what he does."

Tess huffed next to Steele. Her arms crossed in anger over her chest. Steele tried to tune her out.

"But I think we can make a deal," the pastor said. He waved a hand at his men. "Bring out Pagan."

Tess tensed at Steele's side as a man appeared between two of the Chosen. "Pagan!" she shouted. Pagan pulled at the men holding him. They pushed him forward, leading him to the charred, thick beam stuck upright in the ground. They wrapped a rope around him and tied him to the post.

"Tess," Pagan shouted.

"What are they doing?" Tess asked.

The pastor turned back to his men. "They are preparing him for purification."

"Purification? What the hell does that mean?" Tess asked. Her voice rose an octave.

"Tess, you need to go," Pagan pleaded from across the field. His face was swollen where he had been beaten. Men tossed dry kindling near his feet. They stacked wood around his legs.

"Like you purified the homes down the coast," Tess spat.

The pastor lifted his chin high into the air and smiled. "You've seen some of our pacification of the countryside."

This bastard can't be serious. This isn't how terms are met. "Pastor, I thought we were coming to terms?" Steele said, words rushed. "Why are we talking about purification?" Each moment this conversation continued, it spiraled further out of control.

"Sometimes people don't understand the gravity of a situation. The fight for men's souls is sadly never done nor easy."

Tess took hasty steps forward. Guns were brought to shoulders. Revolvers were cocked. All were pointed at the two outsiders.

"Pagan," Tess sobbed at the man. Steele stepped forward and pulled her back away.

"Careful, Tess. We don't want a *misunderstanding*," the pastor said, his voice chilly as a winter morning.

Steele cast his eyes from Pagan back to the pastor, his heart rate going faster and faster. *This shit is about to hit the fan,* his mind shouted.

"Peter's not here. We cannot make the trade today even if we wanted to," Steele pleaded.

"While I want Peter back, it's not the only thing I want to come from this *negotiation*."

"What do you want?" Steele hissed.

"I want our people to be as one. I want you to join us. It's better for your people."

"We'll never do that," Tess spat. Steele held her with one of his arms tight around her tiny waist. The pastor's men laughed at her.

"I think I've given you two a lot to think about," the pastor said calmly.

You sure have, you bastard. "Can you give us a minute?" Steele said.

"Why, of course."

Steele turned to Tess, spinning her to face him.

"We can't fight our way out of here. We can't run. We can only listen."

She looked back over at Pagan. Her eyes were filled with angry tears.

"Leave!" Pagan shouted. "Fucking leave!" Spit flew from his mouth. She gave Pagan a quick glance, but her attention was on Steele.

Her face got close to his. Her eyes glared at him. "I didn't bring you in so you could fold at the first chance you got."

His mouth tightened and he whispered. "I'm not folding. I'm listening to a man who has been pretty darn reasonable, considering that we gunned down eight of his people in the last week. A man who also has a vision, God-driven or not. Think about Pagan. We can still get him back."

"I don't like him. This isn't right. He's threatening us to get what he wants."

"I hate that but let's listen. It may be the only way we leave here alive," Steele hissed.

Her mouth clamped.

They turned back to the pastor. His hands were clasped in front of his body

"Tell us more," Steele said.

"You will join God's Chosen people. All of your people must accept Christ or be purified by fire." His words were as matter-of-fact as if he had said the sky was blue.

Steele laughed a short laugh. "What do you mean purified by fire?" *You know. It's the way he said it, with all the confidence of a deeply religious man. You've seen their handy work.*

"Mr. Steele. We're building Christ's kingdom on Earth. There's no room for those on the sidelines. There are only God's Chosen and those touched by the devil. Hear me. I'm giving you a second chance at peace. I'm giving you an opportunity to give life." Thoughts of Gwen raced through his mind, followed by thoughts of his unborn child. *All you have to do is join and they will be safe. All you have to do is say words you don't believe in because they've been corrupted. No true follower of Christ would murder the innocent for not joining. Yet here we stand. Will you give up your freedom for safety? Will you make others give up their freedoms?*

"We will not," Tess shouted at him. Steele held up a hand in the air.

"We have Peter. Let's trade and we will leave the area for good. No more conflicts. Nothing."

"I'm not afraid of more conflicts with your tiny *band*, Mr. Steele, but you should be afraid of mine." More men walked out into the field. All armed. Some held melee weapons: bats, metal bars, and knives. Almost all had guns. All were ready for a fight.

Fire seemed to burn in the pastor's eyes as if he were watching his vision play out in real time. "I will burn your community to the ground and kill everyone inside. This is a crusade. God wills it. But," he held up a long finger, "I'm giving *you* a choice. Just as God gave Eve and Adam a choice."

Steele locked eyes with Tess. Her eyes smoldered with the ashes of her people's lives and freedom. She would never give in, not even for a chance for peace. They may be all that was left of the United States. They may be the only people left in the world. *At what cost do we make peace? What compromise do we make to stand against the true enemy, the dead?*

Steele eyed all the armed men. The many. The Chosen. Steele was but one man. Unarmed. His only ally nearby, a scrawny unarmed woman. She would never submit, and as her comrade, neither could he. As much as he would suffer for his decisions, he could not submit. Submitting to this man was antithetical to what they believed in.

"I'm sorry, Pastor, you ask too much. We want there to continue to be peace between our groups, but we cannot join you by coercion."

The pastor ran a finger along his temple, dragging down his cheek. "This is unfortunate." He stared Steele in the eyes. The pastor's eyes promised bullets sent for Steele and his friends. Steele knew he'd seen worse.

"I will pray for Peter's soul," the pastor said. The pastor waved his hand. A man bent low near Pagan. Pagan's eyes met Steele's, fear embodying them. Acknowledgment of his fate. Smoke plumed up from his feet. Pagan's feet stamped up and down. Little yellow and orange embers grew into flames around his feet. His mouth opened, and he screamed.

JOSEPH

Cheyenne Mountain Complex, CO

Sirens blared in the hallway, the sound running along the walls. *Awoogha. Awoogha.* Worried, Joseph looked back at the door. They had been inside Byrnes's office for hours.

"What's going on?" Joseph said, covering his ears.

Byrnes's face went sour like he'd eaten only lemons for weeks. "Lockdown." He ripped open the top drawer of his desk and pulled out an M9 Beretta 9mm. He slammed a magazine inside and racked the slide back. He held the weapon pointed at the ceiling.

"Come on," Byrnes said, standing. Joseph stood hesitantly. The lean colonel rounded his desk and pushed Joseph in the back until he was in the hallway. The sirens screamed even louder there. Joseph reached up and covered his ears.

Yellow lights spun overhead, hanging from the ceiling. Soldiers in black gear, MP5s strapped to their bodies, barreled down the hall.

"What's happening?" Byrnes growled, reaching for one and grabbing him by his shirt.

The soldier stopped, eyes angry behind his black mask before realizing Byrnes was a colonel. His eyes cooled quickly. "Outbreak. Corridor Three." Byrnes released him and he sprinted off. Byrnes turned to Joseph, but Joseph already knew.

"That's where Rebecca's room is," Joseph said.

Byrnes's thin jaw clenched. "You should head back to your room and lock the door."

"I will not," Joseph said. His voice bordered on more of a squeak, but determination was there too.

Byrnes nodded at him with a slight dip of his chin. "Fair enough." He turned and chased the soldiers down the hall. Joseph followed behind him. They jogged, the pounding of feet echoing from the floor to the walls and back. White walls zipped by them in a blur.

They rounded a corner, and a squad of black-clad soldiers blocked their path. The man in the rear raised his MP5 9mm submachine gun, his masked eyes watching them. He lowered it a second later when he realized they weren't infected. Joseph thanked God that his training allowed him to identify the threats before he unloaded a magazine into himself and Byrnes. The three other soldiers pointed guns down the corridor, poised and ready to shoot, but held their point of reference. Byrnes and Joseph stepped behind them.

"How many infected?" Byrnes asked.

"Only one, sir. The sensors in room C-3EB were tripped a minute and fifteen seconds ago."

"Good response time, Sergeant." Byrnes nodded to him.

Joseph stepped up on his tiptoes. A lone female stood down the hall and his heart sank in his chest.

His fears took his breath away, tightening his chest like a vise.

Her light blue medical gown hung limply around her. It was twisted lopsided as if she had gotten into a fight and hadn't bothered to fix her clothes. Her dark auburn hair stuck to her neck as if she had succumbed to the disease in a feverish sweat. Her surgical mask hung to one side. Her chin dropped and she stared at them through her eyebrows.

"Background is clear. You are approved to engage," Byrnes commanded. She chomped her jaws together at her former colleague, blood oozing from her mouth in response.

"No!" Joseph shouted. He brushed past them, stepping in front of their guns. The soldiers looked at him, dumbfounded by his actions. One reached for Joseph and he dodged him.

"Dr. Jackowski, what in the hell are you doing? Get back here," Byrnes shouted.

Joseph held up a hand in the air. "Hold your fire," he said. Joseph took a hesitant step forward. Rebecca saw him. She took a shaky step for him. A pale bare foot stepped his way.

"Rebecca," he said, his voice almost a whisper.

A low growl grew in her throat. She lifted her arm up. Blood dripped from the point where she had ripped away her IV. Her fingers curled into a hooked claw. Joseph took another cautious step closer. "If you're still there, please go back to your room," Joseph said, but he already knew.

She shambled down the hall. Her shoulders swayed unnaturally as if she had hurt both her legs. As she neared, he could see her eyes. Pale white orbs, as sure a sign as any that the infection had claimed victory over her body. Nothing remained of Rebecca, the doctor that he had fallen for. The doctor who had worked until her last breath to find a vaccine to save mankind. It had stolen her body, but never her soul. Now this husk hobbled down the hall, hoping to reach him to infect him as well. Kill. Reproduce. Kill. Reproduce. Killing was part of its reproduction cycle, and it wouldn't stop until it completed its mission.

"Please go back," Joseph sobbed. The wetness of the warm tears on his cheeks was distant. "We need more time," he whispered. The living cadaver of Rebecca continued on for him, ignoring him like a jilted lover.

Out of the corner of his right eye, a black gun filled his vision. Boom. Fire burst from its barrel and Rebecca's body became erect, almost as if she were suspended in the air. Her eyes met his, and for a brief second, he thought she was there again. It was like a flash of sadness had shone through the infection, longing for more time. Then it was gone.

A circular dime-sized black hole leaked a trickle of blood out from her eyebrow. The blood dripped down the ridge of her eye socket and around the curve of her mouth. Then she collapsed.

Her body folded onto the floor. She was a forgotten toy tossed away by a child. Her knees bent back and her arms flung to her sides like those of a tormented Shakespearian actor.

Joseph faced Byrnes. Joseph had known she was gone, but he had let himself hope. Hope is what torments the soul.

"Check out the rest of the corridor," Byrnes ordered. He holstered his sidearm and the metal slid over the hard plastic. Black-clad soldiers ran past them, stepping around Rebecca's body.

The colonel's brow furrowed. "There was nothing we could do. Her fate was sealed when she was bitten."

Joseph looked away from the colonel's eyes. He knew Byrnes was right, but the sting didn't leave him. He pushed away from the colonel and ran down the hallway to where she lay. Blood pooled around her head, dark red and almost black. He fell to his knees and took up her hand in his. It was cool inside his warm living hands. Her white eyes stared up at the ceiling, vacant.

Byrnes called to him. "Careful, Dr. Jackowski. Her blood is extremely contagious."

"You think I don't know that?" Joseph snipped at him.

Byrnes's mouth flattened and he sighed. "I cared for her too. She was the last colleague I had and an amazing doctor. I don't want to lose two of my doctors today."

Joseph reluctantly released her hand, setting it gently on the floor. He turned to find Byrnes offering his hand in her place. Joseph glared at him but placed his hand in his.

"For her," Joseph said. They had differences, but this fight was bigger than those.

Byrnes helped him up from the floor. "For her." He sighed and looked out over the mess in the hallway. "I'll get some biohazard technicians to clean this up. I'm going to check on the other doctors."

"I'll dig through her notes and see if she left us anything of value," Joseph said.

Byrnes nodded at him and walked away.

The door to Rebecca's room was only partially open. He rested a hand on it, letting the weight of his arm slowly swing it all the way open. It was dark. Her heart rate monitor was tipped over, and her bed looked like someone had used it as a wrestling mat. IV tubing was strewn on the floor. Her sheets hung off the bed along with a blood-smeared pillow where she had hemorrhaged out of her ears and nose.

Papers lay strewn about the entire room as if she were placing them to potty train a dog. He bent down and began shuffling them together in a pile. Most were his notes. Underneath a pile, he found her tablet. He picked it up and turned it over.

The sirens stopped outside her room. *At least the outbreak was over quick.* He pressed a button on the edge of the tablet and it powered up. The battery bar was still in the green, so it had enough power for him to study what she had last worked on.

He scrolled through her notes. Most of her notes were things they had discussed while she was coherent. He ran his finger along the right side of the screen. Her notes became more short and terse near the end of her page. Single phrases. The cat only has three legs. Can't play unless it has four. Cat needs a leg. *What does that mean?* Her words became more singular down the page.

Cat missing leg. Cat need leg. The satellite virus was behind those incoherent words. A fevered hallucination going back to a childhood memory. Her typing became nothing but a mishmash of letters together and turned into pure gibberish.

Joseph suppressed a tiny chuckle. "You must have had a three-legged cat as a kid," he said to the empty room.

He heard the technicians in the hallway haul her body up and drop her on a gurney.

He studied the phrases again. "The cat only has three legs. The cat needs a new leg to play," he said under his breath. He looked around the room as if she would have left him another clue as to her meaning. Nothing stuck out in the trashed room.

Clutching her tablet he stepped into the hallway. He walked around the puddle of blood that was once Dr. Weinroth and hurried to his room.

KINNICK

Eisenhower Tunnel, CO

From the depths of the dark tunnel, fire leapt with scorching fury for the entrance. It was as if the tunnel were about to spit its inferno back out at the soldiers and cars along the highway. The flames came for them, step by hindered step.

Kinnick watched in horror as the first flaming bodies emerged from the tunnel. Clothes were aflame. Hair singed and burnt from the tops of their skulls. Flesh melted like burning plastic. Their skin was brown and black from the fire but cracked pink below the surface. Regardless of what horrible trauma had befallen the corpses, they still came onward, unwilling to give in to death. Second squad unleashed into the new infected, finishing them off.

"They're coming," Stark breathed through the radio.

"How many?" Hunter asked quickly into his radio.

"Too many. We have to fall back," Stark replied between gasps for air.

"A thousand? Two thousand?" Kinnick said loud into his radio. Angry, he clicked off his radio, waiting for his officer's response.

The microphone popped. Gunfire echoed over the line. "As far…as…we could see."

Hunter and Kinnick locked eyes. Kinnick held his breath as if he would never be able to take another. *Jesus Christ.*

"We need to fall back, Master Sergeant," Kinnick managed to get out.

"Second squad," Hunter started. An infected stumbled through the flames, its clothes alight with flickering fire. Its exposed flesh blackened crisp. It was impossible to tell the infected's gender. It stamped through burning fuel and around the burning wreckage of a car.

One infected turned into three and three into too many as the dead multiplied in the darkness of the earth. It was as if the tormented souls marched from the fiery bowels of hell itself.

"Fire!" Hunter screamed. His SCAR was to his shoulder, cracking rounds quickly. As he moved to the side off the highway, hundreds pushed their way from out of the tunnel. Arms and legs were alight and the infected continued onward as if nothing was wrong. Bullets ripped through organs and flesh, pieces of flesh blown straight off their bodies.

The infected poured out faster than 1st and 2nd squads could shoot. The dead surged around the cars, flooding onto the road. No gunfire could slow them down enough to make a difference. A private was bulldozed to the ground, screaming as the burning infected scorched his skin with their scalding hands. They immediately tore into his flesh with mouths afire.

"Up the hills," Kinnick screamed. He sprayed rounds out of his M4 in their direction. They weaved in and out of the highway debris, racing for the rocky terrain. Kinnick cut through the cars, running for the mountainous hills that made the Eisenhower Tunnel a necessity. From behind him, he could hear Elwood's entrenched hillside squad firing from the other flank. He knew they wouldn't be firing close to 2nd squad, leaving the most threatening of enemies unhindered in their pursuit.

The screams of Stark's 2nd squad sounded off as they were caught from behind. They had no clear path to safety, trucks and cars blocking them. A smoky haze filled the air clouding everyone's vision. Visibility low, Kinnick found himself zigzagging and banging into cars as he followed close behind Hunter.

Hunter jumped the hood of a car, firing both left and then right as he ran. Kinnick started to lag behind. He dodged the open door of a GMC Yukon, his shoulder catching it painfully on the way by. When he looked back up, Hunter was gone. Smoke, infected, and fire took his place. Kinnick's heart felt like it was going to explode in his chest.

Glancing to his left, and only a car away, an infected closed in on one of his men. Kinnick squeezed the trigger of his carbine. His first round exploded in its shoulder, causing its arm to flinch backwards and dangle like a Christmas stocking as it hung by only loose flesh and shredded ligaments. Kinnick rushed his next shot. His second round caught it in the collarbone, denting it inward. Following up his first two shots, his third hit its open mouth. The back of the infected's skull blew out, causing the top half to dip in front, its mouth snapping closed.

"Hunter," he called out. Black smoke sat low in the air blanketing rock, man, and concrete alike. Kinnick scanned left and right, peering through car windows and over car rooftops. He coughed and spit on the ground. "Where the fuck are you?" he yelled. Stinking, flaming flesh rounded a car. Kinnick instinctually point shot his M4. It was more muscle memory than actionable thought. The infected's head popped as a round went into its temporal lobe. His mind discarded his action as reaction before the infected rolled forward into a pile of bones and skin on the concrete.

Finding himself holding his breath, he spit the smoky taste from his mouth. He wheezed as he ran for large jagged rocks on the hillside. His body was only beginning to realize how exhausted it already was. His feet hardly obeyed as he attempted to make it up the incline.

Slinging his M4 behind him, he clambered up on all fours, reaching for a rock and then another. His men fought for survival up the rocky pine-filled slope, slowly being pursued by infected.

"To the top," he choked out. Infected were the only ones to hear him. Dozens followed his voice, struggling up the hill much as he had done. Kinnick leaned upright. He shuffled his feet using a rock as a stepping stone to propel himself farther up the hill. The only way to go was farther up the slopes.

Tall spire-like pine trees coated the hillside like a thick toupee leaping up before him. He clambered on up the slope, making for the trees, crawling part of the way on all fours like a dog. Sucking in wind, he peered over his shoulder. Infected were still on the hunt behind him.

Twisting back around, he fell onto his backside. His legs thanked him.

His mind screamed danger. He jammed his palm down onto his Beretta M9 9mm pistol. He wrapped his fingers around it, feeling the coarseness of the grip. He pulled it free of its holster and fired into the oncoming pack.

Kinnick's heart's rhythm exploded in his chest. The tension coursing through his veins caused him to jerk the trigger too fast, causing most of his shots to go low left. Two infected dropped to the ground before his mag ran dry. He crawled upright and ran into a cluster of trees more closely pressed together.

His feet dug into the loose gravelly rock. The ground seemed to chew up his steps, sucking him down into the earth. The infected walked as far as they could; some fell and clawed the earth trying to reach him. He scrambled around a tree and put his back against its solid coarse trunk. His heavy breathing rubbed the bark as he caught his breath. He could hear the infected's hasty pursuit. He looked to his left, and a man in camouflage hit the ground with a grunt.

"Sir, help." The soldier crawled toward Kinnick's spot. Kinnick recognized the short corporal, named Davis, from Stark's 2nd squad. Shadowy forms closed in on the soldier from behind.

"Behind you," Kinnick yelled. He raised his sidearm, slipping over the loose sloped ground for the soldier. Click. Click. Kinnick's finger worked the trigger but nothing happened. In his panic, he had forgotten the reload. Almost numb fingers reached for a new magazine on his hip. Davis rolled over onto his back and sprayed bullets into the infected, but they were too close and he was aiming instinctively center mass. They fell upon Davis before Kinnick could get his magazine seated and the gun operational.

Davis screamed as their teeth tore off his nose and part of his cheek. Kinnick stopped and steadied himself, shooting three rounds. Two for the infected, one for their newest indoctrinated infected. Moans flowed up the alpine mountainside and hundreds of forms walked through the trees.

Kinnick ran farther up the slope. His quads shook, giving everything they had. Breathing burned his chest, and his calves were filled with as much blood as they could hold, but he continued to dig his feet into the rocky slope, showering the infected behind him, struggling through the rocks and steep incline. His vision was blurred with stinging sweat. Blood pounded inside his skull, and his vision was a haze. Dark shapes ran down the slope ahead of him. *Dear God.* Kinnick stopped standing upright. *This way too. I'm done and I killed all these boys.*

The ones coming down the hill were different than the ones coming up the hill. They held their guns in a meaningful way as if they were ready to use them. The lead man neared Kinnick and he recognized the brute.

Stark bounded down the hill with fifteen men at his back. He slid on his ass part of the way down. He leapt up, his carbine bursting fire past Kinnick. Stark's gun blazed so fast it sounded like it was on full auto. Kinnick went to his knees, crawling in the dirt until he felt a hand on his belt.

"Move your ass, Colonel," Stark yelled in his face. Veins bulged in Stark's neck.

Kinnick mountain-climbed his feet but mostly scrambled until he was upright. Several agonizing minutes later, he reached the top of the ridge. His legs were overcooked noddles. He was so fatigued that he was afraid he might actually be having a heart attack as pain shot down his left arm and up into his neck. He forced himself upright and joined his men, aiming down the ridge. *Don't have time for that.* He shook his arm out, trying to catch his breath.

The remnants of Stark's 1st squad fired down the steep slope into the infected. Kinnick took up his carbine and listened in misery to the faint calls for help through the gunfire.

A private struggled through the trees. Two infected converged on him and dragged him down from behind. The private crawled, hands gouging the earth as he tried to escape. He spasmed as the infected dug their hands into his lower back pulling pieces of bloodied uniform, skin, and chunks of kidneys from his body. They shoved the bloody guts in their mouths, tearing into the meat while his soldier convulsed in shock on the ground.

"Where's Hunter?" Kinnick shouted. His carbine pinged as he fired it.

"Don't know, sir," Stark said over his shoulder. He slung ten rounds in quick succession, dropped his magazine then reloaded by shoving a fresh one in its place. "Not going to matter if we get overrun," he shouted.

Kinnick picked out a pack of the dead scrambling up the slope and pulled the trigger repeatedly. The bodies stumbled and jerked as rounds penetrated their rotting flesh. He calmed his breath and lined up his sights on an ugly infected's head. The carbine sounded off and the infected dropped to the ground to be trampled by the other dead. It didn't cry out when struck. It didn't scream when its guts were splattered against the rocks. When limbs were severed from their bodies or their bones broken into tiny white fragments, they only let out a low moan like a distant train.

"Get those 2-40s going," Kinnick yelled over to the remainders of 2nd Platoon. Two soldiers laid prone on the ground. One hastily flung out the bipod legs of an M240B machine gun. The supporting soldier laid out the belt of ammunition. It thundered out rounds. A fast-paced, dud-dud-dud-dud spewed from the barrel. It hammered at the infected gathering along the slope. Guts sprayed out their backs as bullets raced through rotting flesh. The hot rounds penetrated multiple bodies, going through entire groups of the dead. The infected knocked into one another, the incline of the hill causing some to collapse and roll into the others. Hasty feet flattened the rest.

A truck roared on the cluttered highway before Kinnick saw it. A white semi pulled a long silver cylindric fuel tanker behind it. Infected were brushed to the sides as the truck divided them into two halves on the edge of the road. An infected clung to the passenger side door, pulling itself alongside the driver. It fell backward as bullets punched through the door of the truck. With a crunch, the driver hit an abandoned car and shoved it to the side like a bigger sibling would a smaller as they raced for presents on Christmas morning. The semi slammed perpendicular to a smoldering car near the entrance, t-boning it several feet. The force of the impact drove the car sideways into the median. The infected swarmed the semi, beating it with fists and the weight of their lifeless bodies.

Kinnick's radio crackled. "Who's that guy? Do you want us to clear out some space for him?" Elwood said. His voice was skittish as if he would sound the retreat at any moment. The glass shattered on the driver's window. Arms shot through. Heads exploded and the bodies fell back onto the others.

"Hold your fire, Lieutenant. We don't want to hit the fuel tanker."

"Copy that, sir."

A man's head popped up from a rescue hatch atop the semi. He looked around before he pushed his arms through the opening. A soldier pulled himself up from inside the semi's cabin. Kinnick raised his binoculars back to his eyes. A brown bearded soldier huffed as he pulled himself free. *Master Sergeant Hunter.* The man crawled across the top of the tanker as hundreds of infected assaulted the semi beneath him. Kinnick glanced at the remainder of 2nd Platoon.

"Stark, how many of your men are operational?"

The bull of a man stared down his firing line.

"Fifteen, Colonel. Farrell is a bit banged up, but he'll fight."

Kinnick pointed. "Move down the ridge."

Stark's eyes flashed. "Sir?"

Kinnick pointed. "Fire your way down the hill, and clear out a path for Master Sergeant Hunter. Do not hit the tanker."

"Second Platoon, you heard the Colonel. Clear a path for the master sergeant. Move!" Stark screamed. The soldiers ran down the ridge directly perpendicular to the tunnel. They fired between sprints. Kinnick ran with them, following a scrawny soldier tasked with carrying a light machine gun. Dust rose up as boots beat the rocky ground with tread. As they grew close to lining up with the edge of the tunnel, the squads split into a V, aiming down the hill.

"Don't hit the truck," Stark screamed at his men.

They fired into the mass of infected, bringing them down in slow, controlled shots. Hunter stood, feet widespread, balancing atop the tanker. He quick-fired into the infected's heads, and the bodies piled up around the tanker. There was a method to his extreme violence.

As the infected thinned, Hunter jumped down from atop the silver tanker, using the pile of dead to break his fall. He rolled over the fallen bodies, all that his kit would allow. The infected swiped, grasping hands reaching for Hunter and missing. He pushed up onto his knees and scrambled upright. He lowered his head and sprinted for the hill. He cross-checked an infected woman in the face and bounded up the slope. Second Platoon slow-stepped down the hill, closing the gap between themselves and the insane master sergeant.

Hunter hustled up the hill. Infected would turn and lunge for him as he ran the gauntlet of the dead. Most he ignored on his way by. Others he popped off rounds into when they were too close. The steep incline caused his cheeks to puff out and turn red as he ran. The gap between Hunter and the infected widened.

Hunter raced past 2nd Platoon and they retreated back up the mountainous slope. Kinnick panted as he saddled up alongside the master sergeant. Hunter put his hands on his hips trying to breathe.

"Been awhile since I ran up a fucking mountain. Wahoo," he half-yelled.

"Glad to have you back," Kinnick said, clapping Hunter on the back. Hunter stood, taking a big breath, his mustache quivering beneath his greedy oxygen-ingesting.

"Let's seal the deal," Hunter said with a wink.

"Stark, you don't by any chance have a rocket I could borrow?" Hunter asked.

The linebacker smiled. "Alexander," he called over his shoulder, "would you oblige the master sergeant?"

A helmeted soldier jogged up and handed Hunter a foliage green AT-4 anti-tank rocket. Alexander bowed his head as if he were a squire handing a legendary knight his sword. The master sergeant winked at the young soldier and hefted the 84 mm unguided single-shot rocket launcher up onto his shoulder, taking aim at the fuel tanker. He flipped open the sights and lined them up.

"Clear," he shouted, ensuring no one was unfortunate enough to be behind him. A moment later, a single shot roared from his launcher. Flames burst from the back of the AT-4. With a screech, the rocket penetrated the tanker. The ground shook as fire exploded outward into the tunnel and the infected.

Hunter turned to Kinnick with a grin under his bushy beard. "That should do."

"That'll do." Kinnick clicked his radio. "Elwood, you may clear out this area. Second Platoon is coming your way."

Kinnick nodded to Stark. "Go ahead."

"Be a pleasure, sir," Stark grinned. "Let's mop 'em up." He held his hand in the air, spinning it in a short circle, and pointed his men in the direction of the remainder of the enemy.

TESS

Temple Energy Plant, MI

"Bring me your people, Steele. We will not wait long," the pastor shouted with a smile. His long-fingered hands wrung themselves together.

"God wills it! God wills it!" shouted the pastor's men, hoisting their weapons high in the air.

Flames licked Pagan's legs with their orange viper tongues and he howled in searing pain. His eyes fell on her for only a nanosecond before he forced them shut, his voice rising in agony. His eyes had shouted regret. Maybe it was for never saying how he really felt about her. Maybe it was for something he had done, but he would have only a few agonizing moments to straighten it out in his mind.

"You bastard," Tess spit at the pastor. Steele pulled at her waist with his hands. She shook him off. "We will never surrender. I swear it. You'll see my face before you die."

The pastor shook his head in disappointment. "Such a misguided creature you are, Tess. God's love will warm your heart one day, child, of that I have no doubt. His embrace will burst you with his love."

Tess shook. Her body screamed fight or flight. She leaned toward fight. "What more do I have to give? What more do I have to lose?" she screamed. *Better to go down swinging.* She took a lunge at the pastor, but powerful arms encaged her.

"We can't stay," Steele said from behind into her ear. His words were nothing to her. He carried her backwards, and she fought and trembled as Pagan screamed with everything he had inside him. He would continue to scream until the nerve endings in his skin were seared away by the flames, however long it took. Five minutes, seven minutes, until his epidermis split and the fat leaked from underneath the destroyed layers of flesh or the smoke overcame lungs.

She kicked out. She kicked back at Steele. The heel of her foot met his shin. "Let go, you bastard," she screamed aloud, but her screams paled in comparison to Pagan's. The notes of agony taking every ounce of breath away from him.

"They will pay," Steele whispered to her over and over. Moments dropped into the bucket of eternity. Dazed, they saw the chain-link fence open and close. The sneering pastor's men turned into round-trunked brown maples, skinny lakeshore pines, and slender white birches. Steele released her and she clutched a maple overlooking the power plant. Tears gripped her eyes. The gray smoke was rising from the field, dispersing in the air.

Steele armed himself next to her, holstering his M9 Beretta and tomahawk.

"We can't let them do this," she croaked between sobs, leaning on the tree more than standing upright. The fire crackled below, totally engulfing Pagan.

Steele threw branches and twigs to the side, uncovering a black-stocked Remington 783 .300 Winchester hunting rifle. Releasing the bolt backward, he put a brass-encased round into the receiver, locking it forward with a snap of his wrist.

Pagan's head lolled from his left to right, his mouth was bent in a painful smile, his lungs spent from screaming. *Have the flames already licked away the flesh of his face, leaving him with a permanent skeleton's smile?*

For a moment she hoped that Steele might try to save him. "What are you doing?" she spit out. Steele put the hunting rifle to his shoulder. His eye hovered near the optics.

"Mercy," Steele said from the corner of his mouth, and the rifle cracked out of the forest. Pagan's head slumped to his chest, a tormented man put to final rest. And tears rolled down her cheeks.

"We run," he said. He slung the hunting rifle over his shoulder and forcibly grabbed her hand. His hand was hot and rough in her's. Tree limbs whipped them while they fled through the forest gauntlet. Sand flung from their feet into the air in a rushed ferocity. They didn't care about tracks. The Chosen knew where their camp was. They knew where they went. It was only a race against the clock before they came for them to exact their price, to force them to live under their unholy regime or be put to death by fire.

Everything happened in a daze. All the trees that passed her were hazy. Her muscles burnt beneath her skin, lactic acid building up, but still, a level of numbness filled her to the very core. An emptiness that made her long for something to believe in. Something to make her feel whole. An emptiness that nothing in this world could ever fill.

Her lungs stung and she ripped her hand free from him. She doubled over, labored breathing exiting her chest. "They're monsters," she breathed.

Steele sucked wind. "They are," he said worriedly, eyes scanning their surroundings. He didn't sound confident.

"I will kill every…single…one. I promise you," she said.

"But first we have to get back. Figure out a plan," he said.

A twig snapped nearby. Her heart leapt from her chest. *They couldn't already be here, hunting us like dogs.*

A form came from beyond the trees. Its jaw hung loose, hanging by white tendons to the infected's skull. Steele bounced upright and met the dead with the butt of his rifle, slamming downward until with the stock until the infected was destroyed. The Chosen were not the only enemies who roamed the countryside.

"Come on," he said. She followed him unwillingly through the trees. Her anger caused her to drag her feet, slowing her down. This anger was willing her to stay put and fight for Pagan's honor. Her man. Her partner from the beginning of the planet's descent into hell. The man had survived the ugliness of fighting religious zealots in a foreign country only to be murdered by religious zealots in his own. A man she was comfortable around and safe. A man she loved. A man who was dead. She never actually believed he would die. Never. Even when they had fought packs of the infected, she always knew he would be there with that damn goofy smile on his face.

The other part of her followed behind this other bearded man. A man who had stepped up into Pagan's place. It was this part that let her follow Steele and trust his intuition. It took everything in her to give in to this man, but at the same time, it felt right. His internal resolve and willingness to do right glowed before her. She felt bound to him like she had never felt for another man. She had experienced many lovers but not a love like this. Keeping her eyes on the center of his back, she ran behind him taking the hills, sand, and felled tree trunks in determined stride.

Eventually, trees gave way to the asphalt road. Steele sprinted across it. A motorcycle lay on its side in the ditch.

"Thunder did what he was supposed to," he said. Steele heaved the four-hundred-pound beast upright. He mounted the motorcycle, looking to her to join him. He held his hand out expectantly. "Hurry," he said, rushed.

Her eyes never left his. She bypassed his hand, cupped his shaggy cheeks, and brought him in close. Their lips locked and she kissed him with all the feeling she had left in her. He slowly pulled away, his eyes wide in surprise. Fire surged through her veins. It wasn't the anger that drove her but something else entirely. Something she hadn't felt in so long.

"I-um," he stuttered. She put a thumb to his lips.

"Don't say anything. You'll ruin it." She swung a leg over the back of the motorcycle and settled in. When she wrapped her arms around his torso, he revved the engine, speeding down the road. She could feel him breathing as the wind whipped them. Tucking her face behind his back, she felt at ease, his closeness tempering the sting of loss. His closeness filling in a piece of her void.

Before long, they found themselves at the entrance to Little Sable Point, and she was hesitant to give up her stranglehold on his body.

"Tess," he whispered. "We're here." He kicked the motorcycle stand out with his boot. He gradually released her from her hold on him. They dismounted the motorcycle.

"Are you okay?" he asked, eyes worried.

"Pagan's dead and they're coming for us," she said.

Her world spun and she landed in his arms. He scooped her up, carrying her through the camp. Everything happened as if she were a mile away in the clouds. People shouted around her. Darkness draped around her like a death shroud. The last thing she remembered was Steele yelling as he stared down at her, his eyes frantic.

STEELE

Little Sable Point, MI

"How fast can we get this camp mobile?" Steele asked Thunder. Thunder scratched at his bandana running along the brow of his forehead.

"Me and my boys could hop out of here in ten. It's everybody else that will slow us down. We gotta get trailers hitched, the semis are done for, not enough fuel, and we have to make sure we got all the supplies we can manage." Steele grimaced as the retreat to-do list grew longer and longer.

Turning to Ahmed, he said. "I need you to grab one of the bikes and roll up to the Lakeshore intersection with Larry. No shooting. The moment you see anyone you report back here as fast as you can."

"Don't leave without me or you won't get those hockey tickets when this is over," Ahmed said. He hefted his M4 and gave Steele a mock salute.

"We won't. Any chance I get to see the Caps go down, I'll take," Steele said after him. *I'd be surprised if any of us leave here.* Ahmed disappeared into the camp.

"How many trucks need fuel?" Steele asked Thunder.

"Just over half."

"Goddamnit, man. How's that possible?"

Thunder scratched his belly as he shrugged. "Some people rolled in here on fumes. Others siphoned the gas off for the scouting vehicles, even the motorcycles. Not many thought past their own escape." The wheels on the back of a pickup spun, and a family drove away. *Every man for himself now.*

Steele wondered how many people would still be at Little Sable if they had gas.

Steele shook his head in disgust. "We can't haul the food trailer without at least one semi."

"No, but we can start loading up the backs of the campers and pickups."

He looked out over the protective ring of vehicles. "Find the fuel; I don't want to leave anything behind. I'm going to talk to the volunteers. Reconvene in about thirty."

"You got it." Thunder slogged off toward his motley crew of bikers.

Steele spied Max standing nearby looking more scared than anything else. Max held his gun in his hands, his face twitching under the stress.

"Max, grab the rest of the volunteers and have them meet me by the lighthouse.

"Ye-e-es, sir," Max gave a weak salute and ran off, almost tripping over himself. *I'm not sure I can handle his death on my head. He's only a kid. A kid who wanted to fight.*

Steele paced near the lighthouse, his M4 slung around his front. Max arrived with Steve in tow. Moments later Margie arrived, holding her bolt-action hunting rifle along with long-haired Gregor and Hank. Hank looked exhausted from the effort. Bengy stood with his M1 Garand held in one hand. The old man appeared unafraid, revealing not even a sliver of doubt.

"Where's Nathan and Jason?" Steele addressed the whole group but stared at Max. His responsibility was to find the volunteers and bring them in.

"I-I, couldn't find them," Max said.

"I gave you one fucking task and you couldn't even do that," Steele shouted at him. Max's cheeks reddened and he stared at the ground. Steele took a moment to calm himself. *What good am I doing yelling at the boy? Can I actually blame anyone for running? We will all be dead in an hour anyway.*

"It's not your fault." Max looked up, relief washing over his features. "You're fine, kid."

"We're here," Nathan shouted. His dark skin contrasted greatly with Jason's pale complexion. They hustled in and took their places amongst the rest.

"Thanks for showing up," Steele said, hoping his unhappiness was conveyed by the tone of his voice. The volunteers shifted anxiously on their feet. People ran to and fro as they tried to gather all their belongings. *What do you got, Steele? A ragtag, half-trained group of scared people.*

"When you volunteered to defend Little Sable Point, you knew it wasn't to only defend against the dead." He locked eyes with each person in turn, making sure everyone knew he spoke the truth.

"You knew that someday, some prick was going to come down that road and try to take what's yours, harm your loved ones, and leave you for dead. It's inevitable. It's unfortunate. But you're ready," he said. His volunteers looked at one another, a fraction of pride overcoming their fears. He adjusted his neck to hide his lie and continued.

"The people that are going to come down that road are fanatics. They have perverted their religion so much that if you don't join them, they will murder you. I don't know about you, but that doesn't sit right with me. They don't sit right with me. I'll be damned if they harm a single person in this community." He stopped in front of Max, dusting off the boy's jacket.

Max watched his every move in wonderment with wide eyes, eating up his words.

"There's going to be a lot of them. They're going to have guns. It will be loud and people will die, but we have an advantage. We know where to hide. We will fight and run, fight and run if we have to until everyone is safely on the road. Little Sable *will* live on."

Max cheered loud, raising his rifle in the air. Everyone looked at the goofy teenager. He looked momentarily ashamed by his own outburst. "I'm wi-ith you," he said.

"It seems like the only way," Margie said to the group. The men nodded, grim determination settling on their features. They were stronger together.

"We aren't alone. The Red Stripes are still here. They will fight." A glimmer of hope danced among their eyes.

"Jason, you hop up in the lighthouse with Trent. Take a deer rifle. If things kick off, aim for the guys that look important. The rest of you buddy up and spread out. Remember, when the shooting starts, you hide behind wheel wells and engine blocks. Anything else bullets will go through. This isn't the movies." He left out the part about how some bigger rounds would go through those too.

"If you see something, sound the alarm," he said and marched off to find Thunder.

***

Two hours later, Steele leaned on a pickup truck waiting for Ahmed to come ripping down the road on his motorcycle. Then the fight would be on. But so far, everything was quiet. He snatched up his M4 and silently patrolled along the perimeter. People packed and prepped their vehicles for departure.

Steele walked past Margie, who was crouched against a car. He squatted down next to the gray-and-auburn haired woman.

"You need some water?" he asked, offering her a water bottle.

She gave him a side glance and shook her head. "I'm good, Captain." Her eyes flitted back out toward the line of trees facing the perimeter of vehicles.

He put the water back in his cargo pocket. "You know I'm not a captain, right?"

She only addressed him for a second from the corner of her eye. "I know you aren't, dear. But the boy, Max. He hangs on every word you say like it came from God himself. He adores you and needs a hero to believe in to get him through this." The woman, about the same age as his mother, smiled sadly at him, her cheeks quivering a bit.

"You understand?" she asked as if he were a young man.

He gave her a slight nod.

"Let the boy idolize in peace and don't be so damn hard him. He's had it bad enough."

Steele sighed. "You're right. I'm trying to show him that being a man isn't something you just become one day. It's not a number. It's something that goes deeper. It's your commitment to your fellow man and your drive to do right conditioned through discipline to oneself." He took his turn looking out the barricade into the beach-like field before them. Dead yellow grass lay flat before the long line of trees. A road cut through the trees. Even now, they could be winding down the road to reach Little Sable Point or stalking through the trees. *No, the pastor wouldn't sneak. It's not in his modus operandi. He has God on his side, and he will come with the full fervor of assured victory and guaranteed salvation. When it's time, we will send him along to find his salvation.*

The touch of her hand against the side of his face startled him. Margie's brown eyes stared into his. "I see hope in you. You've given us something, even if it's a chance to die with a bit of dignity."

He ground his teeth, looking down before he answered. "You won't die," he said, blue eyes blazing. "We'll live."

"I know, Captain." She let her eyes fall back on the field.

"Keep a look out, volunteer," Steele said. He stood back up and marched back down the sparse line. He nodded to Gregor. The long-haired brute nodded back, his gun laid out on the hood of a truck. Steele's feet padded the sandy ground, squishing as he walked. He was stuck in his troubled thoughts before Thunder's hefty frame waved him down, half-running his way.

"We're going to have to stash the food to run. Not enough fuel for Bessie's semi." His eyes read Steele, looking for chinks in his armor. If Steele broke, the Red Stripes were gone without a backward glance.

"Your boys don't look like they would take well to siphoning anyway." *Best to laugh away your misfortune.*

Thunder cracked a smile. "No, they wouldn't.

"That food's important. We don't have much to stand on without it. Make sure to keep Bessie in the loop. I don't want her thinking we robbed her."

"She's onboard and there's enough," Thunder said.

Steele nodded. "Me and volunteers will man the perimeter while you and your club load up some of the pickups. How long you need?"

"About an hour."

Steele eyed the sky. The sun was cascading west toward the lake like a slow meteor. "It'll be dark by then. You think we should risk it?"

"I don't think we have a choice."

"I got this feeling that the noose is tightening every moment we stay here."

"I feel it too. It's time to roll. I'll give a holler when we're ready," Thunder said.

"Stick to the plan, Thunder." Steele's eyes read the man. *Can I trust you to not cut and run? We can only do this with you.*

Thunder nodded. "You can count on us." The older man's eyes looked through Steele as if he were only seeing a transparent screen door.

Steele bowed his head and jogged over to Tess's dingy off-white camper. Kevin sat outside, a bottle of whiskey in his hand. "We're getting close. How is she?"

"Haven't heard a peep." Kevin wavered and leaned closer to Steele, whiskey hanging on his breath. "Don't tell her I told you, but Gwen's in there too." Kevin raised his eyebrows and burped out the side of his mouth.

"Shit." *Both in there at once. Jesus.* "Thanks, buddy," he said quickly.

"You're welcome, Cap'in," Kevin slurred with a fake salute.

"Grab Red Rhonda and get this thing hitched. We're leaving soon."

"I'll see what I can do." Kevin stood up, wobbling for a moment while he kept himself from tipping over.

"Can you even drive?" Steele said.

"Always drive a bit better with some booze in me."

Steele snorted and stopped short of opening the door. *This may be the most dangerous door I walk through.* His hand hovered over the round door handle. He hesitated to walk into whatever potential hailstorm of womankind that awaited him. *I'd rather face armies of the dead. I know what I get with them. These two?* He gulped.

He stepped inside the musty smelling camper. He expected an ambush of insults, evil looks, and jeers. With a bit of hesitation, he put one tentative foot over the other. When he looked up, the two women saw him. Tess peered at him from beneath her blankets. Gwen sat on the edge of her bed holding a bottled water. Both sets of eyes watched him. *These two sitting together? I can't believe the universe hasn't imploded in on itself.*

He stood in the aisle of the camper. "Hi there, ladies. How you feeling?" he asked passively.

"We're fine," the women answered in unison. They gave each other a knowing look of accepted rivals. Tess sat up and Gwen handed her the water. Tess gave her a smile and Gwen returned it. *What do they have, some sort of ceasefire? I don't want to know what happened here. The only thing a ceasefire means is they have found a common enemy. Me.*

"I'm glad you're both feeling better."

"Any word on leaving?" Gwen asked.

"Thunder is getting the food from Big Bessie into some pickups. When they're loaded, the camp moves."

"What about the pastor?" Tess said and coughed into her hand.

"We've got the volunteers set up and ready to cover our retreat if need be. Shouldn't be more than an hour," he said.

"Our packs are in the corner," Gwen said, face unmoving, a statue of an ancient Greek goddess. *She can't possibly know about the kiss. I didn't even do it. I was a victim of a forced osculation.*

"You guys can stay with me while we travel," Tess said. Her eyes were pure amusement, and he squirmed under their gaze. "I think it's important for the co-leaders of this community to have easy access to one another."

"I agreed with her and said we would talk it over," Gwen added.

They are trying to murder me with stress. Steele scratched his beard, thinking for a way out of this conversation that was clearly a trap to make him say something wrong. The faint sound of Red Rhonda idling nearby was his savior. *Kevin, you're a gift from God.*

"That must be Kevin. I'm going to help him get this thing hitched up."

Their eyes didn't move much, neither indicating pleasure or heartbreak at his departure. He darted out of the camper. Red taillights glowed brightly in the dusk, shining light on a red pickup. Kevin's head stuck out from the driver's side.

"Where do you want this thing?" Kevin yelled.

Steele waved him back. The truck angled sideways, missing the hitch.

"Stop," Steele yelled. The pickup jerked as Kevin hit the brake. A few more inches and he would have rammed the camper. "Hold up. Start over. It's crooked."

Kevin stuck his head out of the window. He looked backward trying to figure out his angle. "Sorry," he yelled.

"Drunk ass," Steele said under his breath. "Second times a charm," he yelled forward at Kevin. The truck revved forward and the taillights flicked on again, shining red and glowing white. Steele waved him back.

A loud pop sounded off. For a moment, Steele thought it might be a tire exploding or the pickup backfiring. Steele eyed the tailpipe of the pickup.

"Jesus, Rhonda," he said. He waved his hands at Kevin. "Stop. Stop. Start it again," Steele said, holding a hand in the air. Two more pops echoed out in the night. Confused, Steele looked back to the entryway of Little Sable Point. Headlights beamed, gleaming away the night. Trucks bounced down the road.

"Kevin. Get this thing hitched," Steele mumbled. He found himself running for the entrance as gunfire kicked off. The rumble of motorcycles vibrated the air like rolling thunder.

Holding the M4 in his hands, he sprinted. His feet pounded the sand. *I knew it. I knew it.* But surprise still crushed him as he approached the impromptu community gate. The pickups that normally sat in place had been rolled to the side. The last motorcycle sped past, joining the swarm of crimson midnight bees quickly disappearing around the bend in the road.

A person lay in the sand. Margie held his head up, her hand pressing firmly on his chest.

"What happened?" Steele shouted at her. She cradled Steve in her arms. *You know but you refuse to see.*

Margie looked up at him, tears in her eyes. "They killed him. He wouldn't let them leave with all the food, and they shot him for it," she sobbed, shaking her head. Blood oozed from between her fingers as she tried to hold his blood in.

"Who shot him?" *The plan. All my men were too spread out to help.*

"The Red Stripes."

KINNICK

Dunluce Pass, CO

Skinny pine trees clustered all over the rocky, tawny landscape. The pass was near the top of a mountain, and the elevation was far above sea level. They seemed to be closer to the sky. The site for the battle had been unknowingly picked by a railroad company in the late 1800s. The company had dynamited and carved a path over and through the mountain in an effort to connect the profitable coasts of the United States.

The brown rocky rooftops of other mountains stood tall in the distance. The taller ones were capped in white snow. The mountains were divided by a natural split formed by water millions of years in the past.

Kinnick stood in the center of the road that they were to hold. Dirt and dust had settled upon it as cars stopped using it. The road was long and led down the mountain, hugging its sides the entire way. No rail prevented cars from going over the edge. The other side of the roadway was a rocky hill leading only up. Determined evergreens clung to the hillside like stubborn, bent old men.

"Reminds me a bit of Afghanistan," Hunter said. He spat black juice from his mouth, splashing a rock and leaving residual spit on his boots. "Aside from the paved road."

Kinnick eyed the roadway. The last bit of it he could see rounded a bend, zagging across and back down the mountain.

"We'd be in better shape if there was no road," Kinnick said.

Hunter took in the land. "It's kinda fucked up thinking that we've been doing all this fighting and dying here instead of some shithole foreign country."

Kinnick sighed. "That's why we're here. To make sure this country stays in one piece."

Hunter smirked. "Don't want California floating off on us."

"Floating off would be better than nuking it."

Two days had passed since the barricade of Eisenhower Tunnel. They had destroyed all the infected on the eastern side of the tunnel. They had reinforced the tunnel with a host of trucks stacked in a massive line across the entrance.

The smell at the tunnel was so bad and the men so tired, they dug in and slept on the ridge the first night. It took them another full day to ruck to Dunluce Pass. Kinnick's legs were so sore he could hardly walk. He settled for a painful hobble to get around.

Kinnick estimated the distance of the stretch of road until the bend before it fled behind tall hills.

"How far do you think it is to the bend?"

"Eh, about four hundred yards."

Kinnick nodded. "Plenty of good firing lines."

The grade in the roadway incline was shallow, but the steep rocky hillside leading up from the road provided good protection from the infected as far as he could tell.

Hunter pointed to the hill above the dusty road. "Good ambush positions." Then he pointed low. "Nothin' 'cept a billygoat could get up that way. It's an ideal position."

The infected would either take the road back from the living or be stuck. "A bottleneck with no alternative way through the mountains en masse," Kinnick said with a nod.

His men stood nearby. His leaders on the eve of the coming battle. Elwood stood with a slight hunch, helmet under his arm. His platoon sergeant, Sergeant 1st Class Putnam stood a step behind him. In his early thirties, Putnam looked likely to give Stark a run for his money in a liftoff. Next to him was Sergeant Matthews, thinner with the look of a long distance runner.

"Men, you see that sign there?" Kinnick pointed to a cherry-red-colored sign nearby. His men's dust-covered heads looked over at it. "It says Dunluce Pass. 11,293 feet. There." He pointed. "About a hundred feet behind us is the choke point." He pointed at the highway that appeared to be cut straight out of the rock with dynamite over a hundred and fifty years ago. Thick white and brown lines cut horizontally across the cut rock. It gave the appearance of a layered club sandwich crushed by millions of years of pressure.

"That is the hole we must plug with our lives. Our entire mission hinges on us holding this pass. For if we fail here, the infected will roll up what's left of the United States military, and before that's done, the rest of the country will be destroyed by thermonuclear warfare."

Stark's eyes were fierce. Elwood listened intently weighing his words. Hunter spit again on the rocks.

"We are going to stagger our fire teams." He turned to youthful Elwood. "Lieutenant Elwood, your platoon is mostly intact. Our defense is going to center on you holding our flank. I want your two best fire teams about two hundred yards down this road. Get them up on the ridge in the rocks and pines. It's steep and the dead are slow."

"It's good ground," Hunter added.

"Master Sergeant, how many rounds per soldier?"

"Rifleman about eight hundred. Each machine gunner has twenty-five boxes of ammunition."

Kinnick nodded. "It'll have to do." He looked back at Elwood. "Every fifty yards, I want another one of your fire teams. As the fighting gets thick, they will fall back to the next fire team. So, as we get pressured, we will apply more concentrated firepower."

"I will get a team together and line the roadway with claymores," Hunter said.

"Excellent," Kinnick said and nodded.

Stark viewed the terrain. "Plenty of ground that the infected have to cross in order to reach this point."

"There will be plenty of them to cross it," Kinnick said. The broad-shouldered soldier stared grimly, looking out over his surroundings.

"Lieutenant Stark," Kinnick said. Stark faced Kinnick again. "I want 2nd Platoon on the road. Pile up rocks, trees, whatever you can get your hands on to slow them down. You are the short end of my L in the anchor. Your team will be putting rounds head-on into them. Their only path is through you. Your men have suffered some casualties. Can I count on you?"

"We are the Regulators, sir. Always ready to mount up."

"Good. I never doubted you."

Kinnick pointed back behind the pass. "Gentlemen, that copse of trees beyond the pass is our fallback point."

A small circle of tall pines sat through the pass on a low hill. *The dead will be able to traverse the slopes. By then it might not matter.* He wondered if the famous Spartan King Leonidas felt like this when he measured and weighed the terrain for his final stand at Thermopylae.

"If we get pushed from there, we will regroup on the other side of the bend in the highway. There we will bound and cover as we make a tactical retreat." *Like Custer at the Battle of Little Bighorn? He had more men and fewer enemies.*

"It won't come to that, sir," Stark said.

"I pray it doesn't," he said. They stood a moment in silence, each man contemplating the death that marched for them.

"You are dismissed. Master Sergeant, a word," Kinnick said. The men threw up salutes. With a crisp hand, Kinnick returned the salute. His officers and NCOs left to go about their pre-battle preparations.

Hunter walked with him through the pass. They stopped and Kinnick looked up the side of the rockface. He patted the sheer cut rock with his hand. It was rough and coarse on his palm.

"We can't bring this down, can we?" he asked his Hunter.

Hunter stared up at the rock. "It crossed my mind, but I don't have enough C-4."

"Damn, if we had some air support that would make a world of difference," Kinnick said. "Even a single gunship would level the odds. At least a bit."

"We gotta face this for what it is, not what we want it to be," Hunter said.

Kinnick gazed at him a moment. The master sergeant met his eyes and his drifted out to the mountain range.

"I'll get something rigged up. Can't promise nothing," Hunter said.

"Thank you, Master Sergeant. Carry on."

Three hours passed and Stark's men had erected a barricade that looked more like it belonged in the Civil War than in the modern era. Rocks were thrown about the road, anything to provide an obstacle. M240s were set on the fallen tree logs, each manned by a gunner and an assistant gunner.

Kinnick sat in the fallback point of the trees. His men had thrown up a high-frequency radio tripod with a long-wire antenna. It attached to a satchel-like pack containing the radio itself. It looked more like a large handset connected to a battery pack. It allowed him far-reaching access to other radios but limited reliability dependent on a host of factors.

Turning the knob on the brick, he skipped over to his desired frequency.

"General Daugherty. This is Colonel Kinnick, over."

Static burst through the radio phone. He clicked over another channel.

"Lieutenant Wyman, this is Colonel Kinnick. Status update, over."

More static groaned from his earpiece. Kinnick eyed the puffy gray-clouded sky. A layer of depressing cotton candy blanketed overhead. *I wonder if it's the cloud cover or some sort of solar flare that is keeping us offline.* He set the radio down.

A faint voice cut through the static. A ghost in the airways. Long-distance echoes. He had heard men talk about it in the past. *Were they picking up somebody else out there? Or were they picking up radio transmissions from the past? Or were they bouncing transmissions of a faraway planetary body?*

"Sir," the voice breathed. Static cut in. Kinnick could hear someone talking, but it was faint as if the man were under water.

"Lieutenant Wyman? How are you holding? Over."

"…thousands…we must," Wyman said, his voice cutting in and out.

"Lieutenant, you *must* hold the pass. I repeat. Hold the pass at all costs," Kinnick said into the phone.

Gunfire grated from the radio, sounding like a firework display. "…repeat, over?"

"Hold the pass," he said in the phone. He held the phone next to his forehead while he listened to the static.

"These fucking radios."

Hunter sat nearby, back against a tree.

"It's all we got," he said.

Kinnick wanted to chuck the piece-of-shit phone and smash it into the rocks. *Of course, my phone wouldn't work when we need it.* He settled for squeezing the hell out of it.

"I know that, Master Sergeant. Doesn't mean it's not a pain in my ass." The air had chilled as the sun dipped a yellowish-white orb behind the clouds.

His high-frequency beeped and sputtered. He clicked the dial back a frequency.

"Colonel Kinnick," he answered.

"...General Daugherty."

"Sir, I didn't expect..."

"No time...need...out."

"Sir, my mission is to hold the passes, over."

"Hundred...thousand...coming."

"We can handle it, sir. The men are ready."

"...death awaits," the general's voice cracked on the other end and the call ended.

Hunter perked up as he listened to the conversation. "What's got him in a tizzy?"

"I'm not sure. I couldn't piece it all together, but it sounded like he wants us to bug out."

"Doesn't surprise me. Send us out here. Get us all chewed up. Give back the ground we just took."

"I know this ain't your first rodeo."

Gunfire rippled in the distance, the thud-thud of machine guns firing. The sound traveled along the mountains. Hunter looked down the highway. Kinnick's two-way radio buzzed. "Sir, we got contact," a frantic Elwood said on the other side.

"How many, Lieutenant?"

Claymores burst in the distance followed by the sound of an M240 machine gun, carbines, and rifles.

"They are supposed to wait for the claymores until it gets thick," Hunter said. He stood and angrily stared down the roadway.

"Lieutenant?" Kinnick said into his mic. Hunter stood, staring at him with the eyes of a wolf.

"Lieutenant?" Kinnick shouted.

"Come on, Colonel," Hunter said, hoisting his SCAR. They ran for the pass.

STEELE

Little Sable Point, MI

"I will not leave you," Steele repeated. It was the tenth time he had assured them he wouldn't flee. The scared faces of about eighty people stared back at him. He stood head and shoulders above those that remained, looking down at them. Anyone that had a working vehicle was already gone. The camp had disintegrated around them in the night. After the Red Stripes had fled, most of Little Sable Point had followed.

The left behind had gathered in a mob. Fear rippled through their ranks like an angry ocean. Steele stood on the back of Big Bessie's mostly empty semi-trailer. A few boxes remained that hadn't been stolen by Thunder and his gang. Big Bessie stood to the side, big arms folded across her chest.

"We don't have enough fuel to get everyone out of here," he said, his voice booming. "The pastor and his men are coming." People in the crowd moaned in misery. "We will tighten our ranks and fight. It's the only chance we have." *We will die for it.*

"What are we going to do without the Red Stripes?" Scott shouted. He wore glasses and a dirty untucked button-down shirt. He seemed out of place with a 12-gauge shotgun in his hands that Steele thought he would be better suited for a keyboard and a monitor.

"What about my children? What will happen to them?" Harriet hollered. She cuddled two young kids in front of her.

"I have trained some fighters. The pastor and his men are not trained soldiers. They are regular people." He cringed at the word regular. Nothing about those people was regular. "We only need to hold them off, put up enough of a resistance for them to decide we aren't worth it."

A man waved his hand at Steele in dismissal. "You're crazy to think you can stand against all of them. I'll be in my camper spending time with my family. You should all do the same." The man gathered his wife and kids, walking away.

"You would rather sit by and watch the slaughter than fight for your family?" Steele screamed at the man.

The man turned back, looking over his shoulder. "What did you say?"

"I asked if you would sit by while your friends and family are murdered?"

The man turned all the way around. "I'd rather be with them when it happens than fighting some battle we can never win." He put a reassuring hand on his young son's shoulder and walked away.

Steele watched him go along with the others. "We can win. We only need to survive." The crowd murmured a dull moan. People walked back to their shelters and vehicles. They needn't go far as the circle of vehicles had shrunk over the last few hours. Steele had made them pull the remaining fueled vehicles in tight, leaving very little common ground around the lighthouse. "Be ready to fight," he shouted after them. In minutes, he was alone with only his volunteers and a few others. Max watched his every move. Gregor nodded, determined. Jason held his gun tightly in his hands.

"We ain't going to last long without food," Big Bessie said, her voice more like a frog's than a woman's.

Steele hopped down from the back of Bessie's trailer.

"I'm not worried about that," he said.

"Why's that?" Big Bessie said, cocking her head.

"You can't eat if you're dead."

The heavyset woman breathed hard, staring at him. "Do what you gotta do then and make sure we survive. 'Cause I'm planning on finding that asshole Thunder and getting all my food back." She held up her tire iron threateningly. "To think that bastard was sweet-talking to me. Said I had pretty eyes."

Steele wanted to avoid that lover's quarrel. "If only it was that easy." He turned toward his small group. They stood piecemeal before him, spread out as if they didn't trust what was about to happen, feet stuck in the places they had stood amongst the crowd. His small group of confidants—Kevin, Gwen, and Tess—stood waiting for him.

"Not the most inspiring speech I've heard," Kevin said with a hiccup. He wiped his mouth with the sleeve of his ACUs like a drunk ROTC student.

"They all left, so I would say they agree with you."

"I've got an idea for the next one," Kevin said.

"Great. You got until the pastor shows up. Not sure how many more speeches I'll get after that."

The slender man visibly gulped, his Adam's apple jiggling in his throat.

"Take Jason and Gregor and go check on Ahmed and Larry while I talk to Gwen for a minute."

Kevin nodded and the men disappeared. "The rest of you, man the barricade."

Gwen looked at him, her eyes watery in the moonlight. He stepped up and took her hand in his. The lighthouse loomed like an ancient tower. Tess hovered a few feet away, watching them. He ignored her dark eyes.

"You're planning on making a stand here?" Gwen said.

"Yes. I'll make a stand here."

"No, we'll make a stand."

Steele shook his head and squeezed her hands. "No, you'll leave here and won't look back," he said more flatly than he wanted. *That did not come out right.*

Her face twisted in the shadows. "Excuse me?" she snapped.

"He's right. We shouldn't risk the baby," Tess said from the side.

Steele gave her an angry look.

"Nobody asked you," Gwen said over her shoulder.

"Can you give us a minute?" he said to Tess.

Tess sighed and disappeared.

When she was out of earshot, Gwen spoke up. "I understand she is concerned about the baby, but that's none of her business. You're mine. I would rather die than let you fight this battle on your own."

"Don't worry about her," he said, glancing in the direction she went.

"I'm not worried about her," Gwen said. Venom oozed from her lips. "She told me all about your kiss."

He felt his cheeks redden as bloody embarrassment raced to his face and anger bubbled inside him. "I don't have time for this right now. You have to leave."

"Like hell I do. She said that you were an unwilling participant and I believe her. But you should have told me."

"I'm sorry, but it doesn't matter now. You can't stay. People are going to die tomorrow. Knowing the pastor," his voice dropped to a whisper, "he will kill all of us if he wins."

Her eyes widened. "What about all that brave, we-only-need-to-hold-them-off talk?"

"It's just that. Thunder's gone. I only have nine barely trained fighters plus anyone else who gives a shit about their families. I can't let it end here. Our story doesn't end here." He glanced down at her belly. "My story won't end if you live on. My blood will run through our child's veins. It gives me peace with what is to come."

Her eyes looked down at his chest and back up to his eyes.

"I cannot leave you, even if it means that we all perish," she said.

"Did you see all these people holding their families in terror? They won't fight with their families on the firing line. I need you to take the children and the elderly away from here. As far away as you can get. We can't fit everyone, so you need to take the most vulnerable."

She shook her head furiously against his wishes. "No. This is my fight too. I can fight better than most of them."

He squeezed her hands. "It's our fight. You said you want to make a difference. You're more than a gun on the line. Your task is so much more important. It is to run and make sure these families survive. I will deal with the rest and when it's over, I will find you." He looked over his shoulder into the night.

Her lips drew downward, her eyebrows closing down and in. "There has to be another way," she uttered. Her voice was almost as small as a child's. "I don't want to leave you again."

"There isn't another way. I will find you when this is done." Silence divided them. Time trickled by. The moon covered them in its own spotlight. They were frozen criminals in the night.

"We have a responsibility to protect the children from this madness." She grabbed the collar of his ACU jacket and pulled him close, his face only inches away from hers. "But you find me, Mark Steele." She pulled him closer and planted a kiss on his lips. Their lips locked in something so real and organic; it was the love they felt inside and out.

She loosened her hold on him for a moment, looking him in the eyes. "You find me." She looked around him. "I'll gather the elderly and the children. Speaking of which, I think you have a volunteer you need to speak with." She straightened his collar and gave his chest a pat with her hand. She turned around and walked away into the night, and he exhaled.

Goddamnit, this sucks. He watched her swaying hips disappear into the darkness to Tess's camper.

A timid shadow approached Steele. Max had been standing there watching them the entire time. Steele had known it, but Gwen had needed his full attention.

"I will fight with you, Captain," Max said. The boy looked scared but seemingly older. He gripped his gun in his hands. *He is still too young for this world. If I could spare you these things, I would.*

Steele waved him closer. "You're a good kid, Max." He put an arm around the scrawny teenager. "Come with me, I have a special mission for you."

Max's eyes lit up, staring up at his hero. "Wha—t k-k-ind of mission?"

"Follow me," he said. He patted the teenager on the shoulder, releasing him.

They walked in silence. Reaching Tess's camper, they stopped.

"I'm going to be honest with you. This is the most important mission. This isn't guard duty or watching the road."

Max's eyes grew large.

He's more of a kitten than a lion. Steele gripped the teenager's bony shoulder. "Can I trust you with this task?"

"Of c-c-course."

"Now, I need you to be on your A game. Alert, quick on the trigger." Steele flexed his finger up and down. "And be a team player. No questions asked." He eyed the young man with hard, scrutinizing eyes. "Can you promise me to do this?"

"Yes, sir," Max snapped at him.

"Good." Steele pierced him with his eyes. "You are going to go north with Ms. Reynolds. She is going to need your help and your protection."

"You-you want me to leave Little Sable?" Sadness crossed Max's youthful features like he'd been picked last in a dodgeball game.

"Yes. Gwen will be going north, and she needs someone to protect her." *She doesn't need one, but she's getting you. He has to believe in fighting for something.* "You have good eyes and a good head on your shoulders. She will need your help. You know why this is important, right?"

"Because she's your lady?"

"Yes, but even more so, she's pregnant, and I will not have anything happening to her or our child. Do you understand? I wouldn't send anyone else on something like this."

Max blinked and smiled. "I-I do. But what about the pastor?"

They both turned to watch a single motorcycle headlight rumble down the road. Steele eyed it, knowing the omen that the two-wheeled rider carried.

Steele put a hand on his shoulder. "You leave the pastor to me."

JOSEPH

Cheyenne Mountain Complex, CO

Joseph double tapped his finger on the tablet and a document opened up, filling the screen.

"Did she ever mention anything about a cat?" Joseph said.

Byrnes's forehead creased in confusion. He glanced down at the laptop on his desk.

"A cat? Like Fluffy or something?" Byrnes said.

Joseph gave him a curious look and handed Byrnes the tablet. "See for yourself. This is incoherent at best."

The colonel swiped the tablet with a finger and studied the next page. The fluorescent lights in his office were on full blast now rather than the pleasant dim reading light given off by a lamp.

The colonel had closed the door as he spoke with Joseph. He had told Joseph it was so they could concentrate on their task, but Joseph knew it was to give them a few more minutes in the case of another outbreak. To accentuate the fact, the colonel's M9 Beretta 9mm laid on his desk, ready to be scooped up at a moment's notice.

"The virus attacks the frontal lobe causing it to swell and bleed in the brain. It's possible that she was experiencing hallucinations caused by her condition, forcing her mind into a loop of a childhood memory." He looked over the tablet at Joseph.

Joseph pushed his glasses up the bridge of his nose. "I don't know. I can't remember her mentioning anything about a cat."

"Neither can I." Brynes handed the tablet back to Joseph. "I'll think on it. But right now, I've tasked Dr. Hollis and Dr. Nguyen to study the process the virus is going through from entrance to activation within the dead cells. This thing is remarkable. Makes you wonder if God is trying to send us a message."

"Not the message I'd hoped for," Joseph said and eyed the colonel. "I suppose it was only a matter of time before Mother Nature turned the tables on us."

"Or flipped them over on us." Byrnes looked back at the laptop. "We are almost positive Mother Nature is behind this and not some bioweapon. We've found no biosynthetic materials or any evidence of gene splicing."

"I'd almost rather be going up against a bioweapon. If someone can engineer it, we could probably un-engineer it pretty quick."

Byrnes's eyes lit up. "Could you imagine if we could control this? Basically, we could give it a limited lifespan of about twenty-four hours. We could drop it on known insurgent areas and let them eat each other alive. Next day, we roll in and clear out the rest. Bingo. Problem solved."

The horrifying images of the outbreak in the village of Kombarka, deep within the Democratic Republic of the Congo, flashed one after another through Joseph's mind. He gulped down stomach acid, witnessing again the terror and fear surrounding the people, hearing their screams as they were torn apart by their neighbors and loved ones. "Let's not imagine it that way. Let's imagine it on the endangered species list."

"Or getting us off that list," Byrnes said. He checked his watch. "Come on. Let's get to the lab and check on the team."

They suited up in their blue biohazard suits in a sterile room. Each man checked the other for breaches in his seals or punctures in his suit. After a breathing and comms test, they entered the compression chamber. White gas pushed out of the chamber and the doors rolled open.

The other doctors were already inside the lab. Dr. Hollis looked up at them as they entered. He looked like a light blue, almost ripe blueberry. Joseph nodded to him. Their suits crinkled as they walked to the other doctors. Drs. Nguyen and Desai were crowded around a plastic, covered incubation chamber. Dr. Nguyen's gloved hands were stuck inside the chamber. The thick gloves gave him an extra layer of protection from the virus inside.

He moved liquid from one tube to another while Dr. Desai studied the liquid through a microscope that brought up the image she viewed on a flat screen nearby.

She gave him a sad smile from behind her plastic mask when he got close. "I heard about Rebecca," she said. Her voice crackled over the comms headset, making her sound a planet away.

Joseph frowned. "She spent her every waking minute working until she turned. Some of it got a little cryptic at the end, but her contributions have been outstanding."

"She was a top-notch physician," Dr. Desai said. She turned back to her work. Cells danced on the screen. Joseph stood in silence for a moment. He was tired of ripping open the scab of Rebecca with the wound so fresh. The only way to keep his mind off of her was to work.

"Have there been any new developments?"

Dr. Desai pointed at the screen. "We know that the satellite virus initially uses the monkeypox as a vector but can only succeed if the cells die or the host dies. Then after the cells die, the virus goes to work. The more dead cells, the faster the transition from alive to infected dead."

"I know, doctor. I've been grappling with this idea since we discovered it."

"Well, on a good note, the satellite virus is like any virus. It holds genetic material that it implants in healthy cells. It rewires the cell's function and puts out its own instructions. The only difference being that it waits for the cell to die before activation. Its genome is comprised of over two hundred thousand base pairs, albeit much less than a human. The problem we have is figuring out which combinations of code does what for the virus."

"So, where's the off switch?" Joseph said.

She glanced back up and her dark eyes gave him a disapproving look. "You know we have mapped the entire human genome over the last fifteen years, and we only understand a fraction of what gene combinations do. This testing, with limited time, will be difficult to discover. However, there is something somewhat unusual I wanted to show you."

She hovered her cursor over an image and double-clicked it to zoom in. It focused on the part of the cell that looked like a capsid, and it inserted the viral genetic data into the cell.

"Look here." She pointed with a blue-gloved hand at the screen. "There is a reason Primus Necrovirus started as a satellite virus. It has only managed to use a single glycoprotein on its outer membrane viral envelope to attach onto new cells. Not very efficient."

"That's why in the early stages it relied on the monkeypox as a vector to host cells."

"Correct. It's a vulnerability point. If we can modify its receptor so it cannot penetrate a cell but the body still recognizes it in dead or live cells, it will have an almost zero chance of infection. Or so I can theorize at this point in time."

Almost zero. "So we have to remove the current receptor, modify it, reattach it, and test it. Without the monkeypox to assist in transmission, we can inoculate people against Primus Necrovirus without risking infection."

"That's correct. However, there are at least two different forms of the virus that we are seeing," she said. She looked back at her microscope. "There could be even more."

He nodded remembering the people in the Congo jungle. "The strain with the host virus, it needs the monkeypox virus to transfer until the host dies. Then there is the current one where the satellite virus is on its own."

"Those are the main culprits. As far as the original virus goes, monkeypox is a relative of smallpox. If you are inoculated for smallpox, you should have a smaller chance of contracting monkeypox. The problem is, people have stopped being inoculated against smallpox because the first world is free from it. Dr. Hollis has been working on an enhancement to the smallpox vaccines. What if we blended the vaccines together? The modified protein receptor Primus Necrovirus and the enhanced smallpox vaccine. Perhaps that will do the trick. Give people full immunity to both the original variant and the mutated virus."

"We will have to test it on people to make sure it works," Joseph said, cringing inside his suit. People would most certainly die because of their unsubstantiated experiments. "But we don't have a choice."

"This will not be pleasant," Dr. Desai said.

"I agree. This will not be pleasant," he echoed, watching the virus dance on the screen.

GWEN

Northern Michigan

Gwen gritted her teeth to stem the flow of emotion that washed over her, ebbing and flowing like a tide. *You don't have time for tears. You have more responsibilities than tears.* The steering wheel was rough and worn beneath her hands; little black flakes peeled off and stuck to her fingers and palms. The night seemed to push in on the RV from all sides, making her headlights dim. It was as if she were driving down a wooded tunnel. Her headlights, faint from age, did almost nothing to aid her.

Children sobbed in the back. The elderly sat, heads bowed, arms wrapped around the youngsters. Max sat in the pilot's chair next to her. He nervously scanned the area outside the window, bent forward in his seat as he tried to see everything going on around them.

Anyone who was a liability in a fight was with her. Dr. Thatcher sat with his little Pomeranian, Gordon, on his lap. Gordon's little orange head bounced from person to person, shaking with fright.

She watched the road, struggling with every mile of distance between her and Mark. *I should be with him. His fight is my fight. If I can't fight for my baby's life, then what can I possibly fight for?* She wanted to scream, laugh, shout, and giggle at the same time. *Damn hormones. If my body could just pick an emotion and roll with it, I would appreciate it. Mark.* Flashes of his laughing face bounced over her eyes. *He did this to me.*

She could see Max watching her out of the corner of her eye.

"What?" she asked.

"Are you okay, Ms. Gwen?" Max asked from the co-pilot's seat.

"What? You don't think I can drive this thing?" she spat. She gave him a dirty look.

"No, -no, ma'am."

"Don't call me ma'am. What am I, your fucking mom?"

"No, Mrs. Steele."

She looked at him, furious. "I'm not married either, nor should I be denoted by my marital status. Do you understand?"

"Yes," he mumbled.

"Can't you see I'm fine?" she yelled at him. His eyes widened, and he scootched away from her in his seat. He held a .22 rifle between his legs.

"Well, Max, let's talk you through it," she chided. "I'm in charge of the safety of twenty-six people, most which are under the age of eight. My *baby daddy*, and not my husband in case you were confused, is playing George Armstrong Custer against a bunch of fanatical Jesus freaks." She stopped, forgetting where she was going with her harangue. She held up a finger, remembering. "Oh yeah, I almost forgot. Everyone else in the world is an undead walking cannibal that will stop at nothing to kill and eat you." She took her eyes off the road to give him the most irate of stink eyes. All confidence the teenager had disappeared, and his shoulders hunched, drooping lower than normal.

"And my hormones are making me feel a little bit-," she was cut off.

"A little bit crazy," Max said, his voice a fraction of a whisper.

"Crazy? Did you just call a pregnant woman crazy?" she said, her mouth hanging open. *The nerve of this ingrate. This kid doesn't know anything about anything.*

"Umm," Max dragged out. He looked like he was about to open the door and tuck and roll out onto the roadway.

"You, you little boy. You have no fucking idea what crazy looks like," she said, swinging at him. He dodged her swipe, bending down low into the passenger side.

"I'm sorry," he yelped.

"You'd better be, and keep your eyes peeled for infected. The last thing I need is to end up stuck in some horde."

She checked her rearview mirror, glancing at the people in the back.

"Everything is going to be all right," she said in her best motherly voice. The voice that came out of her was not her own. *Oh, my God, I sound like my mother.* The crying continued from the back.

She looked back in the mirror. The older folks looked like they were on their last leg. A few of the older women held children in their arms, whispering words of comfort. All the children cried except one.

A little blond boy sat on the far back bench. His legs didn't touch the floor; they dangled off the seat swinging back and forth. He wore baby blue overall shorts with a white turtleneck as if someone had dressed him up for a summer picnic. *It's him.* She slammed on the brakes. People cried out, startled. The inertia tugged them forward in their seats.

"What are you doing?" Max's voice came out as a hesitant squeak.

She turned around. The space where the boy sat was empty.

"Where's that little boy?" she cried out.

Dr. Thatcher looked around. "They're all here," he said. Worry crossed his fleshy face. "We have been driving nonstop since Little Sable."

She slammed the RV into park and stood up, leaving the driver's compartment. She stepped over young and old alike. "He was sitting there," she said. She pointed down to an empty spot on the bench.

"Where's the boy?" she asked everyone. The children looked scared.

"Gwen, everyone is accounted for. Everyone we started with is here," Dr. Thatcher said. He stroked Gordon's head with a heavy hand, making the dog's eyes bulge out more than normal. "I'm positive."

Gwen bent low to a little girl. Her hair was in a dirty snarled black ponytail. "Where's the boy that was here?"

"I don't know," the girl said in a mousy voice.

A freckled-faced girl next to her spoke up. "There's no boy," she said.

Gwen thrust a finger at the empty space. "Yes, there was a boy sitting right there." She wanted to pull her hair out. *What's happening to me?* She let her hand fall on her forehead, massaging her brow.

"Ah. Ms. Gwen," Max said from the front.

"What, Max?" she yelled back at him.

"You better come up here."

"Can't you wait a minute? I'm trying to figure this out." *Or am I crazy?* She started counting the children and then the adults. She only got to five before Max spoke up again.

"Ms. Gwen. We should go." She could hear him rolling the manual window down in quick circular loops.

"Just wait, Max," she said, starting her counting over again. *One. Two. Three.*

A gun boomed in the vehicle making her jump. The children started to frantically scream. Her ears rang with high-pitched whines and screams.

"Goddamnit, Max!" She brought a hand up to her ears. She leaned down, looking out the front of the RV. Max's gun boomed again. A figure stumbled and fell. A figure in a mass of hundreds. The infected came and the kids cried in the back of the RV, all except the blond boy just out of reach.

STEELE

Little Sable Point, MI

The taillights of the camper disappearing down the road were seared into his mind. Steele had stood motionless for minutes after they left, watching the night as if he thought she might come back. Knowing that she went into an unknown that was plagued by the undead and riddled with death but would still be safer than staying with him at Little Sable made his insides swirl in a pool of uneasiness. *Is this land even worth fighting over? If they die, you sent them to their deaths from the safety of this community with nothing but a teenage boy and a pregnant woman to fend for them.* He shot air through his nose trying to relieve his stress. *It's done. She's gone. The plan is in motion. Now you can fight this dirty war without the innocent getting in the way.*

He marched to the trailer holding Peter. Margie sat in a chair outside the trailer. The older woman stood as he approached, gripping her bolt-action hunting rifle like she was going to use it to club him over the head with it.

"It's only me, Margie," he said softly. She relaxed a bit in the moonlight. "How about you get some rest? We've been at this all day. Save some of your strength for tomorrow."

"Captain." She exhaled a deep sigh, smiling faintly in the dark. "I've been through longer nights than this. Parenting isn't a nine-to-five gig."

Steele smiled back, lips closed covering his teeth. Her words reminded him of something he may never experience. "I'm sure it's not, but I need to talk to our captive alone for a minute. Can you send Jason over here in about thirty?"

"I sure will, Captain. I think you did right by sending Max away with the others. He's a good boy, but I'm not sure he's ready for this. And the children. Sparing them this may save their souls."

"Or I could be sending them straight to their deaths."

Her eyes were pools of black shadowed by the night. He couldn't tell if she blamed him, pitied him, or respected what he had done. "You made the right one," she said, squeezing his arm on the way by.

Steele jangled the chain as he undid the lock. He let the anticipation of his arrival dig into Peter's brain. Peter shifted inside, his every move echoing in the empty trailer. Flicking on his flashlight, Steele shined it on the man in the back. Peter covered his eyes with his forearms.

"What? What do you want?" he said. The man was terrified and recoiled from Steele's presence. He would probably never really recover from the mental strain of waterboarding. The feeling of drowning, the water filling his throat, and the terror of not being able to get air to his oxygen-deprived lungs would stick with him. Those experiences would cloud his dreams, forever turning them into nightmares as he slept.

"Came to check in on you," Steele said.

Peter seemed to recognize every part of his voice, and he shrunk smaller in the light. "Steele. No. Don't come back here. I told you everything," he yelped. He shifted himself into the corner of the trailer, legs kicking outward. Steele slowly walked along the inner trailer to the cowering man in the back.

"Settle down, man. I'm not going to hurt you," Steele said, grabbing the chain that connected Peter to the trailer wall. The big man flinched.

"What are you going to do to me?" Peter asked, his hands still covering his face.

"I'm going to take you back to Temple Energy."

Peter's eyes went wide in the flashlight. "Screw you. You're just messing with me," he whimpered. "You're prolly going to waterboard me again. Or pull off my fingertips. Or cut off my balls!" Peter squealed. The man pushed himself further into the corner.

"I'm not going to do any of those things." Steele pointed his flashlight away from the man.

Peter blinked rapidly in the low light. "I don't believe you," he sputtered.

"Don't," Steele said. He stuck a key into the lock keeping Peter bound to the trailer wall. He unlocked him, freeing the chain away from the wall. He tugged on Peter's chain as if he were a dog. "Come on."

Peter sat in the corner, whimpers coming from his throat. Steele yanked the chain a little harder than he wanted to, and Peter tumbled upright. An outline of a person stepped in front of the trailer doors. *Too early for Jason.*

"Where do you think you're going?" came Tess's voice. Steele relaxed a bit.

"I'm taking Peter back to the pastor," he said, flat out with it. *No time for deception.*

"Why? We can use him as leverage if the Chosen come."

"We can use him as leverage now and maybe prevent them coming at all."

"What gave you that idea?" she said.

He jerked Peter's chain. "Take a seat," he commanded the broken man. Peter sat in the trailer doorway, his head bowed.

"I got this message earlier." He unfolded a piece of paper and handed it to her. She turned on her flashlight and it shined bright on the yellow legal paper, illuminating the words almost too transparency.

"You're kidding me," she said. She looked at him. "You believe this shit? It's a trap."

Steele reached over and snagged the paper back. He held it in his hand like it was a golden ticket.

"Sure sounds like it."

"He wants to meet you in the middle of the night at the roadblock. Far enough away from us where we can't help. This is suicide."

"Maybe." He was glad he couldn't see her well in the dark. The disapproval on her face wouldn't help.

"Why are you doing this? If they kill you, we won't last ten minutes against them," she said. *Less than that.*

Steele pointed to the paper. "He's offering us an opportunity to live. We only need to pay a tithe to live within his kingdom. We give Peter back as a symbol of good faith, then no one else has to die." He folded it up and put it in his breast pocket.

"And you believe this bullshit? The guy *burned* Pagan alive. How can we come to terms with a person like that?"

"I don't know if I will ever come to terms with that, but this is a chance that people here won't have to die. You saw his group. We're sorely outnumbered and outgunned." Steele gave a look over at Peter—he knew he was listening—and Peter dropped his gaze back to the ground like a whipped dog.

"I don't think you should go," Tess said, her lips crunching together.

"If there's even a small chance I can prevent the upcoming bloodshed, I have to do it."

"I picked you to help me because you have half a brain, and now, Pagan is gone which unfortunately means you're it." He felt that he caught a hint of deceit in her voice as if she had forced herself to say it. "And when they crucify you or whatever medieval bullshit they decide to do, I will have no one to help me keep this place afloat." Steele grimaced at her words.

"I'm only doing what you asked me to do. And that's protecting these people."

"A leader takes a stand. They don't die shaking hands with fanatics," she snarled.

Maybe she's right. The only way to curb their fanaticism is to stand against it. "It's the best the I can do."

They stood in silence for a moment, dissatisfaction settling in the air like an ugly cloud.

"I'll remember you, Mark Steele, after they butcher you and burn your corpse." *If I'm lucky.* "The last knight of the apocalypse." She planted one right on his lips, shocking him. He could feel his cheeks turning red. *Is it because Peter is watching? Or is it because Gwen isn't here? Or did I enjoy it?*

"Are you going to tell Gwen about that one too?" he said quickly.

He thought her eyes were playful and sad in the dim light. "She and I came to terms over you. I was supposed to get you administratively. But it looks like that's coming to an end with your daring ploy for peace."

She turned and walked away, her thin form disappearing into the night. This interaction made him glad he hadn't told Gwen about his secret rendezvous with the pastor. *I'm going to pay for this.*

"Chicks," Peter mumbled, shaking his head.

Steele gave him an eye with a twist of his head. "Come on, Peter. I've got a surprise for you." He yanked Peter's chain and he tumbled off the back of the trailer. He caught himself before he hit the ground.

"I-I, don't like surprises."

Steele grinned at his captive. "You're gonna hate this one."

***

Waves crashed on the nearby beach. It sounded like an ocean, but it was the call of fresh water. The moon glinted off the whitecaps as they repeated their endless assault on the shore. The two men walked slowly down the center of a two-lane road. The white moon was the only light illuminating the way ahead. Maples and oaks hung over the road like overarching fingers of a tree giant.

Steele gave Peter a shove in the back for encouragement. The man sobbed a bit in the night, making him sound like one of the infected. Peter passively resisted his every push like Steele was forcing him down a pirate's plank.

"Sack up, dude," Steele said behind him. He scratched under his jacket with the hand holding Peter's chain.

Steele kept his M4 at his side. His other hand rested on his carbine. His tomahawk lightly tapped his thigh as they walked. The presence of his sidearm weighed on his hip.

Peter mumbled through his gag. His curly hair bounced in the dark as he tried to look for infected threats ahead.

"You know the way." Steele shoved him. "Quiet." *I don't know who is more nervous, me or him.* Steele's eyes scanned the terrain. It looked familiar, but the woods and the beach at night all pretty much looked the same. They had ditched their pickup over a mile back so as to not give away their presence.

Steele's heart sped up as he noticed a darkness forming across the road ahead of them like a gate. It was a thick dark line. Steele knew it for what it was. The roadblock. The hair on his neck stood up as they neared the felled tree with every step. *Someone else is here.*

Steele tightened his hold on the chain, forcing Peter to stop. They stood motionless in the night. The sound of waves battered away at his confidence. They awaited the sound of the dead. Eerily, they had seen none between the two camps. *This pastor guy must be good at what he does.* Peter shuffled his feet, scraping the pavement.

"Quiet," Steele shushed, looking over his shoulder.

A beam of sunlight hit them. Steele quickly recognized it as a deer shining spotlight. Thirty-two hundred lumens carved through the night, bringing Steele and Peter into the spotlight as if they were two actors on stage.

In the darkness, he hadn't noticed them. The men had only been darker shades of night. He couldn't tell if they twitched or moved or were nervous, only that they stood silent and waiting.

"Drop your gun," commanded a voice from the trees. Steele set his gun down on the ground, not letting his fingers move an inch on Peter's chain.

Individual lights sprang up in the trees. Hundreds of flashlights flicked on like torches. People were on the beach, in the forest, they lined the top of the log. They rested guns across their chests or held them lazily toward the ground. He was no threat, and they knew it. The lights enveloped them, closing in within ten yards as they surrounded them. Steele pulled Peter's chain tighter into his gut, feeling his knuckles close to popping on the metal. They all stood watching Steele and Peter for sixty tense seconds.

A man walked through the circle of lights. His tall form was clad in all black, the only visible part his gray hair. His men parted before him like a flock of sheep for their shepherd. He walked into the ring and stopped. He clasped his hands behind his back and looked at Steele. His eyes finally fell upon Peter and a smile curved on his thin lips.

"Peter, my son, you are alive," he said. Peter mumbled loudly through his gag, pulling on the chain Steele had him bound with.

"Not so fast," Steele said to Peter.

"I'm going to be honest, Mr. Steele. I thought you would have put him to death by now in retaliation for the cleansing of Mr. Pagan. I'm somewhat impressed if not confused by this. Vengeance is a normal human response following anger and resentment. But you have held off. I'm curious as to why?" His eyebrows rose in anticipation of an answer.

"I'm tired of having needless blood on my hands," Steele said, his eyes ripping the pastor. The pastor nodded with a slight grin.

"I know you see my actions against the nonbelievers as unnecessary bloodshed, but I can assure you that this is God's will."

"I'm not here to debate God's will." Steele shifted his feet.

"I'm not sure you get to make the rules, Mr. Steele," the pastor said.

"I came to make a deal," Steele said. His voice was flat. He made sure to keep his eyes on the pastor.

"Ah, yes. A bargain. You may commence," the pastor said with a wave of his hand.

Steele licked his lips. "You allow us to live within your Kingdom of God and we will pay your tax. You can have Peter as a show of our good faith."

The pastor walked forward to them, foot by slender foot, his boots clicking on the pavement.

"Yes, the letter. It's a good idea, no? Two peoples living in harmony."

Steele almost choked as he said the words. "It seems reasonable."

"Reason. It does seem reasonable. But how do I ensure that your people keep their word that they will pay me what is mine on a regular basis for our *protection*? I would like to avoid anything like what happened to Peter's ill-fated peace-party."

"What did you have in mind?" Steele said cautiously. This man was as wily as the devil himself.

"I would like long-term assurance."

"I'll see what I can do." Steele watched the man as he paced.

"I want your camp's children. All of them."

Steele gulped hard. *Thank God I sent them with Gwen.* Steele's eyes narrowed. "You know I can't ask that."

"I can promise their safety, more than you can. Of that I'm certain. They will be fed, clothed, even schooled while under my care. They will be warm when winter hits Michigan, and I assure you, it will be soon and it will be harsh along the lake."

"How could I ask these people to give up their children?" Steele wondered aloud.

"It's that or they will all die tomorrow. Think about it logically. I guarantee their safety. It's all a parent can hope for in the end time. Freedom from worry. They will be part of the Kingdom of God. His living legacy here on earth. We have largely cleared this whole area of infected. I send out teams on a daily basis to spread our reach. You can be a part of this cleansing. A part of God's solution."

Would I ask Gwen to give up our child to them for assured safety? How could I ever ask people to give up their children or die? "You know I can't ask people to do this. We will send food and supplies as we find them, but no children."

"I'm not asking what you're willing to do. I'm telling you," the pastor growled. "Those are our terms."

"I can't accept them," Steele said. He wrenched Peter closer to his body, using him as cover. Steele knew that the pastor would eagerly martyr Peter if it came to a shootout, but it was better than taking rounds to the chest in the open.

"Pride cometh before the fall, Mr. Steele. Then again, that trait seems to run deep in your veins," the pastor said. A smile crept upon his lips as if he knew a secret. His eyes met Steele's with cold knowledge sitting inside them. Steele's hand tickled his side as it itched for a gun to hold. The men in the circle seemed to read his mind. Guns lowered and pointed at him from all around.

"You don't know anything about my family," Steele hissed.

The pastor looked down at the ground and shook his head as if he were disappointed in Steele.

"I know you and your mother are a lot alike." A slimy smile grew on the pastor's lips. Steele's stomach twisted in aversion to this man.

"Where is she?" Steele growled. *If I bend and roll, I may be able to get a shot off before they waste me and probably each other in the chaos. That bastard is close enough for point shooting.*

The pastor's eyes held almost mirth around them as if he took pure joy from Steele's torment. "We've sent her back to her maker."

"Fuck you," Steele snarled.

The pastor sighed. "No need for such harsh language. She could not overcome her pride before she perished in the flames. Even when I offered her a chance to use her God-given gifts to help others." Steele glared, his nose flaring. "I see her in your eyes." *He can't fucking know that. How could he?*

"You don't know shit about her."

The pastor's forehead wrinkled in concern. "Sure I do, Mr. Steele. I burned her house to the ground with her and her lover inside. Not too far from here." He pointed. "I'd say about eight miles south down the coast."

"You lie!" Steele yelled at him. Peter whimpered through his gag as Steele jerked his chain. *Her house was burnt down.*

"I don't lie, Mr. Steele. We could have used the top surgeon from St. Anastasia's North Shores Hospital."

The blow took the wind out of him. It was too much. The pastor knew too much. The world grew distant. His heart pounded in his ears. His vision blurred a bit with each heartbeat, coming back into focus for a moment then blurring again. His breathing grew labored and shallow in his chest.

The pastor's eyes weighed Steele's distress with ugly concern. "Maybe we would do better speaking with somebody else from your community. That tomboy. What's her name? Tess?"

You already knew. You already knew in your heart she was gone. Fuck.

Steele reached his hand into his pocket. His eyes never left the bastard's. His fingers locked around a rectangle remote detonator in his ACU pants. Guns cocked. Two hundred eyes stared down sights at him. Peter's body shook as he sobbed in front of him.

"Nobody moves or we all go boom." Steele lifted his hand in the air.

The pastor's eyes grew wide as recognition settled upon him. Men holding their flashlights took worried steps back.

"Don't worry, gents, a few feet won't make a difference, I made sure of that." Steele removed a thick coat wrapped around Peter's shoulders revealing tan blocks of C-4 connected with wires strapped to his chest.

"He's bluffing," the pastor hissed like the vile viper he was. He took a step back toward his men.

Steele spun around, making sure everyone could see that Peter's chest was strapped with explosives. "Don't even think of shooting me." Steele held his hand with the detonator in the air. "I let go of this detonator and it's enough to kill everyone here. Enough nails, marbles, and bolts to shred the very flesh from your bodies." He turned toward the pastor. "The marbles are courtesy of the children," he said with a wicked look in his eyes.

The pastor's face turned into an evil snarl.

Steele addressed the rest of the pastor's men. "Even if you did somehow crawl out of here, you would die with no medical aid. Not to mention the attention it would bring from the dead. Imagine crawling away from here mangled until the infected caught you." He gave the pastor an extra cruel look. "It will send you to hell faster, pastor."

The pastor lifted a hand in the air. "Now, Mr. Steele, no need to be hasty. We came to parley, not for more violence."

"You came to intimidate, murder, and enslave us. You murdered my mother. She never hurt anyone. And I would rather see every single man here dead than have that befall Little Sable. Even if I have to sacrifice myself."

"No one has to die," the pastor said. His hand wavered in the air, visibly shaking.

"Shut up," Steele spat. "I'm making the rules here. Now, I'm going to leave you Peter, and I'm going to go back to my home. If I think someone is following me, he goes boom." Steele spun Peter around in a circle so everyone could see. Nervous eyes stared back. "If I don't feel safe on my way back, he goes boom. If I don't make it back in exactly twenty minutes, one of my buddies makes it go boom." He stopped and glanced at his watch. "The countdown has begun." He bent low and snatched up his carbine off the ground.

Steele swung the carbine around, pointing it at a few of them. "Now, I never want to see you assholes again. My group is gone, so leave us be."

Peter cried through his gag.

"It's okay, Peter," the pastor said, leveling his chin at Steele.

Steele let Peter's chain drop. It clanked as it hit the ground, making Peter jump. Steele placed his M4 over his forearm, still holding the remote detonator clacker in his hand. He pointed his carbine at the pastor.

"I could kill you now and have every right to do so, but not today. Enough blood's been spilt."

Steele walked backward, spinning in circles, taking his turn pointing his gun back at the men surrounding him. They parted wide for him and he backtracked. They watched him with wide eyes. Others had a cold look in them as if they didn't care if he blasted them fifty feet into the air, obliterating them into tiny pieces of charred flesh.

"I won't warn you boys again. If you come to Little Sable, you *will* die." Then he turned and ran. After one hundred yards, he shoved the detonator in his pocket. He ground his teeth in rage as he ran and pushed his sadness and fear into the pit of his stomach through the pain.

GWEN

Lakeshore Drive, MI

The wall of death advanced in their direction. They were all dead, but they still moved like the living. Slower, but alive in the sense that they moved with a singular purpose. The ones wearing clothes wore them disheveled and torn, most hanging by bare shreds as if they had been shipwrecked on a deserted island or had survived a bear attack. Blood stained their clothes and skin alike, most drying in ink-like stains coating their bodies.

The necks of the newly infected were swollen, lymph nodes four times their normal size protruding from their skin like hideous hidden plums. Red blood covered their bodies, but they were few. The dead that had been decaying for weeks dominated their ranks.

The infected that had been killed in the beginning were gray. Their flesh hung from their faces, drooping beneath their eyes and jawline. Their mouths hung open, revealing chipped, broken, and missing teeth. Puckered bullet holes painted the exposed skin of their bodies. Arms hung by mere tendons. Crippled, bent feet dragged behind them, anchors from being assaulted, run over, and maimed. They didn't care what horrible fate befell them now. Only the virus remained, pulling their strings in a shoddy uncontrolled manner, one ugly footstep after another. They moaned, an evil call to arms picked up by all like an angry pack of wolves.

Gwen ground the gearshift into drive and hammered her foot down on the gas. The old RV lurched as if it had forgotten that she required its full power. It was an old war-horse, spurred into the fray by the sharp spurs of its rider for one last battle.

The RV creaked its way to ten miles per hour before the first bodies ricocheted off the front and sides. The dead glanced off the grille of the metal beast. They spun and twisted as they were shoved to the side. The unlucky ones were dragged under the wheels, causing the RV to lurch and shake. Hands pounded the doors. Nails screeched down the sides.

"Keep going," Max yelled.

Cries of terror shrieked from the back. Her speed hovered at about twelve miles per hour, and the old RV took the flesh of humans in its heavy determined stride. The RV shuddered, its shocks bouncing as they absorbed the bodies underneath its wheels. The whirlwind of flesh, hands, and bodies came to an end. She felt the steering wheel stiffen and the steering column lock up in her hands. She wrenched on the wheel, fingers gripped tightly around it.

"I can't steer," she yelled. She muscled the steering wheel, inching it onto the road, but finally, she couldn't budge it. She stared at her white knuckled hands, unable to steer the vehicle. "I can't steer!" The RV could only go straight in her last direction. It stayed true to its current course and motored undeviating into a ditch, launching itself into a coastal forest full of trees with trunks the diameter of teacups. Her chest caught on the steering wheel as they crashed. The air was forced from her lungs. "Uff," she breathed.

The headlights were shadowed by the dried leaves of fall trees. Branches pushed onto the windshield as if they tried to hold them back. Her eyes fogged and it took multiple blinks before she could see clearly again.

Her hands immediately went to her stomach. She stared down at it, hands feeling across her belly. She coughed. *My baby*, her mind screamed, but she had no time to think about the potential danger to her unborn child. The RV leaned forward, its front end pressed tight against trees.

"Damn it," she swore.

The door swung open and Max jumped out of the RV.

"Max," she screamed. His .22 banged out two shots.

She fumbled with a silver button door handle.

"Hurry, Ms. Gwen," Max hollered.

She grabbed her M4 from between the seats. She slid off the seat and out of the RV. A dead woman reached for her with skinny arms, using the side of the RV to get closer to Gwen. Gwen squeezed the trigger and the M4 bop-bop-bop-bopped. Her last round struck home. Gwen grimaced, her stomach and chest in pain, impossible to tell which was worse or if one was caused by the other. Hunched over, she rounded the RV.

Freshly crushed corpses lay scattered along the road. The bodies were the worst roadkill disaster she could have ever have imagined. They crawled for them. Their fingernails scraped until they popped off their fingertips, but the clawing of the concrete didn't stop. It wasn't the ones mangled on the roadway she cared about; it was the ones that walked and doddered in her direction. Too many of them staggered her way. Max fired his small caliber rifle hurriedly.

"That door will never hold them," she cried out. She let off three single-round shots, rushing her trigger. Only one corpse fell.

"We've got to get them on top," Gwen yelled. She hustled for the side RV door and ripped it open.

Max's gun continued to bang in the background.

Terrified eyes looked back at her. Gordon barked shrill notes into the night.

"Everyone get on top of the RV. Hurry," she said. She ran for the red emergency hatch and pulled hard on the red levers. Popping it backward, she opened it up and the night sky appeared draped above her.

"Dr. Thatcher, I need your help. Ben and May," she said to an old couple, "we will hoist you up first and hand you the kids. They nodded.

"Of course," Dr. Thatcher said, setting down Gordon. Gordon did circles on the bench seat, yapping as he went.

Gwen waved at a little blonde girl. "Lacy." The little girl jumped into her arms. Dr. Thatcher helped her push the children one by one through the hatch. After the fifth child, the pounding came on the door. Only a few hands.

"Hurry, Doctor. That door won't hold long," she urged. One after another, they lifted them up. More hands joined the others on the door.

Pounding echoed inside the camper. The glass on the camper door broke. Mangled, rotting flesh pushed its way through the broken window.

She took a foot to the face as she hefted the doctor up and through the small hatch. The RV rocked as the dead surrounded it. The door dented inward, bending in the frame, the weight of the bodies pressing into it.

Dr. Thatcher's face peered down at her. "Here," she shouted, handing up her M4.

The door weakened, gaps widening. The door gave way and they stumbled inside the RV. Without looking, she jumped up, grabbing Dr. Thatcher's fleshy arms. Ben grunted as he helped Thatcher pull her up. The sharp sting of fingernails raking across her butt cheeks and into her thighs seared through her pants as they pulled her up from below. The dead moaned below her, almost as if they were saddened by her departure.

She collapsed on top of the RV for a moment, breathing hard. She squeezed her eyes tight, catching her breath.

When she cracked open her eyes, the kids, on their hands and knees, looked at her. She almost relaxed. *Max.* Her eyes shot open as she remembered the teenager was still below.

"Max?" she shouted. She stood up, ignoring the burning down her backside. She circled the roof, leaning backward to balance and keep from sliding off the top.

"Gwen," mumbled a voice. Max stood wedged between trees near the front of the RV. He had weaseled his way through the tightly grown trees. She raced to the front end of the RV and dove down onto the roof.

"Grab my gun. I'll pull you up," she said. She held the M4 by the stock, reaching it out. Grabbing the barrel of her weapon, he jumped on the hood of the RV. Fear encased his eyes. The dead pushed through the trees, stretching out their wicked fingers for him.

"I gotcha," she said. Both hands on the gun, she heaved. His feet scrambled, trying to get a grip up the windshield. He wasn't the only one. Dead hands gripped around his legs. He kicked wildly trying to get them away. More arms reached for him.

"Don't look down," she said. His hands grasped the gun tight, and the barrel started to slip through her fingers. His eyes locked onto hers, frantic.

"Don't let go," he squeaked. His freckles were almost white in the headlights. His hands slowly slipped off the stock of the gun. Inch by inch, he was overpowered. She was thrown backward onto her rear.

"Gwen. Gwen. No," he shouted. She flipped the gun around and leaned over the edge of the RV.

Max's screams penetrated the night. "Ah. Ahh. Ahhhhh!" The infected tore into him. Their fingers penetrated his body, sawing through flesh and muscle alike. They scooped out his insides until his lungs gave out, and he twitched as they ate his body. Headlights revealed the whole gut-wrenching episode like an old drive-in horror movie.

Gwen stared in shock, her mouth partially open until she could tear her eyes away from their kill. More white eyes stared back at her, their arms grasping for her like she was a rockstar onstage playing a guitar solo. She stood up. The children looked at her through scared eyes. She slung her M4 on her back. She only had two full mags. Not enough bullets to even thin them out.

"Come here," she said to them, kneeling on the RV for balance. It rocked as the horde below tried to get on top. Banging into the seats and tables, they fumbled around causing the large vehicle to shake.

"All the kids, come to me." The children crawled to her on their hands and knees, sliding over the roof. She brought them in close and hugged as many of them as she could tight.

"Shhh," she whispered. She sniffled back tears. "We must be quiet."

Little Lacy snuggled into her and wrapped her arms around Gwen.

"Will they go away?" Lacy asked, looking up at Gwen.

"If we are very quiet, they will leave us alone. Which means no crying." She wiped a tear from Lacy's eye. "There, there." She stroked her cheek for a moment.

The older adults scooted in closer, sliding over the roof.

She put her arms around more of them. "Now, we can't cry or they won't leave. Okay?" She made sure to eye the adults as well then back to the children. "We're going to use our imaginations to make up a story about going to your most favorite place in the whole entire world. Then when they're gone, everyone gets to tell their story, okay?" She wrapped her arms around more of the children, shushing them. "Be quiet and think really, really hard…ready? Go."

She held as many of the children of Little Sable Point as she could manage while the infected clambered below. After thirty minutes had passed, she stared off into the distance, watching one child who hadn't joined her.

The blond boy sat on the edge of the roof. His feet dangled off the edge. He giggled and pointed at the dead below. He turned, staring at her with a smile on his face as if he were watching the monkeys at the zoo. She bit her lip, holding back her tears. He turned back around, wiggling with mirth. *I am bringing him into a world populated by only monsters.*

STEELE

Little Sable Point, MI

Steele rounded the bend in the road to Little Sable Point, taking it too fast. The back end of his pickup truck spun out, fishtailing across the road. He corrected the wheel with a sharp jerk of his hand and it begrudgingly straightened out. He sped for the pickup-made entrance of Little Sable. When he got close enough, he slammed on the brakes. The pickup screeched, sliding to a halt on the sandy road. He snapped the driver's side door open and hopped out. As he walked for the entrance, no one challenged him.

He climbed over the car blocking the entrance. A small feminine shadow ran from her RV. She jumped on him, wrapping her arms around him. He hugged her for only a moment before he pushed her away.

"I thought they would murder you like cowards," Tess said.

"They would have, but they didn't have the opportunity." He handed her the explosive clacker.

She spun the remote around in her fingers. Her eyes questioned him, looking for an answer. "What does this do?"

The sun was beginning its daily rise over the land, emerging in the east and settling upon the west. He dug around near the tire of a camper, kicking sand away with his foot from the back of the tire. After a few moments, he bent down, using his hands to scoop away the sand.

She waved the clacker at him. "What does it do?"

He uncovered a bag and picked it up, throwing it over his shoulder.

He smiled at her. "It detonates explosives."

An unsettled look fell upon her as she set it on the hood of a car very gently.

"Where did you get explosives?" she said.

Steele marched away from her. Time was against them. As seconds seeped away, the pastor would realize he had been duped. Then it was a race to mobilize his forces. He walked over to the lighthouse, Tess lagging behind. Opening the door, he grabbed his tactical vest and checked his mags.

"Thunder had them."

Her eyes searched for answers in his. "He gave them to you?"

He ignored her and he scooped up magazines and placed them into his pockets. He made sure the hawk was secure on his belt. He ran a hand down the blade. A few chips had been taken out of it, but it was still a killer in a close-quarters fight. He glanced up at her.

"No. I stole them and hid them because I knew we'd need them for something."

She watched him. "Why did they let you go?"

"I made it look like Peter was wearing a bomb. It was believable enough, but it won't be long before they figure out I was lying." He stood up, meeting her eyes. "The pastor admitted to murdering my mother." The words stung his mouth like he spit fire.

Her dark eyes spoke of only vengeance. "They're rotten to the core, but mark my words, Steele, we will have our vengeance." Her eyes blazed then softened. She squeezed his arm. "I'm so sorry. You're sure? He had proof?"

Steele sighed, allowing himself to grasp her words. It was fact that his mother was gone. Not missing. Murdered. "He knew too much about us."

"He's an evil man," she said, nodding.

"If I was here, that wouldn't have happened. She would still be alive." He stared at the ground in anguish.

"No, you would have been murdered too. You have been given a chance to save people from that fate."

Steele nodded and pushed his emotions deep inside. "He will pay and then we will mourn."

He put his arms through his tactical vest and strapped it tight. He checked his magazines inside his vest. Their weight felt good and solid on his frame. "I had to give peace a chance. Now they can have their war." He slung his M4 around his shoulder diagonally. He walked away from her yelling at the ring of cars. "Larry. Jason."

The two stood sleepily. Larry scratched at his bald head, and Jason rubbed his eyes.

"Hurry up now," Steele shouted. Larry pulled a shirt on, and Jason fumbled with his shoes and gun at the same time.

"Hope you got enough sleep because today is the day. Can we get Trent up there?" Steele looked up at the lakeshore lighthouse.

"I can," Jason said.

Steele judged him for a moment. Jason wasn't the best shot in the group, but he wasn't the worst.

"We'll get you and Trent up there. Larry, get all the rest of the volunteers here. Rouse the rest of Little Sable up. If they can shoot, find them a place and get their guns ready."

"Yes, sir," Larry said and ambled off, swaying as he walked like an ape.

"Tess, can you find Ahmed? I need his help. And Kevin, wake his drunk ass up." Tess jogged off.

The sun creaked higher in the sky and dawn embraced them. The sun topped the trees like a match as he prepared for the coming storm. The volunteers trickled in along with Kevin, teetering from the effects of alcohol, and a tired-looking Ahmed.

"Bring it in close," he commanded. The group of volunteers took timid steps forward. "I ain't going to bite. Now bring it in." They came in close enough. *Do I only have sheep? Are there no sheepdogs among them?*

Steele crouched down, bending his knees. Taking a stick from the sand, he drew a large circle around a rock. The stick squeaked as it dug into the granules of sand. "This is us."

He snaked a line in the sand leading up to the circle. "That is the only road into Little Sable Point." He drew x's around the road. "If they want to get here fast, they will have to use the road. If they want to ruck in through the forest, they can, but I don't think they will. They smell blood in the water. And they're angry."

"How many of 'em are there?" asked Gregor, his long thick black hair draped about his neck like a mane.

Steele looked up at the man. "I estimate they will have at least five hundred."

The eyes of his nine volunteers betrayed their fear. It oozed out of the group like a stink they couldn't get rid of.

"But there's only about fifty of us," Hank said, massaging his scantily hair-clad temples.

Steele nodded. "I know that, Hank. So we're going to have to be smarter, tougher, and craftier than they are." He looked down at his sand map.

"I want to funnel them through here." Steele let his stick run down the line representing the road. "I want to keep them stacked up and easier to shoot, unable to concentrate any sort of firepower on us." He looked up at them. Margie nodded. Nathan studied the map. "So let's get some vehicles here and here." He scrawled small circles along the road. "But not too many where they think it's a trap, but enough for them to have to go our direction."

"Even then, what are we going to do?" Larry asked.

"Glad you asked. Next, I want crossing fields of fire. The cars are going to force them here. This will be our kill zone. So I'm going to need two volunteers here and here." He lightly drew lines in the sand, making Little Sable Point Lighthouse the bottom of a triangle.

"When will we know to fire?" Margie asked. She stood, her deer rifle upright on her shoulder like a Civil War soldier.

"We want them to get all bunched up. Once about half of them make it through our vehicles, we will open up, but not until then, or they will realize it's a trap and try something else. If everything works out, it will cause confusion amongst their ranks and make them think they are up against a larger force." Steele eyed them. "I'm going to put Trent and Jason in the lighthouse, but I need a third. Takers?" Trent nodded and Jason looked pleased. Eyes fluttered around from person to person. Steele heard a few names muttered.

"Bengy?" Steele asked. *If I can take the old man farther from the fight, I should.*

The white-haired man shook his head no. "Can't see that good no more, boss. Best to leave younger eyes for faraway tasks."

Steele's eyes fell upon the middle-aged mother. Her eyes were nervous but fiery. "Fair enough. Margie, I want you up in the lighthouse."

Margie smiled. "It would be a pleasure, Captain."

Steele stood up and wiped the sand off his pants. "Everyone is dismissed. They are coming. Let's roll those cars into place on the double, anything that is out of gas. Ahmed, come with me."

Steele turned to leave and Tess planted herself in front of him.

"What about me?" she said as if they had been dating for years.

"What about you?" he retorted.

She looked to the side for a moment. "Where do I go?"

"Where do you want to go?"

She licked her lips. "Aren't you supposed to tell me? You told everyone else where you want them."

Her coal-like eyes watched him.

"Stay with me."

Her lips curved.

"I thought you'd say that."

"Come on." He waved her toward the sandy dune-grass-covered field leading to the trees surrounding their lighthouse encampment. They trekked over the loose ground to a line of coastal trees made up of thin needled red and white pines, balsam firs, buttonbush, cedars, and birch. The trees doggedly lined the field as if they were nervous about growing closer to the water.

Steele stopped and tossed his bag in the sand.

"Ahmed, you want to start prepping?"

The Arab-American man smiled. "Like Pittsburgh?"

"Just like Pittsburgh. We still have a few tricks up our sleeve."

Ahmed began pulling large rectangle bricks of C-4 from his bag.

Steele turned back to the tall red-brick lighthouse. It spired toward the sky, the tallest building for miles along the coast. Its black observation deck at the top had a large glass bulb encased in glass. He gave a wide wave of his hand over his head. The glass-encased room at the top of the lighthouse turned yellow and orange as it erupted into flames. Steele waved and one of his volunteers manning the elevated sniper nest waved back.

"It's lit again," Tess said.

Steele looked down at her. "I want them to know exactly where we are."

JOSEPH

Cheyenne Mountain Complex, CO

Joseph bowed over his microscope, twisting his needle a bit to the left side of the single Primus Necrovirus capsid. He snipped the viral receptor off the viral protein coat, leaving the rest of the virus intact. The cut was sufficient, leaving the cell with an oblong yet smooth outer surface.

Inside another needle was a microscopic shaving tool. He pressed it near the outer protein coat of the virus. Carefully, he shaved the area where the receptor had been. It was the only way to ensure he could attach the new receptor. The work was painstakingly precise; if he ruined the capsid, he would be back at square one. He would have to prepare a different cell all over again, lengthening an already arduous process.

"Dr. Desai's a superstar," he whispered to himself. He picked up another needle holding her modified receptor, twisting it in his hand. Her ability to modify the receptor with such speed and attention to detail accelerated their testing timetable by weeks if not months. He had spent days in the lab assisting her with preparing specimens for trial.

Nice and easy. Nice and easy, he told himself over and over. He took the needle holding the new receptor and pushed the modified receptor into its place. It attached to the virus protein coat, becoming one with the Primus Necrovirus. The modified receptor would not allow the transfer of genetic material but would allow the body's immune system to identify it for destruction. He moved the virus into a vial.

"How are you coming on the test specimens?" Byrnes said. The man wore the same blue biohazard suit that Joseph wore except Byrnes was tall, giving him the look of an intergalactic spaceman from another planet. His eyes were stern yet sullen behind his plastic mask.

"Almost there. I'm worried about the dosing combined with the smallpox. I'm not sure how to portion the specimens in for the live testing. Any slight deviation could lead to any number of complications including infection and death," Joseph said.

"Or nothing at all. If we don't try, nothing will matter because we will all die in this mountain tomb."

Joseph gulped down the acidic bile rising up in his esophagus. *Kill or die, or wait and die.*

"There will certainly be negative side effects." Joseph looked at the colonel in worry. "Who would volunteer for this?" he whispered. He looked at Dr. Hollis. "People are going to die."

Byrnes mouth twisted and pushed air through his nostrils. "I have soldiers that will do it."

"Volunteers?" *More American fighting men at risk because of me.*

The colonel blinked. "Not exactly." His calculating eyes lost a hint of their iciness. "I don't like it either, but it's a necessary risk. Get this right so I don't regret my decision. I will be in the observation room with Dr. Hollis. You understand the protocol?"

"Yes." Byrnes had instituted a new protocol that insisted only one doctor interact with potentially infected persons at one time unless absolutely necessary. It was a fail-safe so an outbreak couldn't take them all out. *We learned from our mistakes.*

Joseph looked at Dr. Hollis, who looked like a blue marshmallow in his biohazard protective suit, and almost envied him. If this experiment failed, Dr. Hollis wouldn't be the one holding the dripping syringe, that guilty man would be Joseph.

The doctor arranged the vials in order. A slender, bifurcated needle syringe sat next to each vial. Joseph studied each vial clearly marked for trials. These could mean the death of innocents or life for others. Something that his team had created to help mankind continue its desperate struggle against the dead.

Dr. Hollis gave him a hopeful smile. "We have smallpox vaccines stockpiled around the country. If this works, the altered combination of the two vaccines could save a great many lives. I never thought we would even get to trials."

"Me either." *That's a big if.*

"We are confident in our altered smallpox vaccine samples. It's the Primus Necrovirus vaccine that has not gone through any real testing." Dr. Hollis pointed a blue finger at each vial next to the bifurcated needle. "Based on Dr. Desai's calculations, we are looking at one dose or point five milliliters of altered Primus Necrovirus for test subject A, two doses for B, three doses for C, and four doses for D. Do you remember the number of times needed to administer the vaccine properly?"

"I remember, Doctor. The vaccine will need to be administered with the double-pronged needle and jabbed into the skin at least fifteen times."

Byrnes's voice crackled and echoed through Joseph's earpiece. "Dr. Jackowski, we would like to begin trials immediately."

"Okay," Joseph said softly. With a look at Dr. Hollis, he grabbed the tray. His hands shook. He didn't think he was this scared when he had killed a man, an American soldier. *How many more will you kill? How many more will the Primus Necrovirus kill? More, more, more,* echoed in the back of his head like an angry raven that sat on his shoulder.

Dr. Hollis gave him a sympathetic smile that didn't help. "I will work on preparing more of the smallpox for the next trial. Good luck," Dr. Hollis said. He tried to give Joseph a comforting smile.

Joseph left both of the doctors as they continued the splicing work and smallpox prep for future tests. Time would forever be their enemy. *Odds are, we will have to test the vaccines again and again.* Joseph physically shook the thought from his head. *People are going to die from this. It's for the greater good,* he told himself.

Glass doors slid open and he entered a room with four soldiers sitting on metal medical tables covered in thin, almost transparent, white paper.

He stopped when he saw his subjects. The soldiers wore only foliage-green briefs and tan undershirts. They all covered their chests with their arms in the cold room. Two soldiers in biohazard suits stood near the door with guns.

The subjects stared at him. His tray rattled in his hands. The vials rolled back and forth on the tray.

"You may approach test subject A," Byrnes echoed. He watched through the glass wall. A young white soldier with pale skin looked worried.

"You may approach test subject A," Byrnes repeated in his earpiece. Joseph hesitantly walked forward and set the tray on a cart next to the test subject. He picked up the needle and dipped it in the vial filled with the dual vaccine.

"Pull up your sleeve," Joseph commanded. His lips were dry, so he licked them, but his mouth and tongue were dry too, and all it did was scratch his tongue.

The young man complied, bringing up his sleeve with his other hand.

Joseph brought the needle near the soldier, pretending the young man was a testing dummy.

The soldier flinched and Joseph stopped half-way to his arm. The soldier's eyebrows rose on his forehead.

"Shouldn't there be like a syringe, not just a needle?" Subject A said.

Joseph pulled back, holding the needle in the air. "No, this vaccination calls for only limited penetration into the skin by a special two-pronged needle."

"Is it gonna hurt?" he asked.

Joseph twisted the needle looking to see if the liquid was on the tip.

"Just a small prick. Your arm might be sore tomorrow around the infection site. Eventually, it will blister and darken and you will probably have a tiny scar." He caught himself. "I mean injection site." *Or you will turn into a monster.* He gave the boy a weak smile. "Honest mistake."

The soldier gave him a confused look. "Whatever."

"How about you lay back on the table?" The young soldier nodded and leaned back. He laid down, letting his arm fall to his side.

Joseph gripped his upper arm, pulling his skin taut.

"Ow," Subject A objected.

Joseph rose an eyebrow.

"Your hand is freezing," Subject A said.

That's because I am more nervous than a virgin on prom night. "Just relax," Joseph said. He waited for a moment, hand hovering over his arm.

"Something wrong?" the soldier said. He looked up at Joseph, mistrust surrounding his eyes.

"No. Everything's fine." Joseph exhaled and jabbed the needle into the young soldier's arm. The two-prongs entered the upper layers of his epidermis. With a firm and steady hand, Joseph pricked the skin over and over: *Thirteen. Fourteen. Fifteen.* The trial vaccine entered the man. The first live human test. Joseph couldn't set the needle back down on the metal tray fast enough. He stared at the soldier, expecting him to turn on the spot. The soldier stared back.

"You okay, Doctor?"

Joseph smiled. "Of course." He shakily placed a folded piece of gauze on his arm and taped it down. "Keep that on for the next couple of days."

The young man pushed on the gauze, looking down at his arm. "Ow, that does sting, doc." The man sat up and massaged his bicep. He gave a nasty glance down the line of soldiers. "You hear that, Coyle? Your arm's gonna hurt." Test subject D looked even more terrified on the other end.

"You're just messing with me, Riley," Coyle called back.

"Quiet," Byrnes's tense voice boomed over the PA.

"It really hurts," Riley joked. He shook his hand out while still holding his arm with the other.

"Shut up, man," Subject B said.

"Fuck you, Tyler," Riley said back. He continued to rub his arm.

"Yeah, you're going to get us in trouble," said Subject C.

"Quit whining, Rodgers," Riley said over to him.

The men quieted down. Joseph administered each test subject with the proper dosages. The soldiers sat up and quietly chatted with one another as Joseph moved to the edge of the room fearing the result. Now, all they had to wait was a week.

***

Seven days later, Joseph had the men back in the room. They had been observed for a week to see if there had been any adverse reactions to the vaccines. It also gave the bodies amble time to build immunity to the viruses. Two different soldiers were in the room this time covered in their blue HAZMAT suits.

Joseph rolled his medical cart in. Atop the cart sat a shiny metal tray. Small red vials of infected blood, newly infected blood of the standalone Primus Necrovirus. This is what they had to beat. The monkeypox battle was mostly won.

Byrnes's voice buzzed in Joseph's earpiece like a mosquito. "Move to the next phase, Dr. Jackowski. Men, be ready for any adverse reactions." The posture of the soldiers in biohazard suits changed. Their bodies bladed into a semi-firing position, guns pointed downward, but ready to bring up to their shoulders at any moment. The young soldiers noticed.

"Hey, what's got you spooked, man?" Riley called over.

"Watch where you're pointing that thing," Coyle said to the man across from him. Joseph brought his tray over. Riley looked confused.

"Doctor, this is supposed to make it so we can't turn Zulu, right?"

"That's correct."

"Then why are the guys with guns getting ready to put us down like dogs?"

Joseph looked back at the soldiers and back to Riley. "Precautionary measures."

"Precautionary for what?"

Joseph tried to give him a smile. It came out as a grimace. "Just relax and lay back please." The soldier complied. *Good soldier. Follow orders. Die for your country.*

"Make more of a fist for me, Riley." The shoulder flexed his hand and pale blue veins began to bulge up. Joseph took the syringe and slipped the needle point into his arm. Joseph stared for a moment at the infected blood in the vial. Blood to blood contact would certainly infect the soldier and Joseph was doing it on purpose. He pushed the syringe together on itself and it closed. The red liquid disappeared into young Riley's arm. Joseph quickly removed the damning needle and put it on the tray.

"Damn, Doc. That one was worse," Riley said, sitting up. Joseph ignored him and moved to the next person and repeated the process all the way down the line. Within seconds of injecting Coyle, Riley, Subject A, started to yell.

"Ahhh! That hurts." Riley started scratching his arm. He flexed his hands, rapidly clenching his fingers. He bent over double on the table. The other three watched in horror. Riley's fingernails dug into the flesh of his arm, causing blood to spill out.

One of the guards took a step forward, raising his weapon to his shoulder.

"Stand down, Connor. This could be only a side effect," Byrnes said through the headset.

"It burns," Riley screamed.

Subject B, Tyler, began to shake on his table. His body convulsed, muscles spasming erratically. "What the hell's wrong with them?" Coyle shouted. "Come on, Rodgers." Coyle pulled Rodgers away from the others. They stood against the wall, watching their comrades change. Joseph took a step back as both the guards pointed their weapons at the men.

"Stand down," Byrnes screamed in the headset.

Riley pushed off the table and lunged for Connor. It was fast, like a defensive end off the ball. Rounds exploded into Riley's chest, spraying blood all over the white sterile room, but it only slowed him down. He grabbed Connor by the shoulders and the two went to the ground. Riley tried to claw his way into his biohazard suit. The other guard spun and opened up on Riley, hitting the young soldier in the head. He collapsed on top of the guard, blood pouring out of a dozen infectious bullet wounds.

"You okay?" the shooter yelled into his headset.

Connor pushed himself off the ground and stood up. He put a gloved finger through a hole in his suit hesitantly. He looked from the hole to his fellow guard. "Don't shoot, Wood. He got through my suit, but I think I'm good."

Tyler crashed into Wood, knocking both them back into the wall. Wood and infected Tyler bounced off the wall and went to the ground. Joseph sidestepped for the other two test subjects.

"Stay close," he yelled at them. While the guard wrestled Tyler, a short-barreled M4 clattered onto the ground. Connor turned for them, his eyes now white. He stumbled for Joseph and the remaining subjects. Joseph clenched his fists, preparing to fight. Coyle punched Connor in the face, and both he and Rodgers kicked him down. Connor was slick with blood; he slipped and crawled across the floor after them.

"Get out of there," Byrnes screamed into Joseph's earpiece. "We are going to zap the whole room."

"No," Joseph breathed. "C and D are still good."

"It's a bust. We are going to put them all down."

Joseph ran for the compression chamber. *3-7-1.* Beep-beep, beep. He mashed in the code and the door slid open.

"Come on," Joseph yelled. Rodgers and Coyle ran inside the chamber and the doors closed. A loud thud sounded on the door.

A bloody biohazard face-shield stared back at them. Chunks of flesh still stuck to the plastic. Connor pounded the glass with an open palm, his eyes white as chalk. He was joined by an infected Tyler.

The chamber on the other side opened.

"Come on," Joseph said. They stepped cautiously into the other side. Soldiers charged into the room, all guns pointed at them. They all put their hands up. Blood dripped down their bodies and ran off of Joseph's suit. Byrnes followed the soldiers inside.

"You can stand down. We were prepared for this. These men are under strict observation until we can sort this out. Mack, take your squad and put the infected down. Hudson, get these men out of here." Black-clad soldiers stacked on the compression chamber.

Joseph unzipped his biohazard suit and removed his earpiece. "Those two look good," he said to Byrnes.

Byrnes eyed the young men, wet with blood and chilled by the sterile cold, holding themselves for warmth.

"They should have already shown signs of infection," Joseph said.

"Let's observe them for twenty-four hours before we jump to any conclusions. I am optimistic, Doctor. We may have created a vaccine for this thing," Byrnes said. He gave Joseph the only smile Joseph had seen him give yet. "We will revisit the issue after twenty-four hours. Hudson, I want these two in holding cells. No regular rooms like Weinroth." The word "Weinroth" stung Joseph. "If they turn, they will be confined in the least destructive place possible."

"Great." *I should feel grateful and happy that we did it, but I feel dirty.* Yet his mind drifted to the men he had just experimented on like mere lab rats.

"Go, go, go," a soldier shouted in the background. The soldiers disappeared inside the lab and gunfire popped off.

"Let's go," Hudson said. Hudson pushed Joseph in front of him and the group of nine filed into the hallway, the test subjects in the middle. Boots quickly trod the sterile white floor along with the bare feet of the remaining subjects. Down two corridors they walked until they reached a steel-doored elevator.

"The holding cells are down three levels," Hudson said.

"It would be easier to study them here," Joseph said.

"We do as the colonel orders," Hudson said. The reflective doors opened. The group squeezed into the elevator. Guns jabbed every which way. Gear stuck out from their vests. The soldiers pressed close to one another and their charges.

"All I know is that it's as deep as we can go," Hudson said and pressed a button at the bottom of the control panel. The doors rolled shut and the elevator dropped, beginning its descent and sending Joseph's gut lurching. Men shuffled. Boots shifted. Vests creaked and slings groaned.

After twenty seconds, there came a cry. "Oww," someone groaned from the center of the group. Heads turned on shoulders, but there wasn't enough room for people to turn. Joseph, surrounded by the group of large soldiers, couldn't see anything

"Ah. My stomach."

"Quiet over there." Hudson pushed the bottom button again. It glowed a pale yellow, muffled by the sheer number of people in the elevator. "Wish this thing was faster," he said with a side eye to Joseph.

"There's something wrong with him," came Rodgers's voice. Joseph could catch glimpses of Rodgers's closely shaved head swiveling back and forth in concern for his fellow soldier. "You're a doctor, do something," he said loudly in Joseph's direction.

"Ahhhh," Coyle yelled. He tottered, swinging his head wildly. Shoulders pressed into others.

"What's wrong with him?" yelled one soldier.

"Somebody get hands on," screamed another.

Elbows drove the subjects back into the other soldiers.

"He's turning," Joseph screeched, but he was drowned out by the other men.

Coyle sunk his teeth into the face of the man next to him. They were so close that it was only a matter of stretching his neck. Guns were twisted. Pinned in-between bodies, legs, and torsos, every soldier flagged the others.

"Grab him," someone called out.

A round went off, causing a deafening explosion in the small enclosure. A soldier fell into the others, gripping his knee. Gear-clad men crushed Joseph into the corner as they tried to get away from the infected. Men screamed as they were mauled. Bodies smashed into one another, and the air felt like it was being sucked out of the small confined space. Gun smoke filled the elevator. Warm liquid spurted into the air and onto the walls as blood was freed from their greedy bodies.

"Shoot him," screamed Hudson. He was pinned on top of Joseph, his arm trapped in the air, still holding his sidearm. With the blood, it was hard to tell friend from foe as the soldiers struggled with one another.

Joseph did the only thing he could do. He inched his trapped hand to the control panel. His whole body was being crushed into the wall by Hudson's back. Hudson's head spun back and forth as he wrestled with one of his men. Crimson blood had doused everyone. Joseph couldn't tell who was alive or dead. Joseph smashed his finger on the panel and pressed the only other button not lit. Soldiers screamed. The elevator announced its arrival. Ding-ding.

The doors rolled open and the mass of bodies collapsed onto the floor. Guns clanked. Bodies thudded. Joseph crashed onto the floor. Men slid on the ground.

The clicking of computer keyboards stopped. Civilians and unarmed military personnel looked up from their screens. A man stood, mouth agape, headset over his ear. A woman wearing glasses peeked over her cubicle like a prairie dog. Joseph crawled away from the mass of bodies writhing in mortal combat on all fours.

"Infected," shouted a man. People screamed as the newly infected pushed themselves upright, newfound fresh victims awaiting their bite.

STEELE

Little Sable Point, MI

The midday sun did nothing to warm him. The wind off Lake Michigan pierced his clothes like stinging bees. The sun shone down, failing its most primal task of warming the Earth as if it too had forsaken them. He paced behind the cold dead vehicles, his mind unable to rest.

The pastor had murdered his mother. Now he was coming to murder the men and women of Little Sable Point and indoctrinate their children into his corrupt church. Steele tugged at his beard as he paced, working himself up. *What kind of son am I? She needed my help and I was off gallivanting the world instead of protecting her from that monster.* His mind blamed him. *You wanted to make peace with the man.* He spit on the ground, glancing up at the flames pouring from the top of the lighthouse.

He had kept the fire lit inside the tower as a taunt to the pastor.

Kevin watched him.

"Steele. I was thinking about that speech." Steele passed him, marching back and forth.

"What about it?"

"You could do some FDR. Nothing to fear but fear itself."

Steele passed him again, going the other way. His M4 was slung across his body. "Nah, too cliché."

"Or Patrick Henry, give me liberty or give me death," Kevin said, waiting to see if Steele would bite.

Hand on his carbine, he passed by again. "Fitting but too hostile."

"Churchill?"

Steele stopped in front of Kevin. "How about some whiskey instead?"

"I can help you there," Kevin said, handing up a bottle of the honey-colored liquid. Steele took a pull, long and hard. He wiped the extra with the back of his hand. The booze burned down inside his belly. Lack of food made him feel the effects of the alcohol almost immediately.

He looked out on the field, soon to be a field of bloody misery and mournful wails of the dying. Grass stuck up in clumps for a hundred yards, mixed in with sandy clay. After the sandy field, a line of trees stood for about a half mile to the main road. A smaller two-lane road went from the lighthouse parking lot, cutting through the forest.

He glanced at the men and women that sat near the cars whispering to one another in nervous anticipation. Even if they won this contest, many of them would die, and he would be responsible for their deaths. *My list will grow longer today, but what choice do I have?*

"Tess, want some?" Steele said. The liquid sloshed as he waved it in her direction.

She held out her hand, taking the bottle. She took a big swig and handed it back to Kevin. Kevin handed it to old Bengy, and the Korean war vet looked at the bottle.

"Haven't drank in thirty years, but who wants to be sober for this anyway," Bengy said, looking at the bottle with some apprehension. He held the bottle to his lips, tipping it back toward the sky. He looked at the bottle. "Damn, I miss the stuff," his voice sounded gravelly after the alcohol.

Tess looked out at the line of trees. "You think they forgot about us?" she said.

Steele watched the concealing trees. "No. They're coming. I assure you the pastor does not forget easily. And I'm sure he won't be happy about us taunting him with the lighthouse."

Tess glanced up at the lighthouse. "That used to be a beacon for the refugees. Now it is a call to war." She turned back to Steele. "Let the bastards come. I'd love to send a few rounds their way," she said with an air of confidence that Steele did not have.

He stared at this fiery black-haired woman. "Anyone excited for war has never experienced anything but peace."

***

An hour passed in uneasy silence while the people of Little Sable Point waited. A few piled sand up around the cars, trying to harden their position, until shouting came from the heavens.

"Steele! Steele!" Margie shouted from the lighthouse. She leaned over the edge waving at him. Her fist pumped toward the trees in front of them three times like a referee.

"Hold your fire until you get the signal," Steele shouted, looking out. He hoped it would be enough. It had to be enough.

Steele hoisted himself up on the hood of a pickup.

"People of Little Sable Point." He waited as all his people's eyes looked up at him. "This is our hour of greatest need. You stand on the front line of a battle, not only for survival but for your very freedom. The pastor's army of fanatics comes to force you under a yoke of tyranny. He wishes to make you slaves to his religion, your lives only purpose to worship him." All eyes were upon him, people silent in contemplation. "It's better to die a thousand deaths than to live for one *second* in servility to these people." He pointed out as the first of the pastor's convoy emerged from the trees. "I do not shy away from this battle. I embrace it." He held his carbine in the air. The people of Little Sable Point let out a ragged, if timid, yell.

"Nice speech," Kevin said up to him.

His friend helped Steele down. "We need it. You have to fight for something," Steele returned, hoisting his M4 carbine to his shoulder.

The pastor's men in pickups slowed down, swerving around stranded vehicles. Steele pumped his fist at Jason above and Gregor down the line. Gregor climbed on top of a camper before laying down prone. Steele turned to the left side, pumping his fist up and down. Larry and Hank did the same.

A car sat about seventy five yards out, an old clunker that his crew had pushed out in neutral.

"Don't fire until they are past the tan Honda," he shouted at the people around him. They looked nervously down their sights. *I will be lucky if they hit the ground. We only need to last long enough.* His eyes rose to the sky momentarily. *Long enough for a divine intervention.*

Two pickup trucks pulled out onto the stretch of land between the forest and the vehicle-encircled, red-brick lighthouse. Men held on in the pickup beds, their guns pointing outward. *Only two?*

His attention quickly returned to the road when the high-pitched whine of a diesel engine caught his ears. A semi without the trailer barreled into view, a hulking heavy hitter of the trucking world.

It was followed by the crunch of metal as it smashed through obstacles knocking them left and right. Steele lined up his red dot optic on the driver. *I should take him now.* Instead, he watched as the semi took on the two vehicles blocking its path like an offensive tackle driving them backward. The back vehicle rolled on its side and flipped end over end. It was enough.

Blockade free, the convoy of the Chosen drove onto the sandy field pickup after pickup. An old yellow school bus eventually stopped and men ran out, taking their places among the trees. They lined the area between the forest and Steele's few entrenched defenders. Minutes ticked away from each of their remaining lifespans as the pastor's men filled in the gaps. Too many guns pointed in Steele's direction. More men leapt from trucks, taking up firing positions. They spread out, wrapping around the flanks of Sable Point in a horseshoe of metal and flesh. *Did I make a mistake by not lighting them up on the road? Should we even have planned our defense around the lighthouse?*

A final black, relatively clean SUV rolled behind the others. It stopped near the center of the newly made line. Steele pointed his gun in that direction, letting his optic do the work. A tall gaunt man exited the rear passenger side door. He was dressed in black, a hammer hanging from his belt.

"I see the pastor has made an appearance," Steele said to Kevin.

Kevin leaned over the hood of the pickup, looking down the barrel of his M4 carbine. "So this is the guy who's been causing us all these troubles. Seems a bit old to be bothering us, don't cha think?" Kevin said, his foot tapping the sand about a thousand times a minute.

Steele peered down his line. His men and women looked around, not knowing if they belonged in the fight. They internally debated if they could still run and make it.

"Steady now," Steele yelled out. He was cut short by the electronic, megaphoned voice of the pastor.

"People of Little Sable Point."

Steele's eyes narrowed. *That's my line.*

"We're here because a certain man claiming to be your leader has led you astray. He leads you with half-truths and lies. He desires only power for himself."

Steele felt the eyes of his followers fall upon him, considering the pastor's words. *Will they hand me over and be done with it?*

"You needn't worry where your next meal comes from. You needn't worry about those infected by Satan's Legion. You needn't fear at all. Look at all my men. My community can provide all these things for you. Food. Shelter. Safety. Salvation."

The uneasiness from Steele's followers laid heavy upon them. He could feel their eyes upon him. *What would stop one of them from putting a bullet in me and ending the resistance? Nothing.* Steele took a moment to covertly scan his surroundings.

"Why do you all so badly want to die? Has there not been enough death already? I only ask that you accept Christ as your savior and join us."

Voices murmured back and forth. He could hear their voices.

"It can't be that bad."

"It's better than dying."

"We'll finally be safe."

He didn't know who said what and it didn't matter. Fear was driving them. Fear and the hope that somebody would figure everything out for them. *I must help them see.*

Steele called out from his vantage. "Don't you see this man has a serpent's tongue? He murdered my mother when she wouldn't join him. I watched him murder Pagan. The pastor would rather burn Pagan alive than trade him back to us. By God, he's no saint. He's a monster. He promises you safety but at the price of your freedom. He promises you food so you will worship him as a demigod. He gives you shelter in exchange for your soul for he knows no God but himself. Don't let him fool you. He offers you only chains. Americans don't wear chains."

The few remaining in Little Sable stayed in their place. They quieted down. Steele exhaled.

"That could have gone bad," Kevin said.

"You weren't considering switching sides?" Steele said.

"Some food and shelter does sound nice."

"I won't stop you," Steele said, watching the man out of the corner of his eye. It was not lost on Steele that he had killed Kevin's brother. Did it matter that Kevin had hated Puck's guts? Kin was kin.

Kevin shook his head. "No. No. I prefer a good book to subservience."

"Glad to hear it," Steele said under his breath.

The pastor's voice boomed. "I give any man or woman a pardon to join me now. Before this gets ugly."

Steele peered down his ragged line, the remnants of a community forced into action. His people looked scared, but their backs were to the wall, and the only way out was to fight like the devil through the pastor and his followers.

Steele brought his attention back to Kevin. "I'm thinking we should get this thing started before anyone gets lured in by his poison apple. Care to do the honors?"

Steele dug in his cargo pocket, revealing a rectangular green remote detonator also known as a clacker. When the green remote was squeezed, it depressed the black button and detonated the explosives.

Steele passed the detonator to Kevin.

Kevin's hand trembled as he took the device. "I…Wow. I never thought I would be the one to lead an attack." His long face showed all his nerves. He held the green remote in his hand, palm open, afraid to close his fingers around it as if the device itself could blow him up.

"Here, take this," Tess chimed in, handing the bottle of whiskey to Kevin. He grabbed it with one hand, took a long swig of booze, and handed it back, his eyes never leaving the detonator.

"Press here?" Kevin asked pointing at the device.

"Squeeze that puppy until it goes boom," Steele said.

"What say you, people of Little Sable Point? You have ten seconds to make up your mind. Hand over the scoundrel and be done with this madness," the pastor bellowed.

Kevin motioned for Tess to give him the whiskey back.

"Ten, nine, eight..." the pastor's voice echoed.

Kevin took another swig of booze and closed his eyes.

"Give them a little taste of freedom," Steele said with a grim grin.

"Seven, six..."

Kevin nodded and clicked the detonator a bunch of times in his hand.

"Five."

The treeline on both flanks of the pastor's line exploded in a roar of fire, timber, and smoke. Men were thrown into the air and onto the ground. Trees fell in a dozen different angles. Men collapsed onto nearby trucks. Chosen soldiers crawled on the ground. Trucks burned. The pastor's men ran to help the injured. Chaos enveloped the pastor's line.

Steele's followers cheered. Many turned his way, eying him in surprise, and for a change, hope. Steele looked down his sights. The pastor crouched low, watching his men scramble in disorganization. Steele grinned. "Nice work, Kevin."

"I can't believe that worked. Where'd you get that?" Kevin said, his eyes wide.

"Just a little reappropriation of materials before Thunder deserted us."

Bullets thudded into the pickup. Steele knelt lower behind the walls of the pickup bed.

"Open fire," Steele screamed. The command was repeated down the line.

Steele let off a three-round burst near where the pastor had been, but their tall leader had disappeared. He turned his red dot to a man aiming over the cab of a pickup and sent a single round his way. The man flinched as the round entered his shoulder through his collarbone, and he disappeared behind the pickup. If the clavicle was shattered, the man would be out of the fight permanently, unable to shoulder a weapon. If it wasn't, he would bleed out by the time the battle was over.

As more of the pastor's men regained their feet, they started firing into Little Sable's protective vehicle concealment. Metal and plastic punched inward as bullets penetrated cars searching for Steele's volunteers. Dud. Dud. Holes appeared to the side of Steele. He took cover for a moment, catching his breath. Tess knelt next to him, ducking her head.

Looking down the line, Steele flinched as more bullets screamed above him. Many of his followers hid behind vehicles, seeking reprieve from the building onslaught of enemy rounds. Every now and then a volunteer would lean over, spraying bullets everywhere. Steele crept to a different part of his pickup truck, bouncing upward as he took aim. He shot at three men pinning down his shooters on top of the camper. His rounds forced them into taking cover.

He felt an impact behind him. A different noise than the gunshots, it was like someone had dropped a sack of groceries off a building. He took cover, staring at the remains of Jason near the lighthouse. Brains leaked from the spot where his head had smashed into the pavement, caving in his skull. His legs twisted outward at the knees, white bone and red flesh spraying the ground.

"Keep firing," Steele shouted, but the rounds kept coming. The faint sound of the diesel engine whined again and then it chug-chug-chugged. The semi rolled over the ground and men fought from behind it. Some of the Chosen rode atop its fifth-wheel, coupling like a tank desant.

"They're going to ram us!" Steele shouted. He spun past Kevin and moved down the line at a crouch.

"Shoot the truck," he yelled at Alex on the way by. The college student stood up and fired a couple of rounds before taking cover again.

"Shoot the tires," he screamed at Bengy as he ran past. He didn't wait to see if the old man heard him. Steele bounded upright and put three, three-round bursts through the windshield. The semi kept coming. Either the driver was hidden, or they had managed to find a way to have it run by itself. Steele ducked back down as the glass of a car window burst and bullets zipped through the car around him.

Bullet holes dotted the front end of the truck as if it had chickenpox. Its front wheels were deflated, but the truck came onward for their tight defensive ring. Steele put down a man hanging off the back of the semi. He fell underneath and disappeared beneath the tires. Another man filled his place, impervious to the danger. The semi gained even more speed, its engine roaring. Foot by bloody foot, it traversed the ground beneath it.

Steele put another magazine through the front grille.

"Reloading," he screamed. After punching the magazine release with his index, he snatched a new magazine from his vest pouch and slammed it home. He hit the bolt release button, ready to go. It was too late. He could only watch as the semi barreled down on them, its charge uninterrupted by anything Steele could do. It drew closer until it was about to impact Steele's line. He dove down onto the ground.

Metal screamed on metal and crunched, concaving as the semi crashed into the middle of a camper. The semi punched through the center of Steele's line like a harpoon through a fish. Smoke and debris filled the air. The contents of the camper exploded out into Steele's camp like a tornado had hit a trailer park. It was eerily silent for a moment as both sides stared at the destruction.

A few moments later, men that had been following the semi ran through the gap. In groups of two and three, they rushed inside the compound. Orange flames exploded from the ends of their guns as they let loose on the members of Little Sable Point. Steele couldn't tell who was who now. Kevin and Tess were lost behind him. He had no idea where anyone was in the smoky haze.

Steele bounded upright and moved with speed to the semi, now sitting exhausted, a war elephant riddled with arrows, gasping its last breath after having penetrated the enemy line. Steele scanned. *Have to stem the tide or we are overrun.*

A man in jeans and a tan hunting vest ran for him. His shotgun boomed from the side of his hip and birdshot pellets tore into Steele's leg. The pain stung, but his adrenaline did what it was designed to do: It dulled the pain enough for him to ignore it.

"Motherfucker," Steele screamed at him. Steele sidestepped on his good leg. *Always get offline.* He fired three rounds, prepping his trigger on each single shot center mass and then transitioned upward, placing one through the man's chin.

"Fuck," Steele cursed again. He let himself breathe and glanced down at his leg. He knew he had been shot, but didn't know how bad it was. Too much stimuli was happening around him. He knelt down and slid next to a car, his affected leg hesitating to obey. He cupped his groin, holding his boys tight. Nothing burned there. No blood. No flaps of skin. The fabric of his ACUs was torn and shredded. In the center of his thigh, he stuck a finger through a tear and wiggled it around. It always takes a minute for the blood. He removed his finger. Crimson liquid covered its tip. *Jesus Christ. No time to worry.*

Steele stood and went for the gasping semi. With each step, some of the adrenaline wore off. With every movement, he could feel more of the small pellets riddling his leg like needles hiding inside his flesh and his muscles. Weapon in the high ready, he hugged the edge of the truck.

Two men ran through the wreckage of the camper. Steele tapped his finger quick on the trigger and they collapsed.

Steele closed in on the semi. He jumped up on the step and ripped open the truck's door, thrusting his gun first inside. He looked inside the cab. Dead blank eyes looked at him, the driver's body riddled with bloody holes. Hopping down, he felt the pain of a thousand stab wounds shooting up his leg from the bird shot.

Steele hobbled for the gigantic rubble-ridden hole in his line. He couldn't tell how many had gotten through. *Ten?* Trucks sped across the field for the gap in Little Sable's defenses. The pastor could smell that victory was at hand and had sent all his men forward. *We had a good cause.*

Kevin stumbled up, blood running down his face, arm in arm with old Bengy. Steele grabbed Kevin by his shirt.

"Both of you get out of here." Kevin nodded, his face wide-eyed in fear.

"Okay," Kevin breathed. Bengy halted with a hand on Kevin's chest.

"Old Ben, we need to leave," Kevin said hurriedly.

Bengy unraveled himself from Kevin's arm and held up a hand. "It's okay," Bengy said with a nod.

Steele knew the stubborn look in the old man's eye. "Find anyone that's left and leave," he said to Kevin. Kevin rushed away, momentarily stopping to help up an injured man. Bengy stood, watching him go. The old man smiled as if he were remembering a life long past in a moment. He sighed.

Steele gave him a sidelong glance as the trucks raced for the chink in Sable's perimeter armor.

"It's time," was all the old man said.

Steele nodded. The man would make his stand here. "I suppose it is."

Steele collected himself and stepped into the gap. He steadied his breathing, stopping short as he sent a burst of rounds through the nearest pickup window. The driver slumped down, causing the truck to ram into another portion of Sable Point, sending Chosen out of the bed of the truck into the air. Their forms writhed, twisted, and crashed into the ground.

Shooting, Steele let his M4 carbine sing away, round after round, note after note. Bengy's M1 Garand added its harsh booming tones to Steele's quick, lighter notes of gunfire. For a brief moment in time, they sounded like a gunfire duet.

Soon Steele found his gun dry, no magazines left in his vest, and he transitioned to his M9 Beretta. He capped rounds at three men, giving each one a round as he transitioned targets. As he turned back to address the two still standing, he hardly noticed something bite into his strong-side arm. His arm fell to his side, limp. He opened his right hand and switched the firearm over to his support hand. He canted the weapon slightly more than normal and unloaded it at the driver opening the door of the nearest pickup truck. Bullet holes littered his windshield. The driver slumped in his seat.

It was at that moment he noticed how quiet the world had grown around him. Steele turned to look over his shoulder. Bengy lay in the grass behind him. Dune grass tapped his weathered face and his chest was flat, his wood-stocked Garand still clutched in his hands. *See you soon, old-timer.*

The trucks stole his attention away. They rumbled within ten yards of him and formed a semicircle around the hole in Sable Point that Steele and Bengy had plugged with their bodies. Over a hundred men encircled him, their weapons lined up in his direction. They walked forward as if they stalked him, only stopping when they were close, waiting for the command to pulverize his body with lead.

"I want him alive," came a voice from the back. The ranks of the Chosen parted in reverence and the pastor walked forward as if he glided atop the dune grass and sand alike.

Steele lifted his arm upright. He narrowed an eye and ignored the natural movement of the gun. The trigger snapped back. Click. The pastor did not flinch. He walked with impunity out of the folds of his army and into the open with Steele. A shepherd among his flock. He drew himself upright in front of Steele. His chin rose upward, and his look was one of a disappointed father.

"Drop your gun, fool," the pastor said. "Your defiance is over. You've lost."

Steele met his eyes and dropped the gun. *I might be able to send the hawk through his skull before they annihilate me.* The gunfire lessened now. A tat-tat-tat snare drummed out. A few single round shots. Little Sable Point had been overrun fast.

Steele cross-drawed his tomahawk from his belt with his off hand. He gripped it tight. *I need a single second and a half. The hawk will need two full rotations to hit him square in the chest. Wind shouldn't affect the throw, only whether or not they can shoot me before I get the throw off.*

"Surrender, Mr. Steele. There is no need for more bloodshed. Your tenacity is unmatched but lacks the power of God. Much like the fallen angels, you were a dastardly opponent but destined for defeat from the very beginning for God's victory is assured," the pastor said.

Peter's blond curls shook as he bobbed his head in acknowledgment of their victory. More of the Chosen pushed forward to get a glimpse of their defeated enemy. They sneered at Steele and jeered him. The pastor spread his arms wide like a soaring eagle, giving a shout.

"God wills it!" he shouted. He raised his arms high in the air looking to the clouds.

"God wills it!" he shouted again, pumping his arms toward the sky.

"God wills it!" they all shouted. The pastor's men echoed the call of victory. Over and over, their cheers went up to the heavens, filling the air that had once been buffeted by gunshots.

Other captives were led to where Steele stood. Tess was manhandled next to him, her eye black.

"Fuck you," Tess shouted.

Margie's body was thrown down at Steele's feet. She lay unmoving, blood coming from her head. Nathan and Gregor were shoved next to Steele. Other men and women from the community cowered in their small defeated circle of people. Too few of them had made it.

"What have I done?" Steele lamented aloud. Warm blood ran down his arm, dripping off his fingers like a leaky spigot. Drip. Drip. Drip. His lifeblood leaked out onto the sand. *Who were you to lead these people to their deaths? Who were you to stand up to the many with so few? Who were you to have hope? Who were you? I am…*

He let his tomahawk fall from his fingers. Pain shot down his arm from destroyed nerve endings. He grabbed the shredded flesh where his tricep used to be. Holding it, he tried to keep push it back in. His leg didn't seem so bad now compared to his ruined arm. The shouts of his enemies echoed in his ears, almost sounding far away.

The pastor stepped closer, waving his followers down to silence. Steele leaned on Tess, taking weight off his leg.

"That's better, Mr. Steele. Finally, we have a bit of cooperation. Many good men were martyred today fighting for God. Many people could have been given life, but instead, you are responsible for their deaths." *A weight I will carry with me until my last breath.*

"The tree of liberty is watered with the blood of tyrants and patriots alike," Steele managed to utter. His voice seemed almost soft under the oppression of the pastor and his men.

"Ah yes, Patrick Henry. Misguided use of the phrase, but you are adamant. The way of the Lord is a refuge for the blameless, but it is the ruin of those who do evil. You are a tumor that needs to be cut away. Better to be done with it than wait. You are unable to be redeemed in God's eyes, of that I am sure. Peter, gasoline."

Peter grinned as he carried the gas cans forward.

When Peter got close, he hissed. "You deserve this." He tossed the oily liquid on Steele's clothes. "For what you done to me. For the good brothers and sisters you killed today." He splashed the gas on Steele's face.

The gasoline stung his eyes. Steele turned his head away and squeezed his eyes shut. Other Chosen came forward with more cans, tossing their contents upon the people of Little Sable Point. The oily liquid burned his wounds as it flowed over his body. He would soon burst into a screaming ball of flame. The pain that would envelop his body would be infinitely worse than what he currently experienced. Steele wiped it away from his eyes with his good hand.

"No, please," his people screamed.

Gregor stood tall, letting the gasoline drip along his skin and down his long hair.

"Please, please, please," a woman cried, her chin to her chest. The Chosen continued to dump fuel onto their battered bodies. It drenched their hair and faces and soaked their clothes. The terrifying apprehension of being burned alive rippled through them as if they were already on fire.

"No. No," screamed Donald. He tried to run for the Chosen. A gun boomed and he clutched his stomach, sinking to the ground. Donald moaned as the Chosen dragged him back to the remainders of Little Sable. They dropped him and the man groaned on the ground. Nathan rushed forward and put a hand on his wound.

Tess hugged Steele's body tight, and he draped his damaged arm over her shoulder. She held him up more than he held her. It was the smallest of comforts in a world that was about to be set afire and burnt to nothing.

"It's okay," he whispered. "The children are safe." *Gwen is safe along with our child.* Tess sniffled into his chest.

"Fuck them," she said into him. "Psychopaths," she sobbed.

"It'll be okay, Tess," Steele assured her. Empty words for an empty world. A world that seemed to take pleasure in snuffing out life wherever it found it.

Tess wiped gasoline from her face, blinking up at him.

The pastor smiled wickedly at him. "No enemy of God can stand before him. Now we must pray." The pastor turned his eyes to the sky and clasped his hands in front of his body. "I send your souls to hell in God's name. May you languish there for an eternity with no reprieve for what you've done to God's Chosen people. Amen." Amens echoed from his followers.

A slimy long-haired fellow flicked a lighter and smiled. He handed it to the pastor. The pastor held it up for all his followers to see. They cheered in joyful bliss. Their fists jabbed the sky. Their shouts rang true in victory.

The pastor walked for them, lighter in hand, and stopped. The flame of his lighter whimpered and disappeared. He stared at the suspect lighter, a brief moment of doubt dancing across his face. He looked at the lighter and back at Steele as if he had committed some sort of witchcraft.

"Devilry," the pastor said.

A wind came off the water, blowing into the groups of combatants on the field. It died down and the pastor flicked his thumb again. And again. His followers were quiet as they watched their leader struggle with a simple light. The ragged remnants of the Little Sable Point community held their breath.

Steele's legs shook as if the ground itself vibrated beneath him. He stared at his feet for a moment. Blood, sand, and filth stained his boots. He was unsure if he was almost done bleeding out and likely to collapse.

Others felt it. They stared at the ground in alarm. They looked about, uncertainty clouding their faces. A soft far-off rumble became a deafening roar.

Men at the back of the pastor's army shouted and pointed. The Chosen soldiers ran, looking for cover. Guns cracked, and Steele saw them now.

Atop their steel steeds, they rode across the paved ground. Their engines roared out and the earth trembled beneath them. A single, red-bandana clad, gray-bearded man led hundreds of two-wheeled demons. He pointed a short shotgun with one hand and it ripped fire into the pastor's men. Black leather covered them. Half helmets. Skull caps. Biker vests flapped in the wind as they raced for the pastor's men. Guns blazed in their hands and the Chosen soldiers fell into confusion.

Thunder took his motorcycle into the field of battle, his honor guard of Red Stripes around him. Fat Half-Barrel sprayed buckshot with his sawed-off shotgun into a group of Chosen. They fell to the ground, crippled in pain. Garrett capped his handgun, aiming left and right across his handlebars, a wicked grin under his beard.

They raced past the pastor's men, shooting as they sped by. Some riders put their bikes down as Chosen bullets struck them, but they were few. The motorcycles split down the middle, encircling the Chosen. Chosen soldiers threw down their guns and tried to run for the trees.

The pastor locked eyes with Steele. He wavered, turning around and watching his people be surrounded in horror. He knew now that his end was near. Steele coughed a bit and smiled.

"You. You wretched devil. You planned this?" the pastor sputtered, anger creasing his aged features.

Steele released Tess and bent down for his tomahawk. He felt every pellet in his leg. He felt his lifeblood leaking from his arm. His fingers wrapped around the oily gasoline and sand-covered shaft, making it slick with coarse grime.

More of the pastor's men threw down their guns and put their hands in the air. Steele hobbled forward. With each step Steele took, the pastor grew older. Steele placed the axe head of his tomahawk onto the pastor's long crane of a neck. The pastor shifted his chin up and away from Steele's blade.

Steele looked up at him, making sure his eyes never left the pastor's. "He's a bit late, but my man showed when he had too."

The pastor's mouth twisted and he spat on the ground. "Damnation is eternal for enemies of God."

"Let me know how that works out for you."

Around Steele, Thunder's bikers disarmed the Chosen soldiers. Hundreds of bikers moved through them. Wild-eyed women. Braided-goateed men. Shiny bald heads. Long unkempt-haired women and men alike. All rough people sporting colors of different motorcycle clubs: black wolves, coiled steel snakes on a yellow background, playing card eights, skulls and gears, the reaper standing over a coffin, and seven naked women holding swords.

Motorcycles rode down the retreating men that fled the field. A few gunshots were heard over the motorcycle engines, but the battle was over.

Steele could only grin at the pastor. A shadowed man moved nearby. Steele yelled over at a confused Peter. "Let's put those gas cans down. We don't want you hurting yourself." Peter's face dropped as if Steele had physically beaten him again. Peter set down the gas cans, taking a step away, hands in the air. He lowered his eyes.

The Red Stripes rolled close before cutting their engines and dismounting their motorcycles.

"Thunder," Steele yelled out. He removed his axe head from the pastor's throat. The gray-bearded man swung his big belly off his chopper and adjusted his pants.

"Steele," he said, almost as if he were a proud father. A wide grin revealed his teeth underneath his thick beard. "Saw the lighthouse blazing from five miles out."

Steele limped forward, his hand still squeezing the hell out of his tomahawk.

"Good," Steele said. When he got close to Thunder, he punched Thunder square in the nose, knocking the old man back onto his ass. Half-Barrel put his sawed-off to the side of Steele's skull.

Thunder's hand leapt out to his man. "Half-Barrel, no!" He lifted a hand to his nose, examining his own blood with a twist of his fingers. "I deserved that."

"You sure as hell did. You killed Steve. That wasn't part of the deal," Steele's head felt like it had been stuffed with cotton. His legs felt weak like his muscles were leaving him.

Thunder stood. "He tried to stop us. He was going to shoot us."

"That's good training," Steele said, breathing hard. His heart pounded in his chest. He collapsed, his body meeting the ground with a thud. The sky turned black above him.

KINNICK

Dunluce Pass, CO

"Status?" Kinnick yelled into the mic of his radio as he ran. His face hardened as repeated gunfire echoed off the rocky slopes. Kinnick bounded right up against Stark's Platoon. The men supported themselves against the barricade, waiting with nervous eyes. Stark gave him a fierce look over his shoulder.

"Elwood? What's your status?" Kinnick breathed.

Kinnick stood tall in the pass behind his men. His breath came out shallow in his chest. His hands were slick on his M4 carbine. "Come on, Elwood," he said under his breath.

Gunfire boomed. High wails and deep moans bellowed from around the bend. Undead voices echoed up the road following the rocky slopes into the pass. All the voices blended into a single hell song that sucked the pure natural silence from the mountain pass.

Within moments, the front ranks of the dead stepped forward as if they were part of an ancient undead phalanx of hoplites. Undead bodies tripped and fell as bullets zipped through them, spraying flesh and blood onto the concrete. They marched at a slow determined rate, letting their brethren be trampled where they fell with no regard for them.

Fire blazed through the mountain trees where Elwood's fire teams were set up in ambush above the road. The left flank of the undead horde withered under machine gun fire from the slope. The dead on the right flank were pushed off the mountain roadside, driven over the edge by the butchered bodies of their fellow infected.

A minute raged and the fire team on the ridge made headway decimating the dead with fiery lead. Until the reload.

"Fuck," Kinnick swore. A private on the barricade firing line let his carbine go, firing.

"Hold that fire, private," Stark screamed at his man. The dead surged forward as the bullets ceased to hold them back. Hundreds pushed over each other, slipping over the slick blood spilt on the ground. Exposed intestines tangled around their legs brought them down, but they persisted, knowing nothing except death to all things living.

"Colonel. Elwood. Position one." A hard breath pushed into the mic. "Positions one and two are gone. Turner, Singer, and Montero are dead. There are too many."

"Keep those M240s going."

"Yes, sir."

Moments later, the machine gun was up and running again. The infected twitched as bullets entered and exited their bodies. An infected was cut in half as he climbed the hill for Elwood's fire teams. He continued to crawl until an M4 round through the skull stopped him.

Kinnick's master sergeant stood to the side letting off single rounds, dropping pack leaders with individual bullets. The horde surged forward ignoring bullets and the soldiers on the hill alike.

"Don't fire until you see the white of their eyes," Hunter shouted, but it was too late. His voice was overcome by hot lead, as Stark's Platoon unloaded into the horde. Claymores exploded farther down the hill.

It's too early Elwood. It's too early.

Kinnick let his radio drop to the dirt. He hefted his M4 carbine and joined his men on the line.

"Hold this pass, goddamnit," Kinnick screamed at them. He wasn't sure they heard. He may have only said it to give himself courage. His M4 carbine's bolt pumped in almost slow motion as the ejector flung out spent cartridges from his extraction port. Dropping his mag to the ground, he shoved a full one in its place, reloading. Bullets thudded into the bodies. He aimed high for their ugly curdled milk-colored eyes, ending their pitiful existence with every round fired.

The heavy lead smell of spent cartridges and brass hung over them, enveloping them in a cloud polluting the mountain freshness. Gun smoke that surrounded them dissipated into the air, and tiny specks of white fluttered down, finding a way in the madness battle.

"You got your snow," Hunter shouted at him. He laughed a wild roar. He screamed at the top of his lungs. "Get some, boys."

Kinnick put out a hand, his fingers outstretched. A small, jaggedly individual sterling white snowflake rested gently on his hand. It stayed for a moment in his palm and then melted into a droplet of water. His eyes veered skyward.

The little flakes of white taunted him as they floated upon the bodies of the infected, most still moving, others trampled beneath their feet. If the snow had come a week ago, none of these men would have had to fight here. They only would have needed to sit and do a boring overwatch while letting Mother Nature do the work of blockading the passes.

The dead pushed forward, not driven by courage or even fear. The need to murder every single one of Kinnick's men is what kept them going. These undead monsters wanted only to feast upon their corpses. The unlucky ones would stand up again as infected blood raced through their veins, giving chase to the men that had been brothers only moments before.

"Get those 203s going," Hunter yelled.

Multiple single shot M203A grenade launchers thumped 40mm grenades into the mass of bodies. Limbs exploded outward, splashing into pieces and red mush upon the rocks. The bodies piled up and no piece of road lay untouched by the dead.

Stark's Platoon gave up a worn-out cheer. Hands slapped backs. Smoke settled down on the road in a gray fog.

"Stay alert," Hunter said into the smoke. "Reload those mags," he shouted. Men hurriedly complied, heads bobbing as they looked from their mags to the road. "You know these bastards will come again." The sound of clinking bullets dominated the air. Raw fingers struggled to push down, mag springs fighting their tired fingers. They moved more from muscle memory than concentrated effort. Corporal Burbeck stared out, his eyes wide and unblinking, as his fingers shoved rounds into a magazine.

Kinnick's hand fell upon his radio. "Lieutenant Elwood, do you copy, over?" Kinnick said.

Static buzzed. He gazed along over his remaining soldiers holding the pass. *I could send a fire team up the left flanking slope. Split your little platoon into little pieces and then they will die in little pieces. What can you hold this with when they come again?*

"Lieutenant Elwood?" he said letting the mic depress. "Fuck me," he said under his breath.

"Get those boxes of 7-6-2 rounds up here," Hunter yelled at two men from 2nd Platoon. They ran off looking for giant boxes of belted ammunition.

The master sergeant turned to Kinnick. "Want me to run up there?"

Kinnick eyed the slope. Forms came from the trees. One fell down the elevated slope.

"Infected," Hunter hissed. He fired six shots before they went down. "I think that last one was one of ours."

"I know," Kinnick said. *Write those men off for dead. We are the last.*

His radio buzzed. "Colonel," a man whispered. Kinnick held the microphone up to his lips while he watched the ridge.

"Lieutenant Elwood? Sitrep, over?"

"We've been overrun. They butchered them. The ugly bastards didn't even blink." His voice shook, sobs coming through the radio.

Kinnick eyed his master sergeant. "That little shit is laying down up there?" Hunter grabbed the mic from Kinnick's hands. His beard touched his chest as he yelled. "Elwood, you stupid pussy. Die like a man or get your ass down the hill. You ain't helping us right now."

"Yes. I…I…I'll wait for them to pass. Yes." Seconds ticked by as he rustled over the radio. "They're eating Sergeant Putnam," he sobbed.

Kinnick grabbed the mic back from Hunter.

"Soldier. Get your act together or you will die," Kinnick ordered. A minute passed and screams permeated the hillside.

Kinnick closed his eyes a moment. Hunter frowned, his eyes gliding to the top of the slope. A bloodied man stumbled down the slopes. Rock and gravel rolled in front of him, tumbling down the hill at his feet. His boots dug into the loose rocky soil for traction.

"Will you look at that?" Hunter said.

The man slipped and ran down the hillside, a slight hunch in his back.

"Everyday I get surprised," Kinnick responded.

The man stumbled into the pass. His chest heaved, stretching in and out. Hunter raised his M4 to his shoulder.

"Don't shoot," Elwood cried at them, holding up his bloodied hands.

"You bit?" Hunter yelled.

"Nah. No," Elwood stuttered. His young eyes were clear and wide, no sign of infection.

"Let him through, Master Sergeant," Kinnick said. Elwood crawled over the barricade, taking refuge behind Stark's Platoon. "You did what you could." Kinnick's brow creased. "No one else?"

"I don't know, sir," Elwood said panting. "It was chaos. They were all over the slopes."

Kinnick patted the young lieutenant on the arm. His arm shook beneath Kinnick's hands. "Master Sergeant, get this man a gun."

The master sergeant chucked an M4 carbine at the young officer. "Be a pleasure."

Elwood caught the M4, eying it as if it had sold him out in the past.

"We need everyone in this fight. No time for anything else," Kinnick said.

Elwood's wide camel-colored eyes blinked. He gulped and nodded his head once.

"Here they come," a private yelled from the front. Forms emerged from the mountain's gun smoke haze. Both Kinnick and Elwood faced the threat.

"The dead," Kinnick whispered. With no machine guns hitting their flank, the horde came on uninhibited. With torn clothes and matted hair, dead gray-skinned infected came for them. They dragged their battered, maimed limbs behind them. Torn flesh flapped free like the wing of a lazy bird. They came for revenge against their camouflage-wearing foes.

The undead ranks were so swollen that those on the right side of the horde were pushed off the edge. They fell soundlessly from the mountains, arms still stretched for Kinnick and his men.

"Fire, fire," Stark screamed at the men. His colder than ice eyes blazed as he yelled. Kinnick shouldered his carbine, letting it kick away at the crux of his armpit. He aimed at their heads, firing faster than he should. It seemed the only thing to do. Shoot as fast as he could at the mass of people. Unload everything they had. When they found Kinnick and his men later, they wouldn't have a bullet left.

Brains ejected backward as bullets entered their skulls, but their effort, even with the machine guns rattling away, did little to stop the mass of the undead. It was war, but there was no glory to be found in this battle of extermination. It was mere slaughter. During the minutes of heavy gunfire, the dead had forced themselves to within yards of the makeshift barricade. Guns blasted and no one could hear.

In the madness, Hunter, standing near Kinnick, sprayed bullets into the dead. It was impossible to miss. Kinnick took a step back as infected men grasped Hunter's gun over the barricade. Their hands slipped and their flesh burnt as they pulled at the barrel of his gun. Hunter wrestled his weapon away from them, getting closer to their grasping hands in the struggle. They were a stinking monstrosity of heads and arms and legs. One leapt forward, reaching for Hunter. It's hooked and broken fingers plunged into Hunter's face. He recoiled backward, holding his face. Blood oozed white and red between his fingers.

Kinnick shot into the horde, pulling Hunter back by his tactical vest with his other hand.

"Fallback point," Kinnick yelled. He led Hunter back ten feet. His master sergeant bent at the waist trying to hold whatever was left of his eye in. Stark held the barricade. Throwing down his M4 to the ground, he snatched up an M240 from the hands of a disemboweled man. He held the weapon to his shoulder, and with the other hand, he let the linked ammunition drape over his arm. His gun ate the ammo fast as he unleashed it into the faces of the dead. His shoulder rocked in time with propulsion of bullets from the gun's barrel.

"Arrrrgggggh!" he yelled as he blasted into his foes. Hands grasped for him, tearing his combat uniform. Kinnick turned, still holding Hunter, shooting the undead off of Stark.

"Fall back," Kinnick screamed. Stark's Platoon started to backpedal. Private Warren turned and ran for the pass, followed by Burbeck.

The high-speed rattle of bullets stopped and Stark swam the M240 machine gun back and forth into the gory skeletal faces of the infected. An infected man caught Stark's arm in his mouth, tearing tissue free. Stark recoiled in horror. The infected stuffed Stark's flesh into its mouth. Stark punched its face in, knocking it back into a thousand others. He went to punch them as well, and this time, their teeth clamped down and took the fingers off his hand. He held his hand up in front of his face, watching the blood spurt from his stumps. Other hands reached him and yanked the soldier over the barrier.

The remainders of Stark's Platoon broke at the fall of their leader.

"To the rally point," Kinnick shouted. His men ran. Those nearest the barricade were swarmed over. A private screamed as ten infected tore around his body armor, digging blackened hands into his neck in-between his collarbones.

Blood pounded in Kinnick's head as he ran. His heartbeat echoed in his eardrums as his feet struggled to run over the roadway. He chanced a glance over his shoulder. Hunter clapped his firing device together as he sprinted behind Kinnick. Clack. Clack. Clack. A moment later, claymores lining the pass exploded outward into the dead. Bodies crawling over the barricade were shredded in place, stacking them atop of one another. The barricade grew taller with the bodies of the infected.

"That bought us a minute," Hunter grunted from behind. They retreated for the rally point. The rough, rocky landscape gave way to a small round of trees on a tiny hill no more than twenty feet of elevation from the road.

Kinnick's legs burned with lactic acid. His arms screamed in exhaustion. Spent, scared men collapsed in the small grouping of trees.

"Your eye," Kinnick said.

"I've seen worse," Hunter returned. Blood continued to ooze between his fingers as he ripped open a trauma pack from his cargo pocket. He wrested out gauze and grunted as he stuffed it into his torn eye socket. Gauze ends stuck out of his eye like pink cotton candy.

"Here," Kinnick pulled out a tan bandage, winding it around his skull. The master sergeant held a painful smile.

"It's fine. We gotta get these boys back in the fight," Hunter said.

Scared eyes looked back at Kinnick and Hunter. The soldiers were at the end of their rope. Death came for them, and it took them fast and without remorse. *I should have fought for more men. Now, I have led these brave few souls to their deaths. Fool.*

Hunter read the look on his face. His single eye darted back and forth. He nodded and did his due diligence, setting the men to tasks, knowing that it would be their final assignment.

"Corporal Warren, get that machine gun set up. Burbeck, lay out the 40mms. You got to hit that pass over and over when they get through the wall. Paterson, you keep Warren in the fight. We got at least five more boxes of the 7-6-2 for the 240. Remember your lineage, Bunker Hill Brigade. Always steadfast, fight like the devil, and don't give an inch to the bastards."

Kinnick pulled out his high-frequency radio. He stared at the dusty handset in desperation. He twisted to the corresponding channel and pressed the handset to his ear. The radio beeped at him. *No point in having pride now.*

"NORAD Operations," a voice said on the line.

"This is Colonel Kinnick. Requesting air support, danger close. We've been overrun."

Gunshots popped off nearby.

A new voice came on the line. "This is General Daugherty."

Not you. "Sir, this is Kinnick. We are requesting close air support and exfiltration. Our hold has been broken." Snow flurries continued their downward descent from the sky and through the trees.

"I'm not surprised to hear from you, Kinnick, but I'm not happy about it either."

"Sir, we are being overrun. We need immediate assistance."

General Daugherty paused.

I don't have time for pauses.

"There's nothing I can do. It's out of my hands."

Was that remorse in the general's voice? No matter now, we are all dead.

"I understand, sir," Kinnick said, eying the pass with dread. Dead hands pushed their way through the barricade with the sheer weight of numbers. The bodies stacked on the barricade were pushed all the way to the other side. The dead crawled over the bodies of the slain, foe and kindred alike.

"Thank you for your service, Colonel. Good luck."

"Copy," Kinnick mumbled.

Kinnick hung up his radio handset. *Bastards.* It was a weird feeling knowing that he would soon be dead. It was a rough feeling knowing that his military was going to abandon them in a mountain pass in their own backyard like some abused dog.

The enemy closed around them. Their heads swayed like buoys in an endless sea of flesh. The 40mm rounds thudded and exploded in the pass. He felt detached from this reality as the grenade rounds pounded the pass.

The faint moans of the dead scratched his ears like fingernails down a chalkboard. The machine gun pounded away at his skull, but it was the screeching of aircraft that caught his attention. It was something that he was accustomed to, having been a pilot in what seemed like a previous life. He ignored the march of the dead, his eyes drawn to the gray billowing clouds.

The high-frequency radio beeped. Kinnick snatched up the handset. "Colonel Kinnick, this is Raven. Heard you boys were in the thick. Permission to engage the pass, over?" a voice crackled over the radio.

"Raven. General Daugherty said we are on our own. Where'd you come from?"

"Battle-axe and I overheard your conversation with the general. We thought we would lend you boys a helping hand." Kinnick was dumbstruck. He turned around in a circle, looking in the sky for them.

"Jesus Christ, Raven. We are on our last leg. Fire away."

"Better hunker in real tight, Colonel, 'cause it's going to get hot."

"Everybody, danger close!" Kinnick screamed. Hunter shot him a confused glance with his one eye. "They're coming in hot."

Kinnick hopped down prone. Rocky earth ground into him. Dust puffed into the air. Seconds dragged by like the feet of the dead.

"I'm out," Warren yelled over his shoulder. The dead still poured through the pass. The onslaught of death ever approached Kinnick's men. Thousands of moans cried victory as their feet pounded the earth with every step.

"Keep firing," Kinnick shouted at his men. The bullets of so few did little to thin the massive army of infected. The undead absorbed the bullets and the fallen alike, replacing their dead with even more infected. In no time, the infected were a few dozen steps away.

The dead looked like people now. Mouths hung open. Heads tilted atop mangled necks. Shoulders drooped, attached to bullet hole riddled bodies. Gray skin sagged over skeletal frames. Disheveled, filthy hair coated scarred faces and lipless mouths. Some of their lips had been rubbed away from all the feedings. Dead white eyes zeroed in on their next victims. The dead could smell victory and the flesh of men alike. Kinnick and his men would be dismembered as the horde passed over them. The front ranks of the dead would feed on them while the others would continue their drudge for the rest of humanity. The infected would march into Colorado and finish off the last bastion of the United States government in the Golden Triangle. And mankind would go with a whimper instead of a roar into the annals of earth's long history. Extinct.

Kinnick flipped a switch on the lower receiver of his gun. He took aim and let his carbine fire repeated three-round bursts. It did little to the mass of humanity. It was as if he shot a concrete wall. The infected reached for him with rotting, mangled fingers on broken hands.

Shroom! Shroom! The earth shook as the jets went by. The ground began trembling beneath the assault from above. Fireballs erupted into fiery fingers that reached for the sky. A deafening roar assaulted his eardrums and an inferno rolled down the roadway, annihilating the infected.

The dead nearest them were sent off their feet. Others near the pass were incinerated into flaming dust. Kinnick covered his head with his arms as pieces of charred flesh, rocks, and wood rained down on them. An infected head plopped down within feet of Kinnick, rolling to a halt near his leg. Its mouth lay permanently open, its skin charred black. Kinnick swatted it away with his free hand and grabbed his carbine with the other. He stood up to get a better view.

"WaHoo. Get some," shouted Burbeck, raising a fist in the air along with his M16A4.

"How about them apples?" Warren called out at the rocky terrain of smoldering infected. Bodies that hadn't been completely incinerated were aflame in blackish heaps of gooey flesh. Paterson stood up and wrapped his arm around Warren. The dead only caught in the shockwave were getting back to their feet.

"Don't celebrate too early," Hunter said. "Let's clear them out."

His remaining men smiled as they put bullets into the crawling dead. Hope had replaced certain death. Five minutes later, Kinnick joined Hunter, looking over the pass of death.

"We did it, sir. Nothing like a little air superiority."

Kinnick grinned as his stomach warmed with the turn of fate. "Can't say I've ever been more proud."

Hunter offered him a salute. The rest of his men did the same. Tears came to the corners of his eyes as he returned their salute. *I can't believe we held them.*

"Let's get Daugherty, that snake-bastard, on the line. Tell him we did it."

Hunter grinned beneath his bloody brown beard. "I'd love to see the look on that prick's face when you tell him we held."

"We will soon enough, in person, but first, let's give our saviors some love," Kinnick said. He picked up his radio handset. "Raven, there are some real grateful men down here. Thank you."

"Least we could do on our way by."

"Way by?"

The microphone cracked and shifted to only static. Kinnick glanced at the sky wondering, what the pilot meant.

Over a minute later, he saw the white flash and his gut sank as low as it could go in his body. He was far enough away where he could look right at it. It seemed more like a sun in pencil form leaping up from a mountain hundreds of miles away. A gray plume of smoke shot upright and curled over on itself thousands of feet in the air. *Salt Lake City?* Kinnick closed his eyes, opening them as he could feel the boom run across his face. Tears flowed freely down his cheeks, driving off his chin now. *Roooaarrrr!* The boom echoed from mountain to mountain.

Everything he had fought for and his men had died for had been in vain. Entire cities were being annihilated as thermonuclear warheads slammed into all of the population centers of the western United States. Kinnick dropped to his knees, letting his gun fall from his grasp.

"The bastard. He did it. He really did it," he said aloud, but no one heard.

STEELE

Pentwater, MI

He awoke before he opened his eyes. He listened briefly, wondering if he had passed on. No heavenly trumpets awaited him. No din from a Valhalla battle. Not even the darkness of nothing. Only pain met him. Pain that pounded through his arm and leg assured him he still remained in the world of the living. He peeped his eyes open. A woman's heart-shaped face looked back. He knew in an instant it was her. Until the day he died, he would recognize it. Gwen's nose sniffled and she ran a hand across it. She half-laughed, half-cried.

"You're awake," she whispered. Her voice was genuinely happy.

Steele groaned, feeling the full extent of his injuries. His arm burned and his leg throbbed like someone was pushing on his small pellet wounds.

"I suppose you're going to tell me I'm lucky to be alive," he whispered, his voice crackling in dehydration.

She placed a bottle of water to his lips, and the dryness of his throat scratched as the water went down. After a gulp, it wouldn't go down and he spit up some of the liquid onto himself. He brought his arm that wasn't agonizingly filled with pain across his mouth.

"How long have I been out?" he asked, twisting his head to get a good look at his other arm. It rested on his chest in a sling, and white bandages wrapped all the way around it. The bandages were tight and his arm was hot underneath them, screaming in pain for air. "Let me swell," his wound seemed to whisper.

"You've been in and out for two days. One of the War Machines is a retired corpsman. He did the best he could, but the arm is," she stopped mid-sentence. She gave him a sad smile that made his heart drop. "Time will tell."

Steele lifted his head off his pillow. He wiggled his fingers a fraction in defiance at her claims.

"Fingers still work," he grunted. After putting his head back on his pillow, he lay silent for a minute, exhausted by the small effort.

He took in his surroundings, not recognizing the dorm-like room he lay in.

"Where are we?"

"Pentwater Fire Department. That's where the bikers dropped us off after the attack."

"What attack?" Steele's heart jumped. Instinctually his eyes darted around the room for a weapon. "Pastor?"

She shook her head. "Hundreds of infected on the road. We were trapped, but Max, he helped save us."

Steele smiled and coughed a bit, bringing a fist to his mouth. "There's no way you needed saving. Where is that young buck? I want to tell him I'm proud of him." He stared at her, awaiting her reply. He blinked. "That stupid kid. Bring him in. Let me see him. I'll give him a noogie or something. "

Gwen glanced nervously at her hands. She clasped them tightly in front of her. Tears filled her eyes. "He didn't make it."

Steele let his head rest back on the pillow and squeezed his eyes shut. *Goddamnit. You weren't supposed to go on the list, kid.* He took in a deep breath and let out a sorrowful sigh.

"How many of us made it?" he asked, fearing the answer and keeping his eyes closed.

"Many," she said. He cracked his eyes open and eyed her suspiciously, knowing that it wasn't beyond her to withhold some part of the truth.

"I don't believe you."

She raised an eyebrow in defense. "You don't?"

"I want to see everyone. Help me up," he ordered. He waited a moment when she didn't help. "Please?"

She stared back, her hands clasped in her lap. Her eyebrows raised up a bit, the mother coming out in her.

"Don't you practice your mother face on me," he said, raising his eyebrows back at her. He knew one eyebrow wasn't going up as high as the other due to the scar tissue covering his scalp.

"No. You need rest." Her eyes dared him to say otherwise.

"I can rest when I'm dead."

Her eyes narrowed. "If you don't rest, you will *be* dead." Her face took on a defiant demeanor. The two were like a pair of mules pushing over an inch of ground.

"You at least have to let me take a piss."

"Fine," she said. She handed him a crutch and wrapped her arm around his body, helping him sit up. Pain shot through his arm, taking his breath away. He gave her a wince-filled grin.

"Are you sure?" she asked.

"Yes. Give me a hand." She placed a gentle hand on his back, helping him upright.

They stood and he wedged the crutch in the crook of his undamaged armpit. Hobbling, he marched for the bathroom door. After relieving himself, he made good on his promise and went for the dorm room door. She let him go but stayed glued to his side. He wasn't sure if she was sympathetic to his plea or simply letting it go. Because if she didn't want him to go, he would have been easily led back to his bed.

He stepped into the hall and limped down the whitewashed corridor, wishing he had stayed in bed with every damaged step.

"One step at a time," he said to himself. His pace was painfully slow. Literally anything moved faster than him. Turtles. Sloths. A snail. But he moved with determination. He didn't know why, but he felt like he had to.

A familiar face emerged from a small dorm room just like the one he had been in. The middle-aged woman smiled at him as he hobbled past.

"Margie," he said with a smile. She was all right. "Good shooting out there." She reached up and touched his face. Her lips curved like a proud mother, her eyes wrinkling in the corners.

"Thank you," she whispered. "He's up," she shouted. Others came to the doors. Bald Larry gave him a grin and gripped his good arm tight.

"You did us proud," Larry said with a nod. "You did us proud."

Hank and Gregor were there.

"You guys did well out there," Steele said to them. They both nodded.

"Thank you, Captain," Gregor said. He wiped a strand of hair out of his face and put a large hand on Steele's shoulder. Steele was too tired to fight them on it.

"Alex?" Steele asked. The two men shook their heads no. Another name for the list. He wrapped his fingers around the worn metal hammer dangling from the chain around his neck. *Jarl. Wheeler. Andrea. Barnes. Lewis. Max. Alex. Bengy. My mother.* The last one stung the most. He wasn't there when she needed him the most. *And all these others from Little Sable I couldn't save.*

"Kevin and Ahmed?" he said urgently to Gwen.

She smiled. "They're here. In the kitchen," she said. He hobbled down the hall a fraction of a step faster.

He found the pair eating soup from cans at a long table that once served the squad of firefighters when they were on call at the firehouse.

"Yay, the big guy's up," Kevin exclaimed, throwing his arms in the air.

Ahmed grinned. His stubble seemed to have turned into a jet black beard overnight, the same with his shaved head. "It's good to see you, my friend."

Steele looked at the ground and back at Ahmed. "We need to find you a set of clippers. Your hair looks terrible. I'm going to start calling you my chia pet," Steele laughed. Ahmed felt his bristly scalp.

"You survived all this to come in here and tell me I need a haircut?"

Steele laughed. Pain went through both his leg and arm. "Ow. Don't make me laugh."

"When we're done with my hair, I'm taking it to that squirrel's nest on your face."

Steele ran a hand through his beard. "Not until the playoffs are over." Steele stopped smiling after a moment.

A certain sadness washed over them. They would never watch hockey again, but they were alive.

Steele glanced at Kevin. “Good to see you in one piece.”

“So you really took that Víktov Hill strategy to heart? Battle wagons, militia, ambush. Like a true commander.”

“History will always play a role in the present. It’s only a matter of seeing where it applies, but I’m hardly a commander.”

“Call it what you want, but you won a great battle out there.”

“Thunder won the battle. We held the ground long enough. More stupid stubbornness than anything else.”

Kevin gave him a knowing smile. “Jan Žižka would have been proud.”

Laughing, Steele shook his head at the former history teacher. *We fought because we didn’t have a choice.* “Lofty comparison.”

He left the men and crutched for the stairs. He traversed the stairs one at a time using his crutch and Gwen, jumping on his good leg one at a time. As he hopped to the bottom, ten bikers hung around drinking beer and talking. They gave him curious looks. Food was stacked throughout the firehouse.

Down the way, short-haired Tess sat talking with Thunder. His nose was puffy and swollen, making the biker look more like Santa than a rough motorcycle gang leader.

“You’re awake,” Thunder boomed, his belly jiggling. A broad smile stretched across his gray-bearded face.

Tess stood and put her arms around Steele gingerly. He could feel Gwen tense up on his other side. Gwen’s grip tightened around his body.

“I was worried,” Tess said. She ignored Gwen and hugged him tighter.

“I’m glad you’re okay,” he said softly down to her.

She pushed him away. “A lot better than the likes of you. Not sure I’ll ever get the stink of gasoline off me,” she said with a smile. She gazed up at him, her dark eyes sparkling. “We did it, Steele. We defeated those whack jobs.”

“We did.” He looked around her. “Speaking of which. Where are they?”

She pointed to a rectangular brick building. “Thunder has them all corralled in the school gymnasium over there.”

“Plenty of guards and we keep ’em locked in,” Thunder said.

“Isn’t that a fire hazard?” Steele joked.

Thunder gave him an evil grin.

"That's a risk we're willing to take," Tess said.

"How many of them are in there?"

Thunder gestured at the gym with a hand holding a beer. "Eh. I'd say about two hundred and twenty or thirty. We left over a hundred at Little Sable Point for the dead. I'm not sure how many escaped."

"They're probably regrouping as we speak at the Temple Energy Plant." Steele's mind raced at the potential for another fight.

"You thinking about taking care of them?" Thunder asked. Steele shook his head no.

"That's mostly women and children now. Any remnants of the Chosen will be on the defensive from either us or the dead. Let's think about it for a few days."

"You know what they say about seizing the initiative."

"I do, but I'm not sure acquiring another five hundred prisoners will be great for our food situation."

"Their wounded?" Steele asked.

"They insisted on tending their own," Tess said.

"Make sure they have adequate supplies. We aren't monsters."

Tess's face grew dark, but she nodded.

Thunder scratched at his bandana. "They may have some supplies that we can use back at the power plant."

"I'll think on it," Steele said, feeling the exhaustion of his injuries and decisions alike.

Thunder gave him a grave nod. "You do that. When you're feeling a bit better, I will introduce you to some of the clubs."

Pressing his lips flat, Steele let Thunder know he appreciated him not overwhelming him with a bunch of new faces in his injured state. The other man nodded.

"I look forward to meeting some of the members of Rolling Thunder."

"Ha. That's got a nice ring to it," Thunder said with a laugh. "Boys got some chicken cooking over there. You want some?"

Steele's stomach grumbled in response. Not having eaten in days was catching up with him. "That'd be nice. Gwen, you think you could go with

Thunder and find us some food?" he asked as sweetly as his pain would allow. Her face strained, and she eyed Tess untrustingly.

"Yeah, sure," she said like a viper, giving him eyes that said if he wasn't injured already, she would be doing it for him. She walked off with a backward glance at him like a warning shot across his bow. Without her support he sat, mostly fell, down into a nearby lawn chair. Tess dragged a lawn chair and took a seat next to him with a smirk. She shoved her hand into a cardboard box.

"Beer?" she said, holding up a can.

"No, thanks. It'll put me back to sleep. No craft brews?"

She cracked open the top of the can and slurped a sip. "At this point, it doesn't matter. Beer is beer."

Steele breathed a laugh.

Tess took another swig, watching Gwen and Thunder. "You can tell her not to worry. Our near-death experience won't change our working relationship. I'm not going to steal you out from underneath her," she said, acting as if he had no say in the matter.

"Well, I'm sure she appreciates that."

"Crossed my mind, though," she said with a smirk.

Steele shook his head with a laugh. "I bet it has." *But I have bigger fish to fry*, he finished in his mind.

Her playful look sobered. "I'm still glad we found each other. I'm not sure Little Sable would have weathered the storm without you."

"Little Sable never would have made it this far without someone like you at the helm," he said.

She flashed him a smile. "Don't make me blush."

"I hate to say it, but despite what we did, Little Sable Point is gone," he said. He shifted in his seat, painfully adjusting his weight.

"I know, stupid. But the idea behind it, ya know? I think it gives people some hope that things might get back to normal," she said.

Steele looked out over abandoned buildings of Pentwater. The gathering of bikers laughed uproariously. Trash littered the street. Broken glass lay scattered near buildings. Doors lay smashed open. A club of bikers in black-wolf patched vests and with guns drawn, charged into a building across the street. After a dozen gunshots and a few minutes, they walked back out with hands full of boxes and supplies.

"It gives me hope too," he said, staring out at the desolation before him.

JOSEPH

Cheyenne Mountain Complex, CO

The lights were off inside his room. With no windows, the room was black. The only light crept in underneath the bottom of the door.

Joseph's back was against the wall, and his hands were wrapped around his knees, holding them together. He had heard a man screaming as he dragged himself down the hallway.

"Be quiet," Joseph whispered into the darkness. The man never heard him.

The man's screams were horrible. His skin screeched on the floor as he crawled. *Screee. Screee.* The gradual scrape of clothes and flesh on the hard floor came to a stop. More footsteps came down the hallway, but Joseph knew better than to hope. It wasn't the first time the infected had come. The steps were followed by low moans.

"No. Please," the man sobbed outside his door. The voice pled for them to stop. Splashes of something hit the floor. The man's screams became cries and the cries became gurgles. Bones popped. Tendons snapped. Followed by the chomping of flesh and the clicking of jaws. Then there were only the distant gunshots. An hour passed and the infected finished their dastardly deed and left Joseph alone.

The gunshots had come in intervals as if different groups of men were clearing the areas already cleared, or maybe the first group through hadn't survived the clearing.

Booms thundered on his door as if the person were trying to punch their way inside.

"U.S. Army. Anyone alive in there?"

"Yes." Was all he could muster.

Joseph reached up and clicked the bolt open. The door cracked open and armed men pushed their way inside. Flashlights pointed every which way. The lights illuminated Joseph, revealing drying gore splattered all over his clothes.

"Let me see your hands," the soldier screamed through his mask. Joseph timidly put them upward.

"I'm not infected," Joseph growled. "I'm Dr. Jackowski."

The soldier looked him up and down. "We've been looking for you. Get in the back. We'll take you to the collection point."

The soldiers were armed with miscellaneous weapons. Two men were heavily armed in black tactical gear like Hudson's squad that had been ripped apart in the elevator. Masks, gloves, and helmets covered them. They held short carbines in front of their bodies. One of the men wore civilian clothes but had a tactical vest over his torso with an MP5 strapped to his chest. The other two men wore combat uniforms but only had pistols in their hands.

Joseph was pushed to the back of the squad of pieced together soldiers. He joined a couple of people huddling near the back. A woman with glasses cried. The man wrapped his arms around the woman. "Shhh. It's okay, Megan. These men will keep us safe," he said.

Her head shook side to side in a tepid no. "They grabbed Stephen from my arms and ate him," she mumbled. "They said we would be safe inside the mountain," she whispered. Her words were guilt-ridden, barbed arrows into Joseph's soul. *I caused this.*

They avoided a puddle of crimson liquid and bits of a uniform as they followed the soldiers like elementary students following their teachers on a field trip. The soldiers checked room to room for survivors. Quick knocks. Quick questions to determine if they were alive. The group's progress was painfully slow down the hall.

Joseph recognized the double door at the end of the hall. Bloody footprints stained the floor, leaving long streaks across it.

One of the heavily armed soldiers leaned back. "Wait here," he said in a gruff voice. He eyed them over his shoulder. "We're going to clear the main room. Yell if somebody comes up behind us."

The soldiers filed up on either side of the door. The squad leader held up his hand. Three. Two. One. He displayed with his fingers and the squad of mixed personnel disappeared into the office.

A man growled and someone fired their gun in a short staccato of bullet notes. Joseph crept down the hallway after the soldiers.

"What are you doing?" the man behind him hissed.

"I've got to see something," Joseph said.

"They said to stay here." The man's voice came out in a whine. Megan continued to cry on his shoulder.

"I know." Joseph ignored the man's pleas for him to stop and walked inside.

Cubicle walls were knocked over onto desks. Blood covered the floor where people had been consumed or turned into infected. The squad had cleared corners and made its way cautiously forward to the bloodbath around the elevator. The soldiers twisted back-and-forth, guns searching for threats. Joseph followed behind them thirty feet behind them.

"Help," echoed out from the elevator.

Shouts sounded out. "Drop the gun," screamed the soldiers. Metal clanked on the ground.

A man emerged from the elevator where he had been hiding. Dead soldiers were strewn around him. His body was covered in dried brown blood as if he had been swimming in a cesspool of death. Only his eyes were gore-free. His shirt and briefs were stuck to his skin. Bites decorated his skin. His arms and shoulders were covered with open wounds in the form of bite marks. Blood seeped from the indentations in his skin.

"He's been bit," shouted a soldier. He pointed his pistol at the man. Guns lifted to shoulders and they sidestepped away from one another in an effort to not get stuck in the crossfire.

Gauze had been stuffed into a hole in his calf and bandages had been hastily wrapped around both his arms.

"I…I…Please don't shoot. I'm okay," the young soldier stuttered. Joseph jogged closer to the group. *It can't be him,* he thought.

The soldiers exchanged looks. The squad leader, the most heavily armed soldier, turned back to the young man. "I'm sorry, buddy. It's been a rough day for all of us. You know a bite means. It's only a matter of time. Our orders are clear."

The young, shaved-head soldier shook his head, looking from gun to gun. "No. Come on, guys. Same team."

Joseph eyed the squad leader. The squad leader's finger tapped the receiver of his carbine three distinct times, and a man in only a tactical vest and civilian clothes moved to the side.

"Make your peace, brother. We won't let you turn," the squad leader said. The other soldier crept up from the side, gun pointed at the young soldier's head.

"Wait," Joseph screamed. Guns whipped his way, and for a second, he knew they were going to shoot him.

"Get back in the hallway," shouted the squad leader, pointing a gloved-finger at him, his other hand still on his carbine.

"No." Joseph gulped.

The soldier's eyes went wide and he marched for him. An iron grip crushed into Joseph's shoulder. "What's wrong with you? Can't you see it isn't safe?"

"Don't shoot that man," Joseph shouted. The squad leader shoved him backward. Joseph stumbled back.

"Get back," the squad leader shouted. He pointed a black-gloved finger at Joseph. "He's infected. We've let him live too long as is," he hissed through his mask.

Joseph gave him as fierce a look as he could muster. "That man is living proof that we have found a vaccine for the virus."

The squad leader looked back at the bleeding, bandaged man in his briefs. He released Joseph and pointed back. "Him?"

"Yes. Subject C is the only one who hasn't turned when bitten." Joseph eyed the young soldier standing there practically naked. His skin was pale beneath the blood. Joseph added hurriedly, "We must get him medical treatment and pray he doesn't turn."

***

Forty-eight hours later, Subject C, Private First Class Rodgers was confined and under constant monitoring in the quarantine wing of the BSL-4 lab. Joseph watched him sleeping on the other side of a camera.

"No sign of infection," Joseph said to Byrnes. The gaunt military man rubbed his chin and nodded his head.

"I can't remember the last time we had any good news. We will continue monitoring him for any changes."

"I'm thinking another week and we will be almost positive that the recipients of the vaccine will not turn infected. Its replication cycle is so fast that every hour he doesn't turn, I am more sure it worked. Two to three weeks, and I will be comfortable for expansive distribution among the soldiers."

"What if there are long-term effects?"

"Nothing is more long-term than death, but we will use it on a few squads to begin with. Men involved with some front-line work. I can live with some irritable bowel syndrome, or something like that if it can keep these guys fighting long enough to win."

Joseph didn't like it but had to agree. This vaccine would provide soldiers and civilians with an opportunity to live through potential infection. The infected could still murder them, but vaccinated victims would not contract the disease by fluid transmission or bite.

Byrnes nodded thoughtfully. "The outbreak was terrible, but we did it, Dr. Jackowski." Byrnes wrapped his arm around Joseph, cupping his shoulder. The tall colonel smiled down at him. Still a sad man, but happy in this brief moment in time.

"We did," Joseph said. Joseph gently released himself from the colonel's grip. "I'm going down to speak with Richard."

Byrnes watched him for a moment before he spoke as if he tried to understand him. "What is your loyalty to that guy? He's the cause of all of this."

Joseph looked down. Patient Zero had caused him nothing but pain and suffering. Men had died to help Joseph find him. Men had died controlling him.

Rebecca, a woman whom he had fallen for even as she slowly succumbed to Primus Necrovirus, had died because of him. This had all been because of one person who had unknowingly spread the virus to an unsuspecting planet. Yet, in the end, the virus was to blame, not the man that contracted it. Richard Thompson, Patient Zero, would get the blame if someone ever wrote about the virus in a history book, but he would also be the man who saved mankind from it.

"I dunno. But I want to tell him that we did it. That we couldn't have done it without him."

Byrnes nodded his acceptance and Joseph left. He walked quietly down the hallway, to his room. He donned his HAZMAT suit, undergoing all protocols.

Gasses released as the pressurized doors opened up to Patient Zero's white sterile room. His heart monitor beeped. *Beep-beep, beep. Beep-beep, beep.* Patient Zero's chest rose and fell. Joseph hesitantly approached the bed, remembering the time he had been in the room with Rebecca and Patient Zero had infected her.

His blue-suit-booted feet crunched like plastic beneath him until he was alongside Patient Zero.

"Richard," he whispered. Richard's fingers were limp and lifeless. He took the man's hand and squeezed. Patient Zero's hand felt almost artificial through his biohazard suit. It was like squeezing the hand of a mannequin.

Bandages covered the countless incisions where the other doctors had sliced him open for observation. One bandage covered his forehead where they had taken a portion of his frontal lobe. It had greatly diminished his communication abilities. His eyes fluttered and cracked open.

"It's me, Joseph. Do you remember me?" He gave Richard a faint smile.

Richard's pale white eyes blinked acknowledgment, a faint milk-chocolate brown hidden beneath their whiteness.

"I came here to tell you something."

Richard blinked his almost white eyes again. Drool dribbled down his chin from the corner of his mouth

"We've come up with a vaccine. It's more of a miracle than real science, but it worked."

Richard's eyes blinked rapidly. Joseph squeezed his hand.

"We couldn't have done this without you. It was your cells that allowed us to find a way." *And Rebecca.* "I just wanted you to know that. You have saved a lot of lives. And you took Rebecca's." A flash of anger bubbled in Joseph's gut. "You took hers. You took the woman who was to be my partner in this. You took her and made me watch her die." He found himself crushing Richard's hand in his. Richard's eyes blinked fast. Joseph let go of his hand, staring at his own.

"Why am I even bothering? You can't even speak on your own behalf." Joseph shook his head in frustration. He stared at the white walls. Pure and snow-white and sterile, but also, devoid of feeling and emotion.

"No, it's not your fault. It is the virus's." His eyes dropped back down on Richard's incision-covered body. *Look at his man. More scars than Frankenstein.* The man stared back, a primal form of relief in his eyes.

Willing or not, you both gave your lives for this.

From the corner of Richard's eye, a tear trickled down his face.

"Goodbye, Richard. Your part is done, but this war is not over."

Richard would continue to be observed in his diminished state until his heart gave out. After his body was put down and incinerated in the flames of a cremation furnace, the war for the living would continue. Richard, Patient Zero of the worst outbreak in recorded human history, would be a footnote. The outbreak war would continue until the living became the dead or as long as the infected roamed the earth.

STEELE

Shores of Lake Michigan

White caps on gray water crashed onto the beach below, filling the air with a dull roar. The sky was a lighter version of gray. Dark clouds hung low, racing across the horizon of the giant lake promising rain sometime in the near future. They stood near the edge of the lakeside sloping cliff that dropped almost one hundred feet to the beach. The grass was uncut and overgrown, standing all the way to Steele's knees.

The wind came off the water, whipping his coat that dangled around his shoulders. Steele didn't wear a suit or a tie as was customary before the outbreak. Simple and more functional clothing was appropriate. His sling-propped arm wouldn't allow him to easily wear a coat, so he wore it around his shoulders.

Loose-fitting ACU pants covered his yellow and purple leg that itched like hell. He decided it was a good time to ditch the crutch, having leaned heavily on it for a week. He wasn't sure if a few of those nasty metal pellets were still stuck in his leg or if his wounds were just that deep, but the small wounds ached and itched incessantly. He was only thankful he hadn't taken a slug to the thigh instead. *You would have bled out in a minute.*

Gwen was there with him. The wind attacked her hair, pulling pieces and strands all over her head despite the fact she wore it in a ponytail. Having her nearby comforted him. It gave him some sort of solace in a time that was filled with so much loss. She held his free hand.

She stared downward at the two piles of freshly dug dirt in the ground. Kevin stood next to her, his hands clasped in front of him. Ahmed stood next to him, a shovel in one hand, a black M4 slung on his back. He had insisted on digging in Steele's place. Steele had begrudgingly obliged and watched the burly man go to work on the sandy soil.

There wasn't much to bury, but Ahmed dug full-sized graves anyway. Releasing Gwen's hand, Steele bent down on one leg, ignoring the screaming of his other. He picked up a handful of gray ash and sprinkled it in the hole. Much of it lifted off, the wind carrying it away. Gwen did the same. The only sound was the crashing waves of Lake Michigan. Steele nodded to Kevin and then Ahmed and they followed suit.

Steele looked down at the almost empty grave. The words to say hid from him. *What do you say to the ones who've already passed that you should have already said?* All those missed phone calls. The times when he thought he would just catch-up later. Other things had filled her place.

Work dragged him from corner to corner of the earth as he paid the price of being a counterterrorism agent day in and day out. It was a never-ending battle between good and evil fought in the gray. His mother paid her own price for his dedication to his country. Gwen paid that price. The price of lost time. Time was one thing he could never get back. It made him question whether or not he had made the right decisions even if they were for his country's sake.

His mother suffered in silence, alone, with his father gone, waiting on her only son to return from his modern-day quest. A mother who waited patiently day-by-day, praying that her son stay out of harm's way long enough to make the final journey home. Then tomorrow came and his mother was gone, and he was too late. *I should have been here. I never should have left. Who would I be if I had stayed?*

He bent down again, digging into a handful of smoky ash. "You're going to be a grandma," he said, tears filling his eyes. He bit his lip and wiped his eyes. She had loved to talk about how excited she was for him to be married and have kids. Now she would have a grandchild she would never see. Cheeks she would never pinch. Little feet she would never tickle. A forehead she would never kiss goodnight. Newborn baby smells she would never enjoy. All of these precious things taken from her. Experiences that he would never get to share with her. All taken by the pastor and his men. He suppressed his deep rage for the man.

His fingers closed and he made a fist. The granules crumbled into dust as they were compressed by his palm, and he tossed the remainders into the hole. "I wish it was different," he whispered.

He took a deep breath trying to collect himself. "We put you here because we knew this is where you'd want to be," he said, taking a deep breath. The hugeness of Lake Michigan stretched far and wide as he could see. "You got a great view. Sunset every day. The lake will be here and some trees. We'll bring the baby back so you can meet," he said to her ghost.

He bowed his head in silence, lost in his thoughts. For minutes, the group stood quiet, contemplating all those they never had the chance to say goodbye to. They contemplated all the missed opportunities and missed phone calls to their loved ones, each person and minute, now gone. The wind picked up and a sound came flirting with it.

A slight humming pricked his eardrums. The others heard it too. Gwen looked over her shoulder. Her hair continued to get tossed in the wind. Ahmed eyed the road. Steele turned, shifting his feet around in search of the source. Soon all their attention was in the direction of the street.

"A car?" Ahmed asked. He shrugged his M4 carbine off his shoulders and into his hands.

Steele eyed the road expectantly. *The Red Stripes?* The rumbling grew louder.

"Bigger," Steele said, limping for the charred remains of his family's house. Gwen put an arm around him and helped him to the ground with a grunt. Seconds later, the first truck wheeled by. All tan. Thick wheel treads. The truck looked like it was made from rectangles. A man's head poked out the top of a turret. A camouflaged helmet sat atop his skull. He rested easily on his M2 .50 caliber machine gun, the barrel pointed lazily upward. The Humvee disappeared behind trees and another house.

"Military? Here?" Gwen whispered.

"I dunno," Steele breathed. He kept only his eyes above the charred wood, watching.

A minute passed and another Humvee rolled by, followed by another and another. All bore the same mark: a dark red anvil painted on the side of each driver's door.

"Jesus, look at all of them," Kevin whispered. Humvee after Humvee drove along the lakeside road. Troop carriers filled with soldiers crammed in like a box of bullets were spaced intermittently throughout the convoy.

"Who are they?" Gwen asked.

She was silenced as an airport mobile lounge followed along, its steel-plated windows raised up. Arms and heads stuck out, draped on the sides of the tall moon-rover like vehicle. *Lunchbox.*

Steele swallowed hard, all the moisture in his throat disappearing. His heart pounded his chest. He knew, and it scared him to his core.

"Colonel Jackson."

KINNICK

Peterson Air Force Base, CO

The dark black liquid was too hot. Little waves of heat quivered up as they struggled to free themselves from his cup. He sipped it anyway, feeling it burn his tongue a bit on the way down. *Can't waste the good stuff.*

He gestured his cup at his master sergeant. "Coffee?" he asked.

"I'd love some," Hunter said. Hunter still wore white bandages around his head. They covered his eye along with a black eye patch. Kinnick poured him some coffee and handed it to the man. Hunter took it carefully with two hands.

"Any word from Wyman's platoon at South Fork pass?" Kinnick asked.

"No. But I can't imagine Turmelle going down without a hell of a fight," Hunter said, running his coffee cup into his lip. He noticed Kinnick staring at him and shrugged his shoulders. "Still getting used to it. What the hell you need two for anyway?"

"I'm glad it wasn't worse," Kinnick said to him. Airmen sat at cubicles, facing a giant radar on the wall.

"How's Hawkins doing?" Kinnick said. He had been in nothing but meetings since he had returned.

"Hawk? If we hadn't sent someone to pick him up, he would have waged guerrilla warfare until they were all dead. Again."

"You got one hell of an operational detachment."

"Sins and skins." Hunter put out a hand with a smile. Kinnick locked hands with the man. A cool circular piece of metal pressed flat into Kinnick's palm. Hunter released his hand and a half-dollar sized coin sat in the palm of Kinnick's hand. Across the top, it read "SKINS" in red writing. Beneath that, a skull wore a wolf headdress and red arrows lined the back with a single number "51" at the bottom.

"I talked with Hawk. Well, talked at Hawk. And we decided that we wanted to get you inducted as an honorary member of our unit before..."

"Before it's too late," Kinnick said and returned the smile.

"We never know when our time comes, but when it does, meet it with bullets and a smile," Hunter said.

"Sins and skins, Master Sergeant."

"Sins and skins, Colonel. And I'll let you in on a little secret." Hunter nudged Kinnick. His single eye looked around the room before he leaned in. "You're the first, and probably only, chair force member to be inducted into our ODA."

"It's an honor that I will hold dear," Kinnick said, staring at the coin.

"And I'll see if we can dig up a patch for you somewhere. Your uniform is a bit sparse."

Kinnick laughed. "Much appreciated." Kinnick turned away, looking at the giant projection of the surrounding airspace.

They sat in silence for a moment watching the green planes scoot inch by inch across the radar. Almost all of them floated from north to south.

"No need to go west," Kinnick said. He grimaced, feeling guilt for failing his nation. Large red rings sat around the major cities of the West Coast, projecting the spread of nuclear fallout contamination and other affected areas.

"Colonel Kinnick?" A major said, peering into the cubicles. Kinnick stood up.

"I'm here."

The major nodded. "Please come into the War Room," he said from across the operations center. Kinnick managed his way through the cubicles into the vice president's War Room.

A host of officers sat around the table. General Daugherty was there to the right of Vice President Brady. His mouth was set to an irritated twist and a general air of displeasure to see Kinnick alive. Kinnick took a seat at the far end of the table. Brady's tie was gone today. He wore a simple white collared shirt underneath a navy blue suit.

"We're glad to have you back Colonel Kinnick," Brady said. Kinnick kept his face flat. He was unamused with the man who had ordered nuclear strikes within his own nation.

Daugherty cocked his head to the side like Kinnick was an odd creature. "It's true. I admire your bravery even if it was an ill-advised mission. We clearly need men of your leadership quality within our ranks."

Kinnick gave him a terse nod. *If we only had men of better quality leading us from above,* he thought.

The general cleared his throat and adjusted his glasses. "But the fact remains that the passes in Colorado were not holdable, and we were forced to launch a full-scale nuclear strike against the West Coast."

Papers shifted. Some of the officers stared down at their reports. There was clearly dissent among them, or at the very least, shame.

"As the briefing in front of you states, the strikes were a great success. We are estimating an eight-five percent kill rate within the metropolitan areas."

"One hundred percent kill rate for anyone still alive there," Kinnick said flatly. Heads turned toward Kinnick. Eyes quickly averted. Other stared brazenly, knowing what they had supported.

"May I continue, *Colonel*?" Daugherty said with an emphasis to make Kinnick's rank seem small and insignificant. He was making sure everyone knew that he was in charge and nothing Kinnick could do would change that.

"It's impossible for us to know the number of American deaths in relation to the bombings, but we consider the losses to be negligible."

Kinnick masked his disgust by taking a sip of his coffee.

"Gentlemen, this was the only way. Kinnick, we are aware of the sacrifices that your men made to hold the passes. We gave your plan a chance, and it failed, so we moved forward with a sure thing," Daugherty said.

"You gave me a hundred men when you and me both know I needed hundreds of troops and full air support. It was a suicide mission."

"If it were up to me, I would have given you no one," Daugherty said. His eyes grew angry behind his glasses as he spoke. "You took our men on a suicide mission that you wanted to lead. What about those soldiers we will never get back? Those men who died for *nothing*. Men that could have been ready to fight the bigger battle on the even more important front."

"Enough, General," Brady said. He faced Kinnick. "Colonel. We aren't going to fight you on it. What's done is done. The bombs have been dropped on us, by us." He gestured a thumb at himself. "That's on me."

Kinnick shut his mouth. The vice president was right. Kinnick couldn't change what had happened.

"Do you want to be a part of this military?" Daugherty asked.

What do I have left? He had thrown his hat in with the military since he had found himself trapped within the Pentagon instead of taking care of his family in Northern Virginia. *What about my men out there? What about the Skins? You still have a place here even if the leaders are jacking it all up.*

"I am committed to this country."

Daugherty eyed him suspiciously. Brady patted the general's arm.

"See there, General. Colonel Kinnick is only a bit frustrated. We lost some good men out there. But we must continue. Perhaps the colonel will be a bit more sympathetic with more intelligence."

"Very well," Daugherty said. He clicked his remote control instead of taking a swing at Kinnick.

A rounded aerial view of tan farmland lit up the screen.

"This is from a drone from over western Ohio," he said. Fields flew by as the drone passed overhead of yellow corn husks and brown burnt leaves. The fields quivered ever so slightly.

"Sorry, it's hard for me to see. Is that water?" the major that collected Kinnick asked.

The general zoomed it in. "That, Major, is what's coming west as we speak."

Forms swarmed the fields. None of them stopped as they stumbled forward. Like a river, they only went around obstacles. Thousands. Tens of thousands. Hundreds of thousands.

"There are so many," the major uttered. The words came out soft.

Kinnick closed his eyes.

Daugherty zoomed out. Millions of sand-sized infected walked across the screen. "As you can see, this is the threat we now face. They are gathering, sweeping across the Midwest. This is a mere fraction of their numbers, and they are coming this way."

"How many?" Brady asked.

"Millions. Our best estimates, depending on infection rates, are over a hundred million."

Brady shook his head. He sat back in his leather chair, eyes wide. He held his hands in front of his body, fingers spread out. "Nukes are off the table for this one?" he asked.

"I'm afraid they are if we want to survive fallout. We could get away with it in the west because of the Rockies, to the east we will be contaminated. The land, the people, everything will be poisoned. Those in our bunkers will survive, but for how long with limited supplies, I don't know."

Kinnick gripped his brow, a headache setting in. The situation was worse than he could ever imagine.

"Air assets?" Kinnick said, looking up. He ran a hand along his jawline. He hadn't realized he had grown a grizzled beard.

"Very limited. I believe you saw the extent of our air power in the passes. Our drones are becoming very difficult to control. I don't expect they will be reliable in the near future."

I wonder what they did with the pilots, Raven and Battle-axe.

"Ground?" Kinnick asked, his headache swelling.

"Limited. Don't you see, Kinnick? This is the battle we all fear. The west was only the anvil; this is the hammer." The general looked over his glasses at Kinnick.

"Somebody get me a goddamn drink," Brady said, throwing his hands up. "I thought the nukes were going to set us straight." An officer stood up, pouring the vice president a glass of scotch.

Brady watched him with disdain. "More, Major," he said. The major filled the glass to the brim and brought it back to the vice president, handing it to him gently.

Kinnick zoned out. The officers argued with one another around the table. Their conversations turned to faint chattering in the background of his mind. All he could see were the infected on the screen. Swarms of the soulless marching. *Do they even know why they march?*

They all marched in one direction, toward them. All with a single purpose. The murder of all things living. Daugherty's words echoed in his head. *This is the battle we fear. We are on the brink of annihilation.*

A Message from the Author

Thank you for reading *The Rising*, Book Three of The End Time Saga. I truly hope you enjoyed this installment. I had so much fun putting this one together for you. If you have the time, please consider writing a review.

Reviews are important tools that I use to hone my craft. They help me identify what I'm getting right and what needs work in my writing. Reviews also help potential readers decide whether or not to purchase and read my work. I take them very seriously and appreciate your time.

If you do take the time to write a review, reach out to me on my website *DanielGreeneBooks.com* or email me at *DanielGreeneBooks@gmail.com.* I would like to take the time to thank you personally for your feedback and support. Don't be afraid to reach out! I love meeting new readers.

You can find me on Facebook: *Daniel Greene Books*

You can find me on the web: *DanielGreeneBooks.com*
Or
Email: *DanielGreeneBooks@gmail.com*

The End Time Saga doesn't end here. The fourth installment is coming soon...

A Note

Little Sable Point Lighthouse is a real place in Michigan. I fictionalized the location to fit my needs as a writer, but it does exist. I've been there once and it's a beautiful place with a wonderful beach and views of picturesque Lake Michigan. When choosing a place for the Steele family home, I knew that I wanted to use Little Sable Point Lighthouse as a location for Tess's camp so I placed them in relation to one another. I took some liberties with spacing and location of forests and parking around the lighthouse. If you have a chance, you should consider checking out this wonderful park.

While the Eisenhower Tunnel is a real tunnel in Colorado, Dunluce Pass is a fictional mountain roadway near the Eisenhower Tunnel. South Fork, Independence, and Mosquito are all real passes fictionalized for the sake of my novel.

I've done this in my other books with Pittsburgh, Fairfax, Pentwater, Washington, Kinshasa, Grand Haven, and others. I've fictionalized the places to fit my story better. I try to keep it real enough where the reader could look up a place and see the picture I'm painting, or if they've been there, perhaps recognize the imagery. It's a delicate balance between realism and the fiction of the story.

The same holds true for the military units depicted in the books. I try to create entirely new units so as to not depict a unit in the wrong light. There are a great many veterans out there, and I really want them to find my writing realistic without losing them because everything about a particular unit wasn't spot-on. An extensive amount of research goes into this balancing act and I sincerely hope you've enjoyed this installment of The End Time Saga.

- Daniel Greene
02/27/2018

Special Thanks

No book comes to fruition without the help, assistance and support of a horde of people.

To my wife, Jen: You have been so supportive of me throughout this entire journey that I don't know how I'd do it without you. You've been there through ups and downs and haven't balked at any challenge sent your way. You are a one-of-a-kind woman and I am so lucky to have found you on that night back in 2011.

To my Beta Readers and Contributors (Kevin, Dan, Brady, Jennifer, Beth, Joe, Eric, and Mike): You have done me and this book such a wonderful service. You have helped take my writing to the next the level. Thank you.

To my Cover Artist(Christian): Your work is amazing as always. You really are able to capture the exciting essence of the series.

To my Editor(Lisa): Your thorough and meticulous work on my novel is so important. My deepest thanks.

To my family, friends, and readers: Thank you for pushing me along on this journey as an author. Your support means the world. As long as you keep reading, I will keep writing.

About the Author

Daniel Greene is the author of the growing apocalyptic thriller series The End Time Saga. He is an avid traveler and physical fitness enthusiast with a deep passion for history. He is inspired by the works of George R.R. Martin, Steven Pressfield, Bernard Cornwell, and George Romero. Although he is a Midwesterner for life, he now lives on the East Coast.

Books by Daniel Greene

The End Time Saga

End Time

The Breaking

The Rising

The Departing (Coming later 2018)

78100667R00241

Made in the USA
Middletown, DE
29 June 2018